Alpha Farm
The Beginning

ANNIE BERDEL

A Prepper Chicks Series

For   information contact:

AnnieBerdel@yahoo.com

www. AnnieBerdel.com

DEDICATION

To all the strong Women of The Coop ~
Forever Sister Chicks in heart and soul.
I adore you.

ACKNOWLEDGEMENTS

There are certain people who come into your life that you allow the opportunity to either destroy every dream possible or they take the opportunity to cheer you on from their Balcony in your life.

To all those who have cheered ~ From the bottom of my heart,

I adore you beyond reason.

Abba ~ j'adore!

To my Eddie ~ Always the Keeper of my Heart.

To the Wee Ones I have birthed ~ You are my inspiration and the driving force behind what I do. I will do everything possible to make your life better than mine. After all, if it hadn't been for you, I would have finished this book in half the time!

To Dixon ~ Because I am your human and that makes me happy.

To my mentor, G. Michael Hopf ~ You have been such a huge factor in pushing me forward and watching my dream become a reality. Thanks for answering all the questions and enduring all the name calling.

Eloise Knapp ~ A talent for Graphic Design that has left everyone talking. I only hope the book itself lives up to your artwork. Amazing!

Scott Wilson ~ For seeing me without my make-up on and only making my words better! Your insight is much appreciated!

Niall ~ Just THANK YOU!

To all the Beta Readers ~ YOU ROCK!

FOREWORD

When I was asked to write the foreword for Alpha Farm, I was honored and excited to be given such a responsibility. Writing a book is a doable feat, but writing a novel that both entertains and educates is a winning combination. Annie Berdel delivers on both in this unforgettable novel.

I was honored to write the foreword because this book, though a work of fiction, could also be looked at as a possible forecasting for things to come. Annie has done a wonderful job at giving the reader a look into a possible future our country might have. I have read many books that portend the end of the world as we know it and this one is frightening in its realistic portrayal.

As a post-apocalyptic author myself, I know there are two things we strive to do. My first job and Annie does this, is to entertain the reader, if you don't the reader will lay the book down and never return to it. Second, the author of this type of fiction wants to have the reader leave their tale with knowing something they hadn't before. Annie does this superbly and I, myself, walked away knowing things I hadn't before. Annie's expertise in preparedness shows through the entire book. Her explanations and details can only come from someone who knows how to do the things she writes. This expertise is what gives Alpha Farm the realism and informational curve needed for 'prepper fiction'. She gives us the punch of reality but with her dynamic storyline, gives us the one, two combination of entertainment and education.

My excitement for writing the foreword comes from the fact that I consider Annie Berdel, a good friend. She has been there to help during my career as a writer by giving her time to help promote my works. So when she asked if I could help her write her first novel, I jumped at the chance. It was my unique pleasure to help her along the way as she wrote, in record time mind you, a fully engaging novel with twists, turns while departing wisdom and knowledge on how to survive what just might be coming around the corner. Doing what she did is not an easy task and she accomplished it all by herself with a few tidbits of advice along the way. When you read Alpha Farm you will be catapulted into a story where you'll feel connected to the characters, the story and come away from it wanting more. Her talent is right there on the page and without a doubt this will be the first of many more books to come.

Apocalyptic fiction tends to be dominated by male authors and I believe it's about time that more women jumped into the mix. Annie's contribution to this genre of fiction will be impactful and add to a growing list of young, new female authors. I am thrilled she finally decided to write, only when one makes that commitment can they see a dream fulfilled and influence the world in their own special way.

The realities are this, things are changing and the world we know and love will most likely be completely different and for the worst. Annie Berdel gives the reader a glimpse at our possible future, it is a world that is dark and scary but she also gives you the hope that if you're prepared you can survive what might be coming down the road.

G. Michael Hopf

Bestselling author of **THE NEW WORLD** series

PROLOGUE

She blew out the candle and watched as the smoke drifted toward the stars. What a beautiful night it was. The clouds danced playfully in front of the moon, causing shadows across the open field.

If she stared hard enough, she could just barely make out his figure coming out of the tree line. Tears ran down her cheeks as she tried so hard not to blink, for she knew if she drew her lashes even slightly together, he would be gone.

She turned away quickly...one day soon they would be together again. Until then, she had work to do and these girls needed their Mum to not be so emotional.

Taking a deep breath and straightening her back, Emma turned and walked back into the kitchen just in time to witness the unspeakable.

1

As cheesy as it sounds, she was, in fact, a tall drink of a woman. Back in her day, she could make a man swoon with a flutter of a lash. Ah, those were the days! Awake at the butt crack of dawn milking cows, throwing hay in the afternoon and making the young men stutter in the evening shadows. A small giggle escaped from her throat as she glanced in the mirror. The tinsel in her hair now replaced the sun-streaked gold threads that turned those boys' heads long ago but dang if she had a rosy complexion without nary a wrinkle. Good genes and all that. She would have to thank her parents one day.

Emma drove into town and stopped at the post to gather the mail and catch up on the latest news. Most people don't know the benefits of a small town post office. You see, small town post offices are not only a beneficial link to the outside world, but a gathering place of longtime friends and family. Theories run rapidly at the post, not gossip, but theories. By the time it is discovered that so-and-so got a letter from whats-a-ma-call-it, we also find out where and how world peace can be solved. So is it any wonder that what Emma got in the mail was also a huge topic of conversation. I mean seriously, it's not every day that someone gets a hardcore whisky-making still in the mail, now is it!

She had been waiting for this bad boy for going on 3 weeks now. Emma had the boys at the post load it into the back of her truck, tucking it in ever so tightly as not to get jostled around on her way home. Shen then gave a quick hug to Hazel, the postmaster, and damn near gave herself a heart attack as she tried to help a young mother chase down an ornery toddler before he ran out into the street. She wasn't as young as she used to be, that was for sure.

As she drove up the driveway to the house, she caught a glimpse of him coming out of the greenhouse. Even after 30 years, he still had the ability to make her forget to breathe. Her Tommy. Tommy with his ever-so-slight Brooklyn accent. The man who left the "Big City" to move to her little farm in Ohio. Talk about trying to fit a square peg into a round hole! But they survived. Through all the ups and downs, they had survived and were much stronger for it.

"Hey doll!" Tommy cooed

"Hey, the still has arrived! I think I should give him a name, seems only right!"

"Seriously?" quirked Tommy

"Yes, I've waited for this thing almost as long as I've waited for you to like vegetables," snickered
Emma.

"Whatever" said Tommy "Let's get the new "Man of the House" into the house and get him out of his box.

Working together Emma and Tommy managed to get the still into her studio and unboxed. He was a beaut! All copper and golden in the afternoon sun, he was going to be put to good use in the months ahead.

Back at the post office, talk of the town was how long it would be before Emma was arrested for bootlegging. The argument that ensued had some very valid cross points. Most folks knew how illegal it was to make your own moonshine, but most folks also knew that if Emma was making it, it would be some damn good moonshine!

Emma decided to commemorate her new still with a batch of Apple Pie Moonshine. Actually, she needed to get some ready for the holiday season and needed to give it time to age properly. The still would not be ready for actual use for a few days, but this she could make in her kitchen. She got started by taking a large boiling pot and adding a half-gallon of apple juice, a half-gallon of apple cider, 3/4 cup of white sugar, 1 & 1/4 cups of brown sugar and about 4 whole cinnamon sticks. Bringing all of these ingredients to a boil, Emma removed the pot from the stove and let it cool down to room temperature. Once this reached room temperature, she gradually added a half-liter of 190proof grain alcohol, this time using some Everclear that she picked up in town last week. Taking sterile Mason jars, Emma added a cinnamon stick in each one and filled it up with the alcohol mixture. She then tucked them into a cool dry place for Christmas time consumption. It takes a couple weeks for all the ingredients to jive together, so the root cellar would be the perfect place to hide this batch for the holiday festivities.

While she was into the alcohol, she decided to get her vanilla extract steeping for all the holiday baking she did every year. Taking a couple old bottles she had been saving, she filled each with 40proof vodka. Removing the vanilla beans from their own container, she split each one length-wise to open them up and expose all their internal goodness. Adding about 6 of these vanilla beans in each jar, she tightly screwed on the caps. She gave a low chuckle to herself as she thought about how easy it was to make homemade vanilla. Going to the kitchen cupboard, she moved the two bottles of vanilla already there that she made last year to the front and put these two new bottles behind them. FIFO – First In, First Out. She had learned that a long time ago when she worked in a restaurant and it had served her well over the years.

2

Thinking back through the years, Emma was amazed at how things had fallen into place. Finally able to leave her high stress job in Indianapolis and move back to the farm she grew up on in Ohio, it was definitely a long overdue blessing. Even with her days running full tilt to finalize everything on her bucket list of preparedness, she was enjoying life to its fullest.

Glancing out the kitchen window towards the barn, Emma felt that familiar tug in her spirit to get the finishing touches on her preps. For over 40 years she had grown to recognize that feeling. She also felt that time was running short. Blowing out a deep breath, she wondered how many days were left before all hell broke loose. I mean seriously, how could things get much worse? She thought. The price of food alone had risen more than 300% in just over the last year. Trying to find just the staples such as sugar and flour without them having been modified in some way was damned near impossible anymore. "Damn Agenda 21" she muttered under her breath. "How were people supposed to survive with all this nonsense?"

She laid the dishtowel over the sink to dry and decided to check in with her peeps. She knew there was some bad weather about to hit the Midwest and she just wanted to give a quick heads-up to all those paying attention.

Walking into her studio, she slid down into her chair and flipped on her laptop. Logging into Facebook, she smiled as she recognized her all-too-familiar icon. She still wished she had thighs as thin as this Chick but gave a quick grin at the AR-15 in her hands. Prepper Chicks. It made her heart feel good to know how much her website had helped people throughout the years.

She quickly scanned for news of the approaching storms and highlighted them on her page... "Please be safe peeps" she whispered and said a quick prayer over them.

Over the years she had seen the devastation that these HAARP-induced storms had caused. She remembered in 2013 alone, the amount of destruction from these tornadoes was astounding. One reason she liked being back home was because the surrounding hills deterred tornado activity. All the years she had lived in Indianapolis she never did get used to the sirens going off all the time.

Scanning for other news and knowledge building skills, the time quickly escaped Emma. It was nearly 7 p.m. before she realized how late it had gotten and it was about time for her beloved Tommy to come home. Since dinners consisted of a light salad now that they had gotten older and wiser about their eating habits, she gathered up an old apron and headed out to the garden. How many people didn't have the benefit of fresh organic food, she pondered. Shoot, how many people were lucky in this day and age to have any food at all on their plates? With bread at nearly $10 a loaf, ground beef at $18lb and a box of good old Kraft Macaroni and Cheese at $5 a box, the news of people starving to death in the US was increasing at exponential rates daily.

Hearing that all-too-familiar hum of Tommy's '69 Ford Mustang coming up the drive, Emma gathered her bounty into her apron and stepped back into the kitchen. Dropping the veggies off at the sink, she headed out to meet him. Boys and their toys, she thought. A man his age still driving a muscle car out these old dirt roads ... serves the man right that he has to wash it almost every time he takes it out of the garage. It did make her heart feel good that he was finally settling in here in Ohio. Having survived the last 30 years together, the man deserved much more than a muscle car, she thought with a grin on her face.

There was not a better vision to a man when he got home than to see his best friend waiting for him at the door, and Tommy was one of those men who truly appreciated this simple fact. Having spent the last 10 hours in town teaching a pistol class, he was happy to be back home and away from people. Things weren't the same anymore. There was a real distinction between the good and bad in people that really bothered him lately. You were either both peaceful and calm or had a temper from hell and wanted to make everyone who crossed your path miserable. The stress of everyday life was catching up to people and you could definitely tell who was prepared to endure and who wasn't.

Tommy parked the 'Stang and made his way to his wife. Hopping up on the first step, he turned and wrapped his arms around her and drew her close. The familiar smell of her perfume made his knees buckle a bit.

"Wow, you've gotten taller since you've been away! What's in the water in town?" Emma giggled

"It's always been a misconception of yours, my dear, that you are taller than me. It's simply taken you this long to realize that you were wrong all these years" quipped Tommy

"Oh really? I must have been wrong about a bunch of things all these years then" Emma returned

"Yes, you were. Why you allowed me into your life long ago, I will never understand" said Tommy and he kissed her gently on the forehead. When Emma squeezed him even tighter, he knew she made the right decision. It made him proud to know that his just being here could make her so happy.

Hand in hand they walked into the kitchen. Tommy made his way to the sink to wash the vegetables and handed them to Emma. Emma in turn, began to assemble two plates of fresh vegetables and some cheese. Working in sync with not a word spoken, dinner was ready in no time at all. Emma carried the plates to the table while Tommy grabbed some forks and retrieved beverages from the refrigerator for the both of them.

They sat as they had since the time they were dating, with legs wrapped around each other under the table.

"Anything new in town" Emma asked

"Not really new, everything just seems to be escalating. I'm not sure how people are surviving who weren't prepared for the mess this country is in besides just out and out stealing. Or worse," Tommy replied

Raising an eyebrow, Emma thought about the years she had been telling people to get ready. Whether it was for a natural disaster, an economic crash or WWIII, she knew in her heart of hearts that something was going to happen. It was just a matter of time.

"No need to fret Mama," he said. "Our family is close…all of our kids have moved home. We have everything we need and then some at the farm. People are waking up, just sometimes not as fast as I would like"

"Oh, believe me. I know," replied Emma.

"I know you do, Doll" he said as he grabbed her hand and gave her a squeeze. "If it hadn't been for the information you have put out over the years, a lot more people would be in worse circumstances than they are now, trust me. Any interesting news today?"

"Same ole same ole," she responded. "More upticks in earthquakes and volcanoes. I have been watching HAARP and scalar squares on the weather maps and we are in for a couple nasty days in the Midwest. There is nothing anyone can do at this point to fix the economy and panic is setting in at a fast pace on Wall Street and Washington DC. Most of Europe has been taken over by Muslim countries and they are in just complete chaos. OH! And our mama bunny had her babies today!"

"Well, I am glad to hear some good news in that mess!" Tommy said

Like synchronized swimmers, they cleaned up the table and strolled out to check on the new babies.
The grandkids will get such a kick out of seeing the kits Tommy thought. It had taken him some time to get onto the same page as his wife, but it was hard to deny the obvious after a while. Being prepared, being self-sufficient, as hard as it was in this day and age had allowed them to enjoy a comfortable retirement. While others were fighting daily just to scrape by, Emma and Tommy not only were able to support themselves but also their children and grandkids. It was nice to be surrounded by family each and every day. Each child lived on the 300 acres that the Grands, as the kids called them, purchased...close enough to help yet far enough away for privacy if they needed it. Each family, in turn, had their own gardens and farm animals.

A litter of Great Pyrenees roamed the property and kept a close eye on everyone. Well, every GP except Dixon. Dixon was Emma's dog and stayed close to her at all times. If she left the property, he would sit on the hill and patiently wait for her to return. He was lovingly named after a favorite comic book character of Emma's, A redneck with a compound bow who wore a poncho and road a motorcycle...roaming around killing zombies, a complete rebel. Dixon, there could not have been a better name for someone who guarded her life more than his own.

3

The next morning Tommy and Emma took a walk out back of their property. The farmhouse happened to be part of the Underground Railroad system and had tunnels that ran the length of the property. When they first bought the property, Emma had excavators come in and reclaim most of the tunnels to working condition. Underground tunnels now linked all of the families on the property and a few of the newly built cabins that were scattered throughout the woods.

"Check this out" Tommy said as he pointed to a patch of morels

"Wow, I'm impressed!" Emma exclaimed. Not bad for a city boy, Emma thought.

Tomás Montalvo, Tom… her Tommy had left Brooklyn, New York over 30 years ago to move to
Ohio. What he must have been thinking, she wondered. What an adventure they'd had together. What adjustments they had to make so they didn't kill each other. Theirs was a turbulent affair. They spent the first years of their marriage swinging from one emotional pitfall to another until they finally settled into a nice, warm friendship. They had earned their war wounds and looked forward to tenderly attending to the bruises left from trying to fit Tommy's square dramatic upbringing into Emma's round laidback country lifestyle.

They picked a couple handfuls of mushrooms for dinner tomorrow and continued along the dirt path. Foraging was one important skill that Emma liked to teach at her survival classes and she was quite happy that her husband paid attention for the most part. While Tommy was invaluable with his knowledge of firearms, Emma knew that survival in a down grid situation consisted of a lot more information than just about guns. She had seen the signs coming whether it was economic, environmental, weather patterns, war or over-population, and made it a mission to not only teach herself and her family how to survive off the land, but anyone who would listen.

In 2011 Prepper Chicks was born, a website that people could come to and find valuable knowledge.
While Emma understood the importance of obtaining tangible assets such as food and weapons, she knew knowledge was the most important prep a person could have. In 2013, she saw Moore, Oklahoma hit with two tornadoes within a week of each other that destroyed people's homes, and along with their homes any kind of preparedness assets that they had collected. It took all of 16 minutes to be over. 16 minutes for lives to be changed.

Tommy and Emma continued along the path until they came to a clearing. They needed to get a move on if they were going to get done before the storm hit. Emma had been watching the weather predictions for about a week now and this storm had the makings of a full-out Derecho. Sad how people still didn't prepare for these storms, Emma thought, even though the last one took power out for over 2 weeks in some locations and multiple lives were lost. Emma needed to post some more warnings on her Prepper Chicks webpage when she got back, but right now she needed to tend to her own family.

Sticking close to the tree line, Tommy and Emma walked around the edge of the clearing to a barely seen path that led up the hillside through the trees. Once they got to the top of the hill, they quickly got to work.

Communications with the outside world was a tricky game to be played. While a Prepper understands the need for OPSEC, or Operational Security, a Prepper also understands the importance of outside information. Emma shielded her eyes as she tilted her head back and looked up at the 80' tower. This was Big Bertha, as Emma affectionately referred to her. And what a pain in the ass Big Bertha had been from the start. Emma knew the benefits of having a global communications system far outweighed the hassle it had been to get Big Bertha up and running, but dang if she also hadn't had multiple conversations with her Maker along the way, mostly repenting of quite a few foul words that had made it past her lips.

Here she stood, in all of her glory. 80' of painstakingly manipulated steel and wires. Bertha could transmit to Scotland and back and, as a matter of fact, quite a few evenings were enjoyed with the family afterwards trying to imitate the particular Scottish accent reached out over the airwaves.

Bertha also was an important part of a network of Off-Grid communications between hundreds of Preppers throughout the United States. She had been put to use on a number of occasions when, mostly due to bad weather, the telephone service and even the 911 service were inoperable.

Tommy and Emma needed to make sure she was up to handling the expected 90 mph winds that were being forecast with the storm coming in and so began the task of checking to make sure all wire connections were secure along with checking for any branches that might interfere or cause damage if they rubbed up against Bertha. Big Bertha had a home nestled in a grove of mature maple trees which shielded her from prying eyes both from horizontal view but also from vertical view. Emma had Bertha painted to match the natural landscape and she was nearly invisible to the human eye. Even anyone flying overhead would have a hard time spotting her as her antenna was built to mimic the foliage of nearby trees.

Once they had checked on each of their children and their families, Tommy and Emma settled in for the night ahead. Emma went down through her list of preps she wanted to check before she relaxed a bit.

*Flashlights and extra batteries, especially her Black Diamond Spot headlamp

*Oil lamps topped off

*Two liters filled with water and placed in the freezer to be used if the power went out. Being sure not to fill them too full, Emma only filled them to where the dent in the neck began to allow for expansion, they could be used for a plethora of reasons. Normally she used them in the rabbit cages in the summer to help offset heat stroke, but they could also be used in the refrigerator to keep food colder if the power went down.

*Weather radio ready to go

*Gas cans filled and all vehicles full in case they needed to either run the generator for any length of time or needed to leave their location. Like many farms in the area, theirs had an underground tank to store fuel for the farm equipment.

*B.O.B.s packed and placed in a handy location

*Anything outside that could be blown around by the expected high winds was secured.

*Firearms with extra magazines ready to go

To learn more about Being Prepared ~ Visit our website at
www.PrepperChicks.org

Once Emma was comfortable with the last-minute preparedness plans, she settled into the big comfy chair Tommy had bought her for her birthday 5 years ago. She pulled her quilt over her shoulders as she turned her computer on and started to check all of the weather radars.

This storm was predicted to originate in Iowa...continue through into Michigan and then hit northern Indiana, is where the birth of the Derecho would happen. Along the way, tornadoes...heavy rain... strong winds and even hail would wreak havoc before the Derecho was even formed. To even be classified as a Derecho, this storm had to be 280 miles wide with winds in excess of 80 mph.

Taking a deep breath, Emma knew this would cover most of the state of Ohio. Once it made its turn in northern Indiana, it would travel southeast until it swiped through Ohio. Her home state felt the brunt of the Derecho that passed through two years previous, taking with it 26 lives, millions of dollars in damage and power outages in some areas for as long as two weeks.

Fucking bastards, Emma muttered under her breath. Doing some research years previous, Emma had ended up down a rabbit trail that had landed in the lap of weather modification. It was a harsh reality to learn that several governments were involved in a silent war using the weather to cause misery on the citizens of another country. These unseen agents were using the weather not only to create disasters to harm humans but also to destroy crops... and surprisingly enough, these disasters had become a traded commodity on the stock market. Someone once said never let a disaster go to waste, so why not create the disaster to get guaranteed profit, right?

The problem had since arisen with these idiots trying to play God that things had spiraled out of control to where even THEY couldn't control the aftereffects anymore. What was once a poke and a little laugh has now created within nature unforeseen mega storms that even the demigods could not predict. In 2012, weather modification was used by the Chinese government to ensure that the weather was pleasant for all those visiting for the Olympics. In 1992, the Japanese government created multiple snow storms that ensured that the winter season was profitable for the businesses. In 2012, a freak outbreak of tornadoes in already economically unstable Italy caused the final domino to fall and the country was now bankrupt. And so, the games continued to be played until most of Europe had been centralized under EU control.

Emma leaned back and stretched her back. She needed a break from glaring at the computer screen and decided she was going to surprise Tommy for lunch tomorrow with his favorite cookies because of all the work he had helped her with today. She got up and meandered into her pantry and as always said a prayer of thanks for not only herself having a well-stocked home store but also all of her kids. Growing up on a farm, canning and food storage was always a way of life. But not everyone had the benefit of living on a farm. And not everyone has realized how fragile the food system is in the US. Most people take for granted that the grocery stores always have food, after all, this IS the land of plenty. Unfortunately, that is not reality. Reality is that grocery stores only carry enough stock for 3 to 5 days' worth of sales and then have to be replenished. To be replenished, the stores rely upon semi-trucks to deliver the goods. The infrastructure designed to make all of this happen without the consumer being aware of it is vastly corroding. Not only the sensitive nature of the country's supply chain, but Emma has seen the rush for food staples before a big storm is expected. People wipe most stores clean within hours, let alone the 3 to 5 days of stocked items. In a down-grid situation, this already fragile system would turn into one of the fastest hostile environments imaginable as people fought over what little inventory was left.

Grabbing a Mason jar of chocolate chips and the flour, Emma walked out into the kitchen and sat them on the counter. Turning, she turned the oven on to pre-heat. Unsealing the

Mason jar, she measured out the desired amount of chips and then resealed the jar with her vacuum sealer. Better than leaving them in the bag for long-term storage, vacuum sealing the chocolate chips gave the normal 3-year shelf life another 10 years.

Popping a couple chocolate chips in her mouth, Emma decided that for everyone's benefit, it was best to get these cookies made as soon as possible. Chocolate and cookie dough were a weakness to nibbling. Add them together and there was no way Emma was going to make it out of this baking session unscathed!

Adding a cup of her homemade butter into a large bowl, she added almost a cup of both white sugar and brown sugar. Emma gave a snicker as she added the brown sugar to the bowl. How many people had to throw out their cookie recipes because they realized too late that they had run out of brown sugar? Most people didn't like to store brown sugar because of its clumping abilities. One cup of cane sugar and a tablespoon of molasses and BAM! You have made brown sugar! And as a bonus, you can make the brown sugar as dark and flavorful as you like by controlling the amount of molasses.

Cracking a couple eggs into a measuring cup, Emma realized she hadn't closed up the chicken coop for the night. Normally this wouldn't be a problem, but with the storm coming in, she didn't want the girls getting out and not being able to return to the coop with the high winds. Emma hurriedly mixed the rest of the ingredients together and put the bowl into the refrigerator to chill overnight. She would get to the clean-up in a bit, but right now her chickens needed tended to.

4

Emma sat down to put her muck boots on and instantly Dixon was alert and wagging his tail before her. It was an unspoken sign that adventure was ahead for him when the boots went on. She gave him a quick pat on the head. "Yes Dixon, we need to go check on the girls," Emma said. She bent down to tie her boots at the same time Dixon turned towards the door, giving her a face full of tail fur. "Love that dog," she muttered under her breath.

Tucking a couple dog treats into her coat pocket, she headed towards the door. Dixon had lost some of his hyper behavior as he grew older but he still liked to be nosey when he shouldn't be sometimes. And sometimes his nosey behavior has gotten him into a few scrapes with the local wildlife. He could take care of himself, but it was best to leave well enough alone. Treats seem to help keep him focused as now he knew to check with Emma occasionally when they were out. She always had something tasty to give him.

Emma opened the door and the spoiled puppy bounded out before her. Catching a breath of cold air, she realized the temperature had dropped fast. Grabbing her shotgun, or Mossy as she referred to it, Emma stepped out into the night. The wind had picked up considerably. Stepping off the porch, she looked up and saw the clouds racing by above. "This is not going to be a nice storm" Emma thought. She pushed her hands deep into her pockets and headed out.

Night time takes on a whole different charm on the homestead that a lot of people don't appreciate. It's a time of slumbering dreams and yet a time for a false sense of security. The darkness will envelop you, wrap you in its comforting arms and make you forget that dangers are on the prowl.

Emma walked the path to the coop, letting her eyes adjust to the darkness around her. With the moon playing trippy through the clouds, shadows on the ground were dancing all around her making Emma a little on edge. The winds were masking the normal comforting night sounds, the soft mooing of the mama cows to their young, the owls and their enchanted cooing. The very stillness itself was being disturbed tonight. You can never hear the stillness during the day; it is reserved only for night. It's not a quiet. Far from it. It's peacefulness in perfect balance without the added chaos of the light.

Emma broke the stillness and pointed her flashlight towards the coop. Just as she had thought, the door was still open. Shining the light around the coop, she did not see any of the girls outside. That was usually a good sign. Approaching the door to the coop, Emma rested Mossy up against the outside so she could get the coop door closed using both hands.

Shining the light inside, she started counting chickens. If you've never owned chickens, you may not understand the enchantment that comes with life with this delightful creature. Emma raised her chickens from the egg. They owned her heart. Each with their own personality, she could sit for hours and watch them interact. Each coop had its own pecking order. Piper was the head "clucker" in Emma's coop. She was a Rock Island Red and had the feistiness of an eagle. Emma didn't have the heart to tell her she was just an egg-laying hen. She had stolen Emma's heart. One day when Emma heard a commotion and came to the coop to investigate, it turned out a hawk had gotten into the pen. But Piper, being Piper, had all the other chickens tucked in behind her, her wings sprawled wide and a fierce determination on her countenance. One leg in the air, Piper was in pure battle ready form. Emma had to have a little chuckle as Piper reminded her of "The Karate Kid" when the main character was balancing on one leg, arms outstretched, doing The Crane stance on the pole. Piper had this under control completely but Emma wanted to make sure the hawk got out of the pen alive.

Piper was resting in one of the side boxes and all the other hens along with Tootsie, the only rooster, were all accounted for.

Emma backed out of the coop slowly as not to disturb them and reached for the door to close. That's when she saw them. Two red eyes glowed in the darkness.

Emma slowly continued to close the coop door, trying not to make any sudden movements. She knew what was there in the darkness, stalking, and waiting. She had met this adversary before and had let him live, and now could curse herself for that mistake. He had haunted her... tortured her since their last meeting. Emma knew this meeting would end differently. It had to.

She could feel his breath on the back of her neck, making shivers run down her spine. She knew not to move... but she needed to get Mossy. She knew what had to be done and it had to be in one quick, flawless movement. The consequences of not being able to outperform her adversary would get her killed.

Her breath, just the deafening sound of it, echoed in the night. Beneath her the earth pulsated with each inhale and exhale. Emma remembered back to when she first moved back to the farm. The plans she had... and still had. Slowly she slid her hand along the coop door...feeling the wood...the splinters digging into her fingers. She had to use the door itself for as much concealment as possible. She did not want to let him see her arm move towards the shotgun.

The stillness...that stillness that she found peace in when she left her house just a short time ago, was now taunting her. Like a bully on the playground... "DO SOMETHING" it beckoned to her. "Make the first move" it teased, but she knew better. She had to focus. She had to think clearly. Her fingers hit the cold hard steel of Mossy bringing a false comfort. She had danced with that comfort once before and had been very disappointed. It had cost her dearly, but not this time. This time she knew what had to be done.

Closing her eyes, she said a quick prayer and just as fast reached down the length of Mossy and with one swift movement she lifted the gun as she pivoted and aimed.

Just as quickly, she heard the gravel beneath his feet give way to a chorus of chatter alerting her ears
to the torment to follow. "THERE'S NOT ENOUGH TIME" screamed in her head…."SWING DAMMIT" she yelled at herself, startled as the words escaped her mouth and broke the stillness. He was coming as fast and as hard as he could straight for her. His intention was to kill and she knew it with every fiber of her being. "Nooooooooo" she screamed into the night.

A bolt of white caught her attention out of her peripheral vision. "Oh God, no," she thought. Like a locomotive with no intention of stopping, the white savior covered the distance in an instant, hitting the beast with the red eyes with the force of a thousand crashing waves. Over and over they rolled, ripping and tearing at each other with teeth that devoured flesh and gave no mercy.

Emma quickly readjusted Mossy and took aim. The sights were useless in the darkness. Over and over she tried to get focused on the beast but the whiteness appeared. She silently begged for the fury to stop, for her to be given a clear shot, but nothing was listening to her pleas for help. She was the outsider in this fight, and she was helpless.

Realizing she still had Mossy in her hands, she aimed towards the stars who were taunting her in the darkness and pulled the trigger as hard as she could. The deafening sound made all of nature stop for just a fraction of a second. The stillness returned for all of an instant, but it was enough. Emma took aim and fired. Death had finally entered this battle and ensnared its prey.

Laying in the night, the wolf was motionless. A huge hole had been ripped into his chest. Emma walked over to him and knelt down, placing her hand over his muzzle. No breath left his nostrils.

Emma ran over to her Dixon who now lay on the ground breathing deeply, each breath coming in painful gasps. Streaks of red now intermingled with his white fur, bringing tears to Emma's eyes. "Please no!" she screamed "Oh God, please, please, please" she screamed as she buried her head into his fur. She had to get him back to the house. Somehow she needed to get this 150 lb. dog back into the house so she could tend to his wounds or she was afraid the stillness would envelop him also. "You can't have him," she muttered into the night.

Emma ran around to the side of the chicken coop where she kept her wheel barrow. Bringing it along the back side of the dog, she set the wheel barrow along his spine and laid it down. Slowly she tried to roll Dixon as far back into it as she could. Running around to the backside, she grabbed hold of Dixon's collar with one hand and with her weight bracing down on the wheel barrow, she pushed down. Slowly, the contraption righted itself with the dog tossed painfully inside. Grabbing her shotgun, she laid it alongside the injured dog.

Emma ran to the handles of the wheel barrow and swung it around and raced towards the house. Slicing through the night air she reached the porch and sat it down. Crying out, she yelled for her husband while trying to claw open the door to the house. He was already heading out to find her when he heard the shotgun firing.

"What happened?" Tommy asked, getting caught up in the excitement

"He's back," was all Emma said

It took both of them to get the dog inside the house. Emma began barking out orders to help save her beloved friend. They got him onto the table and Emma began scanning Dixon for injuries. There was so much blood. It had matted Dixon's hair heavily to the point the Emma had to feel through the threads for what she thought was a laceration. To her surprise, she found only minor cuts. Tommy had heated water and brought it along with some wash cloths and they gingerly began to try and wash the blood from Dixon's coat. Slowly the couple searched every inch of the dog for injuries. Emma finally let out a breath and looked towards Dixons face. Walking over to him, she knelt down and kissed him on his cheek. He was snoring.

"This crazy dog is just exhausted" Emma said as tears ran down her cheeks. The tears from Emma's face fell upon Dixon and soaked into his blood stained coat. "Crazy dog," she muttered and reached down and hugged him so tight she could feel his heartbeat against hers. She belonged to him. She was his human.

Trying not to wake him, Tommy set about putting on a pot of coffee while Emma added some helichrysum essential oil around some of the minor bruising and some melaleuca essential oil around the cuts Dixon had received. Dixon started to stir so they moved him from the table to his bed in front of the fireplace. Tommy brought in a bowl of water for him and Dixon took a deep drink. A small fire was burning down so the area was nice and toasty. Dixon fell back asleep almost instantly. He needed rest right now more than anything.

Once they were sure that Dixon was comfortable, Tommy walked over and put his arms around his wife. "What happened?" he asked. Still caught up in the moment, Emma realized she was still wired for the fight. "I need a shower and then we can talk" she said, her lower lip still holding a small hint of quivering fright. Tommy kissed her on the forehead and released her, knowing she needed some time to herself.

Emma walked up the steps to their bedroom loft and walking into the bathroom; she shut and locked the door behind her. She turned on the hot water, as hot as she could get it, and slowly peeled the blood-stained clothes from her body, piling them one atop the other in the middle of the floor.

She turned, opened the door and stepped into the shower. A fog had already begun to envelop the room as she felt the hot water hit her skin. The heat from the cleansing pellets sprang to life and washed over her skin, awakening every cell. She felt the thumping, the reminder of their previous encounter. She slid her fingers alongside her breast and felt the uneven roughness of the scar. She let her fingers dance the full length of the invasion from top to bottom as her mind drifted back ten years.

Ten years ago, she met him. The beast with the red eyes. Ten years ago he had left her dying in the woods. She had gone out to search for some ginseng root when she found the litter of pups instead. Mesmerized by their playful banter, Emma didn't see their father crouched behind her. Emma took a step towards them and the next thing she knew, she had the wind knocked out of her and was lying on the ground. Gasping for air, she reached into her belt for her knife. He lunged at her as she raised her hand up to meet him. She felt his claws dig in to her side as the knife entered his chest. He hit her with such momentum that once he hit her blade, he rolled over top of her and came to rest on the opposite side of her, motionless.

Emma reached down and felt the blood pouring from her side. She felt the forest begin to spin around her and knew she needed to get help fast. She also didn't know where the mother of these cubs was and didn't want to chance the fact of her returning soon. Reaching into her pocket, she pulled her cell phone and hit the speed button for Tommy, and promptly passed out.

Days later she awoke with her husband by her side. That's when she learned of her rescue and of the fact that neither the cubs nor the father were anywhere around when her rescuers arrived.

The water danced around her fingers, gently teasing her breast and what remained of her adversary. He was gone. She felt her body go limp as the sobs overwhelmed her, her tears mixing with the water spraying over her, swirling into the abyss beneath her feet. She cupped her hands over her face and let the pain and fear leave her body, leave her soul. Her shoulders heaved against the weight of this burden she had been carrying. This demon that had been haunting her, watching her from deep within the woods, would no longer torment her.

Drying off, Emma slipped into her bathrobe and brushed out her long hair. She would let it dry by the fire while she sat with Dixon. Looking at her reflection in the mirror, she touched the faint lines around her eyes. Time had been good to her. Quickly adding some moisturizer to her face, she picked up the pile of clothes on the floor and walked downstairs.

Tommy was sitting in his chair quietly waiting. He watched his wife walk to the fire and toss the clothes in she had worn earlier. He watched them burn and sent up a silent thank you that he still had his wife. He understood the symbolism but also knew there was still evil in the world that could bring harm to Emma. She was a strong woman...the bravest woman he had ever met but sometimes he wished she wasn't as independent as she was. Try as he might, he couldn't protect her all the time.

He traced her image against the fire with his eyes and felt a need to comfort her...To hold her in his arms and shut the hurt from the world outside their door. She stood there, staring into the flames, her memories captivating her attention. Tommy stood up and walked behind her, enveloping her in his arms. He loved the smell of her hair, the way her body molded to his.

She leaned back into him just as Dixon stirred, bringing them both back to reality. He was looking for food. He was one hungry dog! Emma knelt down and gave him a big hug and then went into the kitchen to make him some homemade goodness for saving her life.

While Emma was busy in the kitchen, Tommy went over to Dixon's pillow and sat down beside him. Tommy owed Dixon for saving his beloved's life and had no idea how to repay him other than to show him lots of love and take care of all his needs and comforts. As much as Tommy loved his wife, he questioned whether there was another that loved her even more.

"Come on Dix!" Emma yelled from the kitchen. Dixon slowly got off his bed and went to follow her voice. Finding her in the kitchen, his tail began to wag excitedly. Placing his food bowl on the floor, Emma went and filled his water bowl and then sat at the kitchen table to watch. It didn't take long for Dixon to clean his plate. He then slopped up a gallon of water and walked over and drooled all over Emma's nightgown. She didn't care though…she rubbed his ears briskly back and forth and gave him a big hug.

"Outside Dixon" Tommy said as he walked into the room. Dixon lifted his head and looked at him.
He wasn't going to leave her side. He placed one paw up on her lap and just stood there looking at Tommy. "Emma, that dog needs to go outside, and you need to change your bathrobe! If not, you're going to have a big mess to clean up… How about sweet talking him into going outside with me while you change?" Tommy said

"Dixon, go potty" Emma said and the dog got up and walked to the door, waiting to be left out. Tommy just sighed and walked over and planted a kiss on Emma's head. "Dixon and I will be back in about 20… go change… you're covered in drool…and that's not going to cut it if you think you are going to get lucky tonight" Tommy chuckled.

"Don't be out long" Emma sang out as the two walked through the back door. "That storm is about to kick up and fast".

The night ahead was a restless one for Emma. The howling of the wind outside beckoned to her in her dreams, sending her on a journey that she would be hard-pressed to remember as the dawn approached, but would leave her soul with an uneasy feeling that she wouldn't be able to shake for quite a while.

5

"Dixon, in" Emma said as she pointed into her truck. He knew where they were going and wanted no part of it. "Dixon, In!" Nothing. He wouldn't move. Not a budge.

Emma walked around the truck and got in the passenger side. "Dixon, drive!" Dixon jumped into the truck, sitting behind the steering wheel. Emma gave out a chuckle and scratched his ear. "Crazy dog," she muttered. Reaching around him, she shut the driver's side door. Then she slid out of the passenger side door and shut the dog in by himself and waved at him as she walked around the front of the truck. Opening the driver's side door, she pushed Dixon over into the passenger side of the seat. Not an easy feat for a dog weighing 150 lbs.!

They finally arrived at Doc's office. The nice thing about Doc's office was that it really was his homestead. With a visit to his friends, it was easy for Dixon to forget he was there for a reason, and not a pleasant reason this time. Emma wanted Doc to check him out after their encounter last night. The wolf was also loaded in the back of her truck for Doc to examine, just to make sure rabies or some other disease was not involved or communicable since Dixon did sustain some scratches.

"Well hey there, big guy" Doc said as Dixon bounded over to him. Doc knelt down and gave him a rub behind the ears. "How's he doing since last night?"

"Good" Emma said. "Tommy got you all caught up on what happened?"

"Yes, he also told me you were out there at the coop by yourself again. I thought we had a conversation about that already?" Doc asked sternly, looking at Emma from under the brim of his hat.

Emma squirmed a bit, kicking at the gravel under her feet. "It's all over now Doc, bastards in the back of my truck." Emma said as she jerked her head in the direction of her truck.

"Tsk Tsk" Doc clicked with his tongue. "We'll talk about this later" he said as he reached his arm around her shoulders. They both walked together into his office with Dixon not far behind.

Dr. Scott Smalley and Emma had known each other since high school, having dated briefly. They were in the same graduating class. After graduation they went their separate ways but still retained the sweet fondness they had always had for one another. It wasn't the fondness needed to sustain a marriage but more of a deep lasting friendship. They could go for months without talking but be able to pick up right where they left off. Emma was off to see the world when she left home, but Doc stayed in town. He left long enough to go to veterinary school but came right back to his roots. It took Emma a little longer to realize where her heart had always belonged, and when Emma moved back home, Emma called upon Doc numerous times for her livestock. One night while waiting the birth of one of her calves, Emma brought up the topic of preparedness. Turns out they were on the same page.

When Doc was in school, he learned that antibiotics that were being used for animal wellness were, in essence, the same antibiotics that were being given to humans. "The difference" Doc explained one day "Only consisted of dosage requirements and relabeling. You cannot imagine the manipulation in the drug companies out there Emma. Just to get a buck off of people. Sickening"

For more information about using antibiotics in a survival situation, please visit
www.doomandbloom.net/category/antibiotics-2/

Doc walked around the back of the truck and pulled the tarp back. The gnarled teeth of the wolf were extended out from its jaw. "That's odd" Doc thought. He continued to pull back the tarp until the entire length of the wolf was exposed. "Damn" Doc muttered under his breath. Running his hands along the belly, Doc knew. This wolf was nursing. Doc turned and looked out beyond his barn towards Emma's farm. Those cubs were in the woods behind Emma's house somewhere and would be getting hungry without Momma there to feed them. Depending on how far the female traveled, the cubs could be anywhere between there and town. Tilting his hat back, he continued to examine the female until his hands brushed over a lump beneath her fur. If it was what he thought, he needed to get her under a knife and in for a biopsy as soon as possible. Giving a quick whistle, Doc waited for a couple of his employees to help him get the wolf into his examining room.

6

Once Tommy and Emma made sure all was OK at the farm, Tommy threw the chainsaw into the back of his truck with extra gas cans. Emma loaded the back of her truck with medical supplies, her prepper bag and some bottled water and they both headed off to town in separate vehicles. The storm last night was rough, a little too rough and they both wanted to check on some friends in town. No matter how much you talk to people about being prepared, they found that there were still some who just refused to listen and take action. "Those crazy preppers" they would jokingly call them. They weren't always laughing so hard though when they needed to be rescued.

Emma watched as Tommy continued on down the road, but wanting to check on her aunt and uncle, Emma turned her truck onto the dirt road before she reached town. Having time to think about the past couple days, specifically last night, she finally let out a sigh of relief. "Fucking wolves" she muttered under her breath. She had seen a steady increase in their numbers lately. The calls coming in to the dispatch along with the chatter down at the post had given her cause to be concerned. Well, there's one less on this planet she thought as she turned into her aunt and uncle's grass-covered driveway.

Emma stepped out of her truck and quickly realized she must have parked the vehicle by a beehive. Calmly and slowly walking towards the house, she knew if she gave them no reason to attack, they wouldn't. They just wanted to eat and make honey! It gave her pause to think, though: beehives for self-defense of your property. Strategically placed outside your home, could it be used for fortification? She had heard of woven bee skeps during her studies in school where medieval soldiers would throw hives over the castle walls during an invasion. People also used to throw beehives into stagecoaches during robbery attempts back in the Wild West. She would have to dig more into this when she returned home later, as it brought a smile to her face to think about hiding supplies such as an extra firearm and ammo in a hive itself! Which reminded her, she probably needed to lay in some more supplies of Benadryl if this panned out as she thought it might. Giving a chuckle, she would also have to make sure her chickens couldn't get into them, as the cluckers would quickly have an easy snack.

Turning the corner of the house to the back yard, Blu, the resident Chow dog came out to meet her. If you have never seen a Chow, you are in for a real treat. Blu looked like a big, furry teddy bear. As she proceeded to greet Emma, it was quite obvious how she got her name. Blu had a blue tongue. Maybe more of a violet color but with such a strong strain of blue that Uncle Randy decided to name her Blu. It is one of the traits of their breed and one that makes them quite valuable.

Blu had been with the family for quite some time. She had birthed many a fine pup and was now spending her retirement years roaming the property and occasionally being an early warning system. I say occasionally only because Blu also liked to sun herself on the patio and had been known to enjoy herself so much that she has been photographed with a squirrel perched directly above her.

As Emma was stooping to give Blu a fine rub behind the ears, she heard the melodic singing coming from the kitchen window. Her Aunt Amy was canning some of her famous bean soup and keeping her vocal cords strong at the same time...

"Did you hear that lonesome whippoorwill ~ He sounds to blue to cry ~ That midnight train is winding low ~ I'm so lonesome I could cry" Amy sang out, stretching out certain words like salt water taffy being pulled. Amy sang bluegrass on the radio when she was a teenager. She sang with the likes of Hank Williams and the Osborne Brothers. It was a part of her soul and something she handed down to her niece.

Growing up, Emma used to sit around and listen to her aunt, her dad and her grandfather pick the strings of their guitars and belt out a good ballad. There was not much better than the blended voices of family singing. It was a natural intertwining of melodiousness that could never be replicated. Weekends were spent with family friends showing up with banjos, mandolins, fiddles and occasionally a standing bass and music being shared long into the night. And you can't have good music without good food. No one ever starved at these gatherings, as some of the best cooks in the world brought forth their creations to show off. At one such event, Emma was introduced to coconut cream pie that had whipped cream piled so high it looked like it belonged on the top of the Rocky Mountains. One could lose themselves in its deliciousness and have to be rescued before the entire pie was devoured.

It was also at one of these shin-digs that a young man named Scott brought over his drum set to play with the older folks. While being the star drummer in the local high school band was one thing, playing bluegrass was a whole different ball game, but Scott soon caught on. Scott also caught the need to further a relationship with Emma. They had known each other in school but only by passing in the hall-ways. Now Scott was spending most week-ends at her house playing music and their relationship blossomed. A deep friendship developed, unfortunately minus the spark of lust even with all the adult intervention. Scott ended up graduating and going off to veterinary school only to return to his roots years later.

Emma turned her face to the sun and felt the warmth dig down deep into her soul. It was no wonder
Blu enjoyed sunbathing so much. Emma stood and walked into the kitchen as her aunt was pulling jars from the canner. She gingerly set them down onto the towel covering the counter and turned to give her niece a hug.

"Hey sweetie, how's things today?" Amy asked "Good, good" Emma answered.

"Oh really? Cuz I'm not feeling that vibe from you, little one" Amy said.

"Just checking on some folks after the storm. I heard the power was out for a few because some trees were knocked down so Tommy brought the chain saw in town to see if we could help. Wanted to stop and check on you and Unk before I headed in," Emma replied

"No worries here. You know how we are. But it's still nice that you stopped in! Before you leave, I'm going to pack you with some soup though. Folks might need it in town and I've got plenty canned already today. Plus… your Auntie wants to get outside in the sun and if I have to finish this, I will never make it outside before she sets"

"Yes ma'am!" Emma snickered. "Hey, have you seen any wolves around here lately?"

"Blu's been a bit restless at night. She's been making her presence known and keeping the neighbors awake but I don't know if its wolves or not. Why?" Amy said with a lift of her brow. She picked up on the hidden message and felt a little uneasy. Wolves could do a lot of damage on a homestead. She'd seen entire chicken flocks wiped out within minutes.

"Shit" Amy barked, "You need to spill the beans, and fast"

Emma shuffled her feet while looking down at the floor. Her hands deep in her pockets with her elbows locked tight, it brought her shoulders up to her ears. Amy flashed back to when Emma was a little girl and would make the same gestures. Something was up and Amy knew it.

"Had a wolf on the farm last night and wondered if you've seen anything," Emma stammered.

"Damn it. I knew something was going on. Everything OK?" Asked Amy

"Ya...ya... Dixon scared it off" Emma replied leaving out so much information that she felt like she was going to burn in hell if her aunt ever found out.

Emma helped Amy pack up some soup along with some cornbread in case Emma ran into someone who needed it in town after the storm. Conversation turned lighter but Amy knew she needed to do some nosing as she knew there was more to this story then Emma was letting on. She let it go for now, though, because she knew Emma wanted to get into town. But, this was far from over and she knew it.

7

Emma headed back into town, wondering along the way where exactly she could find her husband. It didn't take her long to find him as he always migrated to the worst-hit area no matter what was going on. He always had to be in the thick of things. This was a blessing or a curse, Emma thought, but she could never figure out which one. He won her heart by many things but his compassion for others was a huge part of it. On the flip side, his need to be a social butterfly was a bit overwhelming for an introvert like Emma. She valued and got strength from her alone time. Tommy was quite the opposite. His batteries got charged from being around people. The energy just radiated off of him when he was in a crowd of people. Everyone knew Tommy and he knew everyone.

Finding a place to park her truck, Emma scanned the area. The electric company was already out and had secured the fallen electrical lines. The men who were there were cutting the downed trees up and clearing the debris. The wood would be donated to those who needed it and if anyone didn't want it, the guys would divide the rest into their trucks. The typical gawkers were there with their cameras in tow, being more of a nuisance than anything as the workers had to shuffle them around when they had to remove unstable limbs or fell a tree that was damaged.

Emma tracked down Brian Cottner, the Emergency Management Director, to see how things were going and if they needed her help anywhere. He wasn't hard to find as most of the damage from the storm was contained in one general area. He was, on the other hand, not in one of his better moods. His glossy dome of a head was already turning multiple shades of red she noticed as she walked over to where he was talking with some utility workers. His fingers pointing in multiple directions with arms flailing, he reminded her of an octopus. She would be certain to mention that to him later over a beer. Not sure he would appreciate the humor in it right now though, she thought with a chuckle.

"Dude, how long you been out here" Emma asked

"Dude? Really?" Brian snarled back. Emma raised an eyebrow and Brian noticed. His tone changed a bit. "Since last night, why?"

She took him by the arm and dragged him over to her truck. Lowering the tailgate she demanded he "Sit" as she pointed. Emma went into the cab of the truck and got a thermos of coffee, some soup and a nice helping of cornbread and walked back around to where Brian was sitting. "Here" she said as she started spreading out the food. "Eat this before you harm someone with your bad attitude"

Brian took a big drink of coffee and closed his eyes. "I'm good, thanks for the coffee, though," he said as his stomach betrayed him. The growling didn't stop either and Emma started to grin. "Just eat, you big bald bullheaded dork," she said.

"Ya know, it's a good thing I actually like you little miss smarty pants" Brian quipped as he picked up a piece of cornbread.

"Ya Ya, whatever" Emma replied. "Anyone hurt?"

"No, we were lucky. Just a lot of cleanup this time, but dang if these storms don't keep getting stronger and stronger. It's like someone is intentionally turning up the dial!" Emma spun around and opened her mouth and was about to say something when Brian added, "Oh, and you can keep your weather modification theories to yourself, I'm being serious. You don't need to 'enlighten' me with your intelligence," he said as he purposely added air quotes around the word "enlighten." Knowing he was going to start an argument he wasn't going to win, he quickly changed the subject.

"Could use your help on a new project that I want to get going on" he said

"What is it?" she asked

"This is completely off the record, just remember that" he said

"Alright, no problem," Emma said intrigued.

"I want to get more women involved in security, specifically becoming proficient in firearms. I figure, coming from another female, would help motivate them faster," Brian said

"You have a need for speed on this or something?"

"Let's just say I want to put a wiggle in getting our little community set up to not have to rely on outside 'sources' so much" There were those damn air quotes again, Emma thought.

"Sure, whatever you need. You know that. Anything you want to talk about?" Emma asked

Brian and Emma had been friends for a long time but not always on the same side. Brian, a couple years older, graduated and got a degree in crisis management. Getting wrapped up in all the government enticements, Brian came home with the intention of "saving" his home town, not realizing that they didn't need rescuing. Government hand-outs always came with strings attached and it took Brian a few years of being a puppet to wake up. A few more years of trying to untie all the knots that he himself had created and Brian finally had his community working towards being self-sufficient. Now it was only a matter of tweaking out the rough spots and bringing everyone onto the same page.

"Higher ups are getting jittery," he said. He bowed his head and talked low enough that only Emma could hear him. "They are talking about an overthrow," he said as he raised his head. Looking her in the eyes, gaze as strong as steel, locking her in and not letting go, "a coup," he said without releasing her stare. He watched as her mind started spinning. While her expression never changed, he saw what was going on behind her eyes and it intrigued him.

"Shit," was all she said and turned and walked off.

She knew it was coming. Hell, if anyone was paying attention, they knew it was coming. The natives were tired and restless. The economy was being held up by false, misleading, numbers. Unemployment was so high that a lot of families had already moved in with their grandparents or some other relative who still actually hadn't had their home foreclosed on yet. Going to the grocery store took all of 10 minutes because most people couldn't afford to eat unless they grew their own. Business after business had boarded up or moved on only to find that the only place to move to was out of the country. This country, *her* country, was a mess. And it broke her heart.

People tried to stand up and speak out only to find their voices muffled. Truck drivers and bikers tried to band together and march on Washington only to become a distant memory. With country after country overthrowing its government, it became quite odd that considering the corruption within our own *government* that everything seemed business as usual. But if you put your ear to the ground, and listened, you could hear the rumble... and that rumble was growing. To those who chose to pay attention, they knew the day would come that would change history. It was only a matter of time.

There was a year left until the next presidential election. A lot of people who traveled within Emma's circle had whispered of martial law, of people within the government implementing a false flag in order to stall that very election. If that were the case, they needed to "put a wiggle in it" as Brian liked to say, and get any loose ends tied up in their community endeavors.

Yes, women needed to step it up. Primary focus had been on food preservation and medical training but they also needed to take responsibility for security of their family, their home and their community.

One area of preparedness that women were weak in was, in fact, security. It was the "man's job," right? To be the defender of his woman, his home. But time after time the question arose, what happens if that man is removed from the home? What happens if during a hurricane that man dies and leaves his wife defenseless? His daughters defenseless? They are then removed to a shelter to become someone's new toy because they did not know how to defend themselves. Does not the stronger always conquer? Does not the weaker submit to authority?

Studying the after-effects of Fukushima and Katrina and what happened in the shelters is very eye-opening when it comes to why women need to learn to defend themselves. The occurrences of rape alone rose into double digit percentages over and above what was already occurring before the disaster.

Putting vulnerable people together with predatory personalities is easily a recipe for disaster, sadly at the hands of those reaching out to help them. Add to that alcohol and drug use in a high stress situation with a very low police presence and you have created the ultimate nightmare for a young female with no means to protect herself.

8

It doesn't long for clean up when a community pitches in, and Tom and Emma were on their way home in no time. Tom had the back of his pickup full of wood from the trees they cut up which would come in handy next winter. Backing his truck up into the wood pit, they quickly unloaded it and headed back to the house. They would come out over the next couple weeks and split and stack the wood so it would be ready to use in the years ahead. This winter's wood supply was already moved up closer to the house to be within easy reach.

Dixon came running up to meet them as they approached the house. Their very own White Knight of the Castle. You would never guess that the previous night he was rolling around with a wolf in the middle of a storm. Completely ignoring Tommy, Dixon ran straight to his Lady of the Manor and greeted her with pure, complete Camelot chivalry. One big slopping kiss later they were headed towards the house as Emma exclaimed. "Let's go eat!"

Being tired, they had a light, easy dinner and settled in the living room for the night. Tom began building a fire for the night ahead and Dixon stretched out on his pillow and promptly began snoring. Once the fire caught, Tom surprised Emma by putting on some music instead of turning on the television. Grabbing a quilt and some sofa pillows, and trying to be as romantic as he could, he laid them out on the floor in front of the fireplace. Emma watched him full of intrigue as this was not a usual occurrence in their household. Romance and Tommy were distant cousins. Very distant cousins. Once he was satisfied with his arrangement, he walked over and poured them both a shot of spiced rum. Warming it up in his hands, he walked over to where Emma was sitting and reached for her hand. She was surprised that when she reached her hand out, instead of handing her the rum, he pulled her to her feet. "My love." He said as he handed her the rum with an ever so slight tilt to his head. "Why, thank you, kind sir" she responded with the same faint nod.

"I want to make sure we don't forget to make time for things like this" Tommy said "For quiet times like this with just you...and me... and a snoring dog." He smiled as he nodded toward Dixon.

Tom pulled her over before the fire and they sat on the blanket. Emma nestled into Tommy's arms and sank into a peacefulness that very few experience. He was her rock. With just a touch he could make her world a better place. Sipping on the rum and staring at the fire, Emma's mind started to become quiet. Her muscles relaxed as he stroked her hair. The soothing rhythm of his breathing kept pace with her heartbeat. Over and over his hand caressed the strands of hair...whipping the tendrils with intensity with each pulse. The pressure increased with each lashing until blood began to pour from the wounds. Over and over the whip lashed at her and her screams increased until they escaped from her lips. "Noooooo!" she screamed.

Startled, Tom stared down in horror at his wife. Had he hurt her? Frantically looking for signs of a wound, he finally came to his senses. She had another dream. "Shhhhh. Shhh. It's OK. It's just us. Just you and me. No one else is here. Shhh." He whispered as he held her tight. "I'm so sorry," she whimpered.

Sliding down beside her, Tom took her face between his hands and kissed her forehead. She wrapped her arms around him and buried her face under his chin. This was her comfort.

She had started to have the dreams a couple years earlier. Just out of the blue, for no reason at all. No big traumatic event preceded them; they just began, lasted a couple months and then ended. They always left her screaming out in pain. The only thing she has even been able to remember was that she was being whipped across her back. Deep gashes, over and over as someone was lashing out at her, trying to exert control over her. She fought back both in her dreams and in reality as she considered control a sign of weakness. Her relationships with friends foundered as she fought for some type of domination of her emotions. She suffered. Her friends suffered. But Tommy showed her otherwise. She relinquished control to him, allowed him to consume her soul with only the tenderness his heart knew towards her. He was the keeper of her heart.

Feeling him stir, she tilted her head back and kissed the tenderness under his chin. She needed to be consumed before these emotions began tearing at the recesses of her heart again. She let her lips trail up his jawbone and nuzzle under his ear lobe. Reaching around, he forced her onto her back on the blanket. He knew her body well. He knew how to harness her energy and allow her mind to escape the torment it had endured.

Looking into her eyes, he saw the shadows play across her mind. Trailing his fingers down the chasm between her breasts, he felt a shiver pulse through her body. Her body belonged to him. She could deny him, she could fight him for as long as she wanted but always she had relinquished in defeat.

9

The next morning Emma woke to the smells of bacon and coffee. What a more perfect way to awaken was there? Sliding into her bathrobe, she decided to leave yesterday in the past and live in the now for just a little bit longer. Strolling into the kitchen, she caught sight of her husband staring out the window above the sink. So deep in thought he was. Life was dancing its way through his jet black hair leaving touches of gray giving him a distinguished look. Letting out a deep sigh of infatuation, she disturbed his trance. Turning around, he looked at her and smiled. Their eyes locking.

"I talked to Brian yesterday" he said as he turned to place his coffee cup in the sink

"Oh ya, he have anything interesting to say?" Emma asked.

"Nothing he didn't tell you" Tommy replied sarcastically with a smirk. "You have any plans for the next couple hours?"

"I'm all yours"

"Good, let's do a once over on our preps. Get the kids over for dinner, I think it's time we had a family meeting" Tommy said

"OK. I will call them after breakfast. I love you."

"I love you more, always."

~

The kids started arriving in a whirlwind of loving chaos. While everyone lived on the same property, the acreage gave everyone enough privacy that it still made these events special. Kevin arrived first with his wife Jessica and their two kids, Jack and Janie, 12-year-old twins. Jonathan and his wife Maria arrived with their son Matthew and then Emily and her husband John arrived with their 3 children, James, Amy and Zack

Connor and his wife, Samantha arrived with their newborn son, Charlie and, once again, Lauren brought up the rear, late as always but bringing a double chocolate cake and begging for forgiveness.

Charlie fed and down for a nap, Emma had the boys set up the spare table for all the kids. Lauren took care of the table for the adults and before they knew it everyone was bowing their heads around the dining room.

"Father God, thank you for the many blessings you have bestowed upon our family. Please bless the food we are about to eat for the nourishment of our bodies. We give you all Glory and Praise, In Jesus' name, and everyone said" as they all rang out in chorus, "Amen"

The clinking of glasses and silverware began as food was passed around the table.

"Mumsy, you outdid yourself once again!" Jessica said as the rest agreed with nods and grunts.

Baked chicken, mashed potatoes and the kid's favorite, Emma's homemade noodles.

Emma had made them years ago for a church event and one of the members of her church, Scott was just overjoyed. He referred to them as ghetto noodles because when he was growing up they were so poor that his family couldn't afford the fancy store-bought ones in the bag. They were easy enough to make as Emma had spent years perfecting her version of the plump morsels of comfort.

Taking one cup of flour, Emma would pile it on her butcher-block counter top. Using her fingers, she would make a well in the middle of the flour and crack open two eggs into the shallow pit. Adding a splash of salt and pepper, she also combined a splash of her secret ingredient, evaporated milk, into the well of flour. Mixing the ingredients together, she formed a small ball of pasta.

Dusting the board with more flour, Emma took the ball of dough and flattened it on the board with the heel of her hand before adding more flour over the top. Now it was just a matter of rolling the dough out flat with her rolling pin until she reached the desired thickness.

Lightly dusting the dough once more with just a hint of flour, Emma began rolling the dough from one end creating a long tube of multi layered dough. Grabbing a knife, she began to whimsically draw the blade through the dough to create noodles of different widths. The grandkids loved to slurp up the different sizes of noodles, splashing the rich broth that she cooked them in against their chins. Bibs to cover their shirts were definitely a must!

Once she had the roll of dough cut, she then would begin to tediously unroll the cuts to reveal the noodles. Onto the drying rack they went for a couple hours and then into the pot of homemade chicken broth for several more hours of melding with the juicy fatness from the stock and you had a noodle that once laid upon your tongue, would melt like hot butter on a cast iron skillet over an open flame. Layer those bad boys over some mashed potatoes and it was a marriage made in heaven.

Once dinner was over and the table cleared, the kids went to the family room to play video games while the adults talked.

"Alright kids" Tommy began "We need to get down to business. Heard some reliable chatter yesterday that a government coup could be about to go down and if that doesn't happen a possible martial law imposed to ensure we don't have a change of presidency anytime soon. Either way, things are about to get very sticky and we need to be able to ride it out as long as we can. That being said, I want to review where we are in our preps and what we need to focus on."

Low murmurs could be heard from around the table. Spouses had their heads bowed together in private chatter and then there was Lauren. Not being fazed by the news, she was more intent on a slice of double chocolate cake.

Lauren was really the only sort of non-prepper in the family. While Emma made sure she had a "Get-home-bag" and supplies to last a while, preparedness was never a hot topic in Lauren's world. She was an artist. Artists simply do not think about the future. They lived for the here and now!

To be specific, Lauren was a comic book artist and had her own line of graphic art that supported her monetarily. She also did the artwork for Prepper Chicks when Emma needed something. The problem was Emma never asked. If she did, her request got shoved to the back of Lauren's list and it turned into a struggle to get Lauren to complete anything. It just wasn't important in Lauren's world, whatever it was that her mother did.

"Everyone have their binders?" Emma asked

Each family placed multiple 3-ring binders on the table. Each book contained the same information, contact information to thousands of families around the world who had like mindedness in the area of self-sufficiency and had been vetted as a "safe" family, a list of all the preps currently in inventory, medical history for each family member, an inventory of all equipment along with a maintenance schedule, and a pedigree list of all animals on the homestead.

One by one, the family went through each binder and made sure everyone and everything was up to date. They then began the tedious task of reviewing the functioning of the homestead and adding preps to make is as self-sufficient as possible.

Water – They looked at current water storage. Their goal was enough viable drinking water for immediate use for each member of the family for a minimum of 3 months. Making the calculations out at 1 gallon per person per day, they knew they needed 19 gallons of stored water per day. That amounted to over 1,700 gallons of water for all of them. Being able to replenish that water supply was important. There was a spring on the farm with direct access to underground water. This spring also filled the cow pond in front of the barn. A creek also runs through the property but could easily be dammed or contaminated upstream. Catchment systems were built onto each home's gutter system on the property and a 500-gallon cistern was built underground at each home. Each outbuilding had a catchment system for the various farm animals. Swails were built into the farm as part of their drought resistant system for permaculture and this helped with watering the various fruit and nut trees around the homestead along with the garden. Each family also had a water filtration system for their home water and filtration in their Go-Bags. Inventory was taken for chemicals used for water purification like bleach and for pool shock. Each family took into account their swimming pool which served double duty as a water supply if need be.

Food – Each family had an immediate use food supply of 6 months' worth of food and recipes. Branching off from there were the long term storage items that, because of how they were packaged, would be good for 25-30 years. Replenishing their food supply, they reviewed the lists of non-GMO, heirloom seeds that each family had in stock. There were the immediate seeds they would be planting in the spring, but also a supply that each family kept in sealed Mylar bags in their freezer. Canning equipment was inventoried and projections made for immediate purchase of jars and lids. They also reviewed the livestock they currently had and their breeding charts. Adjustments were made and any immediate purchases assigned to the appropriate person. Bulk seed purchase was addressed to replenish the foddering system they had set up for animal food along with additional nutrients. The family kept chickens, rabbits, goats, sheep, bees, pigs, a couple dairy cows and a couple cows specifically for breeding and for meat. Emma had become a fan of permaculture farming years prior to moving back to the farm and had established a variable food forest that was invisible to anyone with limited knowledge of farming. Planted around the farm was a veritable gold mine of various fruit and nut trees, medicinal herbs, berries and fruit bushes of every kind tucked into every available nook and cranny on the farm including cold-hardy, hairless Kiwi which she grew particularly for Tommy.

Medicine – All training was reviewed and assigned to be upgraded as soon as possible. CPR and basic trauma medicine were immediate needs with alternative medical inventory taken. Essential oils and medicinal herbs were inventoried for each family and a date set to divide herb clusters to each family as soon as spring arrived.

Clothing – Accounting was given for the growth of the children, materials needed to make additional clothing and appropriate seasonal clothing. Maria was a seamstress by trade so could easily replicate any clothing item necessary. Account was also taken for quilts and bed clothes, curtains and upholstery, feminine products such as menses pads and medical bandages.

Security – Guns and ammo were inventoried along with reloading supplies. Notes were made to add additional supplies as soon as possible. Dates were set for additional training and to acquire additional firearms for the kids. Perimeter alarms were inventoried and additional recommendations discussed. An exercise regime was also established to ensure that everyone within the immediate family was in good shape.

Energy – Energy needs were calculated for farming equipment and housing needs. Fuel tanks would be refilled as soon as possible and additional storage was discussed. Solar and wind equipment was inventoried and additional parts would be ordered. Bio-fuel equipment would also be purchased and upgrades added to the farm equipment. Cooking and lighting needs were addressed with an agreement to purchase extra beehives to be used for candle making.

Communications – Ham radio networks would be checked over the coming weeks and equipment serviced as need be. Schedules were reviewed by each family member and accommodations were made to anyone traveling outside the immediate area as a backup if they could not make it home for some reason.

Network – Each family member was assigned a group of people to reach out to for further instructions if certain scenarios fell into place. Further recommendations were made pertaining to individual trades. Accommodations were discussed about and who would be immediately relocating to the homestead if a scenario plays out. Friends and family in the cities who were in the network would be contacted with instructions and also to review their preps. Maps would be updated and travel routes established with alternative routes assigned depending on the emergency.

Government within the Group – Each family member was assigned a specific task within the group to help everything run smoothly. If people were relocating, they too would be adopted into this pseudo -government. At that time, a governing body would be elected. The nice thing about already having a list of people, was they had already agreed to the rules established so they would just need implemented into the group if and when they were to arrive.

Mental & Spiritual – Each family member was accountable to the other and part of that was to pray over each other as a group and individually. Regular time was set aside for fellowship and for instruction. Inventory was taken into account for the further home-schooling of the children. Situational awareness drills were scheduled on a regular basis going forward. Each family member discussed their preferences if in case of death. A designated area was then agreed upon on the farm to be used as a cemetery.

10

"Time to clear the table!" Connor said. "Let's play some Conflicted!"

Playing Conflicted with his siblings was fast becoming one of Connor's favorite things to do at family meetings. They learned so much about each other, sometimes good, sometimes not so good.

Emma discovered the card game Conflicted years ago when a friend was talking about how she was playing it with her friends. Emma was intrigued by the concept so she contacted the creator and not only was an award-winning radio show developed but a long-lasting friendship was formed.

Conflicted is a scenario-based game. A standard deck of 52 cards, each card was printed with a different scenario that a survival or preparedness group could discuss and find solutions to the dilemmas. Knowledge prep was always the neglected prep and the card game was valuable in getting a person to think inside and outside the box. Playing it in a prepper group enabled the members to get to know how the others thought and how they would possibly react, it opened up discussions about humanity and how far a person would go to protect their loved ones, it made you think about your own ethics and how far you would push the envelope and compromise your own morals.

"I want to play the first card tonight," Connor said

Everyone nodded and proceeded to clear the table and Jessica took the kids to the front room and settled them in with a movie. Lauren grabbed some fresh drinks for everyone as they resettled around the table.

"Everyone ready?" Emma asked as she joined her family and heads bobbed up and down

"Alrighty then," Connor said. "Here's your first card.

"One of your friends has been shot in battle, and a field medic told you he will be paralyzed from the neck down for the rest of his life. This is a post-apocalyptic world you are living in and your friend asks you to please have mercy on him and put him out of his misery. His wife and kids have already died and all he wants to do is be with them instead of living in a world as unforgiving as this. Would you have mercy on your friend and kill him or would you let him live? Why?"

"Well," said Kevin, "that's a tough one!" He cleared his throat and continued on, "I'd probably give him a gun with a bullet in it."

"What for?" Lauren said "He's paralyzed from the neck down. He won't be able to even lift it so you are going to have to shoot him yourself cuz he obviously can't."

"So could you kill your best friend if his whole life was already gone and now he couldn't move?" Jonathan asked his brother

Kevin let out a sigh "Ya know. I think I could," he said as he shook his head up and down.

"Really?" his wife asked

Kevin looked down at his folded hands that were in his lap. Kill his best friend. Put a bullet in him.

Kevin wasn't so sure anymore. He needed to be honest with himself and not try to be the tough guy with the rest of the group. He shut his eyes and tried to transport himself to a time and place to try and trick his mind into an answer.

"Curve-ball," Jessica said, "What if it was me?"

"Shit. Really?" Kevin said. "No way. There's no way I could off you"

"The kids are all gone, which would kill me in itself. I'm now paralyzed from my neck down and can't move. You wouldn't put me out of my misery?" Jessica asked as she looked at him.

"Let's go back to the original question" Emily said, sensing the uncomfortable tension between Kevin and Jessica. "I think I honestly could do it and let me explain how. You have to remember," she said with all seriousness, "We are talking post-apocalyptic world here. Our happy little self-absorbed life is over. No more Super Bowl, no more midnight trips to Taco Hell. Lord only knows what we have already seen or have had to endure. Our minds have changed, our thoughts have changed on what is moral or not. We aren't eating or sleeping properly. Heck, I'd probably off both of us together and just get it over with, especially if I already lost all those I care about. Who cares at that point?"

"Well, you could off him and then eat 'em" Jonathan chimed in with a wicked grin

"You're a sick fuck, you know that little brother," said Kevin

11

Kevin and Jessica waved goodbye again as the kids ran back to give Grandma and Grandpa another hug. Their kids still attended public school and had to be up early to catch the bus. 6am came pretty early to a couple of pre-teens and they still had chores to do before bed. Jack and Janie ran on ahead of their parents, who strolled hand in hand towards their own section of the homestead. Reluctant at first to make the move, they both never regretted the decision. It was nice for the kids to have their cousins around within walking distance. Their grandparents had active roles in their lives and saw them way more often than birthdays and holidays like most other kids.

Kevin pulled Jessica back a bit and slowed the pace.

"Everything OK?" Jessica asked

"Ya, I guess. I wanted to get your take on the whole cemetery thing without the kids hearing, though." Kevin responded. "I guess I haven't really thought about that part of all this, but it's bothering me. I'm not sure I could actually bury one of you if I had to. Jesus!" he exclaimed as be ran his hand through his hair, obviously shaken.

Jessica locked her arm into his. "I'm not going anywhere anytime soon, but it's always good to talk about everything. The good parts and the sucky parts, ya know."

"I guess" Kevin stated. "Tonight was a little rough. I'm glad we walked over, I needed the fresh air"

Jessica could sense the little bit of panic in the pit of Kevin's stomach. She had it too, but she was also a mama bear, and she was going to do everything within her power to make sure her family was safely taken care of.

12

A couple days later, Emma drove Dixon over to see his favorite Doc. She wanted to pick his brain on a few things that were left up in the air the last time she was there.

"Hey stranger" Doc exclaimed as he was exiting the barn. He reached down to give Dixon a scratch behind the ears. "How's my favorite wolf fighter?" he asked

"Funny you ask that, Doc," Emma said "It's kind of what I want to talk to you about"

"Everything OK with Dix?" Doc asked with a look of concern on his face.

"Oh no! He's just fine. I just wanted to see if you have gotten any test results back yet on the one I brought you the other day"

"No on the results, but I'm not sure if you realized it, but that wolf you brought me was a female." Emma stopped dead in her tracks.

"A female?"

"Yes, and a nursing one at that," Doc said

Emma stared at him for a minute and then yelled for Dixon to get in the truck.

"Whoa, hold on there a minute" Doc exclaimed as he grabbed her arm "Just where do you think you are going?"

"Damn it Scott, there are very hungry wolf cubs and a pissed off male somewhere between my house and town. Every small child and livestock animal are in danger. I need to go find Brian

so we can start warning people. Now let go of my damned arm!"
she screamed at him as she headed for the truck.

Flooring it, she blew gravel up from behind her rear tires.
"Damn crazy woman," Doc thought and then said a quiet prayer
over her.

13

Emma headed into town. She needed to talk to Brian and put a
plan together to let people know that there could be trouble with
these wolves. As she turned into the parking garage for the local
Emergency Management Office, she realized she had been so
focused on the wolf issue that she had completely zoned out
most of the trip. Taking a deep breath she refocused.
"Situational Awareness" she muttered to herself as she glanced
in her side mirrors. Crime had increased in town recently so
much that one would think her small hometown was a big city.

Unemployment was skyrocketing and people were getting
desperate. Just last week a woman was walking into the local
grocery store with her small child and someone just walked up
and shot her and took her purse. The woman just crumbled to
the ground while her child was still clutching her hand. What
was this world coming to? Compassion and empathy were being
removed from the human language and replaced with rage and
violence. The newest fad in big cities was something called
"The knockout game." A punk would walk up to an individual
and hit them so hard in the face that it would knock them out.
The goal of the game was to only use one punch to knock them
unconscious, which is bad enough, but people were dying from
this senseless act.

Emma removed her handgun from under her steering column and placed it into her holster on her belt. Making sure she had her flashlight and knife, she gave a giggle as she patted her pocket. The triplets, as she called them, were always with her.

Rechecking her surroundings, Emma got out of her vehicle and just stood still listening for any sounds. Identifying her surroundings, a quick scan showed her the exits and surrounding vehicles. She also saw a fire extinguisher hanging on the wall between the stair door and the elevator doors. Walking in that direction, she heard a car door shut. Her head jolted in the direction of the noise but she didn't see anyone. Taking a deep breath she quickened her speed.

Another car door closed and a woman appeared. Emma recognized her from the post office. "What was her name?" Emma thought. She hadn't lived in town long as Emma remembers her signing up for a post office box for her mail delivery. Angie. Angie was her name. They had talked briefly at the post as Emma had given her some general directions towards the grocery and library in town. Angie was a nurse from Memphis here visiting her mom but was in the process of buying a small apartment so she could visit more often. They could also then use the apartment for Angie's other siblings when they also came into town to visit their mom. Emma said hi as they both moved towards the exits to the lower levels.

They were halfway to the exit when the man appeared. Haggard in appearance, he made the hair on the back of Emma's neck stand on end. She knew to trust her senses. Her gut was telling her to get the hell out of there and fast. The man got to the door before her and stood off to the side. "Odd," Emma thought. Why not stand in front of the elevator doors like everyone else? Angie stopped in front of the elevator and pushed the button. She turned and looked at the man and began to engage him in conversation. Well, maybe she knew him?

Emma's mind began to run through possible scenarios. She decided her best option was to take the stairs down to the main floor. Getting caught in a closed elevator with someone who gave her the willies was not her idea of a good time. Making an excuse that exercise was good for the heart; she quickly dodged behind the door and began her descent. Listening behind her, she did not hear the door open or close.

It was a quick trip down the one floor to where Brian's office was located. As she exited the stairwell, she glanced at the lights on the elevator that showed what floor it was on. Nothing. No lights were lit. That means that they did not use the elevator and they were still in the parking garage.

Emma quickly found Brian's office but his secretary said he hadn't returned from lunch yet. Glancing at her watch, Emma was about 20 minutes early. Something wasn't right here, Emma could feel it. Pacing back and forth a couple times, Emma told the secretary that she had forgotten something in her car and would be right back.

Once in the hallway, Emma un-holstered her Glock and checked to make sure she had a bullet in the chamber. Double checking the extra two mags she carried, she slid the firearm down behind her right leg, keeping her finger of the trigger. Once she entered the stairwell, she stopped and listened. Nothing. The silence quickly enhanced the beating of her heart and it echoed in her ears like the drums Doc Scott used to play in high school.

Ascending the stairs one by one, Emma was as quiet as a cat sneaking up on its prey. Stopping at the top of the stairwell, Emma listened. Muffled noises. Emma couldn't make them out. Faint rustling. Taking a deep breath, Emma slowly cracked open the door and waited. That's when she heard the noise that made her heart stop. The muffled noise became clearer. Taking her cell phone from her pocket, she quietly dialed 911 and whispered the address into the handset.

Sliding the phone into her pocket, she said a quick prayer. Opening the door wider, she exited the stairwell and stopped. Listening intently, the sound was coming from where she had parked her truck earlier. Taking a hard left, Emma walked down several rows of cars and aligned herself with where she was parked. Crouching down, she looked under the cars in the direction of the sound.

What she saw next made her blood boil. A coat, the same type of coat that Angie was wearing earlier was on the ground. Emma could see red hair spilled over a face that was pushed down into the pavement. Emma's eyes scanned the rest of the body and that's when Emma saw a knee bent beside the coat. A knee that was clothed in the same type of blue-jeans that the man was wearing earlier. It was quite obvious now that someone, someone wearing the same coat that Angie had on was being raped by someone wearing the same pants the man had on earlier.

The sirens could now be heard, getting louder as they came closer and closer to where Emma was. She knew the man heard them also as she heard him start to bark commands at Angie. "Don't get up.
Don't look at me. Stay where you are or I will kill you" was coming out of the man's mouth in a coarse, raspy tone that made Emma think of pure evil.

Emma knew if something didn't happen soon, this vile excuse for a human would get away. She quickly eased herself to the next aisle and came within a car of the man. Using the neighboring car as cover, the scene before her made her sick to her stomach. The man had Angie on her stomach with both of his hands clenching her naked hips. Her nylons had been ripped from one leg and still covered the other, the clasp of the garter belt fighting to hold onto the top of the stocking. Her skirt had been pushed up her back and her panties shoved aside exposing her smooth porcelain and now quite vulnerable flesh. The man was kneeling between her legs, his hairy buttocks still covered by his shirt thrusting his manhood with such force it caused his shirt to swing back and forth like the temp of a grandfather clock. He was oblivious to Emma sneaking up behind him. His focus was on the woman before him and the sound of the sirens coming closer and closer. His mind was calculating the time he had left, silently cursing that he was quickly coming to an end before he was ready.

The creature lying on the ground underneath the man was helpless. Having lost the senses to fight, she just whimpered. Emma used her lowest octave and yelled "I have a gun and will shoot you if you don't get off of her and get on the ground NOW!"

The man froze.

His hands still on the woman's hips, he slowly disengaged his penis from within her. "I need to stand up," he said as he started to raise his hands.

"Get on the fucking ground now," Emma screamed. Her voice cracked. "Damn it," she thought to herself.

"No....no, it's OK", the man stammered, "I'm going to just stand up now" as he backed away from the woman.

"Don't fucking move you piece of shit," Emma yelled but the man was ignoring her and continued to move back and quickly tuck in his penis and zip his pants.

"Lady, I don't know what you think you are doing, but this is none, of your business what I am doing here with my friend. You best be on your way and right quick," he said

"I am telling you to get on the ground now."

The man was now on his feet and standing. He slowly turned and faced Emma. His eyes now glued to the gun.

"Well listen, bitch, you want a piece of this too, we can make that happen," he said as he began to walk towards Emma. A flash of light hit her across the eyes as the light reflected off the blade of the knife he now had pulled and aimed towards her. The narrow slits of her eyes drew together and Emma knew it was time to act as this sorry excuse for a man was not going to go down without a fight. Emma braced for it. She knew the impact she would feel in her hands. The power that escaped as she quickly pulled back on the trigger hopefully had the strength to send this piece of shit straight to hell.

Center mass, the bullet ripped into his shirt with such force it shoved him back a bit before he collapsed. Emma's eyes locked on his as the surprise ripped through his face. His eyes quickly turned to white as they rolled upwards and he fell back.

Keeping one hand on her gun and pointed on the man, Emma ran over to Angie. So zoned in on the man, Emma had not heard her screams until just now Angie was sitting up, her clothes still in disarray from her ordeal. Emma sat down and put an arm around her.

"It's over. We need to wait for the police now" Emma said to Angie as calmly as she could.

Angie was sobbing with such force that Emma thought she would hyperventilate. But she was also still alive. Angie heard nothing. Saw nothing. She had escaped into her own private womb so the outside would not hurt her anymore. Her world had just been shattered. Her sense of security had been stripped from her. She clung to Emma for life, fighting to take each breath.

14

Brian was through the door and into the parking garage before the police arrived. His secretary had told him Emma was there and had gone back to her car in the parking garage. When she hadn't shown back up, he went looking for her when he heard the gunshot. He saw Emma shoot the guy, and like an old slow-motion movie, watched him hit the ground.

Using her name, Brian called out to Emma multiple times before she finally heard him. Slowly breaking from the trance, she glared at him with the look of pure hatred on her face. The look wasn't for Brian but all the emotions collected together for the man she had shot. It took her a moment for her to recognize her old friend. Brian talked her through getting her pistol holstered as she kept an eye on the man now lying in a pool of blood on the cold hard concrete.

Taking his phone, he called his secretary and asked her to quickly bring a blanket to the garage. "Just do it," he yelled into the phone and hung up. Looking around, he took mental images of the scene. The police should be here soon, he thought, as the sound from the sirens was almost upon them.

His secretary emerged from the elevator and stopped dead in her tracks as she surveyed what was going on before her.

Brian quickly told her to take the blanket to Emma so she could cover up the woman. "Go to the lobby and instruct the officers on what's going on up here so we don't get shot. Let them know I have this asshole under control, that I do have a loaded firearm and that we are going to need two ambulances." "Yes sir" his secretary said as she turned and ran toward the elevator.

"Oh, and don't let anyone up here besides the ambulance and the police… call the garage attendant and tell him to shut off the entrance"

Yes sir" his secretary said as she disappeared into the elevator

"You OK?" he shot over to Emma

"Yeah," Emma nodded

15

"What the hell are you talking about?" Emma blatantly asked the police officer. "What do you mean by 'Was she asking for it?'"

"Well ma'am, you said you observed them before you went downstairs. Was she flirting with him? Was her blouse unbuttoned too much? That kind of stuff." The officer replied with all seriousness.

"You have got to be kidding me!" Emma exclaimed rather loudly. "A woman is raped and the first thing you think that's the problem is that it's her fault? Really? Is that the training you receive or is this your process of thinking, that it's always the woman's fault? That the woman had to have done something wrong because, Lord knows, no man would ever do this without being manipulated by the female? Seriously? I just witnessed some asshat committing a forcible felony and all you're worried about is if he was coerced into it. I just shot a man and now you are putting me through this bullshit?
What the fuck is wrong with you people?"

Emma was truly disgusted. She left the officer staring after her in the hallway and walked back into the hospital room. She had had enough stupidity for one day and was on the cusp of doing something that would not be beneficial to anyone but damn, if it wouldn't make her feel a lot better!

Angie was lying there in her sterile white bed with her eyes closed. Her auburn hair splayed across the pillow with such contrast that it reminded Emma of Heaven and Hell and what this world was coming to. This woman left her home this morning with the intention of returning tonight, eating dinner, scratching her cat and going to sleep in her own bed, sliding in between her own two sheets and laying her head on her own pillow. Instead, she would be spending several days among strangers, being poked and prodded for information like a common criminal. Emma's eyes welled with tears at the absurdity of this.

Tilting her bad back so the tears didn't escape, Emma took a deep breath. The rage within her needed refocused. It was bad enough what had happened, but to be treated like the victim was a part of the issue, as much to fault as the actual criminal, was beyond Emma's scope of reasoning.

Sliding into a chair besides Angie's bed as silently as she could, Emma waited. She would not leave her here alone. She would not desert her; dismiss the seriousness of this act because it was inconvenient to her. She wasn't just a number to Emma. Could it be part of Emma's healing to help this woman? Was Emma in need of helping her as much as seeking the woman's help herself?

Emma laid her head back in the chair. She mindlessly stared at the ceiling and felt herself relax a bit. Her breathing starting to slow, Emma couldn't escape her mind taking her back to her childhood.

16

Drifting back thirty years, Emma's mind fought against the unpleasantness of her own youth, and lost.

 It was time to go home, and she was tired. Emma had gotten most of the cleaning done so hopefully she wouldn't have to come back. She was uncomfortable being here, in this man's house. He had always made her feel edgy. She didn't like him, but she didn't know what it was about him that she didn't like. Maybe it was just all of him, she thought. But she would clean his house and then she would have the money she needed to buy the bike she wanted. And being 13, a bike was a necessary mode of transportation to her friend's house.

She snuck through the house as quiet as she could. She knew there were other people there, his kids and their girlfriends, but she really didn't want to see them. They teased her and made her feel uncomfortable, just like their dad. Unfortunately they were all together in the living room, Fred, the big slob of a man and his boys Roger and Terry.

Emma took a deep breath. Jesus how she hated this but her want overshadowed her fear and she stepped just barely into the room.

"Can I go home now?" She asked addressing no one. Her eyes lowered and her voice barely
intelligible

"You done?" Fred asked

"Yes"

"Alright, we will leave after I get my shoes on." He grunted

The big slob of a man pointed to his shoes and Emma went and got them. He was so obese that she had to put them on his feet and tie them as he couldn't bend over. His shoes were as wide as they were long, bent down from the swelling in his lower extremities caused by his diabetes. And they smelled. They smelled bad.

She went into the kitchen and washed her hands after touching his feet. Feeling sick to her stomach, all she wanted to do was get some fresh air. She slipped outside figuring she would just wait out here for him.

It was already getting dark. The air felt alive as it stung her cheeks. Could you smell snow? Taking a deep breath, the cold made her happy. The stars were starting to wink as her and she was happy to be finally going home and out of the man's house.

She heard the door open behind her and jerked her head around. He was coming out the door. Turning sideways, he had to descend the steps one at a time holding the rail as not to fall.

Emma caught herself staring at him, at his grotesque body. How could her mom like to date him? He couldn't even walk down the stairs straight! Who walks sideways down the stairs anyways?

He unlocked the car from the driver's side and Emma slid into the front seat. She felt butterflies in her stomach, which she guessed was from the excitement of her finally going home.

They drove through downtown and headed in the direction of where Emma lived. Silence enveloped the car. Emma was comfortable with silence. It allowed her to play around in her mind. She dreamed dreams of visiting far-off places where people did not make fun of her because she was shy.

Emma watched as the houses sped by, catching glimpses into other people's lives. She was happy that people left their curtains open. It gave her the chance to peek into their world and dream of how she would design her life when she got older.

Houses turned to fields and before long they were headed into an area that grew darker as it was densely populated with trees. She knew this dirt road. It wasn't the main road to her house but it would get them there eventually. She could hear the gravel pelting the bottom of the car. "Whatever" she thought, as long as she was going home.

She felt the car slow and the man steered it over to the side of the road. He had to be careful because there wasn't much room until the ditch started. She remembered her dad getting his car stuck in the soft mud along the side of a dirt road and she didn't want that to happen. Sitting up straighter, she felt the seatbelt hug her tighter so she couldn't move much.

"What are we stopping for?" she asked

Silence.

This silence unnerved her. The man put the car in park and turned off the headlights. He unlatched his seatbelt and Emma expected him to get out of the car.

Instead, he moved closer to her.

"You're going to be dating boys soon, aren't you?"

"Um. No" Emma said as she swallowed

Something wasn't right here. Her mind scrambled to figure it out. Her breathing increased as her eyes stared straight ahead. She was so scared. Her arms wouldn't move; her body tightened up.

The man grabbed her chin and turned her face towards him. His fingers dug into her skin.

His hand left her chin and slid down her neck to the top of her small breasts.

Oh God, Emma thought. He shouldn't be touching me like this, this isn't right. Her mind swirled around like a ballerina on crack cocaine.

The disgusting pig tried to turn his wretched body towards her more but the steering wheel jabbed into his fat belly stopping him. His hand flung out and grabbed her behind her head and forced her to strain against the seat belt making it hard to breathe. His other hand grabbed onto her chin again as he forced her face forward to bring her mouth against him. Thrusting his tongue into her mouth, she tasted his vile saliva. Pushing back against him, she managed to dislodge herself from his violation.

"Stop it" she whimpered, drawing the back of her hand across her mouth as the tears started to fall down her cheeks.

Emma jumped as the nurse walked into the room. Sitting up quickly, she brushed her hand across the cold on her cheek. She thought she had moved on from her past, but it had the ability to affect her even still. Grabbing a tissue, she quickly dried the tears before anyone noticed.

17

Angie spent a few more days in the hospital until they released her. Having to endure a rape test, various blood and sample tests and the questioning, Angie was more than happy to leave, only to be met by the fear of being alone.

She had always been an independent type, never wanting to play within the rules established by someone else. She had the sense to choose right from wrong and felt stifled whenever she had to color within in the lines of someone else's coloring book.

She looked over at the woman talking with the nurse outside her door. Emma had offered to let Angie come stay with her at her place for a while. "Give herself some time to heal," she had said. Angie recalled the look in Emma's eyes, like she really understood what Angie was going through. She felt an oddly calm peace when she was around Emma.

Placing what little belongings she had laying around the hospital room into her purse, Angie decided that it was time to accept this helping hand instead of trying to tough it out herself. Yes, Little Miss Independence was going to let someone else take care of her for a while, she thought to herself. Tears welling up, Angie knew it was going to be OK to trust Emma.

Emma walked back into the room with the nurse

"Hey kiddo, she ready to get some real lunch?" Emma asked, trying to remain chipper

Seeing the look on Angie's face, she knew it would be hard for her and her strong desire to remain self-sufficient, but Emma also knew she could help her through this. Angie had demons to face in the very near future, and Emma had every intention of holding her hand on the journey ahead

Emma also knew that Angie needed to learn how to defend herself and getting her out to the farm would enable Emma to slowly open that door without causing more fear. Emma knew what she had to do. She had been throwing the idea around for a while, but it was time to take action and it looked like Angie was going to be her first student and hopefully a valuable teacher in the future. She just needed Angie to see the big picture.

18

Emma and Angie pulled up to the farmhouse as the big fury white mass of drool bounded toward them, his tongue flapping wildly against the side of his face.

"Angie, I want you to meet Dixon" Emma laughed as he peered straight into the passenger's side car window right at Angie

"Um, is he gonna eat me whole?" Angie choked out

"I want you to understand something about that dog. First, he likes women. And he obviously likes you or we wouldn't have a car door right now. Second, he is the gentlest dog but will protect those he likes with his life. He can sense danger faster than any human and has quite a way about him of deciding if someone is good or bad. He hasn't been wrong yet. Stay where you are and I will come around to your side and introduce you both. I have no doubt you will be fast friends."

Angie watched as Dixon bounded around the car to meet Emma. She felt a tinge of jealousy. She had never had anyone love her with the unconditional emotions that Dixon was showing toward Emma.

Emma kneeled before her big friend and took his face between her hands. "Dix, I want you to meet a friend of mine. She's been deeply hurt and needs our help." Dixon, his tongue still hanging out as he panted deeply, looking at Emma like he understood. "I want you on your best behavior" she chimed

Standing, they both walked around to Angie's side of the car. "Dixon, sit for our guest." Angie gave a quick smile as she watched the beast of a dog obey. Angie opened the door and stepped out.

"Angie, I want you to meet Sir Dixon. Sir Dixon, this is our guest, Miss Angie." Right on cue, Dixon stood and walked over to Angie, sat in front of her and held out a paw.

Angie, a look of astonishment on her face, reached out and took his paw. "Sir Dixon, it is my honor" she chuckled. Dixon gave a bark in agreement and Angie let out a laugh, reaching up and giving him an affectionate pat on the head.

Emma smiled. Step one was a complete success.

19

Angie spent the next few days just trying to relax. Time and time again she caught herself jumping at the least little noise. Dixon was a big comfort in that area as he never strayed far from the girls, and in return, Dixon was being spoiled rotten by their guest. They were healing Angie whether she realized it or not, much faster than she could have done it on her own. One of the hardest things to do after an assault is rebuilding trust, and Dixon managed to wiggle his way right into her heart. Being a canine, he didn't carry the same threats, didn't cause the same fears.

Emma handed Angie a cup of coffee as she walked into the kitchen. "Sit down, let's talk," Emma said with just the slightest tone of seriousness that it made Angie take pause.

"I want to talk about some training I have going on and wanted to know if you might be interested in helping me out," Emma inquired

"Well, OK," Angie let out a sigh of relief. She thought Emma was going to ask her about what happened in the parking garage and she had no intention of talking about it yet.

"Good. Our local Emergency Management director has asked me to put together a class geared toward women and handguns. Guys have a hard time getting their point across about drawing from a holster when they tell us to just move our boobs out of the way." Emma rolled her eyes and Angie let out a giggle.

"Ya, would be kinda hard to show the technique, I guess! OK, so what do you need from me?"

"Well, how proficient are you with a handgun?" Emma asked

"My dad has a shotgun, my brother has rifles but not much in the way of handguns. I dated a guy once who had a revolver but I didn't much care for it."

"So, first steps first. Let's sit down and go over the pieces and parts of the various kinds of handguns. One thing that I have learned over the years is how differently men and women learn. The male brain has a much better time handling mechanical device such as handguns or even a motor vehicles. They can look at a diagram of something they are trying to build, and most times, they can get it together without too much trouble.

They might have some pieces and parts left, but it will more than likely function," Emma said as Angie gave a smirk

"Women, on the other hand, learn best when the fundamentals of shooting are broken down into smaller segments. They need time to chew up each part and digest it before they move onto something else. We like detailed instruction and the necessary time to practice each step," Emma explained.

"I like that, yes. Makes perfect sense to me. I walked into a gun shop one time down in Memphis. The guys treated me like a brainless bimbo," Angie added

"That isn't going to happen up here," Emma chirped. "I think I've threatened every gun salesman in the state on treating a woman with respect if she came into his shop. But remember, it's also up to us to gain knowledge beforehand. Think of it like buying shoes," Emma explained. "You kind of know what you like before you go into the store. Once you get there, you try on several styles until you get what fits right. Think of it the same way with buying a gun. Most ranges will rent out various styles and calibers. Try out as many as you want until you get the one that works best for you. Not what your boyfriend or husband thinks or what the salesman is trying to sell you, but what actually feels right to you."

"Great analogy!"

"Well, here's what I have in mind. I have a small assortment of guns here. We will spend some time talking about them, getting to know them and then when we feel comfortable, we will go out back and do some practice shooting. I have some targets that Tommy and I use in the back field that we can go and plink on. We can take our time and not worry about gawkers," Emma said

"Awesome. Last time my boyfriend took me to a range to shoot, I was like the only girl in there. The guys were all watching and made me feel very self-conscious. Not fun at all. And then every guy in there kept telling me what I was doing wrong to the point they all had me confused."

"We'll take it a step at a time, and I want you to understand there is a lot more to shooting a gun than just pulling the trigger.
"

20

Emma and Angie spent the next few days sitting at the kitchen table, guns and gun parts spread about. Tommy smiled when he walked into the house to the smell of gun-cleaning solvents. "How many guys get to be this lucky?" he thought to himself.

"It would be nice if there were more trainers like you," Angie said to Emma

Their friendship had blossomed over the last week. Angie was starting to sleep better, even with Dixon on the bed with her. Her spark was coming back so Emma pushed forward with her plan.

"Well, you seem to be picking all the information up right quick. A natural, you sure you haven't done this before?" Emma asked

"Ha! You explain things that make sense. Probably because, if you haven't noticed, you're a woman and understand what women go through. Like when you explained about wearing a holster. Do you think guys ever think about how women's pants don't have as many belt loops so aren't as stable for drawing? Or how a woman, gasp, has curves!" she said as she rolled her eyes. "The guys love them curves but don't understand how it makes our holsters do weird things. How about how high our pants are so our holsters are higher than a guy's so our draw is more uncomfortable when bending our arm back." Angie had to take a breath she was talking so fast.

"OK! OK!" Emma laughed "I get it!

"Oh!" Angie was laughing so hard now she had tears running down her cheeks "Let's talk about the boobies! How many guys have a problem getting from a low ready stance and damn near smack themselves unconscious trying to get into a high ready stance when they have to flip up past the ta-tas! I mean mercy sakes!"

Both girls were now just rolling with laughter. It was good to have silly moments, even in the midst of such pain in one's life.

21

Angie was sitting outside sunning herself when she noticed the big truck pulling up the long drive. She shielded her eyes to see if she could get a better look at who is was, but the shadows played off the windshield and she couldn't tell. She reached her hand out and gave the still sleeping Dixon a pat, more for comfort for herself. Emma said he was a great judge of character and he didn't seem overly concerned about whoever was about to invade his territory. Maybe she should just chill, too. She also lightly touched the holster at her hip, just in case Dixon found it more fun to continue chasing the rabbits he was dreaming about.

The truck rolled to a stop before the garage and Angie heard the driver engage it into park. She heard the door open before Dixon picked his head up and looked in that general direction. Before she heard the door shut, he was up and bounding across the yard to meet the visitor.

Angie took a deep breath. "Can't hide forever, girly," she whispered to herself

She stood as Dixon and the male figure came around the garage. "Howdy!" he yelled out with a wave.

Angie examined the scene before her and quickly deduced that they meant no harm. A man and a pretty red dog were being escorted by Dixon to the house. The two dogs, acting like long-lost friends, paid very little attention to the man as they lumbered along.

"Hello," Angie said as he got closer.

Such a kind face, Angie thought and quickly dismissed it.

"Ma'am, My name is Scott. I am the local vet. I do not believe we have met before," he said

"I'm Angie," she said with her arms still crossed in front of her. "Are you here to see Tom?"

"Actually no, more like Emma. Is she here?" Scott said as he made note of the smile that didn't match the body language

Angie was just about to turn and go look for Emma when she came out of the house.

"Hey Doc!" Emma said with a bit of perplexity in her voice "Did I know you were stopping by today?"

"No." he replied "excuse me for a moment" he said to Angie and turned to walk to where Emma was.

Angie followed him with her eyes as he walked away. While it was nice to feel safe with Emma,

Angie wondered when she would feel comfortable again being around a man. While she felt attracted to Scott, she still knew there was a wall up that wasn't ready to come down. "And a damn shame," she muttered under her breath.

22

"So, this wolf they found. How close to town?" Emma asked

"Closer to your Aunt and Uncles then to town" Doc explained

"Shit. I was hoping they were making their way out here. They are getting pretty brave getting that close to the city, don't you think?" Emma said

"I'm having a meeting at the office tomorrow with some of the neighboring farms. I also called Brian and told him to get his ass out here. Can you and Tom make it over?" Scott asked

"You know it. Just let me know what time"

"Why don't you come on over a little early, say around 3? And um, feel free to bring your friend with you" Scott said as he let his head jerk in Angie's direction.

Emma let out a sigh as she knew she would need to talk to Scott about this privately. "I'll see what I can do."

23

"You sure you don't want to ride along? Doc has some has a pretty neat fur family to check out if you don't want to listen in on the meeting," Tommy asked Angie

"No, I'll be fine here with Dixon," Angie chimed. Angie would admit in a heartbeat that neither choice, either going to Doc Scott's or staying alone for the first time since the attack, were settling with her comfortably, but life had to go on. She had grown stronger over the last few weeks and it was time, she felt, to take the next step.

Emma walked into the room and put her arm around Angie. "We won't be far and we won't be gone long."

"Yes, Mumsy," Angie said as she rolled her eyes like a teenager being left alone for the first time

Tommy gave a chuckle. "Mumsy," he said under his breath, shaking his head back and forth. Holding the door for his wife, they left for Doc Scott's meeting.

24

"The wolf we had the tracker on has traveled a farther distance than any of us thought he would go, and he's just a pup. Makes me think any adult out there is pretty much covering an area the size of the Tri- County as part of their territory," Doc Scott said as he pointed out the diameter of the area on the map.

"Being as aggressive as we have seen them so far has me concerned" he continued. Looking at how I've seen some winter coats coming in on some of the animals, it looks like it's going to be a cold couple of months. Add the cold weather to the aggressiveness we have already seen and we are talking about a recipe for disaster."

"We have 'coon season coming in soon, what do you think we should do?" asked Pete Barbic. Pete was an avid hunter and owned some prized hounds. The last thing he wanted was to lose a valuable dog to a wolf attack.

"Keep them in close. Don't let them get a long lead and keep your ears open. First sign of a wolf and you know there will be more than one in the area. Get out of there and call me with exactly where you were so I can keep tracking their route. We released the one we caught," he said as everyone gasped

"Listen to me before you start freaking out. We put a tracker around its neck so we can follow it on radar and see where they might be making their rounds. Once we determine that, it will make it easier to set up some traps. Right now we are just flying blind on where they might be and that's a lot of territory to cover."

Everyone was shaking their heads in agreement. Two wolves were now roaming around with trackers. That would make it a lot easier to figure out their patterns. The farmers in the area needed to eliminate the threat they caused. One good-sized wolf could create a lot of devastation on a farm. It could completely destroy a small homestead.

"After we plot out some pings from the GPS trackers," Brian chimed in, "We will mesh the data with scat samples and verified interactions. We will then know how they are spending their days and nights and be able to better find their dens. Domestic cats are easy prey, so keep them inside. Mice, shrews and rabbits make up their normal diet but add in the cold weather and you're going to see some odd behavior, some bold behavior if we don't catch them and fast. Late winter is breeding season for wolves so we will see their territorial nature increase."

"What are we looking for exactly, do they look like a big dog?" someone asked from the group

"Not really," Doc said "Most are gray or rusty brown with a bushy tail tipped with black. The tail usually hangs down at a 45-degree angle instead of like a typical canine," as he pointed to a picture of one.

"Keep garbage and pet food cleaned up from outside. This includes anything from around a BBQ grill too. While wolves typically prey on small mammals, they have been known to go after small dogs or cats if the food source is scarce. And if the male dog threatens the territory of the wolf you could have additional problems," Scott said as he looked right at Emma

Emma took the hint. Dixon and the rest of his Great Pyrenees family were in danger on the farm. They would need to take extra precautions until this was under control.

25

Emma was walking back to Tommy's truck when Scott caught up to her.

"Hey, was hoping you would bring your friend along," Scott said

"Ya, we need to talk a bit about that. Listen, don't take this personal, but she isn't ready to get into a relationship just yet. I'm not about to get into her business with you but it's going to take some time for her to even contemplate being social right now."

"Oh, no worries. She just seemed like a nice gal."

"I know hun, but she just needs time. Wouldn't be fair to either one of you right now."

Scott let out a chuckle, "I don't want to marry the woman Emma!"

"Scott, just now is not the time and the one thing she needs right now IS time, just let it go," Emma said with a little too much emotion

"Hey! Geesh! I'm sorry! I just thought maybe we could go out for coffee or something. It's not like I'd rape her!"

The look on Emma's face spoke volumes. Scott knew without asking. He could read his old friend like a well-worn book.

"Oh man," Scott mumbled under his breath feeling like a heel. "Man, I was just joking around, I'm so sorry," he said as he combed his fingers through his hair.

"Let it go Scott," she said as she turned and got into the truck

Scott saw the rest of the group off and decided he needed to go for a walk to clear his head. What an asinine comment to make, he thought.

Giving a whistle for Rusty, they headed up over the back hill. There were some rocky outfaces back there he wanted to check out anyways as they would make the perfect spot for a wolf den.

Picking up a straight branch he spotted beside a downed tree, he used it for a walking stick. He would be sure to add this one to his collection back at the house. Good and sturdy, he would add some paracord around the handle. The last one he designed, he added a compass and a ferrocerium rod too just in case he needed a fire starter when he was out walking. Examining this one, he could easily add a copper end to it to make it last longer. Maybe even brass he thought. Add a piece of pipe and make a secret storage compartment on the end. Now that would be cool, he thought.

A friend of his had visited Ireland and brought him home a shillelagh, a shorter stick which was wielded by all Irish men at one time due to the traditional art of stick fighting in Ireland. From doing a little research, he found out that the British soldiers found it hard to defend themselves against a skilled Irishman wielding a shillelagh without using a firearm, which would cause civil unrest so they banned the short sticks all together. The Irish just made them a bit longer and called them a walking stick to bypass the ban and not a lot could be done about it.

Scott picked up the pace now with his new stick in hand and made it over to the rock outface in no time. Tunnels ran under his farm and connected it to the farms around his, including Emma's. They had all been part of the Underground Railroad at one time. One of the houses over in the next county had been turned into a museum so people could understand and not forget what others had endured back then. If you actually looked at aerial photos of the farms you could see the path if you know what you were looking at. If you looked at the bones of the homes you could also see that the original structures were all built the same too, like row houses. Years of remodels had taken their toll and a lot of the outsides of the homes had completely changed their face.

Scott hadn't been up this way for years. Stopping and listening for a while, he couldn't make out any sounds that he should be concerned about and Rusty seemed at ease. Wanting to check out the outcropping, he was surprised to see where part of the hillside had slipped away to reveal a cave.

"Well heck, what would Ole Tom and Huck do about right now"

Glancing at his watch, he realized he didn't have much time to explore before the sun went down, which meant he would need to make his way back soon.

"Ah heck, I have to at least stick my head in," he thought.

Reaching into his pocket, he pulled out his flashlight, or one of the triplets, as Emma referred to them. He had to admit, she was right. It was good to have a flashlight, a knife and his firearm with him at all times.

Trying to figure out a smart path through all the fresh mud, he finally decided there was no easy way and edged his way along the outside until he hit the hillside itself. He stopped and listened. While many animals used caves for habitat, hungry wolves were not something he wanted to run into while he was alone. He would now have to get dirty but the inquisitive side of him far outweighed and overruled the hygienic side, so in the mud he stepped.

Making his way to the front of the cave quietly, he stopped and listened again. Nothing. Shining the flashlight into the cave, he couldn't see very far. Tree roots hung down and blocked a good portion of his view. Taking the time to log the co-ordinates into his phone, he was going to have to come back another day and check it out further.

Maybe Emma's friend. No. probably not a good idea. Not sure how long it would take her to be comfortable around men again. She kind of reminded him of the cave before him. Completely captured his attention and once he could get past the tree roots, the bad things blocking his way, there might be something even better in the back. "Scott, my friend, your mind works in mysterious ways sometimes," he mumbled to himself. Backing out of the mud, he gave a whistle for Rusty and they headed off for home.

26

Angie hadn't been this relaxed since the rape. Tonight, Emma's kids were coming over for a family dinner and she was invited to stay. She was glad. She had slowly started to get out and even traveled to see her mom in town, but this would be good to be around a group of people who loved each other.

Once dinner was under control and the table set, Angie excused herself to go change before the kids arrived. Once in her room, she stripped and stepped into the shower.

As the water flowed over her, she felt like it was washing away all the bad memories of the past couple months. While she would never forget, each day it was getting easier to breathe, to smile. She dressed quickly and sat down to dry her hair. As the hairdryer blew her hair back, she caught a glimpse of the last remnants of her attack. The scab behind her ear, the ear that was being pounded into the concrete from her attacker's thrusts, was almost healed. She would have no proof of him after that besides the wounds in her soul. Those wounds would take longer to heal and hopefully not leave hideous scars.

Angie entered the room as Lauren, Connor and Emily arrived. Making introductions, they were fast friends in no time. Kevin and his wife along with their kids next, and Angie stepped back to take in the whole scene. There before her was a force like no other she had ever known. A family. Love filled the room with such permeable strength that it overwhelmed her. Gladly someone rang the doorbell and she ran to answer it and made her leave before they saw her tears.

Angie opened the door expecting the last of the kids and was quite taken aback when Doc Scott was standing there. "Hi there," he said just as surprised.

"Hey," she responded and leaned against the door for support

"I knew Jonathan was on his way over and wanted to give him the meds for the goats he ordered a while back."

"Oh, come on in. He hasn't arrived yet," Angie said with a puzzled look "Or at least I think so anyways. There's so many of them!"

Scott grinned, "Yes, just a few. And they seem to breed like rabbits around here."

Scott dropped his eyes, realizing that might not have been a good thing to say. He was quite relieved when Angie picked up on it and gave a giggle.

Tommy walked into the room and almost tripped when he thought he walked in on a private conversation that he wasn't invited to. "Hey Tom!" Scott exclaimed

"Doc. What brings you over?"

"Got the goat meds that Jonathan wanted and I knew he was on his way. Saved him a trip since I was driving passed."

"Awesome! We can get that off our plate tomorrow then. Come on in and sit a spell, I'm sure he will be here soon… might as well stay for dinner too for driving all this way"

"Oh no, no," Scott countered

"Oh please do, I can set an extra plate in no time," Angie chimed in

The trio walked into the family room and Emma caught Tommy's glance. They exchanged raised brows that spoke volumes.

Jonathan and his family arrived and in no time the entire family was all settled around the dinner table. Stories were being shared with the guests that had them laughing throughout the meal and straight into dessert.

"Let's play some Conflicted!" Kevin said. "Let's get this table cleared!"

"What's Conflicted?" Angie asked

"It's a deck of cards with a bunch of survival scenarios all over them," Lauren explained. "We sit around and argue about who has the best solution for each card."

"We don't argue," Kevin said. "We have deep, philosophical conversations that will eventually save the world" which sent all of them into a rage of laughter

"Sweet!" Angie said. "Let's play"

27

"I have the first card," Emma said "And you boys need to listen up. Your significant other develops a fever with a yeast infection. You have no modern medicine as most supplies have been used up. You know the fever is a bad sign and could lead to a bladder or kidney infection. What would you do?"

"Oh wow," said Angie. "I was studying to be an EMT before I left Memphis. Problem is, we weren't' trained for a grid down situation without medicine or a white sterile hospital."

"Well, I can tell you what not to do! Last time we had this question, Connor said to spray it with Windex because that's what he saw on TV!"

"What!" Angie chuckled

"Yes, in that movie about a Greek wedding, the dad was curing everything with Windex," responded Connor

"Hilarious! So what should we do, because I have no idea," Angie asked

"Yogurt, cranberries, garlic are all good for yeast infections. Soak a tampon in yogurt and insert it," Lauren said

"My concern," chimed in Scott, "Is the fever. That's a sure sign of infection. And you said there was no normal human medicine available?"

"Right," Emma said

"Could I use vet meds?" asked Scott

"No one said you couldn't," replied Emma

A grin came across Scott's face as he got up and walked to the fridge. Reaching to the top where he had placed some of the goat meds, he grabbed a bottle and brought it back to the table. "Do your research, but a lot of the same medications we use in the veterinary world, are the same thing in the human world, just packaged differently. This bottle, in the human world, is the same thing as amoxicillin and would help combat the infection causing the fever"

"Wow," Angie replied, "I never knew that and I was studying medicine"

"Not a well-known secret. The pharmaceutical companies don't like that info to get out as the vet meds are a lot cheaper. More and more people are finding out so the companies are trying to get the government to regulate them so it doesn't eat into their profits," Scott said

"Interesting. I need to read up on that," Angie said

"I've got some books for you to read," Emma said. "Doom and Bloom is a book written by a doctor and his wife on grid-down medicine. I think you will find it quite fascinating"

"OK, next question" Jonathan said "You hear a noise outside and realize someone is shoveling snow out of your walkway. You peek through the window and see three older kids with snow clothes on and without thinking you open the door. They immediately push through passed you and into your house. You can't see who they are because they have ski masks on but they start looking through your belongings. What do you do?"

"I would ask them what the hell they think they are doing," Lauren said

"It's three guys versus you. Really? Who knows what they are after? Are your belongings worth more than you getting hurt?" Jonathan asked

Emma shot a quick glance at Angie. She was looking pale and knew where her mind was going. She tried to get Tommy's attention but got nothing.

"What if they were after you and had you on the floor to rape you, would you not struggle to make them go away faster?" Jonathan quipped back

This was going from bad to worse and Emma needed to end this now, but she was too late.

"No," Angie whimpered. "You fight. You fight and you keep fighting no matter what. Because you have to live with the decision you make," she choked out through the tears.

Everyone in the room was looking at her. "Most people think the decision is just to live and there are no consequences to your decision. But there are consequences. Some that will haunt you for the rest of your life. You fight, and you teach your daughters to fight. Don't teach your daughters to be victims. Yes, sometimes your life may depend on you not fighting, there are also ramifications that you will have to live with if you choose not to. I thought not fighting was the right choice once. But I stopped thinking because I was scared. Sitting here with all of you, I realize how uneducated I truly am trying to live in this world and survive. You all have a mom who loves you and wants you to learn so if, God forbid, something happens, you already have an answer in your head on what you would do. I wasn't so lucky. I thought my best choice was not to make a choice. I had no choice to make because I had no training. Your mom is helping me change that and for that, I owe her so very much, because she is helping me get my life back."

There was not a dry eye in the house as they were all focused on Angie.

Angie stood and walked out of the room.

Emma looked at Scott. Something exchanged between them and Scott got up and walked into the other room following Angie

He found her standing in front of the fire, staring into the flames.

"You OK?

"Ya, I really truly think I am" she said with confidence "I think everything is going to be OK"

Scott walked over and placed a hand on her shoulder. "I'm here if you ever need anything"

She reached up and touched his hand. "How about meeting me for coffee tomorrow? I've got some things I need to tell you."

28

The days were starting to quiet down again and Emma didn't want to waste the opportunity to check up on her girls and see how they were doing. Located all over the globe, they were brought together by a calling to be prepared and to protect those that they loved most. Sharing information daily, they built each other up in all areas of preparedness, from canning and water purification to firearms and child care and everything in between. They truly were a remarkable group of women.

Emma sat down in her favorite chair and logged into her computer. While the girls were her utmost priority, she also needed to catch up with her alternative news sites. Not trusting anything the mainstream media had to say, underground news sites had become a necessity to get to the facts. Add to that the connections Emma had with actual eyes and ears on the ground and the truth was breaking free and people were slowly waking up.

Julz was one of Emma's connections. Julz ran a radio station from upstate New York called "ucy.tv" that Emma had a show on a couple times a week to talk about getting prepared. Emma had the utmost respect for the variable Wonder Woman who had painstakingly put together an eclectic blend of journalists from around the world who came together to voice the truth.

Glancing over the recent news, things weren't looking good. Multiple quakes in an area of Louisiana caught Emma's eye. Not much news about it in the mainstream media, but plenty if you knew how and where to get and piece it all together. There were people out there who understood what was happening and tried to get people to listen. Emma listened.

Emma pulled a binder down from her bookshelf and opened it up to the front page. Reading from the
New York Times by Michael Wines...

BAYOU CORNE, La. — It was nearly 16 months ago that Dennis P. Landry and his wife, Pat, on a leisurely cruise in their Starcraft pontoon boat, first noticed a froth of bubbles issuing from the depths of Bayou Corne, an idyllic, cypress-draped stream that meanders through swampy southern Louisiana. They figured it was a leaky gas pipeline. So did everyone else. Just over two months later, in the predawn blackness of Aug. 3, 2012, the earth opened up — a voracious maw 325 feet across and hundreds of feet deep, swallowing 100-foot trees, guzzling water from adjacent swamps and belching methane from a thousand feet or more beneath the surface. "I think I caught a glimpse of hell in it," Mr. Landry said.

Since then, almost nothing here has been the same.

More than a year after it appeared, the Bayou Corne sinkhole is about 25 acres and still growing, almost as big as 20 football fields, lazily biting off chunks of forest and creeping hungrily toward an earthen berm built to contain its oily waters. It has its own Facebook page and its own groupies, conspiracy theorists who insist the pit is somehow linked to the Gulf of Mexico 50 miles south and the earthquake-prone New Madrid fault 450 miles north. It has confounded geologists who have struggled to explain this scar in the earth.

And it has split this unincorporated hamlet of about 300 people into two camps: the hopeful, like Mr. Landry, who believe that things will eventually settle down, and the despairing, who have mostly fled or plan to, and blame their misery on state and corporate officials.

"Everything they're doing, they were forced to do," Mike Schaff, one of those who is leaving, said of the officials. "They've taken no initiative. I wanted to stay here. But the community is basically destroyed."

Drawls Mr. Landry: "I used to have a sign in my yard: 'This too shall pass.' This, too, shall pass. We're not there yet. But I'm a very patient man."

The sinkhole is worrisome enough. But for now, the principal villains are the bubbles: flammable methane gas, surfacing not just in the bayou, but in the swamp and in front and back yards across the area.

A few words of fantastical explanation: Much of Louisiana sits atop an ancient ocean whose salty remains, extruded upward by the merciless pressure of countless tons of rock, have formed at least 127 colossal underground pillars. Seven hundred feet beneath Bayou Corne, the Napoleonville salt dome stretches three miles long and a mile wide — and plunges perhaps 30,000 feet to the old ocean floor.

A bevy of companies have long regarded the dome as more or less a gigantic piece of Tupperware, a handy place to store propane, butane and natural gas, and to make salt water for the area's many chemical factories. Over the years, they have repeatedly punched into the dome, hollowing out 53 enormous caverns.

In 1982, on the dome's western edge, Texas Brine Company sank a well to begin work on a big cavern: 150 to 300 feet wide and four-tenths of a mile deep, it bottomed out more than a mile underground. Until it capped the well to the cavern in 2011, the company pumped in fresh water, sucked out salt water and shipped it to the cavern's owner, the Occidental Chemical Corporation.

Who is to blame for what happened next is at issue in a barrage of lawsuits. But at some point, the well's western wall collapsed, and the cavern began filling with mud and rock. The mud and rock above it dropped into the vacated space, freeing trapped <u>natural gas</u>.

The gas floated up; the rock slipped down. The result was a yawning, bubbling sinkhole.

"You go in the swamp, and there are places where it's coming up like boiling crawfish," said Mr. Schaff, who is moving out.

Mr. Landry, who is staying, agreed — "it looks like boiling water, like a big pot" — but the two men and their camps agree on little else.

Geologists say the sinkhole will eventually stop growing, perhaps at 50 acres, but how long that will take is unclear. The state has imposed tough regulations and monitoring on salt-dome caverns to forestall future problems.

Under state order, Texas Brine has mounted a broad, though some say belated, effort to pump gas out of sandy underground layers where it has spread. Bayou Corne is pocked with freshly dug wells, with more to come, their pipes leading to flares that slowly burn off the methane. That, everyone concedes, could take years.

The two sides greet all that news in starkly different ways.

State surveys show that one of the largest concentrations of methane lies directly under Mr. Landry's neighborhood, a manicured subdivision of brick homes, many with decks overlooking the bayou and its cypresses. Yet only two families have chosen to leave, and while the Landrys are packed just in case, the gas detector in their home offers enough reassurance to remain.

The collapse last year of a side of a cavern more than a mile underground led to a large sinkhole in Bayou Corne, La.

"Do you smell anything?" he asked. "Nope. Do we have gas bubbling up in the bayou? Yes. Where does it go? Straight up. Have they closed the bayou? No."

The anger and misfortune are focused on Mr. Schaff's neighborhood directly across state route 70, a jumble of neat clapboard houses, less tidy shotgun-style homes and trailers on narrow roads with names like Sauce Piquant Lane and Jambalaya Street. There, rows of abandoned homes are plastered with No Trespassing signs, and the streets are deathly quiet.

Candy Blanchard, a teacher, and her husband, Todd, a welder, moved out the day the sinkhole appeared. They now pay the monthly mortgage on their empty and unsellable 7-year-old house as well as the rent on another house. Mr. Blanchard drops by their former home each morning to feed their rabbits and cat, who have lived alone for a year because their landlord would accept only their dog.

The couple rejected an offer from Texas Brine to buy their home, and instead have joined a class action lawsuit against the company. They will never return, she said, because they do not believe the area is safe.

"The point we're at now is what the scientists said would never happen, that this would be the worst-case scenario," Mrs. Blanchard said. "How can you find experts on this when it has never happened anywhere else in the world?"

Mr. Schaff's home also fronts the bayou, and he says he is loath to leave. But investigators found gas in his garage, he said, and he says he is convinced that state officials are playing down the true scope of the disaster.

A wry, amiable man with a salt-and-pepper goatee and glasses, Mr. Schaff said he had planned to retire on the bayou.

"It's my home. I want to die there, OK?" he said, fighting off tears. "I was going to retire next year, was going to do some fishing, play with my grandchildren, do a little flying. And now, this."

Emma thumbed over the date of the article. Almost 3 years earlier and it had gotten worse, much worse since then.

Just recently some seismic activity had cause quite a stir in the MSM which really sent chills up Emma's spine. Digging around, the helicorders started going off not more than minutes after a 6.8 earthquake was registered in China. Could they be connected, Emma pondered.

Emma also noticed a sinkhole had opened up In Kentucky that unfortunately swallowed a lot of very expensive automobiles. Emma dug around until she got the exact location and, getting up, she walked over to her wall map.

Having pinned quite a few events on the map, it was easy to see a pattern developing. Was the New Madrid about ready to wake up? If the bayou were to blow with all the butane that was below it, it would set off a cataclysmic event that would disable much of the heartland of the United States.

Running her finger along the lines developing on the map, Emma thought of the cities in harm's way. Her finger stopped when it came to Memphis, Tennessee. "Shit" she thought and picked up the phone.

29

Emma heard Shelby pick up the phone and then grinned as she heard that long drawn out southern drawl. "Hey girlie girl!" Shelby said

"How's my favorite Chickie this morning?" Emma asked

"Doing well. Just finished making some biscuits so perfect timing as I can talk while they are rising!" Shelby responded

Shelby lived "old school" prepper. It was one of the things that had drawn them together. While Emma enjoyed the benefits of modern comforts, such as electricity, Shelby had stepped completely away from it minus having an emergency phone in the house. Emma learned early on to call about mid-morning as Shelby would be returning from the barn having finished morning chores and would be somewhere in the process of cooking breakfast on her wood stove.

Emma had visited Shelby multiple times over the years and was always in awe of the woman. Emma learned how to pressure can her garden bounty without using electricity from Shelby.

Having given up all the comforts of modern life, Shelby and her husband, whom she lovingly referred to as Mountain Man, had moved their family to the hills of Tennessee over 15 years prior and created a self-sustaining life without the influence of the outside world.

Situated back in a holler, finding her homestead was a chore all of its own. The neighbors, if one were to call them that as they were miles apart, were all related or close enough friends that they were considered family anyways. One does not just pop in because you were in the neighborhood. It took multiple dirt roads to even begin to get to the closest town that Shelby lived near, from there; it was a crap shoot to get to where her land began.

Shelby never got unintentional visitors so when a stranger showed up; it brought the attention of the community into full focus. They were courteous until the intruder left, as courteous as one could be with a shotgun hidden behind their back.

"Have you been able to get into town lately?" Emma asked Shelby

"Not for a couple weeks, why?" Shelby replied as she sat down to listen, giving Emma her full attention.

"Some activity going on. Just be ready and get your hams up and double checked," she explained and then promptly filled Shelby in on what she was putting together.

Shelby was one of the strongest women Emma had ever met and Emma knew it was going to take extraordinary women to be the backbone of her present day underground railroad.

30

"What the hell" Chloe thought as she heard her phone go off. Rolling over, she looked at the clock. "Damn woman, doesn't she ever sleep" she mumbled to herself as she tried to remember what time zone she was presently in.

"Hey Mama" Chloe groaned into the phone

"Chloe" Emma replied in a serious tone.

"Give me a minute, 'kay?" Chloe said as she untangled herself from underneath her latest conquest as slid quietly into the bathroom, shutting the door behind her.

"Bid-ness or pleasure?" Chloe clanged out with a pucker of her lips

"All business" Emma responded and continued to explain to Chloe what was going on.

Chloe was not a prepper in the same sense that Emma or Shelby was. In fact, Chloe made her living by utilizing the oldest profession in the book, prostitution. But she was smart and learned fast.

Chloe and Emma met after a couple years of Chloe stalking Prepper Chicks on Facebook. Chloe was digging around looking for information concerning the nuclear plant that had sprung a leak in Japan after an earthquake. Living on the California coast, it was making her nervous with all the supposed radiation that was leaking into the ocean and hitting her shoreline. Chloe wanted fact. Strong, hard fact, not the bullshit hypothetical crap she kept running into. Rabbit trail after rabbit trail led her straight to Radchick's internet site. Getting the information she wanted, Chloe had to figure out how to handle the ramifications of nuclear waste in her back yard. Digging further, she noticed a friendship between Christina, the admin on Radchick and the admin on a web site called Prepper Chicks. Chloe observed the information exchanged between the two women. Attracted by the fact that it was straight up information without interference of religion or politics, Chloe stuck around, something she rarely did, and little by little she formed a friendship with Emma.

Emma drove out to Utah one year for a firearms class and Chloe drove in from the West Coast to meet up with her. Within a couple days, they were thick as thieves having shared most everything in their lives except Chloe's occupation. Chloe didn't think Emma would understand and didn't want to lose someone she now considered family because of her choices, whether forced or not, that she had made in her life. She wasn't proud of the fact that she fucked men for money, but it was what it was and there was no way around it anymore. She enjoyed the lifestyle that it fueled too much."

"Let's button up any loose ends and make sure we have a clear idea of your direction on the maps before this weekend. I want a general idea of which way you will be coming in, just in case." Emma said

"Let me call you back in Fives" Chloe said and hung up the phone without waiting for an answer.
Turning, Chloe walked over to the bed and briskly woke the man up. "Sorry Shorty but I's got to run. Emergency."

She heard the man groan as they both knew he paid dearly already for the next few hours and leaving early was not on his agenda.

Bending down, she kissed him on his neck leaving a hot trail to the bottom of his jaw. "I'll cut you a free piece of ass over the weekend," she whispered, flicking the outside of his ear with her tongue.

After a quick flick of her bare breast, the man got up and reluctantly got dressed and left the apartment. He knew she was good for it as he spent nearly every Thursday at her place.

Chloe took a quick shower and wrapped her robe around her and put on a pot of coffee. Sitting down at the bar she pulled out a well-worn binder out from the built in bookcase located by her knees. Created to hold cook-books, Chloe had found a much better use for it. She had binder after binder of survival information hidden in plain sight. With Emma's help she had added information that she would never have thought important, like maps. Now Chloe had a binder full of maps for not only roadways but also rail routes, bike paths, aquifers, tributary and topographical maps.

Chloe called Emma back and they spend the next several hours reviewing the maps, and planning.

31

"Goodnight" Tom yelled to his wife, but she was long gone and he knew she wouldn't be to bed for a while. Heck, he thought. He had seen her in the same spot the next morning when he got up. He bought her the chair she was sitting in the first time he had seen her stay up all night laying out plans. He knew she wasn't going to stop what she was doing, as he knew in his heart she was living her calling in life, but she could damn well be comfortable doing it.

Tom walked up the stairs into their bedroom and sat on the edge of the bed. Reaching over, he picked up his Bible and flipped through until he reached the Book of Proverbs. Quickly skimming to the last chapter, he began to read.

[10]Who can find a virtuous wife?

For her worth is far above rubies.
[11]The heart of her husband safely trusts her;
so he will have no lack of gain.

Tommy paused for a moment as his spirit chewed upon what he had just read. He trusted Emma with his life whether she knew that or not. If ever there was someone he wanted watching his six, it was his wife. Not only for the fact that she was an expert with a firearm, but also an expert with his wants and needs, sometimes before he even realized it himself. Letting out a sigh, he continued on.

[12] She does him good and not evil, All the days of her life.
[13] She seeks wool and flax. And willingly works with her hands.
[14] She is like the merchant ships, she brings her food from afar.
[15] She also rises while it is yet night, and provides food for her household, And a portion for her maidservants.

What did Emma call them? "Oh ya" Tommy mumbled "Her Sister Chicks. Those Coop Girls" Tommy breathed in and exhaled "Lord, watch over those Girls of Emma's, they mean the world to her. Let no harm come to any of them and give them the strength they need for the days ahead."

[16] She considers a field and buys it;
From her profits she plants a vineyard.
[17] She girds herself with strength,
And strengthens her arms.
[18] She perceives that her merchandise is good,
And her lamp does not go out by night.
[19] She stretches out her hands to the distaff,
And her hand holds the spindle.
[20] She extends her hand to the poor,
Yes, she reaches out her hands to the needy.

"Yep", Tommy thought as a glimpse of his wife delivering her canned goods to the local shelter flashed in his mind. He gave a chuckle as he remembered his wife talking the pastor into their first ever Thanksgiving dinner that the church opened its doors for. From a mere eight turkeys that were roasted the first year to well over three dozen last year. From the looks of things in town, they will probably need even more. He made a note to remind himself to check on this.

> *[21]She is not afraid of snow for her household,*
> *For all her household is clothed with scarlet.*
> *[22] She makes tapestry for herself;*
> *Her clothing is fine linen and purple.*

Tommy thought about Emma's clothes for a moment. Fine linen was far from being her style. Jeans and a T-shirt might become a fad in Heaven one day Lord, Tommy chuckled. "Oh, and bare feet... can't forget that! Might want to make note of that up there now before she gets there," he said with a smile thinking about everyone running around shoeless.

> *[23]Her husband is known in the gates,*
> *When he sits among the elders of the land.*
> *[24] She makes linen garments and sells them,*
> *And supplies sashes for the merchants.*
> *[25] Strength and honor are her clothing;*
> *She shall rejoice in time to come.*
> *[26] She opens her mouth with wisdom,*
> *And on her tongue is the law of kindness.*

"Well, most of the time" Tom chuckled under his breath. "I think both you and I Lord know this isn't her strong suit!"

27 She watches over the ways of her household,
And does not eat the bread of idleness.
28 Her children rise up and call her blessed;
Her husband also, and he praises her:

"Lord, remind me to do this more often." Tommy asked

29 "Many daughters have done well,
But you excel them all."
30 Charm is deceitful and beauty is passing,
But a woman who fears the LORD, she shall be praised.
31 Give her of the fruit of her hands,
And let her own works praise her in the gates.

Closing the book, Tommy knelt down on the floor in front of their bed, a bed they had shared for more than 30 years. "Lord, protect that woman and give her the strength she needs for whatever you need her to do. I lost her long ago to you, but I trust you with her.... so I guess that makes us partners in a way in keeping her safe." Just then Dixon entered the room and walked over beside Tom and sat down. "Make that the three of us," Tom said as he reached an arm around Dixon and gave him a squeeze.

32

The table was strewn with maps and all kinds of gear. Emma, Scott, and Angie were sitting around the table muttering back and forth when Tom walked into the room.

"Truck and trailer are all ready to go," Tom said interjecting into their conversation.

"Awesome" Scott replied as he quickly glanced up at Tom, "We'll leave in the morning"

"Get in there, get your stuff and get back here," Emma added. "I'm not liking the way things have been rattling down that way."

"Yes ma'am," Scott smirked

"Here's Shelby's number if you need anything. She is a lot closer to where you are going than I am and she knows you will be heading down that day. You will also need this, just in case," Emma said as she laid out a map with highlighted roads. "If that thing blows, Memphis is pretty much toast. Since your house is on the outskirts Angie, your best bet is to head to Shelby's place here.... I've laid out a couple different routes to take in case one doesn't work."

"Awesome," Angie said as she scanned Emma's handiwork

"Let's get these bags packed now," Emma said as she picked up a black backpack

"First things first, let's go through the list and you pack your own bag so you know where what is and how you packed it."

"Thanks, Emma, for going over all this with me these last couple weeks. I would have no clue how to use half of this stuff without actually sitting down with you and using it on our camping trip," Angie said.

"No worries," Emma quipped. "A lot of people call themselves preppers just because they own things that a prepper might have but they never get out and use the stuff. Makes them no more a prepper than parking my bicycle in the garage makes it a car! Now let's do this," she said as she handed the pack to Angie

"OK… Let's go through this list" Emma said " And remember, "COLD" stands for…"

Clean. Clean clothing will retain heat better.

Overheating. Avoid it.

Layers. Strip off outer layers of clothing while performing strenuous work.

 Dry. Wet clothes will kill you."

"Now, the actual list" Emma said

FOOD & WATER
•Minimum of 3600 calories of food per person
•Minimum of 9 water pouches of water per person
•Method of water purification (such as potable aqua or a water filter)
• Small fishing/lure kit
• Canteen and lightweight cooking gear

COMMUNICATION
•AM/FM Radio with batteries or alternate power source
•Whistle with lanyard
•Handheld Ham with solar charger

LIGHT SOURCES
•Flashlight with batteries
•Candles
•Light sticks
•Lantern and fuel

•Road Flare(s)

HYGIENE & SANITATION
•Personal Hygiene Kit
•Toilet paper

•Lip balm

TOOLS
•50 Feet of paracord
•Pocket Knife and Multi-tool
•Rolls of Duct Tape
•Foldable Shovel
•Hatchet or axe
•Sewing Kit

•Compass

WARMTH & SHELTER
•Waterproof matches
•Ferrocerium striker

•Cotton balls soaked in petroleum jelly

•Tent/Waterproof tarp
•Solar Emergency Blanket and High Grade Sleeping Bag
•Hand & Body Warmers
•Poncho
•Lightweight Stove & Fuel
•Wool Blanket

FIRST AID
•First Aid Kit and supplies including tourniquets
•First Aid Booklet/Manual
•Burn gel and dressing
•Snake bite kit

•Insect repellent
•Sun block
•Special medication

MONEY
•At least $100 in small bills in your kit — be sure to include quarters for phone calls

IMPORTANT PAPERS
•Emergency Instructions such as laminated maps
•Copies of documents such as birth certificates, marriage licenses, wills, insurance forms, phone numbers, credit card info, etc. (can be added to thumb drive for light weight packing)

STRESS RELIEVERS
•Games, dice, hard candy

EXTRA CLOTHING
•A complete outfit of appropriate clothing; including extra wool socks, underwear, hat, gloves, belt

•Snow Gaiters and waterproof boots.

"Now, let's go through the truck," Emma said as they picked up their bags and headed outside

- Wool blanket / Sleeping Bag
- Clothing, socks, boots, gloves

- Food and water / fire-starting kit / clean metal container

- First-aid kit including tourniquets
- Flashlight with extra batteries

- Flares / tire sealant / small tool kit and crow bar
- Hand and/or body warmers
- Windshield scraper/broom
- Extra windshield-washer fluid
- Jumper cables or portable jump-starter
- Kitty litter or sand for traction
- Shovel
- Cell phone or CB radio with Solar Charger

They headed back inside. "Scott, how about getting a fire going and Tom and I will throw something together for dinner real fast," Emma said

"My pleasure, after you my dear," he said to Angie as he motioned for her to head into the living room ahead of him.

"Let me do this, I need to practice," Angie said as she walked to the fireplace. Handing the matches to Scott, she said, "I don't need these either."

Taking out her knife and grabbing a smaller branch, Angie kneeled before the fireplace and held the branch up as she feathered some dry wood off it for kindling. Grabbing a piece of jute rope about 4" long, she then began to pull it apart to make a fluffy cloud of twine. Gathering some smaller pieces of bark, she laid the frayed jute inside and set it into the fireplace, then she placed the feathered wood close by and laid a few pieces directly on top of the jute. Getting out the tinder box from her pocket, she pulled out a piece of chaga and laid it in the middle of the pile. Next she took a long narrow rod of ferrocerium out of her pack and held it in her left hand over top of her pile of wood and jute. Taking her knife, she flipped it over and laid the back of the knife against the ferrocerium rod and pulled the knife the length of the rod. Nothing happened. She did it a few more times and nothing.

"Switch the pull," Scott said. "Hold the knife still and pull the rod towards you"

Angie did as he said and a spark appeared. Smiling to herself, she pulled the knife again and sparks caught the jute on fire. Working quickly, she added the rest of the feathered wood until she had a nice base fire going. Next she slowly added the smaller branches. Letting it burn for a few moments, she gave it a couple blows of breath to get the coals burning a bright red. Laying it in the fireplace, she kept adding larger pieces of wood until she had worked her way up to a good solid log.

She stood up and turned to face Scott. She was so proud of herself and took no time in making sure he knew exactly proud she was!

He stood there with his hands on his hips. Across his face danced the biggest grin she had ever seen, and at that very moment, she realized he had stolen her heart.

33

A quick dinner of cold chicken and salad, Emma waited until afterwards to serve dessert in the living room in front of the fire.

"Let's get some early sleep tonight, but I do want to run through some scenario drills while we are sitting here," Emma said

Angie and Scott were cuddled up on the floor in front of the fireplace, the flames dancing wildly behind their backs. "Sounds good," Scott said. "What do you have in mind?"

Note from the Author: To those reading, please take some time and open your mind to the possibilities that are presented in the following Seven Questions. Be honest with yourself. I would love to hear your answers, so drop me an email if you would ~ AnnieBerdel@yahoo.com.

Question One: You are alone, driving out of state when your car dies. Looking around you notice that everyone else's car has died also. Getting out of your vehicle and asking around, you discover that not only are the cars not working but everyone's phones are not working also. You have the sinking feeling that an electromagnetic pulse went off. You are surrounded by strangers from all walks of life. Everyone has limited recourses. Would you join forces or disappear on your own? What would be your main goal after this decision?

Question Two: One of your best friends has been shot in a skirmish and a medic has told you that he will be paralyzed from the neck down for the rest of his life. This is a post-apocalyptic world you are currently living in and your friend asks you to please have mercy on him and put him out of his misery. His wife and kids have already died and all he wants to do is be with them instead of living in a world as unforgiving as this. Would you have mercy on your friend and kill him or would you let him live? Why?

Question Three: The government has collapsed and everyone has been on their own for months. Out of nowhere, six men wearing UN uniforms appear at your door saying they are with the government. They need your ammo and supplies, along with everyone else's, in order to help reestablish order. You and your family must comply or be counted as anti-government radicals. Would you enlist and donate all you have to the new government and be counted as a patriot or would you be labeled as a terrorist and fight them off if you could?

Question Four: Due to World War 3, the infrastructure of society has gone back to a level not seen since the 1800s. Your help is requested in forming the new government and you can change or implement five laws as you see fit. What would these laws be and why?

Question Five: In a post-apocalyptic world, supplies that are not replenished eventually run out. When things calm down to the point where a local economy can start flourishing, what type of business or venture would you like to pursue in order to help rebuild society and take care of your needs?

Question Six: After the collapse, there is a war for resources that involves the entire country. As gun fights break out, the dead begin to pile up. You have lost many of your friends, yet their families are still alive. They won't make it on their own. If you saw this, would you embrace the families of your fallen friends and take care of them with your limited time and resources, or would you leave them on their own. WHY?

Question Seven: The media is curiously silent, but you hear from a traveling nursing friend that in the city 300 miles away, there is a rash of illnesses. One of the hospitals is overloaded. She is worried. How would you handle this news, and how would you go about confirming it? What would be the next two things you do? WHY?

34

Tommy and Emma said goodnight and walked up the stairs to their bedroom. Tom quickly disrobed and slid into bed before Emma came back from the adjoining bathroom.

"You're naked!" she said she slid her body against Tommy's under the big warm quilt.

"And you're not!" Tommy quipped back as he started to remove her nightgown

Emma cradled within the protection of Tommy's arms, looked up at her husband. "This is my favorite place in the whole world," she said as her eyes glistened at her husband

"In Ohio?" Tommy asked

"No no" Emma chuckled "Here, right here, naked, lying in our bed with your arms around me," she said as she laid her cheek against his chest and gave him hug. "This is my secret place where no one else can bother me. This is my home, right here with you. The bed may change, the house or even the state, but here in your arms is home."

She felt his arm move to shut the light off. Or so she thought. He reached down and tilted her chin towards his face so he could look in her eyes.

"I have something for you," Tommy whispered "Because God showed me you were worth more than rubies and I got this for you to remind both of us of that. I forget it sometimes and I'm sorry for that."

"Oh really?" Emma said as she lifted herself up onto one elbow and looked at her husband.

There, dangling from his hand was a ruby heart on a silver chain.

"Oh Tommy, it's beautiful!"

He slid it around her neck as the ruby fell between her breasts.

He kissed her forehead. "I love you."

"I know," she whispered.

35

Angie and Scott made it to Angie's apartment in Memphis without any problems and began the tedious task of packing it for moving back to Emma's farm. Emma took the opportunity, while they were away; to take a walk back to check on the cabins she had built on the property and air them out a bit. She would have guests soon, she could feel it; and she wanted to make sure she was ready for them.

Grabbing her Mossberg and making sure she had an extra magazine for her Glock, Emma packed a small lunch and gave a whistle for Dixon as she headed out. Knowing Dixon, he was lazing in the sun somewhere and would catch up to her soon enough.

Rounding the bend in the dirt path, Emma walked into a far hayfield and headed for a particular tree along the southern edge of the field. Stepping into the woods, Emma felt the peacefulness of the forest envelop her. Stopping long enough for her eyes to adjust to the lack of light, she quickly scanned the area. She loved the woods. It was probably her second favorite place on earth. Maybe it was partly due to her heritage, but it also gave back memories of hunting trips with her father. He taught her how to navigate the woods at night and now she had an uncanny ability go anywhere once and find her way home.

This was her home, she thought, as she walked from tree to tree as she headed toward the first cabin. She had built the cabins years earlier and they were here for a purpose. She boarded them up and only came out a couple times a year to do a physical check of them. When the time came, she would put them to use.

The trail wound down close to the river and back up into the woods. As she cleared a large oak, she stopped. I wonder where Dixon is, she thought. He should have caught up to her by now. That's odd. Making her way to the first cabin, she checked the water pipes, windows and fireplace screen. All looks good, she thought. Double checking the supplies, it looked like nothing had bothered the locked totes. Emma had put these totes out here each spring, exchanging them for the ones she picked up with her 4-wheeler. Inside each tote was an assortment of basic items to last for a few days of being at the cabin. Cooking pots, blankets, food, bottled water, medical supplies and fire-starters for both the fireplace and the small cook stove. A pair of ham radios was also included that Emma had a base unit for back at the main house. While there was no electricity out here, each cabin had a solar battery charger that could easily charge any small appliance or electronic.

Emma stepped out onto the porch and locked the door. Dixon still wasn't there. Looking around, Emma descended the steps and headed off to the next cabin.

36

The second cabin was located along the creek that ran through the property. Still sitting back far enough from the water's edge that someone passing by could not see it, Emma knew that people on vacation sometimes took canoes along this particular stretch and she didn't want them to be messing around the property or breaking into the cabin. The cabin itself was bare bones with just a tote of supplies like the first cabin, but teenagers looking for a place to hang out would find it prime real estate for some late night partying.

Glancing around, Emma took the lower trail that ran parallel the water. She could then circle to the rest of the cabins and exit the woods exactly where she entered without crossing her footsteps twice. She loved this time of the year as the trees were losing their bright green color gifted to them from the hot days of summer. Now, they were journeying into deep blood reds and rustic browns with splashes of yellows and oranges thrown in for surprise. Nature was never boring if one just simply looked.

One would simply think the boulder along the creek bed was put there by nature herself, but Emma had it purposely placed as a waypoint. Tapping the rock with her hand, she made a sharp turn and headed up towards the crest of the hill. Halfway up her ascent, a putrid smell filled her nostrils. "Hmpf," she grunted to herself, "What died out here!" Grabbing a bandanna she placed it over her nose and mouth trying to block out the horrible stench and continued on towards the cabin.

Having just passed a large oak, movement out of the corner of Emma's eye caught her attention. Stopping fast, she scanned the area and caught glimpses of red. Her breathing quickened as she squinted her eyes to try and get a better look. Yes, red and now purple and white. Someone or something was at the cabin.

Slowly taking a step back, Emma tucked herself in behind the big tree she had just passed and listened. She couldn't make out any sounds but dang if she hadn't seen something that shouldn't have been there. "Know your normal" was something a friend had taught her years ago and it had come in quite handy on a number of occasions.

Taking a deep breath to try and calm her nerves, Emma double checked both the Mossberg and her Glock to make sure they were ready if she needed them. While confronting whoever was at the cabin was probably not the brightest idea since she was alone, getting a better idea of what was happening there would enable her to get a plan together as whoever or whatever was obviously trespassing on her land.

Keeping the tree between her and the cabin, Emma took a step back. She could now scan the area on both sides of the cabin without them seeing her. Nothing. She took another step back, with the tree still blocking her. Her ears caught a branch snap. "Shit!" The sounds echoed in her ears as it was obvious something was headed in her direction, the stench was long forgotten, as her other senses kicked into high gear. Raising her shotgun, Emma waited and listened not knowing from which direction her visitor would be revealed around the tree. Sweat started to break out across her brow as she tightened her grip on the shotgun, her finger itching for the trigger.

Expecting a much taller assailant, Emma was a little taken aback when Dixon popped his head from around the tree. Dropping the shotgun, Emma crouched down and gave him a scratch. "What the hell are you doing out here, do you know I could have just dropped you dead?" She barked at him as she rubbed his face between her hands.

Without missing a beat, Dixon walked around the tree and headed back up towards the cabin, Emma, still stunned, just looked on. About halfway he stopped and turned back towards Emma and barked. "That's odd," Emma muttered and decided it best to follow him. She trusted that dog with her life and knew he wouldn't put her into danger. But it was quite obvious he wanted her to follow.

Dixon led the way up the rest of the hill as Emma's senses started to return to a normal balance and the awful stench returned, burning her nostrils.

Dixon walked up the steps to the cabin door and Emma followed, feeling very uneasy. Something was wrong. The door wasn't locked and was sitting slightly open. Dixon nosed his way in and disappeared. Emma took the steps one at a time, trying to see in the door as best she could. The stench was becoming overwhelming. Standing outside the door, Emma stopped. Raising the shotgun to her shoulder, she used the muzzle to slowly open the door.

Little by little the tired sun made its way in the cabin and filled the room. Slowly, the horrible scene inside the room filled Emma's eyes. Old, dirty blankets were thrown about the floor as if someone had been sleeping there and from the looks of the things, whoever it was still wrapped up under one of the blankets.

Dixon stood in the middle of the room, looking back at Emma. Slowly Emma edged her way into the room. The smell now so powerful it made her eyes begin to water. Tears streaming down her face, Emma kept her eyes on the mound. "Hello?" Emma called out.

Off to her left Emma caught the flash of color. Moving quickly, she backed up and ducked behind the wall. The movement came from the kitchen. Without warning, Dixon headed into the room. "What is going on here?" Emma thought

Small, quiet voices. Emma listened with her full attention on the room Dixon had just entered. There they were again. High pitched, she could almost make them out.... "No way", she thought to herself. Take a step away from the wall, Emma slowly moved forward as more and more of the kitchen room was revealed. Finally, she saw Dixon's tail wagging excitedly with his face still hidden. Taking another step, Emma gasped. There was Dixon with two small children, watching over them like the protector he was.

Emma made her way into the kitchen step by step and realized they were the only ones in the cabin.
Trying not to startle the children, their eyes already huge and staring at Emma, she knelt on the floor beside Dixon. "Hello," she said in her best soothing voice. Looking at her, the little girl blinked away a tear and Emma noticed how grimy their faces and hands were. The little boy was a bit older, maybe 5, Emma guessed. Emma reached over and scratched Dixon behind the ear. Both of the children relaxed a bit as they realized she knew the dog.

Just then the boy said something to the little girl. Spanish, Emma thought. They speak Spanish. "Hola" Emma said quietly.

Both of the kids smiled. Emma took a deep breath and smiled back. "Hola, ninos," Emma said through her smile as both kids reached up to pat Dixon.

"What the hell is going on here," Emma muttered to herself as she stood, still smiling down at the kids. "Dixon, sit," she ordered and Dixon promptly sat with the kids. "Stay. Keep them here," she said to the dog.

Emma walked back into the area of the cabin where the blankets were. Shotgun in hand, she approached the large lump under them. Using the end of the gun, she slowly pulled the blanket up. "Oh Jesus," she said. Laying the gun against the wall, she crouched down beside the blanket and lifted the corner, making sure the kids were still in the other room.

The woman's jet black hair was splayed across the floor, a gold comb used to hold her tresses back from her face. Judging from the decomposition of her body, she had been dead for more than a week. Getting up quickly, Emma ran out the front door and through herself over the railing on the porch as she heaved her breakfast into the leaves scattered upon the forest floor. Drying her mouth with the bandanna, she quickly walked back inside and made sure the woman was covered up completely with the blankets. Walking back into the kitchen where Dixon and the kids were, she knelt down and patted Dixon again. She had to get these kids out of here.

Pulling a chocolate bar from her pocket, Emma opened it and gave the kids each a small piece. Grabbing for the food, Emma figured that they hadn't eaten for a while. Standing, Emma told Dixon to follow and beckoned for the kids as she waved the candy in front of them. She had to get them through the other room and out the front door as fast as possible.

"Dixon, home," she commanded and the dog walked to the front door. Stopping, he turned and Emma followed with the open candy motioning to the children. "Ven conmigo," she said brightly to the kids as she motioned towards Dixon.

They walked towards Dixon into the next room, their eyes darting towards where their mother was lying. The chocolate and the dog were now pulling their attention outside.

Emma kept walking, the dog and the kids followed, until they were far enough away that they couldn't see the cabin anymore. Stopping long enough to give them each a drink from her water bottle and another small piece of chocolate, they continued on towards the house.

Getting a better look at the kids now that they were outside, Emma felt they couldn't have been at the cabin for more than a couple weeks. While they were definitely hungry and dirty, they were well cared for prior to their mother's death. Expensive shoes and clothing, hair that had a decent cut, even a gold bracelet around both of the children's wrists were all telling Emma that these kids were not neglected. "How did they end up at my cabin," Emma thought "And what happened to their mother?"

Dixon, Emma and the kids were coming around the barn when they met up with Tom. "What in the world?" Tom said as he took in the party of four.

"They were at Cabin Two. Mom is still there. We need to get a coroner out there immediately with Sheriff Olan. And don't worry, I don't think they understand English," Emma included based on the puzzled look on Tom's face. "We" she said making a big circle with her hand over the top of the dog and kids "Are going inside to get cleaned up and get something to eat. Can you make the call?" "No worries, I'll take care of it." Tom returned. "No sirens"

37

Emma took the kids into the house and helped them take their coats off. While she really wanted to get them into the tub, she knew they had to be hungry more than the dirt was bothering them. They could wash their hands and faces, though. Leading them into the washroom off of the kitchen, she knelt before them and turned the water to warm. Squirting some soap onto her hands she ran them under the water and made lots of bubbles. "Lavar limpia!" she said as she rubbed her hands together. The boy was a bit hesitant but the little girl stuck her hands in with Emma as if it was the same way her mom had washed her hands. Taking a washcloth, Emma dampened it and wiped the grime from the little girl's face. "Oh, you're a little cutie, now aren't you" Emma said as she brushed her hair back with her hand.

"Comida?" Emma asked and both kids nodded. "Lavar limpia," Emma said to the boy and walked out of the bathroom, the little girl trailing behind. Emma sat the little girl at the table and walked to the cookie jar. Inside were packs of crackers for her own grandkids. She grabbed a couple and poured two glasses of milk. Good thing she still had sippy cups around, she thought. She heard the water in the bathroom turn on and smiled, kid knows what he's doing, she thought, his momma was raising him well. Emma sat the crackers on the table and was pouring the milk into the cups when the little boy joined them. Pulling a chair back, he sat down beside his sister. They watched as Emma put the lid on the cup and sat it in front of them. On cue, both bowed their heads. Emma was taken aback. She had to find out what happened here. What brought these children to her cabin and more importantly, what happened to their mom? "So many questions," Emma muttered as she turned to make them something to eat.

The kids were bathed and in front of the fire fast asleep with Dixon on Dixon's bed when the sheriff arrived at the house. Luckily Emma had some pajamas at the house from the grandkids staying that fit them just right until their clothes were finished in the wash.

Emma made them stay in the kitchen so they wouldn't disturb the kids when Ed brought Sheriff Olan into the house. "Sheriff" Emma said as she nodded in his direction.

No love lost between either of them, Emma was waiting for the next election to get Ben Olan voted out of his position. Emma, Scott and Ben had all gone to school together in their teen years. Ben had moved to the area his sophomore year of high school from Chicago and came with the arrogant liberal mindset that his parents liked to flaunt at all the town hall meetings. Ben carried the same mindset onto the debate team. Lucky for Emma, it just gave her more practice in shutting down the arguments against socialism and what our actual rights are under the Constitution with Ben's slant from the left. While Emma began to look forward to their lively debates, Ben silently started to despise the girl who time after time made him look like the laughingstock of the school. It was even more startling that he went into law enforcement after high school and became a deputy in their small county. He was a sheeple, a follower, or so she thought, and that worried Emma in light of what was on their horizon. He obeyed his orders no matter the consequences to the citizens of their town or how much those orders might infringe upon their constitutional rights. Little did she know the scheming that was going on behind the scenes when their old sheriff was fatally shot while on duty. Ben was quickly thrown into the position by a landslide of votes. Emma thought it odd for Ben to gather the majority of votes considering his background until she started asking around town. Small conversations here and there with the townsfolk. All she was hoping for was that nothing happened before they could get someone elected who would back their town and have their best interests at heart, and not sell them down the river to the highest bidder. And Ben Olan smelled like a big old pile of corruption. Several of his deputies had already been busted with prostitutes, and Emma knew the manure only ran up the ranks.

"Where's these kids?" he asked

"They are asleep in the front room with the dog."

"I have someone from CPS on their way out to get them."

"Now sheriff, no need for that tonight. They can just stay here. We can take them into town in the morning."

"Really? You want to keep two mangy kids here that broke into your cabin? Who knows who will come looking for them and from what Tom says, they can't even speak a lick of English" retorted the sheriff

Emma raised a brow and calmly replied "Yes, really. Those children, who I am sure you are referring to have been cleaned up and fed" They have been through a horrible ordeal and don't need to be passed from house to house tonight. For heaven sakes Ben, have a fucking heart for a change!"

"Emma, you and I both know those illegals are nothing but trouble," the sheriff responded.

"These are someone's children, here legally or not!" Emma hissed back. "And they will be staying here tonight so call off your damn henchmen."

Ben knew he was walking into a snake pit at this point and backed down. It was like old times on the debate team and Ben hated the feeling he got when he tried to argue with this woman before him. They made arrangements to meet in town the next day before lunch with the children.

"Any reports of missing kids? A husband or father is out there somewhere. Someone has to know something," Tom asked

"Problem is trying to get them to communicate. They don't like to talk, especially to law enforcement" the sheriff responded

Ben shook Tom's hand as he left without even a word to Emma. Tom carried the sleeping kids one by one into the guest room as Emma tucked them into the big bed.

"Dixon, stay," Emma commanded and the dog promptly lay across the door frame. Being the best protector ever, Emma knew he would keep track of the kids and alert her if they awoke during the night.

38

Emma arose early and went to check on the kids. Dixon was all sprawled out on the floor in front of the door, snoring away; she had to step over him to get into the room. Lifting his head, Emma thought he was giving her his "I've got everything under control" look and she gave a quiet chuckle. Assured that the kids were still sleeping she went back into the kitchen and fixed a big breakfast of waffles and bacon for the kids before they left. It was going to be a long day for all of them.

39

"What do you mean you can't take them?" Emma asked sarcastically. "You were bound and determined to take them last night!"

"They just don't have room nor do they have anyone who speaks Spanish. With Tom being fluent, I thought maybe they could just stay with you until we get this all sorted out," Sheriff Olan replied

"That's fine," Emma replied. "I would be more than happy to help," she said as she walked out with the kids.

Ben sat back in his chair and grinned from ear to ear. "Fucking bitch," he mumbled. Served her goody two shoes right. Always sticking her nose in where it didn't belong and now he would make sure she got stuck with those kids for as long as it took to find out where their father was. Problem was it wasn't top of his priority list and he now had the power to make her sit and stew. He had the power for once and he liked the feeling. She had cost him so much in his teen years. It was bad enough that he had never won a debate against her but it was hard arguing with the girl you had a severe crush on. She had a wickedly quick mind that mesmerized him. With her constant taunting of his loss after loss in debate class, it had been a struggle getting a date from any of the other girls in their school since they all were friends. Albeit a small school at that, but since he wasn't one for the football team it was hard getting a date since everyone knew everyone else and had their nose stuck in each other's business. It wasn't until he had moved away to college had he had his first encounter with a woman, and a pretty miserable one at that. He was attracted to her long black hair and ferocious sexual appetite. She had taught him a lot about pleasuring the lust inside of his soul. It was his first encounter with a woman of Latino descent. She immersed him not only in her culture but also her version of the Kama Sutra in all kinds of public places. The thrill of getting caught was enough to drive Ben mad. He became enraged in his lust for her to the point he was closing himself off from anything and everything that deviated his attention from her, including school. Later, Ben's world crashed around him when another student had taunted his conquest of Ben's girlfriend. "Oh man, don't take it so hard," the kid had laughed in his face. "Everyone knows she was cheap and easy to begin with. Why else would she be with you?"

Ben quickly got up from the chair he was sitting in. His face flushed with anger. He felt a taunting in his groin reminding him of the humiliation he had endured starting with Emma. She would pay, if it was the last thing he would do.

40

Three hundred miles away, Senator Varga was frantically pacing the floor of her apartment. "Damn it. Why can't anyone reach Elsie?" She yelled at the man sitting in front of her as she combed her fingers through her hair.

"Ma'am, I'm sure it's just the area of the country they are in There's not much cell service in that vicinity"

"You promised me nothing like this would happen. I should have known better. How the hell am I going to explain this to my mom? Those children were to be protected at all times and now this bullshit?" Senator Varga was now bent over her desk staring blankly out the window behind it. "I want to know what happened and I want to know where the hell my children are right now!" She exclaimed as her fist hit the top of the desk.

Two weeks prior, Senator Varga had received a phone call that had sent chills down her spine. The voice on the other end, obviously scrambled to avoid detection, was curt and to the point. "Stop pushing for impeachment of the president or your children will die."

The government, our government, was a shambles. Most folks were living paycheck to paycheck or less. The economy was predicted to fall within months but the president of the United States was too busy taking vacations or throwing fancy parties to notice. Any time he felt he was being pushed into a direction he didn't care for, he signed an Executive Order into action trying to scare the general public. Fortunately for him, most of that general public did not realize the orders he was passing could not be enforced. It was purely a scare tactic to get the sheeple under control. Scare them to the point of forcible ownership. He was in essence, creating slaves.

But Senator Varga and others were tired of the games. President Walker was in his second term and it was rumored that he was not afraid to utilize martial law in order to retain the presidency. He had already tested out the populace's reaction by declaring a "Shelter in Place" order on several major US cities during several attempts at terrorist attacks. The citizens obliged and went so far as allowing the militarily armed police to remove them and then trash their homes during a highly questionable house-to-house search for the suspects. Create chaos by using faked terror attacks on your own people to retain control and continuing to bleed the country dry to the point of everyone begging to become a part of a larger world order? Sounds a bit insane, but to those who were witnessing it first hand, you can be assured it was quite real. Senator Varga was one of those with her eyes wide open.

It was after the phone call that Varga understood she had hit a nerve. The nerve ran so deep and was so painful that people would kill her children or anyone else who got in the way, to prove their point and retain control of the greatest nation in the world.

Senator Varga knew what she had to do and phoned an old friend she had served in the military with, someone she knew she could trust.

"Elsie, this is Nina. How's the elderberry bushes I sent you doing?"

Picking up on the code within the opening remark right away, Elsie knew something was wrong. While most people in Washington knew Senator Varga as an avid gardener, the term elderberry was an alert status that Nina had created for a code red situation.

"Ah, not so well Senator Varga. I may

need to get some additional plants soon."

"How about Sunday? I will be home all

day, stop by anytime and pick them up."

"Yes, ma'am. I will see you then," Elsie

concluded and hung up the phone.

41

Elsie arrived at Senator Vargas' home promptly at 2 p.m. on Sunday and was escorted out to the vegetable garden. Keeping an apartment in the city and a residential home just outside the city limits allowed the senator to always have her family close by. Freshly divorced while in office, Nina moved her widowed mother into the country house to help with raising her two children, which was their primary residence. Family was important to Nina and the kids loved having their grandmother around. Spending so much time with her, their primary language was Spanish as that was the only language the old woman spoke. It also allowed Nina the luxury of having a garden, something she was quite fond of. The garden had a dual purpose as it served as an excellent meeting place you see, as Nina was also an apiarist, and who in their right mind would dare plant a listening device in a bee hive?

Walking up to meet Elsie, Nina steered her closer to the colony that was swiftly exiting and entering the white box. She began teaching Elsie about the different medicinal plants that she was cultivating. Handing Elsie a basket, she began to make cuttings of the various plants she was interested in and placed them in the basket as they meandered along.

"Elsie, I need you to protect my children for a couple months. I need you to get them out of here and hide them as I am afraid things are getting very dicey with the situation we are in."

"How are you going to explain your children just disappearing for a while? You know people are going to ask questions."

"Yes, they will be off visiting their relatives before school starts in the fall. Hopefully by the time they realize it's been a little longer than expected, they will be well hidden and safe."

"These relatives, where do they live?"

"I have family in Florida. You need to fly them into Miami and make your appearances. From there I will have a car ready for you to drive them to a friend who lives on a compound outside of Pittsburgh. You will be safe there and among people I trust. You will find all the information you need in the bottom of this basket. Take it home with you." Taking her by the elbow, Senator Varga walked Elsie to her car and placed the basket of plantings in her trunk.

"Thanks for all the advice, I am sure I will be calling for more directions," Elsie said as she turned towards Nina

"I am at your disposal Elsie, as always," replied the senator

The senator waved as Elsie left her drive and turned to go into her house. Taking a deep breath, she regretted what lay ahead but knew it needed to happen to save the country she loved. But for now, she had to explain all of this to her mother.

42

The kids seemed to be adjusting well, especially after Emma had her grandchildren visit. It was also a great opportunity to put some foreign language into their homeschooling endeavors and seemed to be learned a lot easier trying to communicate with their guests than from learning it out of a textbook. Jessica agreed to take the kids for a day so Emma could run into town and see if there was any news on who they were or how they got to her cabin.

This whole scenario was perplexing to Emma. After all, these children just lost their mother and yet showed not much in terms of grieving. There was no identification anywhere on any of them. The kids were well mannered, had rather expensive clothing on including some pretty expensive jewelry. When Emma was helping little Alicia get a bath, she noticed she had a locket around her neck. Opening the locket, a man and woman's pictures were inside. Was this what the woman in the cabin looked like before she died?

Matheo, the little boy, was very polite and looked after his little sister like a doting parent. He didn't say much. The trauma that they just went through might have something to do with that, Emma thought.

He needs some time. "More time," Emma breathed out. "Everyone needs more time"

She pulled into the parking lot of the sheriff's station as Sheriff Olan was leaving. "Well this should save me some time" Emma thought

"Sheriff!" Emma called out

"Emma"

"Any news on the woman from my cabin?"

"Nothing yet but really wasn't expecting anything. Illegals don't talk, you know that. Waste of my time and your valuable taxpayer's money"

Emma let it go, so much to come back with after that little quip, but it would do her no good.

"Alrighty, just thought I would check. I'll check in with CPS while I am in town and maybe check in with you at the end of the week."

"That's fine but I wouldn't expect much news" he said as he turned to get in his car. Quickly turning back around, he raised his finger in the air "Oh, hey, there is one thing. That woman in the cabin. Turns out the coroner said she had a gunshot wound in her stomach area. Maybe she got into it with her illegal baby daddy or something. Don't know but maybe you can use the info."

"Well aren't you all heart sheriff" Emma replied as she walked away

Sheriff Olan watched her stroll off towards her car. "One day, bitch. You'll beg." He muttered under his breath.

43

"Where the hell could she be?" Nina thought as he paced back and forth. So far everything had gone as planned. Elsie flew with the kids into Miami and met up with Nina's Aunt Maria. From the reports in the paper, they were having a grand time reunited with their little cousins.

Elsie had picked up the rental car along with supplies for the trip north. She made sure the kids had good sturdy travel clothes and plenty of things to keep them occupied. They left the following night after everyone had retired for the evening. The only person who knew of their departure was Maria.

"Oh, my sweet bebe's" she moaned as she covered their tiny faces with kisses. "May Saint Christopher watch over you both. Elsie, please, protect these children with your life!"

"Yes ma'am," Elsie replied and buckled both kids into their seats.

Driving from Miami to Pittsburgh, Pennsylvania with two small children was a little out of the norm for what Elsie was trained to do. Serving under the command of Lieutenant Nina Varga, Elsie had trained in the United States Army and spent a few years stationed in Israel training with the IDF. She took an early retirement to become one of the first female private contractors in Saudi Arabia for one of the royal families. She had always protected the wives of the men she worked for, not their children. She was a perfect fit as her Latino features could easily be mistaken for Middle Eastern.

Driving straight through would take her 19 hours minimum. That didn't include potty breaks and food.
If she were alone, completely logical. With two toddlers, impossible came to mind. She would need to make at least one

overnight stop and even she didn't know where that would be until she got there.

Heading north, she made good time with the night traffic. Stopping twice for gas, she was able to make it into Columbia, South Carolina, before the kids woke. A quick breakfast and potty break along with toys and movies ready to go, they headed out. Elsie wanted to make it to Charleston, West Virginia, before nightfall.

Eight hours later, which included six bathroom stops and two stops to see the mountain views, they rolled into Charleston. Elsie found a cheap, clean motel and packed everyone into the room. Checking all vantage points, she ordered dinner from a local pizzeria and by 9 p.m. they were already tucked into bed and saying their nightly prayers.

Elsie had grown quite fond of these children on their trip. They had chatted endlessly about princesses and warriors, favorite cookies and swimming in the ocean at Aunt Maria's house. The next morning as they were getting ready to leave, little Alicia walked into the bathroom while Elsie was brushing her long dark hair. "Here El Le," Alicia said in Spanish. She couldn't quite wrap her little tongue around pronouncing Elsie and it kept coming out as El Le. Elsie looked down and in Alicia's little chubby hand was a golden hair comb. "Oh Alicia, it's beautiful!" Elsie exclaimed to the 3 year old. "Hair" Alicia said and climbed up on top of the toilet. Elsie bent over so Alicia could put the small golden comb in her hair. Both girls were exclaiming with "Ohs" and "Aahs" in the mirror and both agreed, it was hermosa!

44

The compound that Elsie needed to get the kids to was located someone between the northeast side of Pittsburgh and East Liverpool, Ohio. Going straight in wasn't an option as by now, Elsie was sure that someone had figured out the kids were not in Miami anymore. Checking the maps the night before, Elsie wanted to stay out of Pittsburgh altogether if she could. Maybe a six-hour drive from where she was, she wanted to throw anyone off her trail who might be behind here. She would take SR79 north to Morgantown, West Virginia, and then take the scenic route into Wheeling. From there, it would be all back roads and small towns until she arrived at the compound.

Elsie glanced in her rear-view mirror. The kids were dozing in and out watching a movie on the DVD player. Her heart ached for them, for not having a normal life. A child having to go into hiding because of evil people in the world. She understood Senator Varga's vision and her commitment to it. Something in this country had to change and fast. Would these children become the spoils of a war they were too young to even understand?

Elsie began to relax being off the main highway and started to enjoy the scenery. By now they were deep into southeast Ohio and making their way north east. Catching her eye, the gas light blinked on and she cursed under her breath that she hadn't fueled up earlier. Hitting the "find gas" button on the GPS, she was a far cry from the nearest fuel station. Taking a deep breath, she reminded herself that some of these small- town service stations weren't registering on the GPS. Ya, she said to herself, keep telling yourself that. Glancing at the map, she wasn't far from a little town. "Let's just hope they have a gas pump," she said out loud.

Small town it was with barely any homes, but a small convenience store and two gas pumps was all she needed. Elsie let out a sigh of relief as she pulled the car up in line with the pump. Getting out, she surveyed the scene and began the process of fueling the car. Once done, she unloaded the kids to go inside and pay and hopefully find a working bathroom and some hot coffee.

Elsie felt the glares as soon as she hit the front door. They burned beneath her skin, something she hadn't felt in quite a while. Looking around, she was not in a good place and needed to leave as quickly as she came. Quickly spotting the sign for the bathroom, she took both kids inside with her and locked the door. Taking a deep breath, she checked her pistols, both the one on her hip and the one under her arm attached to her bra. Kneeling down, she told the kids to hold hands and that they needed to leave quickly as they were late to where they were going. "No snacks, we can get them the next time we stop. Right now, let's quickly get in the car and get to where we need to go, OK?" she asked the kids as she shook her head up and down. Taking a deep breath, she opened the door and peered out.

It was eerily quiet. She grabbed the little girl's hand as she pulled them quickly down the hallway into the main section of the store. The men were still there. She counted them. Two were missing. Maybe they left, she thought. Taking a deep breath she quickly walked to the door as the eyes drilled deeper under her skin. They exited the store as Elsie quickly picked up Alicia and, grabbing Matheo by the hand, she bolted for the car. Hitting the unlock button on the key ring she threw the kids in the back seat without regards for their safety seats. She heard the door to the store slam behind her.

"Hey spic, you gonna pay for that gas or just steal it. Cuz if you decide to steal it, I might have to just hunt you down and make you pay," she heard from behind her.

She quickly turned around. Three of them were now outside the building, spread apart and staring at her. "I'm so sorry" she stammered. "I forgot. Here, here's the money" she said as she laid the bills on top of the trash receptacle that was between them.

Picking up the money, the man looked at it like it might be counterfeit. "Your pretty little spic ass must be pretty good if you have two bastard kids. Might want to stick around for a while," the man grinned at her showing off his mouth full of half-rotten teeth with a one silver cap.

"Oh, ya ya. Get us some la-tee-no pussy. Maybe the sheriff would like some of this, wouldn't be the first spic bitch he had," the other man said with a deliberate pronunciation of each syllable. All three men were now laughing, talking about calling the local law to come and have some fun too. Seem to be a regular past time for them. Elsie saw her opportunity to leave as they reminisced about the last encounter they all shared after they tied her down.

Elsie turned and quickly got in the car, locking the doors behind her. The men approached the car now, yelling racial slurs and kicking the sides of the car, scaring the children. Elsie quickly started the car and drove off, looking behind her and flipping the men off.

"Fucking assholes," she yelled out loud before she realized it.

Pulling off the road about 20 minutes later, Elsie quickly buckled the kids in their seats. Stopping before she got back into the car, she pulled out a map and scanned quickly so she could get back on a main road. "No more stupid mistakes," she muttered to herself.

She heard the truck throttle down before she saw it come over the rise in the road. Quickly getting back into the car, she pushed the gas down as far as it would go. A little too late though, the truck was upon her before she had the chance to get to full speed.

"Play it cool girl, you got this," she said, trying to convince herself.

"Hey, pull your la-tee-no ass over," the man yelled from the window of the truck

Elsie kept her eyes ahead and kept driving, increasing speed

"Fucking bitch won't pull over! Maybe we need to persuade her," one man said

The front end of the truck swerved and caught her in the front quarter panel of the car. Elsie hit the brakes before it could do any real damage and came up behind them on the other side. Speed increasing, the men were now pissed to be shown up by a girl driver. "Bitch, pull that car over now, this is the law," the driver said as he flashed a badge out of the window at her.

Elsie knew she was in trouble if this was the local law enforcement. No calling 911, she was on her own. The truck had circled back to her driver's side and Elsie gave it a quick glance. The flash caught her eye first and then the sound. The bullet ripped into her side and sliced deep into her flesh.

The shot surprised her as much as the men, as they veered off and disappeared, leaving her to drive off alone. Elsie reached down and felt the blood dripping from her side. Her vision started to drift in and out and she knew she needed to get her foot off of the gas. "Oh God, the kids!" she thought. She had to get them somewhere safe. Looking for a spot to pull the car off the road, she saw the perfect opportunity to lose the car. A creek was visible alongside the road with lots of trees. She could hide in there until she could get help. Pulling the car over, Elsie got the kids out along with their packs. Shoving the car into neutral, she let it roll down the embankment and into the water. She watched it sink.

Grabbing the kids, she set off into the woods. Following the creek for a while, she walked the kids over a bridge that the railway used to get the train cars across the small flow of water. Looking around, she decided to follow the creek for a bit more to see what was off in the distance, if anything at all. The kids were tired, scared and probably hungry. She was exhausted and wanted desperately to check where she had gotten shot. As she peered through the woods towards the top of the hill, she blinked her eyes to try and get clearer vision. The dark outline of a cabin taunted her tired eyes.

45

Sliding her hand gently under the back end of the hen, Emma felt the warm hard shell of the eggs. Not much longer, she thought, and I will have peeps. Feeling sorry for the hen still sitting on the nest, Emma moved some food and water within distance of her just reaching her beak out and taking some of each. Raising kids was such a hard business; Emma thought as her mind went back to the two small visitors. Something was tugging at her gut. Something wasn't right with this whole picture and she needed to find out what that something was.

Picking up the eggs from the nests that had been abandoned, Emma pulled up the end of her makeshift apron and gently placed them inside. Stepping back out into the sunshine, she watched as the two kids followed Dixon around the yard. He truly was a remarkable animal, his coat gleaming white in the sun. He had helped so many people, whether they realized it or not, get through some pretty traumatic events in their lives. Emma adopted Dixon as a pup. Heading out to pick up a couple goats at a neighboring farm, he happened to have been born on the same farm at roughly the same time. He had bounded his fluffy white pudgy puppy self over to her and stolen her heart within the twinkling of an eye. They had been inseparable since.

Dixon turned his head to look at Emma as she came out of the coop. Rescue me was written all over it. Emma knew it all too well. He wasn't as young as he used to be. In his young adult life, he would have been giving those kids a ride around the yard. Now, he enjoyed curling up for a nap instead.

Emma took all of them inside and laid the eggs on the counter. She would get to these later. Nap time didn't sound like a half-bad idea, she thought as she winked at Dixon. Shoes off, hands and faces washed, both kids curled up on opposite sides of the couch. Stretching a quilt over the both of them, she tucked the edges in gave them each a kiss on the forehead. In no time at all, both kids and the dog were fast asleep.

Emma clicked on her computer. It was time to check in with the girls and catch up on some news.
Things were still in a steady slide to hell, but each additional day gave them a little more time to be more prepared than the last.

Hitting the news sources, it looked like rolling blackouts were being planned for several cities across the nation. "That's not going to go over well" Emma thought. How anyone would want to live downtown of a city was beyond her. Whenever they visited Tommy's family in New York, she was good for about three days and she was ready to leave. It was suffocating. And heaven forbid any type of shit-hit-the-fan scenario happened while they were there. Cities, especially the larger ones like New York, Chicago and Los Angeles, were just ticking time bombs. Any city with a by-pass was easy pickings to be turned into an internment camp, or Disaster Recovery Center as FEMA liked to call them now. Her biggest concern was once you entered, would you be able to leave? Would it be for your own good to stay there and would they use force to make that happen? About a year ago, the news was picking up on how even the clergy was getting involved in herding their congregations into these places, but as long and as loud as Emma and her friends were yelling for people to WAKE UP... some still chose to ignore the truth until sometimes it was too late.

Deep in thought, Emma was startled by the back door slamming shut.

"Emma! Emma!" Tom came into the house in a huff along with Kevin.

"Shhhh"! She spat back "The kids are napping...don't be waking them up!"

"Get Jess over here right away, you need to come see this"

Emma picked up on the tone in her husband's voice and knew it had to be important.

"She's on her way," Kevin replied "Mom, get your coat and boots on"

Quickly gathering what she needed, Emma headed to the back door as Jess was walking through.

"Mom, Dad and Kevin are already in the truck waiting for you," Jess said planting a quick kiss on her cheek.

"Kids are asleep in the living room. No idea what is going on so not sure when I'll get back," Emma said to her as Jess just shook her head.

Kevin was waiting outside the passenger side door of the truck as Emma made her way over and crawled in Tommy's truck to the middle. Kevin piled in behind her and before he could get the door closed, Tom was in reverse.

"What is going on?" Emma asked.

"Was down in the lower field this morning checking on the winter crops. You're not gonna like what I found," Tom said.

Tom pulled off the driveway onto a secondary road which ran between the tree line and the railroad tracks that ran across the bottom of the property. Edging into the field planted with winter rye, he turned onto a rail line access road right before the field ended. He was now dead on facing the creek.

Getting out of the truck, he turned to help Emma out but she had already maneuvered out the other side and past Kevin.

Tom walked them both over to the edge of the river bank and pointed. There, just barely sticking up above the water's edge, was what looked like the bumper of a car snagged in some driftwood.

"Is that…" Emma began not being able to pull her eyes away from the object.

"Yep," Tommy replied cutting her off before she could finish the sentence.

"Shit."

"Think anyone is in there?"

"Too late now if they are. Judging from the tracks off the road, it's been a while since that car went in."

"Think you can get a make on it?" Emma asked

Tom looked at Kevin. "That's the plan," Kevin replied and turned to grab his gear out of the back of the truck

Kevin and Tom were both volunteers for the local fire department. Kevin had attended special training for underwater rescue, which they all thought was necessary considering the number of ponds and lakes on the farms in the area, so he had grabbed his scuba gear when Tom had picked him up.

While Kevin suited up, Tom fastened a safety line to the front bumper of his truck. Walking to the corner of the field, he hopped on the rail line that ran across the creek and hopped down on the opposite side of the river bank.

"Throw me that end," he said as he pointed at the line.

Emma picked it up and approached the side of the bank, swinging the end of the rope with the weight attached, she swirled it like a Ferris wheel and lobbed it towards Tom on the opposite bank.

As long as she had known the man, he had never been able to catch anything, which was odd considering the number of awesome Latino baseball players out there. He just wasn't ever going to be one of them, she thought.

Tom tied off the other end of the rope around a tree, making sure it was taut; he then headed back over the railroad bridge to where Emma and Kevin were.

"You ready Moke?" he asked his son, using a family name for Kevin.

"As ready as I'll ever be!"

"Be careful Mokey" Emma said, using a nickname she had given him growing up

Kevin descended the edge of the bank, holding on the safety line that Tom had installed earlier upstream from the vehicle. Riding with the current, he reached the car in no time. Making sure he was a safe distance in case the car shifted, he dove underwater.

Minutes seemed to turn into hours as Emma paced the river bank.

Emma heard a vehicle driving down the main road and she looked in that direction. Luckily they were well protected from prying eyes with the row of trees and brush along the road. No one would ever guess someone was diving into a car in the creek not more than 100 feet away.

Kevin emerged and signaled for Tom to help him out of the water.

Once his gear was off and he was drying off, Emma started with the rapid fire questions.

"Mom, geesh! Give me a second here."

"Alright, alright... Just put a wiggle in it."

The debriefing was easy enough. No bodies found in the vehicle. "Doesn't mean they hadn't washed downstream, just meant that they weren't in the car," Kevin added. Nothing was in the car, actually. Which Kevin found odd. Car was a rental from the sticker on the bumper and he did get a plate number.

"Think we should all Sheriff Olan?" Kevin asked

"No. Not yet." Emma replied, her mind spinning "If there were bodies, then I would say yes but since it's empty, let's sit on it for a day or two. I've got some digging I want to do first."

Kevin and Tom both looked at her wondering what was going through her mind, both knowing better than to ask.

46

Sheriff Olan and his boys hadn't had a good night out in quite a while. "All work and no play makes for very grouchy law enforcement," Ben Olan thought with a smile on his face. He needed to get his self-imposed deputies out of the office and kick back a bit and see what fun was out there. Let them chill and burn off some of that young buck energy they seemed to have.

Calling Deputy Crites into his office, Olan made sure the door was shut behind him and motioned for the man to sit down. "I'm thinking we need to get out, have some fun tonight. What do you say Mike, you game?"

"Sure thing boss, what do you need me to do?" replied the deputy with a grin.

Ben laid out the plan and sent Deputy Crites on his way. They would meet later that night at The Pump, a local convenience store owned by a friend of Ben's. "After all, the more the merrier, right?" Ben thought as he chuckled to himself.

47

Tom dropped Emma off at the house. The kids were still asleep when they returned so Tom took Kevin and Jessica to their home so Kevin could get a shower. They would drive their own vehicle back over later so they could discuss further what they found in the creek.

"You know your mom isn't going to let this go 'til she finds out how that car got in there," Tom said to Kevin on the drive back.

"Ya, been thinking about that. Not saying there was foul play involved but it's not every day someone drops a car into the creek," replied Kevin

"Good, looks like we are on the same page. Let's beef up some security around the farm until we figure out what is going on."

Kevin nodded as he got out of the truck. Turning back with a grin on his face, he looked at Tom and said "Think I'll finally get to take down a drone?"

"I'll see you later tonight," Tom said, just shaking his head.

48

Emma checked on the kids, making sure they were still napping. Grabbing some juice, she sat down at her computer and turned it on.

Pulling down a journal from the nearby shelf, she added today's date and notations on their discovery.

The bright hue of the blinking icon on the computer screen cut through the darkness of the room and caught Emma's attention. Brian had sent her a message on Facebook to contact him for lunch.

"In due time," she muttered.

Her fingers were now flying across the keyboard, opening windows... closing....searching. Trail after trail her eyes darting back and forth keeping pace with the tapping of words being entered.

She knew the rental company.... Now to find their database for stolen vehicles. BINGO Quickly scanning the page, she found a make and model that matched the description.

Missing Rental Cars

Miami - Enterprise Rental Car has reported a 2014 Gray Nissan Murano as not being returned Anyone knowing the whereabouts, please contact Ted Miles at (305) 534-9037 at the South Beach
Branch

Now. To confirm the license plate. That was going to be the tricky part. Calling the police station to run a license check would definitely send up red flags, so that was out of the question.

Digging around on the website, she searched for an office in Minnesota. Gathering the info she needed, she dialed the Miami office and practiced the fine art of bluffing.

"Yes, this is Amy from the Minneapolis-St Paul Airport location. I am calling to get the plate and VIN number on a possible stolen gray Nissan Murano," Emma spoke into the phone. Holding her breath, she waited.

"Please hold for the manager," and she was clicked over to the on hold music.

Shit. Now what? Breathe through it and keep calm, she said as she tried desperately to convince herself.

"Sorry for your hold, my name is Neil and I am the general manager, how can I help you?"

Emma repeated herself and thanked Neil for his time. And then waited. It could go one of two ways.
Either she will need more information of identification or the dude will just tell her no. Listening intently, she heard what she assumed to be Neil, clicking a keyboard.

"Yes, the numbers are as follows..." the voice said finally coming back across the line

Oh Sweet Baby Moses... it actually worked! Emma's was so overjoyed that she got the information that it took her a minute to realize Neil was still speaking in the phone.

"Ma'am! Ma'am, are you still there?"

"Yes, I'm sorry. Could you tell me to whom it was last rented?"

"Um...yes. An Elsie Baretto. Do you have the vehicle there?"

Elsie Baretto....Elsie Baretto, Emma was rolling the name over her tongue, absorbing the familiarity of it.

"Ma'am! Do you have the vehicle?"

"Oh! Um no. No. They don't match. I'm sorry I bothered you." And she hung up the phone.

Emma took a deep breath and stared down at the name she had she had scribbled on her notepad. Elsie Baretto.

"Oh dear God."

Her stomach lurched into her throat. Swallowing hard, she stood up and walked into the room where the kids were napping.

What sweet babies, she thought as she stared down at them. What fresh hell have they been through? Turning, she walked into the kitchen to begin cooking dinner.

49

Dirty, worn jeans and wife beaters looked like the standard attire for the group gathered at the small store. Pickup trucks with 4" body lifts, chrome side-step bars running the length of the cab under the doors and big shiny, black tires filled the small parking lot. Music blared from every window, a cross selection from Megadeth to Skynyrd and some Hank thrown in for good measure. RPMs were being teased and tested as neighbors peered out from behind closed curtains at all the commotion.

Sheriff Ben Olan pulled onto the already crowded pavement and slammed the gears of his Ford F-350 into neutral and teased the crowd before slamming the clutch to the floorboards. Maneuvering the beast into first gear, he slowly pressed the accelerator until thick black smoke rolled from his back tires into the crowd. Cheering was heard as these fine, upstanding citizens raised their beer bottles in appreciation of the true sign of selective breeding. "Boys, we have a skid mark on the asphalt," came the voice over the loud speaker.

Olan stepped down out of his truck onto the pavement amidst his onslaught of worshippers. He wasn't sheriff tonight.... Tonight he was one of the boys. Looking around, he quickly did a head count of all of his deputies. Not one was missing. Makes it easier to cover his tracks that way, he thought with a slight upturn of the corner of his mouth.

Stepping inside the store, he made his way to the counter where his best friend was behind the counter. "John," he said as he nodded in his direction. "Ben. 'Bout time you got here. Let's get this party on the road! I've got an itch I need scratched!" They all filed out one by one, each grabbing a snack on the way out. "I need to move that shit away from the door," Mike thought as he locked the door behind him.

Ben, John and two deputies, Josh and Mark, piled into the back of Deputy Mike's truck along with several cases of beer and hard liquor. Steve stepped in and rode shotgun and made sure they had plenty to drink up front also. Mike started the engine and dropped the truck into gear without warning, almost sending his cargo over the sides onto the ground. Laughter echoed down the road and the truck headed for tonight's hot spot, Emerson Avenue.

50

"Mom, you've been awfully quiet tonight. You OK?" Kevin asked.

"Just a lot on my mind. I was doing some digging around earlier on the owner of that car," Emma replied.

"I'm shocked!" Kevin shot back with a grin.

Ignoring the sarcasm, Emma continued, "I found out who rented the car last and where it was rented at."

"Oh ya, do tell."

"It was rented in Miami by a woman named Elsie Baretto."

"Florida? She have her seasons mixed up? Usually people were heading TO Florida this time of year!"

"No idea but notice anything else? Anything about her name?"

"Not really, why?"

"Baretto is Hispanic in origin."

"And?" Kevin replied

"My two guests are Hispanic."

Kevin stopped and looked at his mom. "You think those kids were in that car?"

"Possibly. Think about it. From where the car went off the road, if they went over the creek using the railway bridge and traveled away from the house, they could have very well ended up at the cabin."

Everyone was silent as they traced the possible steps in their minds.

"You find out anything about this Elsie Baretto?"

"No. I'll wait until I get the kids down tonight and keep digging," Emma responded. "But I can tell you one thing. If she had enough sense to ditch the car in the water, someone was after her and probably still is."

Kevin exchanged glances with Tom. They had figured that into the equation already.

51

Back roads and lots of alcohol later, the boys rolled into a predominately Latino section of the town of Dover. While Dover was not located in the county they had jurisdiction in, it was close enough to the county line to get back home in a hurry if they were called for official business. It also helped that no one in the area knew who or what they were.

Coming to a halt at the stop sign, the boys got real quiet. Mike turned the corner and slowly let the truck carry itself down the side street. Their first victim was in sight.

Sonya was walking home from visiting a friend. It wouldn't take her long as it was only a few blocks and the fresh air and walk would do her pregnant body some good. Placing her hand on her now growing stomach, she felt the baby kick and it made her smile. Shining her flashlight on the sidewalk, she carefully chose her steps as not to fall. Deep in thought of getting home to her husband, she didn't hear the truck approaching.

Mike turned the headlights off on the truck. Slowly coming up behind the girl, he was surprised at how close they got before she noticed them. Ben, Josh, and John hopped out of the back of the truck and had the girl surrounded. Mark kept an eye out for anyone getting nosey in the surrounding houses. One thing they liked about these sections of town is everyone minded their own business. They were outcasts, loners in the country they were thrown into and knew enough to stay quiet and not bring a focus on themselves and anyone they might be hiding.

"Hey baby, whatcha doin' out here all by yourself?" Josh asked as he tilted his ball cap back on his head "You out trying to sell your pretty little ass? Cat got your tongue?" He taunted, knowing she didn't understand.

"Mark, you ready?" Ben called out.

"Yup" he heard coming from the darkness.

With synchronized precision, all three men acted together. John slapped his hand over the girl's mouth while Ben and Josh lifted her from both sides, hoisting her over the side of the truck. By now Steve had climbed in back and as the frightened girl came over the top, both Steve and Mark grabbed her and slammed her onto the bed. Josh and John hurriedly leaped into the back where the girl was being held down as Ben scrambled into the front cab. "Let's go," was all he said as all eyes were on anyone watching from the houses.

52

Taking Emma a cup of tea, Tommy sat down in the chair in her office. She was like a pit bull when she was onto something and knew she was destined to be up all night, or at least until she found what she was looking for.

Search engine after search engine, every rabbit trail was searched and checked against each other. Elsie Baretto had a life somewhere out there and Emma was going to find it. Printing leads, double checking facts, within three hours the office was strewn with papers of information.

Tommy stood up and stretched his back. Walking over, he placed a kiss on the top of his wife's head. "One of us has to be awake with these kids tomorrow. You keep digging, but I'm calling it a night."

Emma placed a hand on top of his on her shoulder. She loved this man and was glad he understood all her quirky, crazy obsessions.

"Dixon, stay," Tommy said and then chuckled to himself as he walked out of the room. Like that dog would listen to him with Emma around...

53

Mike drove the truck off the main road. Slowing slightly, he was looking for the dirt road that branched off the main road that the oil well guys used to check their tanks. "There you are," he muttered as he lowered his headlights and turned onto the path.

The truck bounced from the deep ruts dug into the dirt from the big tankers emptying out the oil.
Straddling the path with one tire in the middle and one up on the side seemed to help a little, but the destination was chosen for a reason. Privacy.

Even with all the alcohol they had consumed, the men had calmed down considerably. John, who had his hand over the girl's mouth was closest to her hair, all splayed out in the back of the truck. Soft as silk, he ran his hand through it. It made his dick hard. Grabbing his crotch with his free hand, he almost lost his balance in the back of the truck as Mike hit a dip. "Dammit Mike!" he yelled out. "No names you dipshit," Brad yelled back.

They were as far back as they could get, so Mike pulled the truck around facing back towards the way they had come in. If anyone just happened back in there, they would see the headlights of their truck first and not what was going on in the back. No homes for miles, they were feeling pretty comfortable that they would not have any visitors. But better to be safe than sorry.

Hopping out of the cab of the truck, both men walked around to the back and let the tailgate down. Grabbing Sonya's ankles, they pulled her to the edge and sat her up.

"Welcome to the party, little lady," Brad said as the rest of the men paced around nervously.

Sonya, her eyes wide open was already in shock. She had heard the rumors. Girls disappearing, but she thought they just were told by the elders to scare the young girls into marriage. Laying her hand on her stomach, she prayed…. And prayed.

"Come on bitch, let's go! Gimme some of that la-tee-no pussy!" Mark said as he grabbed her, ripping her shirt exposing her bra-covered breasts.

"I see boobage! Josh giggled as he reached over and ripped the strap from her shoulder.

Trying to cover herself, the tears started to flow down her face.

"Turn the spic over, I don't want her to ruin my hard-on," Brad said, grabbing his crotch

"But Boss!" Josh whined… "I like those little titties!"

All the men were laughing now. Josh and Mark pulled her off the truck until she was standing on the ground. Josh ripped the rest of her bra off, exposing her completely. Taking turns, the men pinched and twisted her nipples until they were bleeding.

"Enough of this shit! Turn the bitch over," Brad yelled.

Grabbing her by the back of the neck, Mike slammed her face into the back of the truck bed, the edge of the tailgate pushing into her stomach. Lifting her skirt and pulling out his knife, he cut her underwear off, falling at her feet.

"Alright Boss, she's all yours!" Mike said, smiling at the man he admired most in the world.

"Thank ya Deputy, don't mind if I do!" Brad said as he drove his throbbing penis into Sonya. Over and over the men took turns, either holding her head down in the bed of the truck of pounding her with his cock.

Crying hysterically, Sonja felt the small life in her belly get crushed into the edge of the truck bed over and over. "Que Dios se apiade," she whispered.

54

"That blasted noise needs to stop," Emma thought, coming up out of the fog she was in. Reality setting back in, she realized it was her phone ringing.

"Who the heck calls at this hour of the morning?"

She rolled over to try and stop the blaring noise and noticed Tommy wasn't in bed anymore. Glancing at the clock, it was almost noon. "Shit," she muttered

Grabbing the phone she punched the talk button, "Hello?"

"Emma, its Brian. I need to see you right away."

"Today? Or is tomorrow OK?" she asked

"Today," he replied rather sternly and then added, "You feeling OK? You sound tired."

"Ya, I'm fine. About 3 O'clock OK?"

"Is that the soonest you can get here?"

"I'll get there as soon as I can, no later than three," she said and hung up the phone.

Rolling off the side of the bed and wrapping her robe around her, she went into the kitchen. Stopping in front of the sink, she realized how oddly quiet the house sounded. Looking out the kitchen window, she caught sight of Tommy and the kids, Dixon in tow, feeding some carrots to the rabbits she was raising for meat. "The kids look so peaceful here," she thought and poured herself a cup of coffee.

55

Emma quickly showered, dressed and ran out to the barn to let Tommy know she had to run into town for a bit. "Brian called and wants to talk to me about something," she explained.

"Well, be careful," he said as he gave her a kiss. "Kids and I are going to finish with the rabbits here and then go check on the baby chicks. Probably make a little lunch in between."

"I'll be back as soon as I can. I love you," she told him as she held his face between her hands. "Never forget that" They locked eyes for a moment, just a moment, and then she turned to leave.

"Mi amor, de prisa a casa," he said smiling. Both could feel the climax coming, the quickening of life ahead.

56

"Hey sweetness, you ready for an early dinner?" Brian said to Emma as she was walking into his office

"Um, sure, I guess," she said as he about faced her and escorted her into the hallway.

Turning to give a quick wave to Brian's secretary, Emma allowed him to escort her away from his office towards his car.

Once they were alone, Emma just had to ask, "What is going on?"

"I'll explain in the car so hush and act happy."

"Hmpf," Emma snorted. Act happy? What was that about?

Brian opened the passenger door of his Tahoe and Emma got in and slid her seat belt into the lock. Brian did the same and then engaged his firearm under the steering column within easy reach. Emma had done some Force on Force training in Indy at Mindset Laboratory on drawing a handgun from a seated position and she discovered it wasn't as easy as it looked. She quickly sought out the inventor of the vehicle holsters and became a distributor, adding them to her website store.

"Would you tell me now?" she asked as they approached their first red light.

"Something is going on," he replied

"Really, that's a startling revelation!" she snipped back.

Brian turned and looked at her with a surprised look on his face. "Sorry, I didn't get a lot of sleep last night," she said

"Everything alright on the farm?"

"Yes, just animal issues."

"Wolves again? Have they been back?"

"Oh no... not that," she shot back quickly "So, when you say 'something is going on' what are you referring to exactly?"

"Got a call from John Kendrel, he's the Emergency Management Rep for Carroll County. A girl was brought into the hospital last night, pretty banged up. They still aren't sure if she is going to make it. Raped pretty brutally. She's from Emerson... Latino community... and you know how closed lipped they are. Emma, we need answers as this isn't the first girl this has happened to," Brian said as he slid a file over to her.

Opening the folder, Emma caught her breath. "Sweet Jesus" she said, slowly flipping through the pictures.

"Any ideas on who would do this?"

"None," Brian replied, "and we need your help"

"What do you want me to do?" Emma asked

Brian pulled the car into an alley and driving to the end, garage doors opened as he approached. Driving inside, Emma was surprised to see herself sitting in an elevator. Brian punched a couple buttons on his cellphone and the elevator descended into the floor of the building.

Emma was quiet, scanning her surroundings. Not really scared, but hugely inquisitive on what was going on and where they were going.

The car stopped and the gate in front of them opened, revealing a huge warehouse full of individual blocks of computers with a bank of huge monitors on each of the walls. People were buzzing around, talking to each other, pointing at computer screens and drinking lots and lots of coffee. If Emma would remember anything from this visit, it was the amount of coffee cups sitting all over the place.

"Come on, I want you to meet someone," Brian said as he unbuckled and slid out of the SUV. "No chivalry here!" Emma quipped with a grin as she exited her own door.

They walked together to a row of doors on the far side of the room. Brian knocked and quickly entered without waiting for a response.

Inside the office, a rather plump man was sitting behind a mound of files covering a cheap metal desk. Glasses on top of his head, pen behind his ear, he had the air about him of the wizard of Oz.

"John, Emma, Emma, John," Brian said, looking from one to the other.

Emma walked over and reached out a hand, only to be met with a blank stare. Recovering coyly, Emma turned just as fast and said, "Nice place you have here," as she started looking at the files on his desk

"Here, sit," Brian said pointing to a chair. "Let's all chat"

"John here," nodding towards the man behind the desk, "Is my counterpart in the next county over. You are now located in the state emergency offices that were designed in case of a... as you so lovingly refer to things, a shit hitting the fan."

Emma's eyebrows arched as a lopsided smile crossed her lips. "This should be quite interesting," she thought.

"We talked briefly about a possible coup within the government," Brian said looking directly at her

"What you don't know is how much of the present government, and its resources are involved. Each state is currently set up with a ghost, or as some refer to it, a gray government. They have been working non-stop to step in when the time comes."

"Why don't they step in now?" Emma asked

"We still have some things that need to unfold yet. And that's where you and your band of merry women come into play."

Emma sat up straight in her chair. "What are you talking about?"

"Your girls, the chicks, whatever you call them," he said, aimlessly flipping his hand in the air. "You have one mighty network set up across the country!"

"And? You want me to put these girls in danger? And for what exactly? These are moms...and grandmothers for Heaven's sake," she stammered, "NOT flipping CIA agents Brian!"

"Calm your ass down. I don't want an answer today. Just think about it. We are going to need all the help we can get when this goes down…and we need someone to get info out…an old-fashioned, on the ground pony express if the power goes down," he snapped back at her.

"Is that why I am here? What about that girl in the file?" She

shot back. "Or was I just totally set up?" John's head shot up on

cue. "You told her about the girl?" he asked, looking at Brian.

"I had to get her here somehow. Trust me, she wouldn't have come if she knew what I really wanted."

"So this girl is real? Not some story you made up?" Emma asked.

"Oh, she's real all right, and not the first," John piped up now. "Problem is getting anyone to talk"

"Ya, Brian said it was over on Emerson in the Latino part of town," Emma said.

"I'm surprised the poor girl's not dead yet. They took the baby this morning right after they found her. Coroner thinks she lost it at the time of the rape from the bruising and damage," John added

"My God, she was pregnant?" Brian asked

"My guess is, it's someone from outside the community. She was last seen leaving a friend's house and never made it home. Found her this morning dumped behind the local Laundromat. Latinos don't like to talk, but they don't usually do this to one of their own in a tight-knit community. Bigger city, maybe. Not here though."

"How can I help?" Emma asked

Taking a deep breath, John locked eyes with her. "Can you talk with them? You're a woman and I don't have one in my department. Brian trusts you, which is good enough for me. You also know how to protect yourself if something happens."

"Something happens?" Emma asked

"Rumor is they are planning on taking the law into their own hands... I need to get this solved before that happens or a lot of innocent people are going to get hurt."

"I'm going to have to talk with Tom about this first. When do you need an answer?"

"Yesterday."

"I need something in return," Emma responded

"Name it," Brian said

"I need info on this plate, rental info is for an Elsie Baretto. I need to know who she is, where she is from and if she has family," she said as she flipped a piece of paper on John's desk.

The look both men passed between them made the hair on the back of Emma's neck stand on end.

57

Ben kicked back in his chair, linking his fingers behind his head as he took a long puff on his cigar. "Life was good when you were the sheriff," he thought.

Quickly sitting forward, he snubbed out the cigar and picked up the phone.

"You have reached the voice mailbox of John Kendrel. Please leave a message and I will return your call as soon as I can. Thank you"

"Now where the hell would John be in the middle of the afternoon?" Ben thought.

58

"Where the fuck did you get this info?" Brian said to Emma

"Doesn't matter" she shot back a little startled by his reaction.

"Like hell it doesn't! Where did you get this?" his voice several octaves past normal now.

Emma looked at him, afraid to blink. "What's going on?" she finally said

Brian walked over to the door, opened it, walked out and motioned for someone. A young skinny male approached him. Brian said something to him and the kid left. Walking back into the room, Brian shut the door and walked over where Emma was. Grabbing her by the shoulders, he turned her to face him. "We've know each other a very long time" he began "I've always trusted you. Trusted you with my life. I need to know how you know this Elsie Baretto and I need to know now."

Emma sat down. Her mind racing a million miles a minute.

"I have a car in the creek," she said.

Blinking at her, Brian's brows furrowed, "What?"

"There's a car in the creek. I dug a little and found out it was rented to her in Miami, Florida," Emma said.

"Oh God no!" John muttered from behind the desk.

Emma had almost forgotten he was there. She looked quickly at Brian, her mouth still open, a look of confusion on her face.

Brian ran his fingers through his hair as he breathed out the air he had been holding in.

"What the hell is going on?" Emma yelled.

Looking at John, Brian nodded....

"Emma, Elsie Baretto works for Senator Varga."

"Like Varga.... Florida Varga? Like, 'I'm gonna piss of the Prez' Varga?" Emma asked using air quotes in a comical way.

They both nodded.

Emma collapsed back in the chair blowing out a steam of air. "Shit," she said.

"How'd she get in my creek then?"

"Last we can trace, she was heading north with the senator's children to a compound outside of
Pittsburgh."

"Children? What children?" Emma asked.

"Varga's kids. They lived mostly with their

grandmother in Florida. They aren't very old." "Like

maybe 3 and 4?"

"Ya, that's probably about right" Brian added.

"Names are Matheo and Alicia?" Emma asked.

John slowly nodded, his mind quickly picking up that Emma knew more about this than he thought.

"Ah shit," Emma mumbled. "Both of you need to sit down and let me tell you a story"

Two hours later, the three walked out of John's office. The plan was to keep the kids at Emma's safely hidden since the only one who knew they were there was Sheriff Olan. Senator Varga would be notified and plans would be adjusted accordingly.

"Wait 'til Tommy hears all of this!" Emma thought with a grin as she slid into Brian's car.

59

He just stood there shaking his head. What else could he do? He knew there was no turning back, for her, or for anyone else. It was his duty to protect her... protect her not only physically, but mentally and spiritually also. She had saved him so many years ago. A path of self-destruction, a hard life on the streets of New York was a cruel road for anyone, let alone a child. He couldn't blame his parents, they did the best they could with what they knew, who they were. But to her, he owed his life. She was responsible for who he was today, picking him up from the ashes of his own personal hell, for breathing life back into his hardened heart. And his vow was to save hers, if need be. Even if it was the last thing he did.

60

"Senator Varga! Senator Varga!" Deep in thought, Nina did not hear the man yelling out to her until he was right in her face. Stopping abruptly, she looked up at him, her eyes blinking in disbelief that someone could actually get that close to her.

"Yes?" she asked looking around for the men she was paying to protect her.

"Matheo sent me," the man replied.

"What?" she stammered in disbelief. Regaining her composure, Nina motioned for the man to follow her. Swiftly walking past the elderberry bushes, Nina's skirt snagged on a branch. Reaching down to release herself, the man saw how bad her hands were shaking.

"Ma'am. My name is Tomás Montalvo, and this is my grandson Jack. We are here doing some research on the branches of our fine government. Part of my wife's homeschooling right now is learning about the functions of each branch including the House of Representatives, and what better way to do that then to see them first hand."

"But Matheo… what do you mean Matheo sent you?" her lips calmly asking but her eyes scanning his face, begging for information.

Taking the senator by the elbow, Tom lowered his voice.

"Matheo is at my home."

"What? Who are you?"

"Elsie brought them to us," Tom replied.

Nina's composure relaxed a bit, as her mind was trying to make sense of the information.

Tom watched as a well-dressed man came out of the side door of the house.

"Yes, we were wondering if you would care to discuss with my Grandson Jack here your role as a senator within the government."

"It would be my pleasure," she replied, picking up on Tom's cue.

61

With the kids off visiting at Kevin and Jessica's and Tom off to Washington with Jack to deliver his message, Emma sat down and started doing some intensive searching for information.

Senator Nina Varga looks like she has a little bit of spunk behind her, Emma thought. Nina had been in the news a lot over the last few months. The press absolutely loved her for ratings as she, and her constituents, were causing quite a commotion every time the sitting president tried to make a move. It was like watching a well-orchestrated game of block and tackle! "Well done," Emma murmured. Looking through the list of colleagues that Nina had aligned herself with, Emma caught her breath.

"Well I'll be a monkey's grandma!"

There before her, Emma started putting the pieces of the puzzle together. Nina Varga had the total package to pull off what was so glaringly obvious. This woman was going to run for the presidency!

There were plenty of rumors that President Walker would not go down without a fight, and many thought he would use some kind of false flag to pull off retaining his current term. He was at the end of his control over this country. Halfway through his second four years, he had previously tried to sneak a bill through Congress to open up the office of the president of the United States to be able to be elected indefinitely. As long as the people voted him in, he would still be commander-in-chief.

Swooping down like an eagle attacking its prey, Nina had ousted the president's plans. "The last six years had been enough torture for this country and it is time to hand the reins over to someone else before Walker destroys everything!" she had been quoted as saying. And the woman had some strong supporters behind her... friends in high places, as they say.

Emma's mind was spinning with questions. How deep was Senator Varga into the gray government? If she has already attempted to remove her children from Washington, were they planning on a collapse soon? What was coming up next and what could Emma do to get her friends better prepared?
And more importantly, what was Emma going to do with the senator's children?

Emma sat back in her chair and took a deep breath.

She stood and walked over to the window, looking up at the sky, a prayer escaped her lips. "Need some help here Big Guy." In her gut, she knew that going forward it was GAME ON.

62

Johnisse, or Jay as her business associates called her, fingered the fine linens in her closet. Lordy, she thought. How far life had brought her. And how far life was going to take her. She had a plan. She wasn't a hardass for no reason at all. It was all a part of her plan. 2-year, 5-year, 10-year... whatever... she had the plan and was working it. Wrong side of town to penthouse suite. Yes, success suited her. Or success suited her lover. Tiffany was high upkeep and at times Jay's worst nightmare. For what now? 5 years ... 5 years of only the best Jay's money could buy for Tiffany.

Jay let out a sigh. She could handle the high stress of Wall Street. She could take on the "suits" without even breaking a sweat. But something about that woman...that woman

…Tiffany had the ability to manipulate Jay into giving up her right arm if it suited Tiffany. Had she created a monster? Or was she just feeding the monster? Jay couldn't decide but knew it wasn't in any of her plans to correct the issue anytime soon so she just dismissed it. Much like she dismissed the asshats who were shocked when she walked into a meeting and dismissed her because she was black and a female. Jays hunger to prove herself worthy was the driving force behind the determination it took to take her from the slums of Bushwick to the Upper East Side. And nothing was going to take her back to the trash she grew up in and around.

Startled, Jay realized she had let herself drift back to when she was growing up. The smells of Brooklyn in the summertime now made her sick to her stomach. But back then, they were a comfort, a stabilizing factor in her childhood. She closed her eyes and drifted back... she remembered lying in bed, the window open… a faint breeze drifting in coming from the East River…she could clearly hear the siren of the ambulance even on the sixth floor of their apartment building.

Tears began to drift over her cheek as she remembered Nelly. Nelly was her best friend. They grew up together in Brooklyn and lived in the same apartment building. When Nelly was 12, she was raped by a group of boys from the neighborhood. Not long after that Nelly jumped from her apartment window to end the torture she lived with daily after the rape. The neighborhood dealt with her death the best they could, mostly by just not talking about it.

Jay shook her head as if to clear her mind of the memory. Muttering under her breath she wiped the tears from her cheeks. She would be damned if the hard edge she had developed over the years was going to be undermined by a two-bit memory from long ago. Hell, she couldn't even recall Nelly's face no matter how hard she tried anymore…and she did try.

Walking across the room, Jay pushed the button to turn the TV on. She needed to unwind and one fetish that few knew about was watching a show about a man and woman who threw themselves into survival situations and videotaped what they would do. Actually, she could blame it on her old boss who talked about the woman drinking the man's piss to stay hydrated. Jay couldn't believe these people existed outside the loony bin and was intrigued. Hooked from the first show, Jay talked with her boss often about what was going on in the world and how to handle different situations. She learned a lot during that time in her life, not only about business but survival also. She missed those days. She missed the woman who quickly became her mentor.

Picking up the phone, Jay dialed and waited for someone to pick up. It had been a while since the last time they had talked. "Hello," she heard, recognizing the voice on the other end.

"Hey boss!"

"Jay?"

"Yes ma'am! How's life out there in the middle of nowhere?"

Laughing, Emma was happy to hear Jay's voice. "How are you? Where are you?"

"I'm home in New York now and doing great! Just wanted to check in and see how you were doing."

The next few hours drifted by quickly. The two quickly reconnected with nonstop exchange of information.

Johnisse used to work for Emma when they both lived in Indianapolis. Both being transplants from other states, the two had bonded quickly being outsiders to the area. Jay came to

Indy by way of Chicago after leaving New York. She would go back one day but first she needed to make a name for herself.

With Jay losing her mother at an early age, it was easy to get tucked under Emma's mothering wings. Jay looked up to her and learned a lot during the years she worked under her, not just a keen business sense but a lot about how to treat people. Jay had a hard edge to her due to the tough life living in New York but Emma wouldn't give up on finding her soft spot, her sweet side. It also helped to sit around and reminisce about life on the street with Emma's husband Tommy. They had walked the same pavement many years prior and shared a kinship that not many could understand. They quickly melted into something deeper than friends, more of an adopted family without the necessary involvement of blood.

"Oh Emma, I don't think I could do that. You know how Tiffany is. She isn't going to want to leave here."

"Jay, as long as we have known each other, have you ever known me to feed you bullshit?" Emma asked

"No ma'am. No you haven't," Jay replied.

"Time for a vacation then. You need to get to Chicago on business and want to stop over for the night. Just tell her I have some really nice homegrown marijuana to give you. That should shut her up."

"Ouch! That stings!" Jay shrieked.

"Tell me she quit. Just tell me she quit and I will apologize," Emma chuckled.

"No. That should get her there alright," Jay said sadly knowing Emma had found the perfect hook to get her out of town.

"Good. Now start packing," Emma said.

"Packing what? Hell! I can pack for a normal trip but from what you are proposing, we are going to need to invite one of those crazy survivalists along to get us there. How am I supposed to keep Tiffany happy if something happens and we are still several states away? I don't have supplies like that here. Living in Manhattan is like living in the middle of an Island. Well....it is an island but you get my drift. Like freakin' Hawaii!" Jay said, her voice getting higher as the panic began to set in.

"Jay! Jay!" Emma screamed into the phone, "Calm down!"

"Calm down!? You want me to calm down? Seriously? How do you propose I calm down? You have been getting ready for this for years. I got nothing! No supplies and very little Boy Scout skills to get my ass to Ohio!" Jay screamed back into the phone.

"Then the sooner you get out of there, the better," Emma said, barely audible. It was enough to get Jay to listen. "Listen. I know how you feel right now, but trust me when I tell you to get out of there as soon as possible. You have a room here as long as it takes, OK?"

Emma could hear Jay let out a long breath in the receiver.

"I'll see what I can do," Jay finally said. "Let me talk with Tiffany but I want to call you back later... maybe tomorrow and maybe you can help me put something together for the trip. Just in case."

"You know it. Deep breath, chica. You can do this. And when you get here, I am going to turn you into the best doomsday prepper that ever lived!" Emma laughed into the phone.

"Doomsday my ass!" Jay snarled back. "Those people are nuts!"

"Good. I hate lying but you need to get here and we need to talk and put a plan together. I'll have a box of supplies ready for you when you arrive. By then we will have had a drought, or fire or something. I will make something up to tell Tiffany about the lack of sinsemilla to take the heat off of you. Just trust me Jay, you need to get out of the city and soon," Emma said with just a small amount of agitation in her voice to entice Jay to put the plan into action even faster.

63

Senator Varga walked into her bedroom. She was finally alone. No prying eyes or ears to dictate or record her every move. Crossing the room, she walked into her bathroom and undressed, sliding into her bathrobe. She turned and caught a glimpse of herself in the mirror. Raising her hand, she touched the well-earned lines in her face with the tips of her fingers. War wounds these wrinkles were. Battles fought and won... battles fought and lost. Just like the stretch marks that highlighted the landscape of her stomach showing that she earned the title of mother, the fine lines on her face recounted every late night, every disenchantment, every time her heart was broken. Her eyes started to glisten slightly from tears forming as her past flowed through her mind until they gently overflowed and ran down her cheeks. She locked eyes with this person in the mirror staring back at her. Nina's chin rose ever so slightly in determination. She had no choice but to trust these people who had her children.

Drying her eyes, Nina walked into the bedroom. Walking over to her bed, she lifted the blankets and sheets off of the foot of the bed. Wedging her hand down between the footboard and her mattress, she felt around for the groove in the wood. Hitting the edge, she flicked her finger back until the board opened. She reached inside the hidden compartment and pulled the envelope from its hiding place. Replacing the trap door and the blankets as they were, she walked over to her desk and sat down. She took a deep breath and just stared at the envelope. What she was about to do would change the lives of everyone she knew. She only hoped they were ready.

64

Picking up the phone, Emma knew she had very little time to get her Girls into motion. One by one she made the calls, speaking calmly and clearly into the phone with information on what was possibly coming. They had been running drills for years but it looked like it was about time for everything to go "to the quilts" as Emma liked to call it. She came up with the code from some information she had found when she was gathering information on movement of supplies and people during the Civil War. It was confirmed but there were stories of quilts being used to transfer messages back and forth. Different colors of blocks built into the quilt meant different things. Black was always death, blue meant a clear path and so on. Being that Emma already had a network built with like-minded women across the country, it made sense to form Alpha Farms, as she referred to them, to get loved ones home if something happened while they were out traveling or heaven forbid, a real-life down grid situation. These women had come together and formulated an intricate network of routes to be used to transport their college kids, spouses working far from home, whomever they needed to get from one location to another without having to use the grid. Credit cards, hotel rooms, gas stations were all bypassed within this network to enable the travelers safety and operational security among the Alpha Farms themselves.

Hanging up the phone after her last call, Emma said a quick prayer. Knowing that the phone chains were now active gave her a small sense of peace as she knew each call she made would branch out to twenty other calls and so on down the line before all the Girls were reached and activated.

Picking up the phone one last time, she heard the receiver being picked up from the other end.

"Hey stranger," the voice said.

"Time to come home and you don't have much time left. Before you do, I need you to pick up a package for me so listen up," Emma said.

65

Jay walked into the Sporting Goods store and looked around. What the hell was she even doing here? Black people don't come into places like this! Grabbing a shopping cart, she figured she might as well hit each aisle to see what she could find even though Emma had sent her a list of essential items that she said Jay needed to get as soon as possible.

"Alright girl, let's get this over with," she mumbled to herself as she felt the stares in her direction. Looking down, she realized it probably didn't help that she was still dressed in a business suit.

"Oh well! Black successful business women can camp too!" she thought with a grin.

Looking around the store, she was impressed that it was divided into categories much like on Emma's list in her hand. "These people must all be in cahoots together," she thought.

"OK, water. Emma has that as the most important thing," she said as she turned her cart in that direction. Pushing the buggy to the middle of the aisle, she stopped and looked around. "Mercy. Now I know how men feel in the tampon section."

Looking at the list in her hand, she found the type that Emma recommended and threw a couple in her cart and then checked them off her list.

Next on her list was something called a fire-steel. "What the hell is a fire-steel?" Jay mumbled out loud. Looking around, she finally saw someone who worked there. "Can you help me? I need something called a fire-steel," she said to the man.

"I'm sorry, that we don't carry," the man said. "But we do have a fire starting kit. It comes with a Zippo sparking wheel and some cotton tinder."

The look on Jay's face must have priceless as the man just motioned her in the direction to find the Zippo kit. "Are you planning on going camping?' he asked

"Yes, I am going camping. Do you have a problem with that?" Jay replied a little more tersely than she intended. "Listen, I really could use some help here. Some friends invited us on an outing and I've never been off the concrete let alone in the woods," she finally added as an apology

"Then let's get you going. Right this way," the man said as he motioned her down another aisle

Jay spent the next two hours in the camping supply store not only buying most of what was on Emma's list but also listening to the man talk about how to use the items. Exhausted, Jay slid in behind the wheel of her Jaguar and closed her eyes. "Fuck!" she yelled to no one.

Placing her thumb on the ignition pad, she heard the all–too-familiar hum of her little baby. Damn if she didn't love that car! "Call Chinese restaurant" she spoke out loud. The car dialed the number to her favorite eating establishment. Pulling away from the camping store, Jay ordered dinner and hoped like hell Emma had a Chinese joint within thirty miles of her house. If she didn't, life was truly gonna suck.

66

Something woke her out of her deep sleep. She lay there quietly, not disturbing the silence. There was something gnawing deep in the pit of her stomach and she couldn't pinpoint what it was. She rolled over onto her back, noticing the coldness of the sheets on his side of the bed. He would be home soon. He had gone to Washington to give a mother much-needed information. She knew it was the right thing to do, as if she were in the other woman's shoes, she would be deeply indebted to anyone bringing her information concerning her own children.

She stretched her arm out under the blankets and rested her hand where his back would normally be. She missed him. He was part of her own being, her own soul. When he wasn't there, she wasn't complete. When he was there, she gained not only strength from his touch, but peace also. She was such an independent woman that it had been hard to allow anyone into her life, and he had not been an easy fit. They had struggled for years, pushing against each other to retain their own identity, until finally, they stopped and became as one. They now complimented each other in each attribute of their lives and each became stronger because of it.

Arguing with herself, she finally relinquished the fact that she was awake, and needed to peel open her eyes. Doing so, she thought, would be admittance of defeat, that she would not being going back to sleep, but she was fast losing the battle. Groaning, she rolled to her side and grabbed for her phone to check the time. Her eyes parting slightly, she realized it was still dark outside. "What time is it really?" she thought to herself. Finally fumbling for the phone, she picked it up and pressed the button. Nothing. No light, no sound. She must have not plugged it all the way in so she reattached the power cord and decided to wait for a few moments to give it enough juice to turn it on. Laying it back on the nightstand, she rolled back onto her back.

Her eyes fluttered in the night. The moon beams were coming through the window above her bed, making dancing patterns on the ceiling and walls. She hated this the most when he was away, the night. Her mind was being over active and she needed to calm herself.

Her sense of hearing increased dramatically with the limited vision obscured by the darkness in the room. She could hear the faint barking of a dog, probably from her neighbor's house miles away. She closed her eyes again and tugged the blanket up under her chin. He would be home soon, she reminded herself.

She sat upright in bed. A black pit was vastly growing in her stomach. Something was wrong. Her senses fully awake now, she picked up her phone again and tried to turn it on. Nothing. The ceiling fan was not moving either. No sounds. She couldn't hear anything, there was nothing there to break nature's sounds. Sliding out of bed, she grabbed her bathrobe and tried to turn on the light. Nothing. She went downstairs and met Dixon at the bottom of the stairs. She tried the other lights. Nothing. She walked into the kitchen. Nothing was working. She picked up the phone. Nothing. Deadly quiet. Looking out the kitchen window, she noticed the security light wasn't working, just the moonlight danced across the yard. Her heartbeat was increasing, this wasn't right. There were no storms predicted. There were no scheduled rolling blackouts.

Grabbing the truck keys from the hook by the door, she ran to the garage. Sliding the key into the ignition, she turned and got no sound. She knew in the pit of her stomach what had happened. Resting her head upon the backs of her hands still gripping the top of the steering wheel, she prayed. She prayed hard.

67

Throwing the two backpacks into the trunk of the car, Jay knew Tiffany would have a fit trying to get all of her luggage in there along with the two bags. "This just isn't going to work," Jay thought. Piss off Tiffany or Emma, those were her choices. Not much of a choice as she adored both women for very different reasons.

Pulling the bags out of the trunk, she opened the back door and shoved them into the floorboards, one behind the driver's seat and one behind the passenger's seat. "There, that should work. At least now I can get Tiff's big suitcases in the back," Jay thought, pleased with herself.

Looking down at her watch, she got a little antsy as it was now a half hour past the time she had scheduled them to leave. She wanted through the tunnels and off the island before rush hour traffic. They were going to be cutting it awfully close.

Walking back into their townhome, Jay yelled up the stairs. "Tiff, come on! We need to get going!"

"You get me up at four a.m. and expect miracles? Girl! You need to relax!" Tiffany shouted back.

"I know but I really want to get through the Lincoln before everyone else. Just hurray up."

Jay walked into her office and picked up the last backpack. She would wait until they left to take it with them as it had items in it that Jay did not want to forget or risk getting stolen if she left it in the car. Family pictures, important documents like birth certificates and insurance information, both of their wills, address books and a small firearm were all packed in the bag. Emma had talked her into getting the gun even though Jay had argued against it. It wasn't hard to find in Manhattan but Jay knew Tiffany would have a real issue if she knew it was with them.

"Come on baby girl, we really need to get going," she said one more time.

Tiffany finally descended the stairs, high heels and all. Her Coach purse filled with last-minute items that she forgot to pack but knew she couldn't live without. Three different types of lotion were poking out from the top since she had so much in there that she couldn't close it. Around her neck was more gold than was currently stored in Fort Knox, which isn't saying much. Several scarves were tied around the handles of the purse and flowed backwards as she walked, briefly hiding the crammed pockets of her jacket.

"You know, those cows aren't going to care how you look out there," Jay said, trying to look serious.

68

The sun had been up for a while when the first child arrived. Kevin had the look of sheer panic on his face as he yelled out for his Mom. One look at her face and he stopped dead in his tracks.

"All those stories were true..." he asked, more of a statement than a question.

"Yes, all those stories were true," she replied, giving him a hug.

"But... but..." he stammered.

"Kevin, just sit down. We need to talk."

"What's going on?" he asked as he slid into a chair at the kitchen table. Emma poured him a cup of coffee and sat down with him.

"Well, and I hope I am wrong, but here is what I think is going on. By my accounts, some type of EMP has gone off. I woke up last night for no reason. I have to wonder if that's why but it would explain everything not working. We need to do an equipment check as soon as the other kids get here."

"What do you mean 'that's why you woke up'? Did you hear something?"

"I heard nothing… that's the point. No ceiling fan, no ice maker, nothing. I ran out and checked my truck, nothing."

"OK. Wow. All of my life I thought this was bullshit and just played along. Not the prepared stuff, just that someone would dump an EMP off over the US. Out of all the scenarios, that one seemed the least likely. Damn." His face still held a look of shock.

"There's one other thing" Emma added "Tommy and Jack are still in Washington."

69

Before long, the rest of Emma's kids were settled around the kitchen table chattering and comparing notes and the possibilities of the future. Emma looked at each one individually, silently saying a prayer over them. The future lay in each of their hands, Emma thought. "And my grandbabies" she said out loud, turning back to her task at hand.

"What, Mom?" Lauren asked

Taken aback, Emma had not realized her thoughts had escaped her lips.

"Nothing baby girl, was just thinking out loud."

"Come here and sit with us," Lauren said as she motioned to her mom to sit beside her.

The kids had papers all across the table, their prepper notebooks opened and pens tucked behind ears. Emma smiled to herself.

"What do we need to do first?" Lauren asked.

"Let's go check on Bertha and see what we need to replace. Not sure the damage but we need to get communications up and running and fast. Dad have his ham?" Connor asked his mom.

"You know it. He is about 100 miles, give or take. Walking with Jack, he will be lucky to make it 6 hours a day, which is what... almost 3 weeks out before they get here? And that's with no issues. People are going to start freaking in about 3 days tops which is going to put them in a very sticky situation trying to get home. Jonathan can get his truck up and running but that's going to make you all stick out like a sore thumb and probably get shot coming through West Virginia."

"We can take the horses then," Jonathan added.

"Thinking that might be your best option," Kevin said.

"Why don't we just calm down a bit. Your father is with a senator. There might be other options to get him home that we don't know about. Let's get comms up and running before we get ahead of ourselves here. Your dad can take care of himself and his grandson, so don't worry about him. I want them home just like you all do but we can't do it at the expense of a bad move on our part here," Emma stated.

They were all quiet, staring at her. Had she made the wrong move? No. The decision sucked but Emma knew it was the best one. They were safe at the farm and had to get their preparations in high gear here for what was sure to turn into pure chaos around the country. No matter how much her heart was breaking right now, she knew to send the boys out was the wrong move. You just don't sacrifice the many for the few.

70

"You want to take this black woman to go where?" Tiffany asked in disbelief..

"Chicago. And we will be making a couple stops along the way."

"And we can't fly why?"

"There's no airport close to where Emma lives. Come on Tiff. You know Emma and her family. We will stay one night and be in Chicago the next day."

"This is insane. A black woman on a farm in the middle of Ohio with pigs and cows and dirty things. I will be the laughing stock of New York City."

"No one will know. Just tell them we are going to Chicago. End of story. You can shop your heart out when we get to civilization. Promise" Jay said.

"These people are going to freak out. Not only two black women driving through the country but lesbians at that. Lordy, the corn is going to wilt!"

"Tiffany. Emma grows ganja," Jay said.

"Oh! Well you should have said that earlier. When do we leave?" Tiffany said as she opened the closet door.

71

The shaking was horrendous, like someone picked up the entire earth and shook it. The truck bounced sideways across the road with the trailer still hooked to the back which was not the best combination in a situation like this. The trailer, deciding to go the opposite direction, twisted the metal at the hitch making a high-pitched squeal. The pressure was too much and the trailer broke free, falling onto its side and sliding across the opposite side of the road from the truck. Scott got the truck stopped as it slid into the soft gravel along the pavement.

"What the hell?" Scott said. "You OK?" looking at Angie.

Angie was staring ahead. Slowly she pointed and Scott looked in the direction of her finger. The pavement ahead had buckled making the road look like a cheap piece of ribbon candy in a bag full of Christmas mix.

Scott tried to start the truck and it wouldn't turn over. He opened his door and got out, surveying the scene. Grabbing his cell from his pocket, he dialed 911. "Hey Ang.... Your cell working?" he yelled out to his passenger.

Angie dug around in her purse until she found her phone. Pushing the button, she tried to get it to turn on. Getting out of the truck, she walked over to Scott and handed him her phone. "I can't get it to work."

Scott tried her phone and couldn't get it to turn on either. Handing it back to her, he put his hands on his hips and took in the surroundings. From what he could remember, they were well into north eastern Tennessee, almost ready to cross back into Kentucky. They had by-passed Nashville after leaving Memphis, instead choosing to get as far east as they could until they headed north again toward home.

Looking both directions, Scott couldn't see another vehicle, which was odd considering how busy a road this had been already. While not a main highway, it still was well traveled by local folks. "Someone should be coming along soon," he thought glancing at his watch. It was 8 a.m.

"OH NO!" Angie screamed as she ran towards the trailer.

Lying on its side, the trailer had skidded off the road onto the opposite side of the asphalt. The good thing was, none of the contents had escaped as the back door was still latched tight. Not knowing what they would find once they opened the doors was the only question. Scott walked over and examined the trailer. There was no way he could get it upright on his own. He would need to get some guys with some heavy equipment out here to get it back up on its axles, which luckily were still attached to the base. Glancing up and down the road, he still didn't see anyone coming.

Crossing back over to where the truck was located, he figured he might be able to get it started. Thinking it was a kill switch that was engaged, he popped open the hood. Looking around, he found no reason for the truck not starting, and after double checking the battery terminals, he tried to start it again. Nothing. No sound from the starter clicking or anything. Clicking on the radio, again he got nothing. "Hey, go check the headlights" he said to Angie. She looked as he turned them on "Nothing". Glancing up and down the road again, he noticed again no vehicles. Looking down at his watch, the hands were still on 8 a.m.

Scott got out of the truck and walked around to the back where his tool box was. Opening one side of the big silver box, he pulled out a smaller metal toolbox. Opening the box, he pulled out several items including a couple ham radios. Tossing one to Angie, he instructed her to get her backpack out from behind the seat.

"What's going on?" she asked. "Aren't we just going to wait? I'm sure someone will be coming along soon."

"Here's your list... tell me what you think. Nothing in the truck works. No radio, lights, starter or anything with any juice. My watch has said it's been 8 a.m. for almost 2 hours now. Based on the location of the sun, it should be sometime after 10 a.m. There's been absolutely no traffic on the road. We should have had at least two dozen cars pass us by now. And listen. I mean, really listen. Do you hear anything?"

Angie stopped and did as Scott asked, her mind frantically trying to put all the pieces together. Turning, she looked down the roads in both directions. "Birds, that's about it," she replied, looking at him.

"Don't you find this all a bit odd?"

"Scott, please. What is it?"

"I think it's an EMP. I'm not sure about the road, though. All the studies I have ever done never said anything about any kind of wave that went off and disrupted physical objects. It's always been more an unseen pulse that fries the electronics."

"Oh, geez...looks like all my training is going to come in handy" she replied, her eyes wide open.
"Let me get my bag," and turning she walked to the cab.

72

Sheriff Olan tipped his back on his head. His deputies were still not all in his office and he had no way to get in touch with them. All phone lines were down and power was out all over the place. Cell phones, walkies, not even the ham unit had power. Nothing worked and he had no idea why. He needed to get over to the mayor's office and get some answers but none of the vehicles were working which was especially puzzling. Walking outside, he stood on the front steps of his office and surveyed the scene. That's when he noticed the plane. "What the hell" he muttered under his breath.

Heading towards the small local airstrip, a two-seat Cessna was coming in lower than usual, its gleaming white wings tilting back and forth in the sun. "Pull up… " the sheriff muttered under his breath. Olan shielded his eyes and watched as the plane continued on its trajectory. His eyes leaped ahead to where the hotel stood at the edge of the air strip. "PULL UP" he yelled, half expecting the plane to hear his command. "Ah shit" Ben yelled as he watched the plane slam into the side of the building and burst into flames, throwing debris high into the air. "No fire trucks, why are there no sirens?" Ben thought, and then reality hit. Turning quickly, he ran back into his office. Gathering additional firearms and a couple deputies who were there, he had his secretary lock up the building.
"I'm going over to the municipal building if anyone needs me" he said as he headed out.

73

The crowd that was gathered in front of the building was growing larger by the minute. People were nervous and wanted answers. The power was out all over town. Vehicles weren't running. Even the emergency generators were not working. Word was traveling fast through the small town that something drastic had happened.

Brian stood with the mayor on the front steps. He unbuttoned the top button on his shirt trying to get more air. What he had to say was not going to be easy, and he needed to say it in a way as to not cause panic. Scraping a hand through his hair, he stepped forward and raised his hands, trying to quiet the crowd. Picking up the bull-horn, he placed it in front of his mouth.

"Folks! Folks! Please quiet down," he yelled as a faint murmur was heard traveling back through the crowd.

"What's going on?" he heard yelled from the back of the crowd, which did nothing but entice others to yell out also.

"Please, we are trying to explain, but I'll be damned if I am going to stand up here and try and yell over all of you!" Brian yelled into the megaphone.

It was enough to get the crowd reasonably quiet again.

"Here's what we are piecing together, and no, we don't have all the answers yet. It looks like a low altitude EMP was detonated somewhere over the lower 48. Most of the Midwest is without power or communications right now. We are trying to get comms up and running but we are going to need some time. We have some mechanics working on some older vehicles to be used for transportation but we need older models, like pre 1980s, something without damn computers in them. We also have an emergency team at the hospital trying to get their generators going but I honestly am not sure what kind of success they will have. Please. I am advising all of you to go to your homes and stay there while we work through this, but that's all we currently have. The mayor will be speaking again about an hour before dark, so please feel free to come back then, but until then, just go home and stay there.

"What about 911 if we need them?" someone yelled.

"I really don't know. Every electronic looks like it got fried," Brian replied. "We are working on some things but please, check on your neighbors and just stay around your own homes and stay out of trouble. We have our hands full right now."

Brian noticed Sheriff Olan headed in his direction. Waving, he motioned for the sheriff to join him on the steps. Once Ben was with them, Brian mumbled to Ben and Ben then addressed the crowd.

"I am imparting a curfew from sunup to sundown. You will need to stay in your homes until further notice during those times." Murmurs were heard through the crowd. "Don't you mean from sundown to sunup? Or are we allowed to run around like idiots at night?" Someone yelled from the crowd. Ben raised his hand, "It's for your own safety. That's our main priority, and ya... whatever. You want to go out at dark, knock yourself out, but I take no responsibility for your stupidity. There's nothing you should be doing after dark anyways," Ben explained. "Anyone that has a firearm, we might be able to use your assistance. Please meet me in front of my office in two hours as I will be looking at anyone interested in volunteering as a deputy and keeping our fine neighborhoods safe. I will be coordinating all of our efforts with the mayor and with...um... Brian here. Thank you," he said and handed the mega-phone back to Brian.

The three talked quietly for a moment ignoring the crowd. "We will be back here about an hour before dusk for another update. Go home and stay safe," Brian finally said.

The crowd mingled for a while and finally started to thin out, each going off in their own direction. Some town folks stood around and talked some more about the effects of an EMP and the length of time to recoup from the damage. Most agreed it was going to take longer than anyone truly realized.

74

Brian's staff immediately went into action. All information on the long-term effects of an electromagnetic pulse was examined. The startling part was the lack of genuine information they did have. One thing they had learned from over the years was the impact of any kind of blackout. After Hurricane Katrina, a blackout was a major factor in the failure of police, emergency and rescue services during the hurricane, which killed almost 1,500 people.

The blackout caused gas stations to cease operating, paralyzing transportation and greatly impeding evacuation efforts. The Katrina blackout, which afflicted the region for weeks and lasted for months in some localities, so severely impeded recovery efforts that even today, New Orleans and its vicinity is still far from being fully recovered. One thing they did figure out was the key to minimizing catastrophic impacts from loss of electrical power is rapid restoration. Until then, they all agreed, to keep everyone safe, they needed to order everyone to "Shelter in Place."

Brian had a huge whiteboard brought into the main meeting room. On it were listed multiple areas of concern. Some were related only to emergency personnel but the other list was the one Brian was most concerned with, the general public. Based upon data gathered from previous events, within three days, Brian could expect riots to begin. He had to have his team ready. Things were about to get very ugly, and he didn't have the manpower to be able to control it. Martial law or not, there was only so much they could do. Grocery stores and drug stores would be hit hard and fast. Without supplies of medications, the sick would begin to die. He had to prioritize with hospital staff who would be receiving vital treatment.

The elderly would be hit the hardest. Then the people who were physically disabled, those left behind by their loved ones. From there, the next would be anyone who was reliant upon medication or machinery to stay alive. Historically, trying to evacuate swiftly with the elderly or disabled is damn near impossible. With the grid down, a lot of these people were probably already dying. Burial services would need to be addressed so disease does not spread.

Next, Brian needed to get his people prepared for the stereotypical welfare recipients, those people who expected others to save them. These people are the ones who will turn into the aggressors and they will take advantage of anyone. Heaven forbid if this same group of people is addicted to alcohol or drugs. One bullet will not stop them if they are strung out or desperate.

From there we go to the people who are in denial and have done nothing to prepare. These people live in their world of love and peace and soccer games and have minimal skill sets. They make perfect targets as they choose not to carry firearms or anything to protect them. They will react too late; afraid to admit that their democratic leaders will not be there to save them. Heaven forbid they have children. How many would become orphans in the days ahead?

History shows us that time and time again, during a down-grid situation, people die. Those who don't die often times wished they had. The staggering amount of abuse and rape during situations like Hurricane Katrina or Fukushima should be enough to convince anyone to prepare for self-protection. But these things were not talked about. It was an embarrassment to the community. It was a pride issues. It was because it happened mostly to women and children that it was swept under the proverbial rug and truth silenced or even denied in some instances.

Brian stopped and looked at his board, covered in notes and directions to herd people in the days ahead. Herding people was a funny task. Trying to help them, he would be blamed for trying to control them and taking away their God-given rights. And if he didn't herd them, their blood would be on his hands.

75

Tom knew what had happened long before most in the city had figured it out, and he wanted to leave as soon as humanly possible, but he had some planning to do first. Having unpacked his bags, he was putting together a couple lightweight packs for himself and his grandson Jack. Weapons, water purification and clothing would be of utmost importance on this excursion.

Most people would think food would be included, but with Tom's ability to hunt and forage, it was the least of his worries. He needed to stay alive and keep his grandson alive, so firearms and self-protection were top on his list. Time was against them and he was fast losing precious minutes the longer they stayed there. Within days, panic would spread throughout the land and

Tom wanted to make sure he was well on his way home and in the woods of West Virginia if at all possible.

Dehydration was next on the list. Being able to carry the amount of water needed was impossible. One gallon of water minimum per person per day was needed to stay properly hydrated and not lose motor function. One gallon of water weighed eight pounds alone. Add the three weeks that it might take them to get home, and the need to know how to purify water along the route became apparent.

Tom looked through the clothing they had brought along for the trip. Tossing aside the nice dress clothes, Tom pulled together the durable goods. Wool could get wet and still retain its warmth. Tactical pants to help carry supplies that could be evenly distributed on the body. Hiking shoes. While the dress shoes were nice and shiny and looked stylish, Tom had finished reading an article earlier of a man in DC from last winter who had walked home from work in the snow they had received. Three hours later and a hospital visit ensured the man had to have his toes removed due to frostbite. He threw in a hat, gloves, socks, more socks, a jacket and a good shemagh scarf and they were set.

Tom laid out both firearms he had brought along on the trip, his Glock 19 and a folding rifle that accepted the same magazines as the Glock. Handing Jack the rifle, a Keltec Sub 2000, Tom walked him through a refresher course on the mechanics of the firearm in general. Tom's plan was to use Jack as his backup since all he brought were the two firearms.

Double-checking his blades and ferrocerium rods, he repacked all the other odds and ends back into the packs along with the medical supplies.

Next he had his roadmaps spread out on the bed and was discussing with Jack several routes home. In case one path was blocked, they made sure they had multiple backup routes. Jack was scanning the topographical map when the knock came at the door.

"Tomás Montalvo?," which came out more as a statement than a question of identification.

Odd that someone would know they were there, Tom did not relax his grip on the firearm when he addressed the person on the other side of the door.

"Something you need?"

"Commander Kessler," he stated. "Senator Varga would like to have a word with you." The man cleared his throat and continued, "In the bee garden."

"Jack, pack up your stuff quickly" Tom said as he began packing his own bag. "I'll be right there," he yelled out to the man behind the door.

Opening the door, Tom saw a uniformed man standing in front of a military Humvee. "I should have known," he muttered to himself as he was escorted into the back seat. Tom looked down at his grandson sitting on the metal platform between him and the commander. Jack was having the time of his life, as it's not every day a kid gets to ride in a real Humvee and not one of the watered-down, yuppie versions cramming the streets in the civilian world. Tom grinned "Jack, you know what you are sitting on?" "No, Abuelo," Jack replied. "That is a gunner's platform. That's where the guy stands that shoots the big guns. Look up there," Tom said, pointing. "Up there's the gunner's hatch to the top of the truck. He sticks his head out of there to shoot whatever weapon is attached." Jack tilted his head back and ate up all the information that his grandfather was giving him. "Cool!" Jack exclaimed. Tom only wished it was under better circumstances.

The trip to Senator Varga's country home was uneventful as most people were still sleeping when the EMP was detonated. Without all the extra vehicles and traffic controls, the driver made haste in leaving the city behind. Looking back one last time, Tom thought of the days ahead and how much death and destruction would surely follow. This city, once envied around the world for its power, was about to become a cesspool of death.

76

Pulling into the driveway, Tom was astounded at the flurry of activity going on. He and Jack were promptly escorted into what used to be the formal dining room. Stripped of the fine china and the water color paintings, the walls were now adorned with maps and the table was scattered with books and paper pads, full of notes. The commander pointed Tom to a chair and motioned for water to be brought to the table. Sitting silently, he took in the scene before him.

The senator, who was so immaculately dressed earlier, was now in military fatigues. Her hair pinned up and all the useless baubles that women like to adorn themselves with were gone, replaced with just an analog watch. She was making the world spin from her seated position. Tom watched in amusement. She reminded him of his wife, always trying to save the world. A small grunt of a laugh escaped his mouth, which caught Nina's attention.

"Tom! Jack! When did you get here?" she exclaimed.

"Not long. You look kinda busy," he responded.

"Yes, well. A lot has happened in the last 12 hours."

"I missed that memo," he said. "But figured it out the hard way."

She smiled at him. "Let me introduce you to a couple people, and then we need to talk. I have a favor to ask of you."

"Tom, this is Commander Kissler as you have already met. He is my right hand. I've known Sean a long time. If you remember, he was recently allowed the benefit of change of employment from our illustrious Commander in Chief," she stated, rolling her eyes adding air quotes for effect. The men nodded in acknowledgement.

"This is Lt Commander Sam Benteg. Same story. Change of employment after serving our country for 27 years," she said as she shook his hand. "Tom," Sam said extending his hand. Tom reached out and the men exchanged a firm handshake.

"Lt. Miles Cottner, Commander Scott Jeffries and Lt. Tim Eklund, all newly unemployed after serving our great country," Nina added, pointing to the men around the room.

Tom was a little confused. "Why would they all be…" he trailed off.

"Relieved of duty?" Nina asked. "Well, the president doesn't feel he needs their expertise to pull off what he has planned. He knows that these fine men would do everything in their power to stop him and his band of merry men. And they would. These men before you took an oath to this country, something our president has never done without his fingers crossed behind his back."

77

Twisting and turning, Emma woke in a drenched mess. Sitting up, she reached for him but he wasn't there. The room dark, she instinctively made her way to the window seat and sat down. Pulling the quilt around her she stared into the darkness. What a beautiful night it was. The clouds danced playfully in front of the moon causing shadows across the open field. "Lord please," she prayed. "Keep him safe and bring him home." She rested her cheek against the cold glass of the window. Her eyes began to fill, and slowly overflowed down her cheek, the salty warmth forcing her to confront her own fears.

78

Dixon raised his head in a quick jerk, which caught Emma's attention. A low growl escaped his throat sending shivers down Emma's spine. Standing up, Emma and the kids quickly scurried up the stairs into her bedroom on the second floor, taking Dixon with them. Handing both kids a flashlight, she opened the closet door and disappeared behind the clothes. Peeking her head back through, she motioned for the kids to follow her. At the back of the closet was a secret door, used back in the times of the Underground Railroad. The door led to several rooms that squeezed under the eaves of the roofline. Emma had the kids sit down with Dixon on a blanket. "Stay here until I come back and get you," she said as she raised her finger to her lips. "Be very tranquillo." Patting Dixon on the back, "Protect," she commanded him. Not wanting to leave her, he whimpered his discord. "Protect," she echoed.

Lowering the kerosene lamp she was using to light the room, Emma grabbed her Glock and shoved it into her waistband. Making sure she had her flashlight and knife in her pocket, she grabbed some extra magazines and threw them in her pocket.

Just as she turned to pick up the Mossberg, making sure the side saddle was full, she heard what sounded like the train that normally ran through her property had jumped its tracks and was coming straight for her house.

Turning the light off completely, she stepped to the window and looked out. A multitude of headlamps were marching towards the house. Two by two they came until they cluttered her driveway, stopping short of the garage. Men's voices could be heard over the roar of the engines. Shouting orders back and forth, replies following swiftly.

Not quite sure what to make of the menagerie below, Emma slowly crossed the room and began to descend the stairs, her mind agitated with the varied scenes revealing themselves in her head. "This is one of those times where reading too much Tin Foil BS is coming back to haunt me," she muttered to herself. "Remind me to thank Rhonda later!"

She heard him call out to her, his voice cutting through the deafening clutter of noise. "Emma, put
Mossy down before you shoot me!"

Stopping in her tracks, a smile crept across her face.

Propping the shotgun beside the door, she realized her hands were shaking as she turned the doorknob.

Slowly opening the door, there stood her Tommy with the biggest grin on his handsome face.

"Can I help you? You seem a tad lost," she asked, barely able to contain how crookedly happy her lips were curving.

"Yes ma'am, was looking for the hottest Grandma this side of the Mississippi!" he said giving her a wink. "Hi ya, Doll" barely escaped his lips as she flung herself into his arms.

79

The officer coughed trying to get their attention. "Excuse me?" But nothing was working. Trying again, he tapped the man on the shoulder. "Excuse me, Sir?" Finally the couple separated their faces enough that the officer saw his chance to interrupt again. "Excuse me!" he yelled this time.

Turning to look at the man, Tom gave him a grin "Yes?"

"Sir, we need to get the senator in out of the cold" the soldier replied

Forgetting all that had preceded having his wife in his arms, Tom quickly recovered. "Emma, we have guests," he said laying his hand on her cheek. "Let's get them inside and then I can fill you in."

Following her husband's cue, Emma set about putting water on to boil while they started gathering their guests into the house. Tom ushered the woman into the living room and introduced her to Emma. "My dearest, let me introduce you to Senator Nina Varga. Senator Varga, my beautiful wife, Emma." Both women took a few moments and sized each other up. "I believe you have something that belongs to me?" Nina finally said, breaking the silence. "Oh! Yes!" Emma replied and left the room quickly.

Moments later, she returned with the children. As soon as Matheo and Alicia saw the woman standing in the middle of the room, they both let out squeals of joy. Nina dropped to her knees and met them in her arms, melting into each other. "Mama! Mama!" They gushed in unison. Taking each of their tiny faces between her hands, Nina kissed each and every inch of their cherub cheeks, feeling their fluttering lashes tickle her lips.

Emma walked over and slid an arm around her husband, resting her head on his shoulder. They watched the reunion of a mother and her children, forgetting that the world outside was erupting into chaos. Forgetting that the woman on the floor before them, covered in baby kisses, her hair disheveled from tiny hands and arms wrapped around her neck, was the one person who everyone thought could fix the country they all loved so much.

80

Shelby turned the damper down on the stove and checked the pot of water on top. Making sure it was filled for the day, she finished up by throwing a couple logs of wood alongside the stove for supper time. It was expected to be colder than normal tomorrow and she wanted to make sure she could get the house warmed up and the stove ready for their evening meal before heading out to the barn.

Taking a cup from the shelf, she added three teaspoons of dried chamomile flowers into the bottom of it. The yellow of the flowers, even though dull from dehydrating, still brought a smile to her face. "spring couldn't get here soon enough," she thought. She had grown this particular strain from some seeds a friend in Ohio had sent her.

Ladling some hot water from the pot of water on the stove over the flowers in her cup, she sat it down at the kitchen table. Reaching across the wooden surface that had been worn from time, she grabbed the spoon that was in the honey jar and added a heaping amount to her tea. Stirring, she was soothed by the clinking of spoon against the china. This was her favorite time of the day. Chores were done, the children were outside playing and the house was toasty warm from breakfast. She had some much needed time to think.

Picking up her cup, she tilted the edge of the porcelain to her lips. Shelby instantly felt the tickle. Looking down into the cup, she realized she had forgotten to strain the flower heads from the water. Rolling her eyes and muttering under her breath, she pushed her chair back and walked over to the sink and picked up the strainer.

She was about ready to pour the tea into the wire mesh basket when something caught her eye out of the window above her sink. There was her pony Bella jumping wildly around the field. Thinking a snake had gotten into the pen, Shelby picked up her shotgun and headed out. The last thing she wanted was Bella getting bit by a poisonous snake.

Heading over to the fence, Shelby saw the kids playing with the swing in the tree. Looking past them she noticed the chickens were dashing about aimlessly. "That's odd," she thought as she continued towards the pony.

The high-pitched squeal got her attention and made the hair on the back of her neck stand up. Coming from the barn, the sharp groinking bark was coming from the pig pen. Shelby stopped dead in her tracks. Something was wrong and she could feel it riding on the wind. Birds fluttered out of the tree above the kids, sending the sound of agitation through the breeze.

Turning in a slow circle, Shelby watched as the animals around the farm were acting excited... or maybe nervous, she couldn't pinpoint it exactly. "Kids, come along with Mama," she yelled out to them as she waved her arm, motioning them towards her.

The first rumble knocked her to her knees. On all fours, Shelby felt the warm putrid feeling rising up her throat, her head spinning wildly making her not be able to focus. "Momma!" she heard the kids screaming at her. Trying to focus, Shelby raised her head.

The next rumble had her grabbing for the kids and pulling them tight. "God, have mercy!" she yelled out. The next few moments drifted in front of her like an old movie being shown at the local theater. The wailing was coming from beneath her as the soil rocked back and forth. It was cutting into her soul and reminding her of when she gave birth to the child she now held in her arms. The pounding against her pelvis as the new life was trying to intrude into the world she lived in gave her pause to think of the damage the earth beneath her could create.

She heard the glass breaking from the windows in the house before her brain recognized what it was, clear flakes of light splashing out in all directions. The chinking sounds making her think of the porcelain tea cup she was using earlier. Mountain Man had given that cup to her on the birth of their first child. He wasn't an overly emotional man and had no idea how to swim around with the fishes in the pool of romance, but this gift was priceless to her.

Mountain Man. Shelby closed her eyes as a prayer left her lips to be carried on the wind. He had left that morning to go into town to pick up building supplies. She had no idea where he was at the moment. She also had no way to contact him. Looking in the direction she knew he should be, she noticed an enormous dust cloud over Memphis. "Sweet Jesus," she whispered as she stood up, shielding her eyes against the sun.

81

They were running away from the falling buildings, those who could run. They were screaming with whimpered groans, those who could scream. The city was now full of collapsed walls, rubble, blood and tears. There was no one coming to help them, they just didn't know it yet. Their rescuers lived among them, lay among them in the debris. There was just too much damage. A blanket of dust and smoke had been laid over the city, choking off its existence.

The area nearest the river was the hardest hit. Buildings crashed into buildings with no accounting for the lives that now lay buried beneath them, their cries snuffed out. The ones who were able to stay clear of the debris were walking around aimlessly, confused, not knowing what to do next. Tears were mixing with blood and dust, sending rivers of scarlet mud down their broken faces.

The Mighty Mississippi, once tamed by the bustle of riverfront commerce, now devoured the intruders who lined her ribs with such velocity that only small deposits of silt remained. Her bones now stretching wide as brackish water roared northward reclaiming all that once was hers. The damage was unimaginable. From the Gulf of Mexico to Lake Michigan, the once-great United States had been sliced in two. Nations watched in awe as the once-powerful, ego-ridden country was brought to her knees.

The aftershocks were now coming every fifteen to twenty minutes, lasting less than thirty seconds each but causing more chaos as buildings that were haphazardly stacked upon each other continued to fall. Bridges fell like matchsticks being broken and thrown to the wind. The judgment left by the quake was total devastation.

82

The wolf watched from the edge of the woods. He had tasted her blood before and it had called him back. This is where he would wait, hidden within the trees. His chest heaved rapidly with heavy panting. He was agitated, unsettled. He would force her to change her habits. He would bring her into the woods, into his domain. Pacing back and forth, he never lost focus of what his intent was. He would taste her blood once again.

83

The days ahead were a mess of chaos and confusion. Emma tried to get her new guests as settled as possible but it seemed to be turning into a daunting task. The more Emma did, the more they seemed to want. It was to the point that they had taken over the house, garage and most of the side yard completely and Emma was feeling very uncomfortable about that. Tents were erected around the yard where Emma had her garden last year, which just pissed Emma off since she knew the ground was going to be almost impossible to get air into again with how they were pounding it down with all their equipment. She had spent years getting it to how she wanted it, following the instructions of the Back to Eden gardening method. The success she had seen with her crops was outstanding and now to know all of her work was getting destroyed was playing havoc on her blood pressure.

Add to that the imperialistic attitude of the woman who had entered Emma's life. "What was up with that anyways," Emma thought. Female intuition kicking in overdrive, Emma had a feeling there was much more to this woman than she was letting on. It was probably time that Emma had a conversation with her husband about some of Nina's behavior. If there was one thing Emma and Tom had learned in marriage it was the importance of communication, even those crucial conversations that no one really liked to have.

Until then, Emma kept a low profile, mostly just becoming the house maid. Cooking for everyone, cleaning, taking care of Nina's two children, Emma used the opportunities to snoop. For being military and government people, they had no clue about OPSEC, which Emma could use to her advantage. After all, they just thought she was a farmer's wife who just happens to own the homestead where her children had crash landed. Little did they know the extent of contacts and information Emma had at her disposal even with the grid partially down.

84

Chloe sat upright in bed. Sitting as still as possible, she wasn't sure if she had imagined anything with as much alcohol as she had in her system. A low giggle escaped her throat as the funny thought entered her head. No, the hairy bloke snoring in her bed right now was just not good enough to make the earth shake beneath her feet. Nice guy and all, but definitely not someone she could see herself living the rest of her life with. His wallet was the best part of him, fake leather and all.

She slid out of bed as quietly as possible, trying not to wake him. After all, he had paid for an overnight visit. She figured one more good romp between her fancy silk sheets at the break of dawn and she could send him on his way home to his wife with a smile on his face. Walking across the room, she found her bathrobe and slid it on. "What I would give to have a shower about right now," she thought sighing, but didn't want to risk waking the man.

Walking into the kitchen, Chloe turned on the tap. Nothing came out. "That's odd," she thought. Reaching into the fridge, she pulled out a bottle of water and took a drink. The cold water flowed down her throat, smashing through the dryness like flood waters crashing through a dam. Moaning, Chloe sat the bottle down and held her head... cold water down a dry throat gives a massive head rush. Glancing out the kitchen window of her apartment, Chloe noticed how dark it looked outside, odd considering she lived right in the middle of L.A. Walking over, she hit the remote button to turn on the TV... nothing happened. Alarms started going off in Chloe's head. No water, no electricity. Not good signs.

Looking at the wall clock, it was 4 a.m. Most of the people she knew were either working or sleeping, there was no in between at 4 a.m. Looking around, she picked up her cell and clicked it on. While it did have power and the light came on, it couldn't get a signal for some reason. The messages kept repeating that the lines were busy and please try again later. "Maybe it was just a power outage," Chloe thought, but the pit in the bottom of her stomach told her otherwise.

Gathering her clothes as quickly as possible, Chloe put her plans into motion. A quick bird bath using bottled water, dressed and out the door with her bug out bags and Chloe headed for her Jeep. Chloe locked the door to her apartment behind her. Locking the sleeping man inside, she left a note to help himself to whatever he wanted, but she wouldn't be back.

If what was actually going down was what she thought it was, she needed to get out of town and as fast as she could.

85

Angie picked up the map and looked at it. That was one long-ass walk, but it looked like they had no choice in the matter. They had been standing out here much too long and Scott was getting nervous about their exposure.

Angie took a deep breath. Her life had changed so much over the last year, and she had to wonder how much more it would change before it finally settled down.

Kicking a rock with the toe of her boot, she glanced out at the horizon. The sun would be setting soon and they needed to find somewhere to sleep where they would be protected. The truck had broken down that morning and they still had not seen another human come down the road. Add to the fact how the road had buckled and the uneasy feeling in the pit of her stomach that she had been trying to suppress all day kicked in again.

Lucky for them that they were able to get into the trailer and pull some supplies out in addition to their get home bags. Being able to sleep on the cushions of her couch would be nice for tonight instead of the cold hard ground. "Maybe I'll get those set up since Scott is busy with everything else. It would be a nice surprise," she thought to herself. She needed to do something! She was getting irritated and Scott was not being a lot of help. While she understood he had more survival knowledge than she did, she wasn't exactly stupid either. Or at least she thought so with all the stuff Emma had been cramming down her throat these past months.

Angie opened the back doors of the trailer and peered inside. She would need to remove anything she needed now before the sun went down or she wouldn't be able to see. She also knew there was a box with some food somewhere that she could use for a meal tonight instead of digging into their Get Home Bag rations. "Get Home Bags" she mumbled to herself. "If only they would instantly transport you "Back Home they would be even better! And who comes up with these bag names... BOB, Bug Out Bag, Every Day Carry... Everyone had a different name for it. Luckily she had packed hers for the trip home so she knew what was in it and where it was exactly in the bag. Scott said that was important so she could get to the stuff faster if she needed it. She had already taken her hiking boots out and put those on. She had attached the ball-cap to her belt loop for later, but this way she would not misplace it and she knew it would come in handy in the morning without a shower and her hairdryer. Ugh! No shower in the morning already was giving her the heeby jeebies. She tied her jacket around her waist and used the extra space to add some more supplies. Gloves, handkerchiefs and her med kit could now be fitted on top. In the side pockets she knew was her headlamp with spare batteries, spare ammo, a couple lighters along with her magnesium rod, which always made her smile. Lighting a fire without matches or a lighter was one of the first survival skills she had learned.

Her Triplets, as Emma referred to them, firearm, flashlight and knife were in the pockets of her jeans but she had a multi-tool tucked into another pocket of her pack. Para cord had already been utilized in her shoelaces, as pulls on her pack and as a bracelet around her wrist. She also carried duct tape and rock-climbing rigging. Pen and paper to record any events or even to play tic-tac-toe, a fishing kit, water purification tablets along with her filter in her water bottle...deep in thought. Angie was oblivious to the fact that she and Scott would soon have visitors.

86

Brian paced back and forth in front of his desk. "Damn if they hadn't pulled it off," he kept muttering to himself, still he could not believe what had just happened. He had been debriefed but what they had been proposing was just unfathomable.

He was instructed to not tell anyone, not even his closest friends, and since he lived far enough away from the impact point, "His services would be highly regarded in the very near future to help reassemble all the broken pieces of this once-great country back together again." But damn, this was more than he could have even imagined.

What was it they had said, he pondered, "the sacrifice of a few for the betterment of the many" or something like that? "How many lives had just been destroyed?" he wondered. He swallowed the lump in his throat. That was the part that had bothered him the most, the loss of life. Not so much here, but he had to think the impact point had been leveled.

"Time to kick this plan into place," he mumbled as he picked up his radio and called Sheriff Olan.

87

Chloe walked into the diner and looked around. The place was full of people looking for things. Wet things, eatable things, warm things. Their needs never strayed much from those three things. Her eyes drifted from wanting human to wanting human. One single emotion surged through her veins as she realized she felt pity for them. "Lazy ass bastards," she thought.

She was in need also, she realized. Nothing as life sustaining as these poor fools she thought, but a need none the less. Finding an empty spot of wall and placing her backpack between her feet, she leaned back and rested her shoulders for a bit. The prior days started to drift through her mind as her eyes kept close watch on the people milling about the room before her.

Three days ago, she was living her life in Los Angeles without much care in the world. She had gone to the farmers market and picked up some fresh fruit and vegetables, trying to stay away from meat altogether. She hadn't had fish to eat in over a year. That propensity had ended with her research on the Fukushima incident and the fact she didn't like to gamble with her health. She had spent a lot of time reading reports on the hazards of radiation poisoning from the seafood coming in from the Pacific. It was enough to make her change her eating habits completely. Once a staunch bacon and eggs kinda girl, going cold turkey vegetarian was the hardest thing she had ever done in her life.

Two days ago, she had gotten a call from Emma. Be ready. Always ready. Quite honestly, she was tired of being ready. So. Fucking. Tired. She wanted to just stick her head up her ass like all the other people in the world and act like nothing could ever go wrong. She wanted to go to the movies and not think about what she would do if some asshat came in shooting the place up while she was there. She wanted to sit outside and look up at the sky and be oblivious to the straight-lined clouds raining poison down on her. She wanted to just forget everything she knew, but she honestly knew there was no turning back now. She knew too much.

One day ago, she was laying in her bed naked, flat on her back with some guy she hardly knew with his face between her legs. She remembered laying there staring at the ceiling with an occasional groan escaping from between her lips just to keep the man aroused. She knew all the verbal cues to keep his penis hard so she didn't have to waste her time later on, or smudge her lipstick, as a proper lady never smudges her lipstick while fucking. The power she felt from the control she had over these poor slobs was worth more than the money they paid her, sometimes. Money only went so far, but the power, the power had her trapped within its grasp. The power helped erase the memories that kept her awake.

The world tried to cage her in, it tried to save her. Fearless, restless, Chloe had to break free… she had to get out and live her own life. The storm that fused her soul to the ominous chaos of the macrocosm outside was running its course with such a fierce throbbing that at times she thought it would carry her beyond the luminous orbs of light that danced across the night sky.

Today, Chloe was standing against a wall watching all the scared people, people she didn't know. It was easier that way. People had been cruel to her in the past and it was much easier not to care about their souls, she had her own to worry about. Very few people had made it past her bastion of solitude but those who did, Chloe would protect with her own life. Once her heart was freely given, she belonged to them completely. It was a strength deemed worthy by many, a weakness that Chloe guarded with diligence

Chloe watched as the man walked towards her. Her eyes followed his lean body, causing an exhilaration within her that Chloe did not recognize. Catching her breath, she looked away quickly and adjusted her stance. What the hell was that she thought?

"Chloe?"

Startled by the sound of her voice being spoken, Chloe was shocked to see the same man standing in front of her. Blinking, she stared at him with a blank look on her face.

"Are you Chloe?"

Chloe's eyes were diverted to the man's mouth, his lips.

Shaking her head to try and regain control of herself, Chloe finally allowed sound to exit from her own lips. "Yes, yes, I'm Chloe"

As his lips curved into a slight smile, he watched as her eyes caught the movement and her lashes came together slightly. Amused, he knew the effect he had on women. This one was no different than the rest.

"Let's get going then, we have a long distance to cover in a very short amount of time."

Chloe snapped out of her trance. "Wait, who are you?"

"Michael, we had a date, remember?"

"Ah, yes." Chloe bent down and picked up her pack "Let's get going then," she said as she walked off in front of him, not waiting for him to follow.

Michael turned, his brow raised. "Well, yes ma'am!" he muttered under his breath.

88

Sheriff Olen watched as the supplies were being brought into the room. Taking stock, he knew he would need more firepower and more food. Whatever the hell caused this mess was not going to end soon and he needed to retain power in his county. Hell, if he played this right, he could end up with even more territory to control and that suited his plans just fine. Communications were finally coming back online and things weren't looking good anywhere around the lower half of the state and southward.

Handing the clipboard off to one of his deputies, Ben walked back into his office and sat down. He needed to think. He needed to put all the variables of how things may play out in the future on paper and then make sure he was in the best position to take advantage of any and all political power grabs.

Sitting back in his seat, he turned and looked out the window. Besides the area around the hospital where the plane crashed, the town was still in pretty good shape. A couple fires here and there but overall, he had a lot he could work with. This was now his playground and he would be damned to let anyone come onto his turf and mess around. Which reminded him, he needed to have a chat with the lovely Emma. She was becoming quite the talk around here and he needed to see what all the commotion was about out at her farm and put his thumb down on it. He didn't need the bitch ruining his plans, and he would do whatever he needed to retain control of his little kingdom.

89

Outside, Chloe looked around at the few vehicles parked in the lot. A smirk crossed her face as she walked towards the only mode of transportation that could possibly belong to Michael. Dropping her pack, she turned and waited for him to catch up.

"What makes you think this is mine?" he asked as he approached her

"Seriously? Well, I guess it could be that Volkswagen Rabbit over there," she said as she pointed to the little red diesel. "Or perhaps that what....circa 1972 station wagon? I highly doubt it."

"Here, take this," he said as he handed her the helmet. "We have about 200 miles ahead of us. I have an iron butt, but if you have issues just let me know. If not, then we ride straight through. Get a jacket on too," he said. "And you'll have to wear that thing," he said, pointing at her pack

Turning, he swung his leg over the Electra Glide and slid his helmet over his head and started checking gauges.

Chloe grabbed her pack and slid the straps over her shoulders. Grabbing Michael's shoulder, she slid in behind him on the seat and snugged her hair up under the helmet as best she could as she put it on. Wrapping her arms around his waist, she leaned in, feeling the strength in his back against her breasts. That should keep him awake for a while; she thought not realizing a slight smirk had danced across his lips that had earlier devoured her attention.

90

Sheriff Olan was in stunned silence as he rode the bike up Emma's driveway. There were vehicles everywhere. A makeshift tent was set up behind her garage and military personal were scattered around busy working on various projects.

"This is a bit embarrassing," Ben thought to himself as he rode the bike up to the garage. It was one thing to ride the bike around town where no one had any working vehicle, it was another to ride it in here where it made him feel like the hick they probably thought he was. His face quickly turned red as the embarrassment set in, anger taking control of his emotions. "Fucking bitch," he muttered, "I'll teach her a valuable lesson for making me look like a fool."

Parking the bike, he made his way to the back door. He was just about to knock when a couple kids ran out the door with Emma's big mutt of a dog. Raising an eyebrow, he wondered who they were since they didn't look like any of Emma's kin.

Turning back to the door, he raised his hand to knock again when a man appeared. "Can I help you?" he asked abruptly

Scanning the man quickly, Ben noticed the name badge on his uniform. ""Well, not that it's any of your business, but I was looking for Emma, Lieutenant Bower" he replied with a smirk

"Just a moment please," the uniformed man said as he escorted Ben into the kitchen

Leaving Ben briefly, the man walked to the door of the living room and spoke quietly to someone Ben could not see. Ben heard a scuffling noise and assumed someone was sent to get Emma. The uniformed man returned to Ben and asked him if he would like anything while he waited.

"No thanks," Ben replied.

Ben glanced around the house and took in all the changes since the last time he had been there. No wonder the town was talking, he thought. She has a fucking army camped out here.

"Sheriff Olan, what a surprise," Emma said as she walked into the room.

"Emma," he said as he nodded in her direction. "Everything OK here?"

"Oh, just doing some remodeling," she smirked.

"And you need an army to do that?"

"You know how women are! What can I help you with, sheriff?"

"Just checking on the town folks. There were rumors of a lot of activity out here so I thought I would check on you."

"Why Sheriff Olan, thank you for sticking your nose in, once again, where it doesn't belong!"

Ben was about to tongue lash her when Nina walked into the room.

"Senator Varga, please meet Sheriff Ben Olan. He is the local law enforcement around here," Emma said as she introduced the two.

"Ah! Sheriff Olan... So very nice to meet you," Nina said as she walked towards Ben, her hand outstretched.

Ben was quite obviously flustered. A senator, here in Emma's house. What was going on? He wondered, his mind going a mile a minute trying to figure it all out. He was so consumed in thought that he forgot his manners and quickly tried to recoup his composure. Smiling grandly, he turned on the charm.

"Ma'am! I didn't realize we had someone of your stature in residence here! Emma, I do believe you've been holding out on the rest of us!" he beamed.

"Oh, you are a flatterer now aren't you," Nina replied as Ben reached out to shake her hand.

Emma felt sick to her stomach. "Really?" she thought to herself. "Ben and Nina, this might be interesting. Maybe it would take the vulture's claws off of Tommy if Nina had another helpless victim to focus on," she thought as she watched the slow nightmare unfold before her.

"Ben, you should stay for dinner," Emma interjected.

"Yes Ma'am," he responded as he tucked Nina's arm into his. "Looks like you have dessert already here."

91

Angie reached as far back as she could under the pile of furniture. "Damn it!" she swore as her fingers grazed the top of the can. Pushing her shoulder into the chair leg a bit more, she managed to swat the can sideways and send it rolling towards herself. Gathering up all the supplies she had been able to reach, she stepped back outside the trailer.

Looking around, she decided that the best place to begin prepping dinner wasn't far from where she already was. The trailer, even though it had flipped onto its side, had landed flat and was stable. It would protect them from the wind coming down the valley. If she added a tarp or something over the side of the trailer and threw in the cushions from her sofa, they might actually be able to get some rest tonight. All she needed was to get a fire started and soon they would be able to get some food in their systems.

Sam was busy working on the truck. Still perplexed on what happened or why they hadn't seen anyone come down the road all day, Angie had busied herself elsewhere while Sam tried to get the Ford running again. She had managed to get her backpack loaded with everything Emma had taught her and then some. It was hard picking and choosing among all the belongings she and Scott were moving from Memphis to Ohio, but at last the only things she grabbed were pictures and some important documents. Everything else was just stuff. Stuff that wouldn't help her survive.

Angie gathered various sizes of dried branches and set about getting a fire going. She was proud of herself as the spark lit the jute she had unraveled to make a bird's nest. One thing she was glad of was Emma talking her into getting a larger ferrocerium rod. The smaller ones worked, but you couldn't beat the spark her 6" rod put out. Angie had balked at the price, but at this moment considered it money well spent.

Fire going strong, shelter built including soft cushions and sleeping bags, dinner finally drifted under
Scott's nose and caught his attention. Lifting his head from the engine of the truck, he looked around and noticed the smoke coming from behind the overturned trailer. Grabbing a rag that he had laying on the side of the hood, Scott wiped as much grease off of his hands as he could and started to walk towards the smoke and the wonderful smell.

Scott stopped at the corner of the trailer and took in the sight before him. There was the woman he had fallen head over heels in love with. Her red tendrils escaping from under the handkerchief she had tied around her hair. His heart damn near exploded with pride at what she had accomplished. "Wow!" he exclaimed.

Glancing up, Angie shot him a smile. "You hungry?" she asked.

"Famished," Scott replied.

"Well, isn't this your lucky day!" she shot back.

Scott sat down beside the red-headed survivalist and realized how late it had gotten. He had lost all track of time trying to get the truck started. His mind had been working overtime with all the scenarios that were being played out on what actually had happened.

They ate in awkward silence, the stress of the day finally catching up to each of them.

"We need to talk," Scott finally said breaking the quiet.

"Not tonight. It can wait until morning. Right now, I have something else to show you," Angie replied.

Standing and taking Scott by the hand, she led him to where the tarp was. Peering inside, Scott saw the makeshift bed she had made from the sofa cushions and sleeping bags.

"Ohhhhhhh," escaped his lips in a long drawn-out sigh. "That looks amazing!"

A smile spread across Angie's face. She had done it. She had broken through the wall Scott had put up around himself earlier and torn down the stress he was holding onto.

Sliding their weary bodies into the warm, cushiony haven, Angie laid her head on Scott's shoulder as they both drifted off to sleep.

Off in the distance, the ragged stranger walked, placing one tired foot in front of the other. The smell of food had given him the adrenalin shot he needed to keep going.

92

Shelby stared at disbelief at the scene unfolding before her. It was time. Everything she had been preparing for was unfolding before her eyes like a slow-motion movie, and not the way she had imagined it in the least little bit. No matter how much planning she had done, no matter how many supplies she had put away, she had told herself it would never be enough, and she was right.

"Get the animals gathered!! Hurry!! We must get them into the barn!" Shelby realized she was screaming as she was running towards the barn! "Children, we must hurry!! We have to get them penned and we need to get into the cellar!! Help me…we need to get done as fast as possible!" She didn't want to scare the children, but knew it was too late for that. The bewildered look on their faces was enough. She needed their help, though, as she knew there wasn't a lot of time left.

"Bring them all this way!" she yelled as she motioned towards the large doors she was swinging open.

Once inside the barn, Shelby knelt down and pulled two large doors open that were recessed into the floor. With all the loose hay that scattered the floor, not many people knew there were access doors even there. Swinging both wide, Shelby began to descend the earthen ramp under the barn revealing a large room with another door off to the side. There were no corrals or pens down here so the animals would be loose, but it was better than being left up top.

Two cows, a couple horses, rabbits, chickens, goats and pigs were all quickly released into the room and given piles of food. Calculating in her head, Shelby knew they didn't have much time left. Running to the house, she gathered a few quick essentials and ushered herself and the kids through the only door in the big room beneath the barn. Once inside, Shelby got busy giving each child a bag of essentials.

"Only one flashlight on at a time. Let's not waste the batteries," she murmured to them.

"Mama, what just happened?"

"Where's Daddy?"

The questions just kept coming as Shelby's hands continued preparations.

"Come. Sit down here with me," Shelby directed to the children.

"Shhhhh...." she whispered to try and calm their minds.

"Daddy is a smart man and will be just fine. He went into town and should be here by nightfall.
Maybe a little later."

"But what was the big blast? Are we at war?" her eldest asked.

"Honestly, I don't know," Shelby replied. "What I do know is this...."

Softly and with calmness, Shelby told the kids what she felt had just happened in the world above them. Their eyes were glued onto their Mama as she laid out the plan going forward, which included staying in the underground room for a while. Shelby's tone set the precedent for how the children would react to what she was describing to them, and it was important that she remained calm. They had everything they would need for quite a while, but being able not to panic was of utmost importance and without Mountain Man here, Shelby had to do this all by herself.

93

"You have a lovely family, Emma." Nina was trying to start small talk with Emma, more to gain information than to show she cared. She didn't care. She had an agenda that few people were listed on and while Emma wasn't on the list, her delightful husband could very well be used for various purposes.

"Thank you, I couldn't agree more," Emma replied. Emma had sized Nina up the moment she had walked into Emma's house and knew her kind. The woman was out for the next newest and best, disregarding anything used as if merely throwing away trash. She left a wake of burned bridges behind her and never looked back.

The tension between the two women was quite noticeable. It was like watching two wild felines dance around each other, not taking swipes but just waiting for the perfect time to pounce.

"How long have you lived here? It's a beautiful farm you have," Nina asked.

"This land has always been in my family," Emma replied. "It's a part of who I am."

"But what about your poor husband? He had to feel like an outsider coming here."

Nina was digging and Emma knew it.

"Quite the opposite. My Tommy is as much a part of this place as I am. That's what marriage does, it melds the two pieces together into one. Three actually if you understood our religious beliefs. A cord of three is not easily broken."

"Interesting, but I have to wonder if moving to a place where you both were on equal footing is not better for a man's soul, instead of living under the rule of the wife"

"I'm not sure you understand what's good for any man's soul, but I assure you that you have no clue what you are talking about when it comes to my family. No disrespect, but you are merely a visitor here and know little about us to pass such a judgment."

"No. Maybe not," Nina replied. "But I do know that a man wants to rule over his own house and no one given to him by a woman. He needs to feel like a man, not merely a concubine."

Emma could feel her anger swell up within her. "Keep your cool, chickie," Emma said to herself. "It's merely a test to see if she can get your feathers ruffled. She isn't worth it and you need to keep the upper hand."

Grinning her best grin, Emma looked at Nina, "Oh hun, that's what the pool boy is for, right?!" and turned and walked away.

94

Nina's eyes went wide with fury. "How dare she speak to me in such a way!" Livid, Nina just stared at the woman as she walked away. If her eyes could, they would drill holes into Emma's back straight into her soul. Nina envisioned her hand reaching in through those holes and twisting Emma's heart until she died.

Feeling much calmer after releasing some of her anger towards Emma, Nina walked over to the kitchen sink and poured herself a glass of spring water. Looking out the window toward the barn, Nina watched Tom cleaning out the chicken coop. "This place has everything I would need to survive what was coming," Nina thought. Unlimited food, spring water, the total ability to self-sustain herself and with hundreds of acres, it also gave her staff the room to work without being on top of each other. Several of her staff had already taken over some cabins in the woods.

A slow grin crept across Nina's face as she watched Tom work. Not being a country girl like little miss perfect Emma, Nina would need an escort to find her way to the cabins to check in on her people. What a perfect opportunity to get Emma's delightful husband alone. Nina knew the passion that flowed through the veins of a Latino man, and it had been quite a while since she had released her own fervor.

If Nina were to take control of Emma's farm, she had to get Emma out of the way. Killing was killing, and quite messy, she thought tapping her bottom lip with her finger, but a chink in the bitches' armor by fornication with her beloved husband would be quite fun, Nina thought.

Nina sat the glass down in the sink, making sure she left lip prints along the rim of the glass with her dazzling red lipstick. "Game on, bitch," Nina murmured with a grin.

95

Scott tried to open his eyes but he kept losing the battle. Why wouldn't his eyes open? His leg jumped again involuntarily. What the heck was going on? He was so tired and just wanted to sleep. His leg jumped again as he felt something hit the bottom of his boot. The hairs on the back of his neck stood on end as his brain finally circled back around and became fully functioning once again. Again, something struck the sole of his boot.

Slowly peering out from under his lashes, Scott saw the man standing there, a gun pointed directed at Scott and Angie. Scott's brain went into overdrive as he tried to buy more time by pretending that he was asleep still.

Scott didn't have much of a choice after the next kick as the man yelled at him to wake up. Scott rolled over towards Angie and grabbed her before she could get up or scream.

"Slow and easy," the man released the words with the same inflection that he expected his surprised guests to react, slow and easy.

Scott raised his hands in the air as he sat up, trying to get as much of Angie behind him as possible.

"What do you want? Take whatever," Scott said, not taking his eyes from the stranger.

"I reckon I will!" the man replied with such a wicked grin that it made Scott's throat clench.

"Just take it and go," Scott choked out.

"Oh now wait a minute there! I haven't even had breakfast yet. Kinda rude to send me off with an empty belly now, don't ya think? How about you get that pretty little thing hiding behind you out there and fix us men some grub," the man said... and then his voice changed ....low and forceful... "I think you need to remember who's in charge here. Would hate to see someone get hurt."

Without hesitating, Angie crawled out from behind Scott. Stumbling over to where she had cooked dinner a few hours earlier, Angie set about getting a fire going again without taking her eyes off the stranger. Her senses in overdrive, her mind was reeling trying to figure out how they could get out of this situation and no one get hurt. Her main goal was helping Scott and keeping him safe but trying to see his face in the dark and read his expressions was tormenting her. Damn it! Emma was right. They needed to talk about "situations" so they knew how the other people would react. How many times had they played "Conflicted" around Emma's table after dinner? Damn it, Angie wished she had paid better attention. At least now she might have a clue on what was going through Scott's head right now.

It hit her square in the gut like a bulldozer. If the opportunity presented itself, she knew what she had to do. Angie swallowed hard as she remembered Emma's words "Consider it the light switch effect. How fast can you switch yours on? How fast can your mind get from 'Life is all grand, peace love and harmony to I have to do whatever it takes to protect those I love in whatever manner it may take.' The difference in living and dying is how fast you can flick that switch in your head, because the bad guy is already living in your worst nightmare." Angie let her head descend as she closed her eyes. "Lord, please help me!" was all she prayed.

96

The bike sputtered to a slow stop. Of all places, they had to run out of gas now, Chloe thought.
Michael stretched out his cramped legs and balanced the pile of metal while Chloe crawled off, her muscles not cooperating from the long ride.

Chloe slid off her helmet and looked around. A freakin' suburb? Really?

Michael kicked the stand out and propped the bike up. Much more accustomed to riding than Chloe, he dismounted with more grace than she had. Walking over beside her, Michael removed his helmet and surveyed the landscape. "I'm sure there's gas here somewhere."

"You suck at directions," Chloe retorted.

"Oh really? And who the fuck has gotten your fairy ass this far?"

Chloe knew a losing battle when she saw one, but chose not keep her mouth shut anyways.

"Ya, Utah is so far! I guess your tank isn't as big as you think it is!"

"Listen, we are about 400 miles out of Los Angeles. That's what's important. Better this happen now than when we get in the mountains. We need a better mode of transportation anyway. If not, the ride over those bitches is going to be brutal," he said, his chin pointing in the direction of the Rocky Mountains.

Chloe turned in the direction he had pointed and caught her breath. She had never seen them before, the beginning of the Rocky Mountains. Sure, she had read about them in school books, but there's really no comparison to seeing them in real life.

St. George Utah, or Utah's Dixie as some refer to the city as the early settlers grew cotton here, sat at the base of the Colorado Plateau. Red in color from the iron oxide in the soil and rock formations, the view of the mountains reminded Chloe of all the blood that would soon be shed, if not already. So far they had been lucky, mostly just wide spread power outages. Chloe was trying to brace herself though for what devastation lay over the mountains. If what happened was what was being rumored, the ground would be a scarlet red, and not the soft color she was seeing before her now.

Taking a deep breath, Chloe turned to Mike, "Time to get to work, dude. Let's see what we can do."

"I'm thinking a helpless female is going to be more of a welcome sight than a male stranger. All yours sugar plum," Michael replied with a grin.

He was right, again. Being approached for help by a woman would get someone much further ahead peacefully than any man could possibly get. They needed gas, food,…oh, a shower would be great" Chloe thought, new mode of transportation, warmer clothes and water.

"No worries, I got this," she finally said.

Glancing around, Chloe surveyed the houses. Typical suburban homes. Landscaped lawns, no clutter, curtains shut. This might be harder than she thought, that was until she spotted the small motor home parked in the very back of the lot of one house.

"No worries," she muttered again, more to herself than anyone else, as she headed off in the direction of the RV.

97

"UGH! If I hear one more parent talk about how stressful spring vacation is when their kids are home I am going to scream,"

Megan thought as she left the doctor's office. "Why do these people even have kids if all they want to do is send them to someone else?"

Megan buckled her 3-year-old into his car seat, locked the door and made her way around to the driver's side of the car. Taking 30 seconds for herself, she raised her face to the sun and closed her eyes, feeling the warmth penetrate her skin. One must learn to appreciate such warmth in Wisconsin in April, she thought. Last year at this time, they had 3 feet of snow and no sight of spring showing up. This year they haven't seen snow since the middle of March! Just maybe they will have an early spring. How lovely that would be!

Megan unlocked her door and slid into the driver's seat. Glancing in the back seat, she made sure Robbie was still buckled in. Kids his age are better at escaping car seats than Houdini! Poor little guy wasn't feeling his best today though. No fever, but his appetite had dwindled down to hardly anything and he wasn't sleeping at night. Visiting the doctor today, they had drawn some blood for some tests and he had already pulled his SpongeBob Band-Aid off his puncture point.

Megan headed the car toward the grocery store. She only needed to pick up a couple things but noticed Robbie had fallen asleep about a block from the store. Deciding not to wake him, she turned the car toward home. She would send her mom a text later and see if she would pick up some milk and bread on her way over later. She hated to bother her, but Robbie did not need dragged through the store if he wasn't feeling well. Being a single parent sucked sometimes.

Pulling the car into the driveway, Megan tenderly removed Robbie from his car seat and managed to get him into the house without him waking. "I've got this!" she thought as she made her way to his room. Slowly she lowered him into his crib and pulled his favorite blankie up around him. Turning to leave the room, she breathed a sigh of relief and within 5 seconds Robbie was standing at the side of his crib crying.

Megan's shoulders slumped as she turned to pick him up. "Poor little guy," she cooed as she cradled him in her arms. "Oh, mama wishes she could figure out what is wrong!" Megan walked into the living room and sat with Robbie in the rocking chair. Her mom would be bringing her oldest two children home in a couple hours, but right now all her thoughts were on her youngest... Megan began to rock, tears in her eyes and she silently said a prayer and began to sing ever so lightly...

"Hush little baby, don't say a word ...

98

The knock at the door startled Megan awake. "Oh God, please stop knocking!" Megan frantically stood up from the rocking chair and took Robbie to his bed and laid him down. This time he stayed sleeping. Megan heard the knocking again and quickly covered Robbie as she raced from the room. She couldn't imagine why her mom had to knock at the door, she had her own key, Megan thought as she flung open the door.

"Oh. Hello" Megan said as she stared at the woman standing before her. "I'm sorry, I thought you were my mother"

"I really look that old?" Chloe asked

"Oh heavens no! I'm so sorry. My brain hasn't started yet. I was asleep when you knocked. No, goodness no. You don't look like my mother at all!"

"Good! You had me worried for a minute!" Chloe chuckled.

Chloe took in the woman before her. Her instincts kicked in and Chloe had an overwhelming feeling to protect her. The woman looked like she hadn't slept in a long time. Obvious signs of sudden weight loss and dark circles under her eyes, Chloe felt such sadness at the sight of her.

"Oh, my manners! How can I help you?" Megan asked.

"I wanted in inquire about the motor home out back. Is it for sale?"

"Oh. Well, that was my husband's and I don't really know anything about it." Megan replied.

"Will he be home later? Or maybe a number I could reach him at?"

"He passed away a couple months ago" Megan whispered in response.

"I am so sorry!" Chloe said, feeling like a fool.

"No, please don't. He was doing something he shouldn't have been and it caught up to him. Please, why don't you come in and let's talk about it," Megan said, feeling a bit dizzy. The world around her started to spin out of control.

Chloe caught her as she collapsed, barely able to hold her up. "Michael!" Chloe shouted, "Michael, help! Come on dammit, I need some help!"

Michael and Chloe managed to get the woman onto her couch. Chloe ran to the bathroom and found some washcloths. Soaking them in cold water, she walked back to the living room and gently patted them on the woman's face.

ANNIE BERDEL

Megan started to stir. "Get me a glass of cold water from the kitchen," Chloe directed to Michael

As Michael was making his way to the kitchen, Megan came around and tried to sit up.

"Here, let me help," Chloe said, propping her up against some pillows. Sitting down on the coffee table in front of Megan, Chloe laid the cold washcloth across Megan's head.

"You OK, hun?" Chloe asked.

"I'm sorry. I'm not sure what happened. How long was I out?" Megan asked.

"Not long, maybe a couple minutes," Chloe responded.

"When was the last time you ate anything?" "I don't

remember," Megan answered.

"Might have something to do with you passing out. Do you have any fruit or anything?" Chloe asked.

"I think I have bananas in the kitchen."

"I'll be right back. Don't move," Chloe demanded.

Chloe walked into the kitchen and met Michael there snooping through the cupboards. "What the hell are you doing?"

"Looking."

"Go outside and wait, and don't let her see you."

"Ya sure," he said as he grabbed a soda from the refrigerator as he went out the side door.

Chloe grabbed the water and a banana and walked back into the living room.

"Here, eat this. And no talking till you are done."

Megan did as she was told and the color started to return to her face. Feeling better, she sat up on the couch.

"It's been a long day. Sorry to drag you into it," Megan said with a halfhearted smile.

"No worries. But you need to take better care of yourself. Biggest mistake women in general make is taking care of everyone else before they take of themselves. Stop it. And now! Promise?" Chloe asked.

"Promise," Megan replied with a bigger smile.

For the next hour, Chloe sat with Megan and they just talked. Chloe learned a lot about the woman sitting in front of her. She had several children, the youngest being asleep in the next room. Robert, or Robbie as Megan called him, was named after his father. His father had died in a car accident a couple months ago during a business conference in Los Angeles. Tests run on Robert after the accident showed his blood alcohol level to be more than double the legal limit. He was drunk driving, which was bad enough. It still didn't explain who the woman was in the car with him at the time since she had no ID on her. The story cut Chloe to the core. She knew who the woman was. The woman was Chloe. She was a paid escort who made her money during business conferences that catered to married men. Chloe had never seen the impact of what her job did to the other side of her John's life. Now, it was staring her right in the face.

99

Shelby shone the flashlight around the room. Tote after tote lined one wall. Reading the tags as she scanned down them, she found the ones she was looking for.

"Here, help your mama out," she said to the kids.

Each grabbing a tote, they carried them to the middle of the room. Grabbing a knife from within her apron pocket, Shelby cut the duct tape off that sealed the lids shut. Inside she pulled out multiple tarps and had the kids begin unfolding them across part of the dirt floor. Next, they tied them across the ceiling and down the walls, making an enclosed area inside the room. "There, that should keep more of the dirt out," she said.

"Are we going to sleep in here, Mama?"

"Yes! We are on an adventure! This is going to be fun," Shelby replied.

She tried but the looks on the kids' faces told her she wasn't very convincing. Opening more totes, they found sleeping pads to keep them off of the ground and sleeping bags to keep them warm. Being underground should keep the temperature a bit more stable, but it would be chilly to sleep.

Shelby opened one tote that held a camp stove and fuel along with cooking utensils. Digging through other totes, she found hygiene supplies and then food and stored water.

"What would you kids like for dinner?" Shelby asked.

"What can we have?"

"How would you kids like some s'mores?" Shelby asked.

The kids all looked at each other like they couldn't believe what they were hearing. "SURE!" They yelled in unison.

"Hold it together, girly," Shelby said to herself. Funny, though, what thinking it might be your last good days on earth will do to a soul. She looked at each of her kids in the soft glow of the flashlight. She wanted nothing more than to see them grow up and marry off to someone they loved, to give her grandbabies. This wasn't the road she had planned. It wasn't the journey she had asked for, but it was the one that was laid out before her.

100

Angie watched the man from beneath her lashes. He had sat down with his back against the trailer so he could see both Scott and Angie, the gun never leaving his hands.

"Where you folks going to?" he finally said, breaking the silence.

"Ohio," Angie said before she caught herself.

She quickly looked at Scott for a sign that it was OK to answer but his eyes never left the stranger.

"Long way from here, wouldn't you say?"

This time Angie didn't reply. She kept

busy on fixing the man something to

eat. "That truck work?" he asked

"No" Scott replied.

"Why not?" he asked.

"You tell me. I have no idea," Scott said.

"Bit testy are ya? Did I interrupt your beauty sleep?" the man asked looking at Scott. "I'm sure your woman doesn't like being talked to like that."

Scott didn't answer. His face was set in stone looking at the man, not even blinking.

Angie was waiting for any opportunity she could get. Problem was, her gun, knife and flashlight were all over by where she was sleeping under the sofa mattress. While it was good that the stranger couldn't see them, she couldn't get to them easily just yet. It didn't help either that Scott was giving her no clue on what he was planning on doing.

The man startled her when he stood up and walked to her. Pointing to Scott, the man had him move to the opposite side of the fire away from Angie.

"You have anything here to drink?" he asked her.

"Water. It's over there," she said as she pointed to the back of the trailer.

"Don't move," he demanded.

He walked over to where she had pointed and looked around. Angie used the opportunity to try and get Scott's attention.

"Hey! I said no talking!" The man yelled, obviously upset "Fucking cunt. You not understand English or what?"

Walking over, he grabbed Angie by the hair and pulled her to a standing position. Scott reacted and started to approach them but the stranger pushed the gun into Angie's back. "Stop now, bud, or the cunt is going to have a hole in her belly."

Scott stopped in his tracks. Angie's eyes were like large saucers and staring right at Scott, pleading for help.

"Get over to the tree" the stranger said as he pushed Angie in that direction, her back arched as the man pushed the gun farther into her spine.

"Put your arms around the tree," he instructed Scott. "Now lock your fingers and don't fucking move." Scott did as he was instructed as he didn't want the man to hurt Angie.

Reaching into his pocket, the man pulled out some zip ties and rope and handed them to Angie. "Tie his fucking hands together."

Oh God, Angie thought. With Scott tied to the tree it would be up to only her to protect them.

The man walked over and pointed the gun at Scott now and Angie almost fainted. Hurriedly, she did as the stranger instructed.

"Now tie his feet around the bottom of the tree with this," he demanded as he threw the rope at her

Angie looped the rope around the tree looking up at Scott. "I love you," she mouthed. His eyes slowly closed and opened as if in agreement.

The man walked back over to the fire and motioned Angie to follow. "Get me that water before you get over here," he stammered.

Angie fumbled over to where she had left the water bottles the night before. Picking up a couple, she noticed the toothpaste and toothbrushes she had laid out for morning. Quickly grabbing a toothbrush and sliding it up her jacket sleeve, she hurried to the man and gave him his water.

"Can I sit?" she asked.

"Might as well. I don't need anything right now."

"My name is Angie, by the way."

"So? To me, you're just a cunt. Just like all the other women out there," he replied

Angie didn't know how to respond to that. Obviously the man had issues with women in his past and she didn't want to add to it. She figured it would only escalate the situation, possibly beyond her control.

"Do you need anything else to eat?" she asked.

"Sure" he replied and handed her his plate.

They sat in silence for a while the man finished his food. It was too quiet. Angie needed noise to do what she needed to get done. Sliding the toothbrush down the sleeve of her jacket and into her hand, she needed to snap the brush off of the handle. Coughing loudly, she synced the breaking with the distraction of her cough. "Bingo," she thought. Scooting over, she felt around on the ground for a large enough rock that she could file the end of the toothbrush into a point. But it was going to be noisy and she couldn't risk being detected.

"Is there something you need?" Angie asked. "We have some supplies but not a lot. Please, just take what you want and leave us be."

"Aren't you the bossy one?" he replied.

"I don't know why you are doing this. We haven't done anything to you. We were just trying to get home."

The more talking that went on, the more Angie was able to file the toothbrush handle against the rock. She needed to make the best point she could at the end. Chances are she would have one shot at this and that was it. She had to be 100% committed to this, or her plan would fail.

The stranger stood up and looked around.

"What do you want?" Angie asked again, now annoying the stranger.

"I need to take a piss, you gonna hold it for me?"

"Oh. No, I'm sorry." Angie stammered, feeling embarrassed.

"Well maybe you should. Come on and help a man out here," he said grinning at her.

"Leave her alone!" Scott yelled out.

"Or what? You'll pick up the tree and beat me with it?" the man chuckled.

"How about you hold it for me then?" he said to Scott.

Startled, neither Angie nor Scott said anything.

"A lot of years locked up changes a man. The cunt is used materials. You, on the other hand, might be worth the fight." he said directly to Scott.

Angie stopped breathing. "God no!" she screamed out in her head.

The man walked over to where Scott was tied to the tree. There was no escape for him. His hands were zip tied around the tree and his feet were tied against the tree so he couldn't move, his legs apart.

He grabbed Scott's buttocks in his hands. Scott jerked upwards leaving the stranger to let out a howl of laughter. "Relax bitch, it will only hurt for a little while," he whispered in Scott's ear.

Angie wanted to hurl her guts up. Never in her worst nightmare would she have dreamed this to happen. There was no scenario that could have been worked through. She knew what it was like to be raped and wished it on no one, but for a man. It was too much for Angie to comprehend.

Gripping the handle of her makeshift shank, Angie mustered all the strength she could get and lunged towards the man standing behind Scott. Hearing the commotion, the man darted to the right as Angie's arm descended downward and met its unintended target.

101

Brian opened the binder. Before him were the events about to take place in chronological order.

Stage one had begun with the eruption of the New Madrid. Most of Louisiana, Missouri and Western Tennessee were gone, obliterated in the push of a button. Pushed by someone who thought this was all a war game they were testing. In three days another large event would happen that would change even more lives. Situated in Ohio, he should be able to escape the wrath to come. But the poor souls in San Diego would not. Stage Two was about to begin. Closing the binder, he stood and walked over to the window. Glancing out at the changing leaves, remorse hit him square in the gut. What was he doing, allowing this to happen? Not stopping it. These were the good people, right....these people who were giving him orders. Doubt crept into his mind. What if he were doing the wrong thing, what if this whole thing was just another scheme, people no better than the ones whom he thought they were trying to destroy. "Ah Christ, please forgive me," he said as he picked up the revolver.

Click...

Click...

The red gooey substance splattered against the window and ran down the glass as the man's body slumped to the floor.

102

Shelby knew the fallout from the mushroom cloud could reach the farm where they were, but it the initial blast, if it were going to take them out, would have by now. Now she had to wait. Wait and pray. Anything above ground would be contaminated if the fallout reached out to the farm.

The plan was to wait at least 48 hours before leaving the shelter, but not knowing what was going on above was killing her. She needed to know where Mountain Man was, what condition her house was in, the animals. Waiting was frustrating!

"Mama?" Startled, Shelby realized she was deep in thought and not paying attention to the children.

"Yes dear?" she replied.

"Do you hear that?"

Shelby listened, "What is it?"

"Some kind of weird thumping noise."

Shelby listened even more intently. "It's probably one of the cows. They don't like being down here and not being up there munching on grass!"

"There it goes again."

Shelby heard it that time. Her heart rate increased. "What in the world?" she questioned.

"You kids stay here and keep this sealed

shut. I'm going to check on the animals."

"Yes ma'am."

Shelby cut through a small section of the duct tape holding two sections of the tarp together.

"Tape this right back up here," she instructed her son.

Backing over to the door, Shelby listened again. The thumping was a bit louder now that she was out of the tarp. Slowly opening the big door, she entered the larger room with the animals staying against the wall as not to spook them. They knew her and would recognize her scent but she didn't want to take any chances of animals being alarmed.

Stopping, Shelby heard the thumping again, this time picking up faint voices. Hearing to where the dirt ramp was to take her above ground, she cut through the duct tape holding the tarps together. Waiting, she listened "Shelby!"

She recognized her name, and very few people knew about the underground rooms under the barn.

"Joshua?" She yelled out.

"Shelby! I'm up here. Let me in."

Tears began flowing down Shelby's face as she recognized Mountain Man's voice. Her heart broke though when she realized she couldn't let him in the doors.

"The fallout has begun, hasn't it?" she yelled through the door.

"Yes," was the only reply.

"Oh God. I love you, Joshua. You will always be my Mountain Man, but I can't let you in here. You are contaminated. You will contaminate the children and it could kill them!" she cried out, her heart breaking for the man who was a part of her.

"Go to the house, get into the pantry. There's a tote in there marked fallout. Get the walkies and turn them on," Shelby instructed him.

"I love you my Shelby girl" she heard. "I love you."

The hardest decision she had ever made in her life was to not open the door to her husband. It damn near killed her. To make the decision to allow someone to possibly die to save others, all of whom she loved immeasurably, was more than she could handle. Breaking down, she collapsed into the dirt and wailed with grief, the animals starting to scurry around her. The sobs shook her entire body as she realized that that might be the last time she ever heard Mountain Man... her Joshua's voice ever again. Her grief had consumed her as Bella's hoof came down upon her leg, crushing the bone under the weight of the horse. Shelby cried out in horror that matched the severity of the pain. She was alone and there was no one to hear her or to help her.

103

The storm was at least an hour away and would give Nina just what she needed. Walking into the barn, she found her unknowing victim.

"Hey Tommy," she beamed out gleefully.

Looking up, Tom felt uncomfortable that anyone other than Emma called him Tommy. It was her pet name for him, and no one else's.

"Ma'am, please call me Tomás. Emma calls me Tommy and it's her special name, no disrespect."

"Oh," replied Nina, a little taken aback. No worries, she thought, minor setback but she needed to regroup her emotions real fast since it definitely pushed her buttons. "No worries. Tomás is so formal, how about I call you Chulo."

Tom let out a laugh, "Ma'am, that's kinda funny."

"Why? It's most befitting! Nothing better for a Latino friend!" Nina purred. "Say, where are those cabins at anyways? I need to go check on some people."

"Well, which one? They are scattered all over the place," Tom replied.

"I think its number seven."

"That's one of the farther ones in the back. You sure you want to go all the way back there?" Tom asked.

"Oh. Well, maybe you could draw me a map."

"Ma'am, you shouldn't be going out there by yourself. I can take you out once I'm done here I guess.
Can you give me like twenty minutes?"

"You know it, Chulo!" Nina cooed as she walked away.

104

Megan and Chloe were still talking when Robbie woke up. Changing his diaper and grabbing a bottle of milk, Megan put a jacket on him and grabbed the keys to the RV. "Robert bought it a few years ago. We used it every summer for a couple weeks or used it if we had visitors staying, like Robert's brother. I couldn't stand his brother so instead of having him in the house, Robert made him stay out here so they could hang out together instead of disturbing the kids so much." Megan explained as she opened the door.

By now introductions had been made and Michael had joined the group to look through the motor home. It was in pretty good shape other than it hadn't been started since last summer. "With Robert's passing, I just had no desire to come out here," Megan said.

"If you have the key, I'll give it a crank and see what happens," Michael said.

"OH! Hang on a second," Megan said as she fumbled for the keys she had tucked in a pocket. She just couldn't remember which pocket. Without thinking, Megan handed the baby to Chloe so she could find them easier.

A state of shock crept across Chloe's face. She had never held a baby in her entire life. This was entirely too awkward. She was frozen. She may have even stopped breathing for all she knew.

"Come here, baby" Megan said as she reached to take Robbie back. No one but Chloe noticed how uncomfortable she was holding Robbie.

They all walked into the camper and looked around.

"Wow! This is really nice!" Chloe said as she walked around.

"Here's the ignition key, Michael," Megan said as she handed them over.

"Thanks, let's see what she's got," Michael responded and turned to walk to the front of the camper.

Megan sat down with Robbie at the kitchen table as Chloe shortly joined them.

"Where are you headed?" Megan asked.

"Ohio, or as far east as we can get. I have friends on a farm there," Chloe replied.

"Oh wow, that must be nice. I have my mom here but that's it now that Robert is gone. His family drives me nuts and they could care less about the kids."

"I don't have family myself. My friend I told you about, Emma, who I am going to see, is about as close as I will ever have," Chloe responded.

Michael sat in the driver's seat ad put the key in the ignition. "Well, here she goes." After several attempts, the RV started to blow black smoke out the back, but she did indeed start.

Megan and Chloe sang out in unison as the motor started to mellow out and idle. "Yeah!"

"Why don't you both stay for dinner? I even have a spare bedroom you can use tonight and get a fresh start in the morning, shower included."

"Um, sure!" Chloe said smiling. "Thanks!"

"I call dibs on the bed," Michael yelled from the front of the RV.

Megan shot Chloe a puzzled look. "Oh, we aren't together or anything like that," Chloe stammered out.

"Could have fooled me!" Megan said in return.

105

Megan sat up that night talking with her mom. She had made up her mind and was grateful that her mother agreed. It was after two before the woman left for her own house and Megan wanted to get a few hours' sleep before the kids were awake in the morning. She also wanted to talk to Chloe before she and Michael left on their journey.

Passing by the bedroom that her guests were using, Megan couldn't help but notice the door was open.
Glancing in, there was Michael, asleep on the floor beneath where Chloe was sleeping on the bed. "Could have fooled me," Megan thought as she smiled to herself and went to climb into her own bed.

The next morning, Megan had breakfast on the table when her guests finally awoke.

"Wow! I haven't had real food in like forever," Chloe chimed out.

Glancing at the table, Chloe's mouth started watering at the feast before her. Bacon, ham, eggs, biscuits and gravy. Chloe didn't know where she would even start. That is, once she found a seat. All of Megan's children were sitting patiently around the table ready to dig in once the word was given. Each smiled at Chloe and Michael as they introduced themselves.

"Manners are a must," Chloe explained.

"Job well done, Mom," Michael said as he took in the politeness of their host.

Chloe and Michael squeezed in between the kids and everyone spent the next hour having their fill not only of all the food but conversation as well. Megan homeschooled her kids and Chloe was astounded at their ability to hold her interest. Grown adults didn't do that well! As they were finishing, the kids each started to clean up the table without even a peep from their mother.

"I am really impressed," Chloe exclaimed. "Your kids are amazing."

"Thank you," Megan replied. "It's been hard but we have really pulled together this last year."

"Kids, why don't you all take little Robbie into the living room for a while and watch some cartoons. We adults are going to have a cup of coffee and talk some business," Megan said.

The oldest picked up the baby on cue and they all left to go watch cartoons, but not before saying goodbye to their guests.

"Really, Megan, you are doing a wonderful job raising those kids by yourself," Michael said.

"I'm glad you think so. It will make what I have to say next easier," Megan said perplexing her guests.

"I want to go with you. Well, me and the kids and my mom." The silence was deafening as Megan anxiously looked from Megan to Michael and back again.

106

Michael paced back and forth beside the motorcycle, drawing his fingers back through his hair numerous times.

"It's not the end of the world," Chloe said. "They really are a delightful family."

"Do you even know what you are saying? You want to travel with four small children for days across the Rocky Mountains in a cramped camper? Are you fricken insane?" By now Michael was shouting. "So that's a yes?" Chloe asked with a smile.

Kicking the curb with his foot, Michael just grunted.

"Let's just roll with it. Change of plans. No big deal," Chloe said as she tried to swat at his arm.

"You really are insane. My sister is going to owe me big time for this one," Michael replied.

107

Scott cried out in pain as the dull end of the homemade shank caught him right below the shoulder blade. If it wasn't for his arms being zip tied around the tree, he would have crumbled onto the ground. Closing his eyes, it was all he could do to remain conscious as his breathing became labored. He had to focus...he had to stay awake as the woman he loved was in dire trouble. "Fuck!" he yelled out only to send himself into a coughing fit.

Startled, Angie just stood there, unable to move at the horror before her.

The stranger had tumbled backwards and now was sitting on the ground laughing hysterically. "That was just priceless," he howled.

"Oh, Scott!"

"Oh Scott…poor Scott… wah wah wah. Dumb bitch. You got some girlfriend there, Scott," the man said in a devious mocking tone as he rolled over to stand up.

Angie looked back and forth from Scott to the stranger. Her mind and body made no connection as they were wildly working against each other.

The man walked over and was delighted in how easy it was to grab Angie by the back of her hair.

"Bitch, you try that again and I will kill poor little Scott right before your eyes."

Angie's head had snapped back, the stranger pulling her hair so far back that she was having problems standing. Looking in the man's eyes as he spoke to her, something in her soul snapped. Memories came roaring back of a time not long ago in a parking garage. She felt helpless then, but time had changed her. Her eyes became small slits as she glared at the man, not hearing the words he was saying anymore. She refused to be a victim, not anymore. Never again would she endure the terror of her past.

Still holding her hair, the man caught glimpse of the soft flesh of her cleavage straining against her blouse. Pushing her in the direction of the cushions where Scott and Angie had slept earlier, he released her hair as he shoved her downwards.

Angie caught herself as she fell and scrambled backwards towards the makeshift pillows. The stranger, thinking she was cowering in fear was surprised as she quickly slid her hand under the pillow and pulled her handgun.

Locking his eyes with hers, the only words that were spoken were by Angie. "No more," slowly rolled from her lips as the trigger was pulled back. The sound was deafening as the projectile met its target square in his chest.

The stranger's heart instantly exploded as the bullet tore through the flesh. Collapsing in a heap on the ground, he was dead before he hit the dirt.

Angie gathered herself off the cushions and ran to Scott, who was struggling to breathe. Brushing his hair from his face with her hand, Angie saw how pale his face had become. Reaching down, Angie's hand was trailing his back to where the shank was protruding.

"No, don't pull it out," Scott said with panic in his voice.

"OK, OK ... you're the doctor here. Just tell me what you need me to do."

"Is there blood coming out?"

"No, doesn't look like it."

"Good. Leave it in there. I need you to cut me off of this tree. Feet first and then my hands. Is there a chair or stool somewhere close?"

"Yes... in the trailer. I will be right back."

Angie ran to the back of the trailer and brought out one of the kitchen barstools she had packed in there.

"Back it up against my legs... slowly cut me off the tree so I can ease onto the..." Scott caught his breath, now becoming more ragged. "Ease me onto the chair," he finished quickly.

Angie ran back to where she had pulled the gun from and grabbed her flashlight. Rummaging around under the makeshift pillow, she couldn't feel her knife. Flipping the light on, she couldn't find it anywhere. "Dammit" she muttered under her breath. Returning back to where Scott was still tied to the tree, she paused long enough where the stranger was slumped to make sure he was indeed dead.

Pushing the barstool up against Scott's legs, she untied the rope from his around his feet. Checking on him again, she noticed his lips were drying out. Quickly gathering a bottle of water, she was able to get him to take a few sips. Tossing the bottle aside, she went back around to the other side of the tree.

Letting a slow growl of frustration escape her lips, she had to find a way and fast to get the zip tie off of Scott's wrists. Shining the light onto the snap, she realized how thick the ties were. "Damn."

"What's wrong?" Scott panted.

"My knife is gone. I need something to cut through these ties." She glanced up and looked at Scott. She wasn't going to let him die. She just needed to cut through the thick plastic.

"OH! I know!" Running to where her pack was, Angie pulled out her nail clippers.

"You ready?" she asked Scott.

"Ready as I'll ever be," he replied with a faint smile.

108

Getting back to Ohio was out of the question, Angie thought. She had Scott resting on his side, but she had to find help fast, and close. Her best guess was that she had damaged his lung when she slammed the shank into his back, but she was nowhere near qualified to make that determination.

She was able to get him to drink some more water and eat a little bit of food. His color was better but he was in a lot of pain. She was sure he had a reason that he didn't want her to pull the shank from his back, but she couldn't fathom what it was. She had to trust that he knew what he was talking about.

Her best guess was that it was a couple hours now after daybreak. She had moved the stranger's body away from where they were and covered it with a tarp. Before she had left him, she checked his pockets. Little in the way of supplies, the only thing that shed a light into who the man was, was a neatly folded piece of paper. Gently pulling the layers apart, Angie discovered that the man's name was Brian. Reading the rest of the document, Brian had recently been released from prison where he had served multiple years for molestation and rape. Looking at the date listed, he was released the day before all hell had broken loose.

Walking back to where Scott was, Angie sat down cross-legged beside him and sunk her head into her hands. She had to think. She had to figure out how to get Scott medical help. Her mind drifted back to the packs that they had. Angie walked her mind back to when Emma helped her pack them.

"That's it!" she yelled out as she jumped up.

Grabbing her backpack, she searched around in the bottom until she found the plastic Ziploc bag. Opening it, she laid all the pieces of paper out on the ground before her. Looking at the map, she could just about pinpoint where they were currently located. She stuck a small pebble on their current location. Grabbing Scott's bag, she found another Ziploc bag and opened it. Unfolding another sheet of paper, she checked off the co-ordinates of the closest location to where they were. 5 miles. It was 5 miles away. If she could just get Scott those 5 miles, then she knew help would be there. Looking at the map again, she ran her finger from where she was until she hit the circled area. Another 50 miles or so and they could get to a safe haven. Someone Emma trusted with her life. And if that was good enough for Emma, it was good enough for Angie. But first, Angie had to conquer those first 5 miles.

109

Ben smiled at himself in the mirror. Damn if he wasn't handsome. Checking to make sure that what he had for lunch wasn't stuck in his teeth, he splashed on some cologne. Glancing at the bottle, he read the label before he sat it back down on the side of the sink. "Damn shame to waste the good stuff on a spic," he muttered to himself. The problem was, this bitch wasn't one of the party girls, as he liked to refer to them, he had picked up in the past. This one had money and, more importantly, power.

Power excited Ben. He could feel his dick getting hard just thinking about snapping out orders to all the uniformed staff Nina had. If he played this right, the damn army she had with her would soon be doing whatever old Benny boy told them, he thought with a smirk. He just had to kiss Senator Varga's ass for a while. Staring at himself in the mirror, a smile crept across his lips as the realization of how much control he really could have if he really did play this right. What was that called, he thought. Eminent Domain? It would kill Emma to lose her farm, but hey, it would be a matter of national security to kick her cunt ass off of her own land. Oh, this was priceless, Ben thought. This had to be his best plan yet. Priceless. Slamming his hat onto his head, he grabbed his jacket as he ran out the door. He had a date that he didn't want to be late for.

110

Nina walked into the barn and was a little disappointed to find Tom covered in chicken manure still. She was hoping that he would have the decency to at least clean up a bit before he took her out to the cabins, but whatever. She would just have to deal with the smell. After all, most of it was on his clothes and once she was done, he wouldn't be wearing them anyways.

"Hey Chulo, you ready?" she yelled out to him.

"Oh, ya. Give me a minute to finish clipping this hen's wing and we can go," he replied, a chicken tucked beneath his arm.

"Doesn't that hurt?" Nina asked.

"Oh, not at all! It will keep her from flying outside the fenced-in area," he said, pointing in the direction of the field. "If she gets out, it's going to be easy for the coyotes or raccoons to make a meal out of her. It's for her own good."

"Ah," Nina said shaking her head in agreement.

Tom finished up with the hen and gave her a toss as he set her loose. "Wise choice in shoes. Wasn't sure if you even had something to walk out here in as all I've ever seen you in are high heels."

"You been checking out my shoes, Tomás? I'm flattered" This might not be as hard as I had thought, Nina thought.

"They just all seem very impractical for being out here," Tom retorted, bursting Nina's bubble as he walked past her outside.

Nina followed Tom through field after field until finally he entered the woods from the back corner of one meadow. Nina was already exhausted. Her daily treadmill jaunts just weren't cutting it, she thought. Trudging through back country was a lot different than walking in place with her headphones on, that's for sure.

They had made it to the first cabin when Nina had had enough. "Can we take a break?"

"Sure. You OK?" Tom asked. It was the first time he had looked at Nina since they had left the house. Her face was beet red. Tom thought he had pushed her a bit too hard.

"Yes, just need to sit for a bit! Not used to all this walking," she replied. "I think I'll just look around here for a bit, if you don't mind," she said as she walked up the steps to the cabin.

"No problem, I'll be ready to go when you are," he called out but she had already disappeared behind the door.

Nina let out a scream from inside the cabin at the same time Tom realized she shouldn't be in there. Running up the stairs, Tom ran through the doorway. "Damn it," he muttered out looking at Nina.

She was standing there looking at all the blood on the floor

"What happened here?" she asked, turning to Tom.

"Let's go outside."

"No! Is this the cabin?"

"Yes, you don't need to be in here," Tom replied as he reached out for her arm.

Nina pulled away. Walking over, she kneeled down and touched the floor where the blood had dried into the wood. Tears began to stream down her face as she thought about Elsie.

Finally standing, Nina turned to

Tom, "Any idea of who did this

to her?" "No," Tommy replied

and motioned for her to exit the

door.

They walked back in silence, Nina's plans of seduction long forgotten.

111

Nina and Tom were walking past the barn when Ben caught glimpse of Nina with her arm tucked into Tom's. Fury burned deep in his loins. He was waiting in the kitchen for his "date" with Nina and had decided to get a glass of water at the sink when he spotted them. "Wonder if Emma knows about our Latino Lovers," Ben muttered under his breath.

This was a problem. He would be damned if he was going to let anyone get in the way of his plans. Tom was obviously enjoying having another spic in the house, and right under Emma's nose. He almost felt sorry for her. Almost.

Nina and Tom walked into the house and were surprised to see Ben just standing there staring at them. "Ben," Tom said addressing his guest.

"I was wondering if you had forgotten about me," Ben said looking directly at Nina, ignoring Tom's acknowledgement of his presence.

"Oh! No, not at all sheriff. We just ran into a bit of an issue outside. Please, give me a few moments to get cleaned up and wipe this dirt off of me and we can begin," she said to Ben.

Turning towards Tom, Nina laid her hand on his cheek. "Thank you, Chulo" she said before she turned away.

Well isn't that just cozy, Ben thought to himself. Pet names and everything. Ben's blood was boiling within his veins. This just would not do at all. Not at all.

112

Ben shut the door as the last man walked through. Walking between the other two men, Ben moved to his desk and sat down. Opening a drawer, he pulled a map from within and spread it out on his desk. "Here's what we have, boys. And know one thing before we begin," holding his hand up, Ben made a motion like he was cupping something "Your balls are here, I won't hesitate to remove them and shove them straight up your ass if you fuck this up."

Ben motioned to the two men to come closer as they looked at a topographical map of the county. Ben already had lines drawn on it for the men to follow. Ben threw each a pack that had a ghillie suit inside. "You get caught, I don't know you," Ben told them.

Ben then threw several photos on the table. "Gentlemen, your target."

Lying on the table were pictures of the only man who had ever held Emma's heart.

113

Michael looked at Chloe and then back at Megan. "I don't know what to say. You sure you want to do this?"

"I've been up all night thinking about what Chloe told me. Yes. I have never been surer of anything in my life. My home is not here anymore. It's over and I need to do everything I can to protect my children."

Chloe just stood there with her arms folded across her chest, which was pissing Michael off even more. While the hell doesn't she chime in here and help him out!?

"It's a long drive to get to Ohio, you sure your kids could handle that? I'm not even sure if we will be able to find supplies along the way," Michael asked.

"I have a medical background. My mother is an excellent cook and caregiver. We can take care of my kids. I don't need your help there. All I need is for someone to drive that RV. It scares the heck out of me."

Michael let out a forced breath of exasperation. Well, this definitely wasn't in the plan, he thought. Wonder how his sister would react to extra guests. Who was he kidding? He knew exactly what she would do because that's just the kind of person she was.

"Think the motorcycle would fit on the back somewhere?" Chloe finally asked. "We are going to need to measure it. Megan, do you have a tape measure somewhere we could use?"

"Yes, let me get it for you."

Megan got up and left the room, feeling concerned that they might not take her family with them. She knew in her heart, though, that they needed to leave and as quickly as possible. She had felt it for a while now but the feeling was so intense last night that it kept her awake.

"Thanks" Michael said to Meagan as she handed him the tape measure. Chloe followed Michael out the door and down to the motorcycle

"What the fuck was all of that about?" he finally spurted out.

"Keep your voice down," she snapped back.

"You leave me hanging like that and you don't expect me to be slightly pissed?" he shot back.

"Listen, I'm not convinced it's such a bad idea. She had medical training, something neither of us have. She could come in handy. Mama feeds us and all we have to worry about is driving that thing," at which time she pointed at the back of the house with her chin. "Over those mountains and BAM, we got it made."

"Really, little miss I hate kids? Do you know how long this is going to take? At best 3 days."

"Listen, something in my gut is saying take them. I'm sorry..." she stammered. "I just think we need to keep an open mind about this."

Michael put both hands over his face and let out a loud exhale. He knew she was right

"OK, but if anything goes wrong, it's on you," he said.

"Deal, Bandit" she said with a smirk.

"Bandit?"

"Ya, like Smokey and the Bandit. You can play the lookout guy on your motorcycle while I drive the bus."

Michael's face brightened a bit. "I like how you think lady," he said as he swatted her nose with his finger.

Chloe was glad that Michael turned around to start measuring the bike. He missed her face turning bright red as her pulse quickened once again around him.

114

Chloe walked back into the house and found Megan in the kitchen. She walked over and poured herself a cup of coffee and leaned her back against the counter.

"Are you positive you want to leave here?" Chloe asked.

"I am, Chloe. More positive about this than anything that has been going on. Listen, I don't want to cause a kink in your plans, but my gut is telling me to leave and go with you."

"What about Robbie? This trip is going to be really hard on him."

"Well, quite honestly, I think this place is the reason Robbie is so sick to begin with."

Chloe shot Megan a confused look.

"Coffee?" Megan asked Chloe as she poured herself a cup.

"Um, sure. Why do you think this place is the reason Robbie is sick?" Chloe asked.

"It started right after he had his first shots, his vaccinations," Megan started to explain. "He had abnormal symptoms. A low grade fever and tenderness at the site of the injection are kinda normal but Robbie had it four times as bad. He wouldn't eat for weeks and I've noticed a distance in him.
Almost like he isn't there. I started doing some research and the information I discovered scared me to death, Chloe. I cried for days after I found out what was in those shots! How could I do that to my child? The doctor has been throwing around the word autism. Autism, for crying out loud! All because I couldn't take the time to find out what was in those damn shots!" Megan cried out as tears stained her face. "One rabbit trail after another and

next thing you know, I am outside looking at the planes flying overhead. Have you ever heard of chemtrails?" Not waiting for an answer, Megan continued on almost as if purging her soul, "Chemtrails. Those marks across the sky from the airplanes. They should disappear pretty darn fast if they are regular contrails. Chemtrails are what they sound like…trails of chemicals across the sky. They are floating chemicals down on us, for whatever reason, to make us sick or weather manipulation, geo-engineering or whatever, but fact is one of those chemicals is aluminum. There's also aluminum in vaccinations. Now add in the fluoride in our drinking water. Harmless enough right? Fluoride facilitates the movement of soft metals across the blood/brain barrier to infiltrate our brain tissue. Fluoride increases bone and other cancer rates. Cancer is a $500 billion a year medical industry. Don't get me started on the manipulation involved there. It's all interconnected and we don't even know that it's going on! Listen, I need to heal my son and get the rest of my kids safe. I can't do that here. Please, Chloe, let us go with you. I won't even let you pay for the RV if you take us with you."

Chloe looked Megan in the eyes, "We were going to take you before any of this."

"Thank you! Thank you," Megan whispered out through the tears. Jumping up, Megan grabbed Chloe by the hand. "Come on, I have something to show you"

Megan dragged Chloe outside and into the camper. "Check this out," Megan said as she started to open cubby after cubby. "Megan! Where did you get all of this?" Chloe asked in excitement.

Chloe opened several overhead hatches and container after container of dehydrated and freeze dried food containers were neatly arranged by color. Green vegetable cans were all perfectly aligned and facing forward as were all the red cans of dried fruits. "It looks like a fricken grocery store in here!" Chloe exclaimed.

"Medical is all back here," Megan pointed to another cabinet and opened drawer after drawer of any kind of hospital supplies you could think of, all neatly arranged by someone who may have had way too much time on their hands.

"You come out here a lot?" Chloe asked.

"Sometimes, just to escape and cry while my mother was watching the kids. I really had no other place to go," Megan responded.

"You'll need to know about this, too," Megan said as she pulled the cushions off of the long bench that ran the side of the RV. Once inside Chloe noticed some kind of safe that Megan was punching a combination into. Swinging the door upward, Chloe gasped.

"I am quite aware of how dangerous things could get. Be prepared, not scared is the motto, right?" Megan asked with a slight grin on her face.

"Hell, ya!" Chloe squealed out in laughter.

"There should be both a pistol and a rifle for all the adults with a couple spares. Ammo is all under the other seat," she explained pointing to the other side of the RV.

"Remember those rabbit trails," Megan began. "They led from one trail to another. It's scary out there in the world when you realize everything that goes on. I wanted to make sure my family might stand a chance."

"I know some people that would just love you," Chloe laughed out.

"By my calculations, we should be able to get over the mountains and pretty close to where you want to go without any reason to stop except for gas for refueling," Megan added with a look of pleading in her eyes.

"Relax girly. We are all going together," Chloe said as she gave Megan a hug. Chloe could feel the tension in Megan's muscles through her jacket. "Seriously, Megan. You need a break before you do break. You have to de-stress a bit or you are going to make yourself sick."

"It's been a rough time since Robert's death. Longer than that, if I actually admit it. Let me get my family out of here and I'll take a deep breath. Until then, well.... It just won't happen until I know they are safe."

"Well then, we have some work to do. Get your lists going because we leave in the morning," Chloe told her as she gave her another hug.

115

"You did what?!" Emma asked with a bit more enthusiasm than she had wanted.

"She wanted to go talk to some of her crew and I never thought about the cabin," Tommy replied.

"That's odd. Her staff isn't even out there. They have all moved in closer to the house being they are all city folks and not liking being in the woods. Did she tell you that? That she had people out there still?"

"Yes, why? You might as well cough it up because I can see the wheels spinning in that pretty head of yours," Tommy said to Emma.

"Something is telling me to be very cautious when it comes to her. Things aren't as they seem. You might want to think about that yourself there…what is it… Oh, Chulo," Emma said with a snicker.

Tommy took Emma in his arms, "I think you might be just a tad jealous Senora Montalvo," Tommy said with a smile.

"You need to be worried if I'm not," Emma returned as she wrapped her arms around her husband, nuzzling her face into the side of his neck.

"She saw the blood on the floor," Tommy said.

"I could care less."

"You really aren't feeling all rainbows and unicorns for this woman are you?" Tommy asked, a bit surprised. Emma never had a problem with anyone but the sheriff, so it was a concern when she did. Her intuition had never been wrong in the past. In the past though, none of those people lived under his roof.

"Something is just gnawing at me and I can't pinpoint it yet. Just be very careful around her and her people…which by the way, are not in any of the cabins," Emma said.

"Maybe it's time for them to move on," Tom said, feeling uneasy about his guests.

"Been thinking about that. Not going to be that easy. They have set up base camp here. They aren't going to be in a hurry to leave anytime soon."

"Maybe, maybe not. What if we could get her to move in town?" Tom asked.

"Not sure why she would even consider it. She has it made out here."

"I need to go talk with Ben tomorrow. Maybe invite him out for dinner and get him more involved in what's going on out here," Ed said with a smile. He had an idea and for once, it was his idea and not Emma's!

"Ugh. You know how much I loathe that man!" Emma replied. "But I like your train of thought Mr. Montalvo," she said as she nuzzled the tender area of his neck right below his ear.

"I aim to please ma'am," Tommy quipped, feeling his insides puddle into a mess of hot lust.

"Oh really? Let's see about that," Emma smirked as she backed him up until his legs hit the side of their bed and he fell backwards.

116

Ben was sitting at his desk when he saw the back end of a horse stroll by his window. "What the heck?" he murmured to himself.

Rolling his chair to the window, he looked out and the horse was now tied up in the front of the building sans rider. Since the grid had gone down, he had seen bicycles in use more than anything, first time for a horse though. Made sense, though. Maybe he could use this somehow in his plans. There was only so much gasoline to go around for the motorbikes without the semis running. All big rigs had stopped delivering immediately. There were only two vehicles that were able to run in town and that was it. Joey, the local mechanic, was trying to figure out the problem but without parts to order he was limited in what he could do. Horses, on the other hand, could be a big help with his deputies.

"Susan!" he yelled out.

"Yes sir," Susan sang out as she entered the room.

"Can you find out who owns horses in and around town?"

"Sir?"

"We may be able to get the deputies up and around to keep an eye on things better in town if we can get them more mobile. Consider it a return to the wild west," he said.

"Yes sir. I will see what I can do," she said leaving his office.

Ben left his office and made his way towards the front door. Walking into where the duty desk was, he glanced out into the lobby to see Tom Caraballo standing there.

Raising an eyebrow, Ben was surprised to see him there. As a matter of fact, he couldn't remember Tom ever being at the station before.

Curiosity getting the better of him, Ben opened the door to the common room where Tom was standing "Everything OK out at the farm?"

"Oh, hey Ben. Came in looking for you, actually."

"How can I help you?" Ben asked.

"Well, Nina. I mean Ms. Varga and I were talking about what's going on. This goes way above my pay scale. I mentioned that you should be involved in future discussions and she agreed."

"Oh really?" Ben slid out with a smile.

"How about you come out to the farm later this afternoon. Emma is fixing for a sit down around two.
Would be great if you could make it."

"Sounds good. I could actually head out now as it's almost one now. Need a lift?" Ben asked.

"Thanks but I rode in on one of the horses."

"Oh! That was you? I thought I saw a horse stroll past the window. Might have to check them out while I am at your house. See what you have."

"Ya, that you will have to take up with Emma," Tom said "And I can tell you hell would freeze over before Emma would part from any of her herd."

"That could be arranged," Ben thought to himself as he showed Tom out.

117

The black Jaguar looked remarkably out of place driving up the dirt drive. Nina's men stopped it as soon as it had pulled off the main road and after a brief but vibrant conversation with the contents of the vehicle, let it pass to the main house.

Emma turned as she heard the car approach and watched as it stopped in front of the garage, dwarfed by the military trucks parked there also. The passenger side door opened and a spiked heel emerged followed closely behind by an exorbitantly attired black woman.

"Oh Lordy," Emma giggled as she set down the basket of eggs and started walking towards the car.

"Hey boss lady!" Emma heard from behind the car.

"Jay! Tiffany! I am so glad you are here! I will admit, though, with all the excitement, I forgot when you were coming exactly."

"Everything OK, Boss?" Jay asked.

"Oh, we have a lot to talk about," Emma said, giving Jay a quick wink.

"Maybe we should find a hotel in town," Tiffany quickly added.

"Not sure that's a good idea. How did you guys get here? Which route?"

"We came down from Cleveland. We made an unscheduled trip to Niagara Falls before we headed down here and took 90 along the lake. Why?"

"Let's get you both settled and then we can talk. Come on into the house, you both must be famished," Emma said.

"You cooking, Miss Emma?" Tiffany asked "Do you have any of that cornbread you made before?"

"I think I can make that happen!" Emma returned with a smile.

118

They had been walking for over two hours, back towards the direction they had previously driven, when Angie sat Scott down on the side of the road propping him up to sit against a tree. This wasn't going to work at all. It was taking too long for Scott to make any real distance in his condition. He was in too bad of shape to do any walking, let alone another couple miles.

"Drink this," she said handing him his canteen. "I need you to stay here while I go back to the trailer, can you do that without an argument?"

Scott had no energy for a fight left in him. He could barely comprehend what she was saying to him. "Ya, whatever," was all he could muster as a reply.

"Scott," Angie said with striking amount of dominance in her voice. "I need you to stay awake until I get back. Can you do that for me?"

Looking into her eyes, Scott was back in Emma's living room. Back where he realized he first loved the woman kneeling before him. "Pull it back," he said, hallucinations dominating his mind as he first saw her trying to light a fire.

Placing a kiss on his lips, Angie made him as comfortable as she could. "Drink, Scott," she said as she lifted the water to his mouth. "I will be right back so don't go anywhere." "Please God, watch over him," she prayed as she stood up. "This shouldn't take long." she said as she ran back to where they had just come from.

119

Angie did double time back to the trailer; luckily they hadn't gotten too far. She had a plan and only hoped she could get what she needed. She slowed as she came to the small hill in the road right before the trailer had overturned. Walking over to the side, she jumped down into the drainage ditch that ran beside the road. Lying down, she edged her way up to the top of the crest of the hill and watched for any signs of movement.

Nothing. Not taking any chances, she walked a couple feet into the woods and followed parallel to the road until she came close to the trailer. She remembered where she had left the body of the stranger. Hoping to still find him under the tarp, she walked around the corner of the trailer and peeked around.
The lump was still there. Letting out a brief release of air, she quickly moved to the back of the trailer. Working quickly, she found what she was looking for. Pulling her massage table from the back of the table, she quickly took it out of the carry bag. Opening it up, she ripped the legs off the bottom, just leaving the bed part itself.

"This isn't going to work, damn it. This is too hard to pull," she mumbled to herself as she glanced around the box. Sticking out from underneath the sofa, she spotted the shiny metal blades of the sled she used to long to use as a child. Sadly, snow didn't happen often in Tennessee, at least not in the southern part, so the sled was severely neglected. Pulling it out of the trailer, she sat the top of the massage table on the sled. "Better than nothing," she thought.

Grabbing the rope that was used to pull the sled, she started back to Scott with her improvised contraption. This would enable him to lie down while she pulled him the couple more miles that they needed to go.

He needed medical help quickly, she thought. His color was pale and he was beginning to hallucinate. Not good signs. Thinking back to when the truck had stopped, Angie felt a sense of impending doom rise up from the depth of her soul. What the hell had happened? What was going on out there? Quickening her steps back, Angie almost missed the barely visible cloud hovering in the distance. It had to be Memphis, she thought. Oh God, what was going on, she thought. Her steps became more hurried as she got closer to where she had left Scott. Her eyes forward, she should be coming up on him soon. Where did she leave him? Faster she walked, "Where was he, maybe a little bit further," she thought.

The flash caught her eye and made her stop dead in her tracks.

"Oh no!" she moaned.

There beside the tree, barely visible in the grass was Scott's metal canteen glistening from the sunlight, but the man she loved was not there.

120

Walking Jay and Tiffany into the house, Emma was glad they were there. Even with a house full of people, these two were on Emma's side, which gave her a sense of relief. While Nina's people were polite, Emma felt like they were always watching her. Giving her a little chuckle, Emma thought how ironic it was that she felt like they were keeping an eye on her considering how much snooping she had been doing on them. Saps couldn't find the target if it was right in front of them, Emma thought.

Seated in the kitchen, the two guests were enjoying the lunch that Emma had quickly put together.
"How did you get past the guards at the end of the drive?" Emma asked.

Jay chuckled.

"I have my ways" Tiffany said with a wicked smile.

"Ways? You call that ways? Really? This girl here whipped out a can of Angry Black Lesbian on them like a pro!" Jay said in amusement.

"I will take that as a compliment," Tiffany said with a grin.

"Wish I could have seen that!" Emma added, the three women enjoying the hilarity of the situation.

"So what exactly is going on here?" Jay asked.

"There was a small localized EMP that was detonated near Memphis," Emma answered.

"What?! Are you serious?" Both women shrieked.

"I don't think this is anywhere over yet either. My guess is another one will be going off soon, east coast or west, I am not sure yet but I would pick somewhere in California with all the recent quakes there. They pinpointed the Madrid Fault area to try and cover what it really was with some BS about a quake. Being localized like it was, it knocked power out in a lot of the country but really hit from about here south toward ground zero. Any kind of electronics that were not protected got fried. "

"Is that why we didn't notice it was because we were outside the zone?" Tiffany asked.

"Would be my guess," Emma replied. "Parts of the country lost power but cars and some electronics would still work. With us being here, we are getting info from our guests," Emma added using air quotes around the word "guests."

"How bad do you think they got hit down there?" Jay asked.

"No idea for certain but it has to be bad. That area was a mess to begin with and if they hit near the area I think they were targeting, I'm surprised that the Mississippi isn't flowing backwards."

"What? No way," Jay said.

"It's possible. There's a collapsed salt dome down there in Louisiana that has been leaking methane gas for a while now. They hit that area and it could cause a quake like the one that happened back in the early 1800s that did in fact cause the Mississippi to run backwards. Hell, Tiff, based upon reports that I have seen, it could split the country in half and open up the Great Lakes down into the Gulf if that's what they really wanted to do," Emma said.

"I'm thinking Chicago is out of the question," Tiffany said to Jay.

"I'm not trying to cause panic here but I have to be honest with you. I'm thinking if we are this far into the game, New York is out of the question," Emma added.

Jay looked at Tiffany. "Mon Dieu," Tiffany let escape under her breath.

"Plan?" Jay said, looking at Emma.

"OH! You know I always have a plan!" Emma said, smiling at her two guests.

"That's why you're the Boss!" Jay replied.

121

The pregnant girl looked at the stick protruding from the back of the man. Her best guess was that it had punctured his lung to some degree. Based upon his conditions, he needed medical attention immediately or he would die. Now was her time to show her dad she wasn't the screw up he thought she was. Her mind drifted back to a few months prior to when she was still in medical school...

"What the flock of seagulls," Ridley thought as she received her grade. Seriously?! I wake up at 7 a.m. to walk 6 blocks to sit here and take this bullshit from this over-aged, has been, can't find a job so I have to teach, Volkswagen-driving lesbian? Hmpf! Well, whatever! OK, ya, so maybe I should have studied a little more instead of...of... oh wait... there's a party tonight at Elrich Dorm! Yea! My life has been saved!

Ridley spent the rest of her day meandering from one class to another, much like she did every day. Study? Oh heck no, she was here to socialize, or "network" as she liked to call it. One can never have enough friends, now can one! If her social calendar was not full, Ridley felt more of a failure than when she flunked out of one of the $6,000 classes her daddy spent his money on.

Lately, though, Ridley has been feeling uneasy… she just couldn't put her finger on the problem. Maybe a night in would cure what ailing her? It couldn't hurt. But just one night. Anything more than that would be detrimental to her social life. What would people think if Ridley Scott was not out being seen with all the other beautiful people?

With her last class over, Ridley made her way back to her dorm. Too tired to even eat, she melted into her bed and was asleep almost immediately. Sleep was restless. She tossed and turned for a while and finally fell into a deep pool of darkness… fire flaring all around her… screams… oh the screams… covering her ears, she started to run but the screams kept coming after her. Why wouldn't they stop? She noticed she was running through a forest… tree limbs stinging her as they whipped against her body. She had to keep going… she had to get away from the screaming. Suddenly the forest opened up into a meadow… there before her hordes of people… aimlessly walking to and fro. Suddenly the screaming returned…Ridley covered her eyes from the penetrating shrill and noticed the zombies were all looking at her now…arms raised they slowly were approaching her…reaching for her…

Ridley sat upright in bed, hands still over her ears, when she realized she was the one screaming.

Drenched in sweat, she fumbled for her phone and dialed. "Daddy, help me," she whimpered.

Just days later, her father had her pulled from school and back home so she couldn't waste any more of his hard-earned money, as he put it. A few days after that and Ridley learned that all of her partying days had come to an abrupt halt. Ridley was with child.

Now, the soon-to-be mama had to help the man lying on her kitchen table. Her brothers had found him earlier as he was laying along the side of the road almost dead. If she were to redeem herself in her father's eyes, now was her time to do it.

"Mom, I need to get into your stash," Ridley said to her mother.

"I assumed so. Just tell me what you need, little one," Ridley's mom replied.

Ridley, for once in her life, really saw the woman standing before her. She had always thought her mom was a few screws loose with all her crazy antics and even weirder friends. It hit Ridley like a ton of bricks that everything her mother had been talking about was coming true.

"I love you, Mom," Ridley said peering into the woman's eyes.

"I love you too, little one," her mother responded as both women set about saving the man's life.

122

Megan walked through the house she had called a home one last time. Each room held a specific memory, some good, some not so good. Walking into the room she had shared with her husband, she looked at the bed that they had shared since their wedding. Standing at the footboard, she closed her eyes and felt his arms around her. It was hard to let go, even after learning what she had about him after his death. She had married him with the intention of loving him forever. She would, she owed him that. He screwed up. He was human. It was easier to forgive him now than if he was still with them, but forgiven or not, it was time to move on and away from this… from him.

Walking out of the house, she closed the front door and locked it behind her. She was walking away from everything she had given her life for over the last few years. Taking what little she could with the small amount of room they had in the RV, she knew that in a small way she would miss this place, miss her things.

She stepped into the RV and checked that each child was securely fasted in their seats. Robbie would be riding right behind her with her mother close by in case he needed something faster than she could get. She would be riding in the front with Chloe driving to help with navigation and directions. Michael was outside getting ready to lead the way on his motorcycle. The plan was to get as far as they could today. That should get them up into the mountains and ready to descend into Colorado by nightfall. They would make the drop down into Denver in the morning, as the RV would be tricky to handle coming down out of the mountains.

Stopping at the last gas station out of town, the RV, motorcycle and extra gas cans strapped inside the back rail of the motor home all were filled. Chloe was a natural at driving the big rig and Megan had the maps out and highlighted. The trio was off and destined to overtake the mountains as the sun met them as they approached the summit. Pulling over to the side of the road, Megan unloaded the kids for one last look at what lay to the west of the Rockies.

"Beautiful, isn't it?" Megan said breaking the silence.

"Wait until you see what's on the other side," Michael said.

"Never been farther east than this very spot," Chloe chimed in. "This is going to be an adventure."

As everyone was facing west, a bright fireball erupted and sucked everything in its vicinity towards the sky. The enormous mass ascended towards the clouds, rolling over itself until it resembled a mushroom.

"Get in the RV!" Michael screamed.

The women were standing there in disbelief, the children oblivious to what had happened.

"Chloe! Get everyone into the RV now!" Michael yelled again.

"Chloe!" Michael said, now grabbing her arm.

"Wha…What was that?!" she said as she snapped out of her trance.

"It was a nuclear detonation. We need to get out of here now," he replied.

Shaking her head in agreement, she corralled everyone into the motor home.

Putting the large vehicle into drive, Chloe's hands were shaking as she pulled the RV back onto the road.

"This is worse than I thought," she said, looking at Megan.

Far below them, the city of San Diego lay in ruins.

123

"So what's really the deal here, boss lady?" Jay asked Emma as they strolled out to the barn. "Shit got real, didn't it?"

"You know it. At least now you know I'm not completely off my rocker," Emma replied with a smirk.

"I'll admit, I did question what came out of your mouth sometimes, but I figure if I had to have someone's back, it would be yours. After all, you have one of the best grandma tushies I've seen!" Jay said with a laugh.

"I've missed you," Emma said with a sigh. "Not everyone gets my sense of humor like you do. This has got to suck big time for Tiffany, though. Just don't let her near the chickens! Remember that time we had her thinking they would peck her toes off and eat them!"

"Oh ya! I almost forgot about that! I've never laughed so hard in my life! The look on her face was priceless when that big old chicken came strolling up onto your back porch! She didn't wear sandals for months after that!"

Memories came flooding back until both girls had to cling to each other to stand up. Tears of laughter were streaming down both their faces that if anyone had seen them they might have taken them for being in dire distress. Quite the opposite. Emma started to massage her cheeks as they hurt so badly from laughing so hard.

"Sucks that it took all this mess to get Tiffany to visit out here, but I know there is more going on than you're telling anyone. What's the deal? You have that look," Jay asked, turning a bit serious.

"What fricken look are you talking about? The shit hit the fan" and all hell is about to break loose' look or the 'I've got a bitch living in my house that's putting the moves on my husband look,' or maybe it's the 'My country has gone to shit and I don't know how to save her,' look.... Take your pick Jay, few more where they came from too," Emma replied with a bit more tension then she had intended.

"What do you need me to do?"

"Just being here helps. A lot of things I can't share with just anyone. I've freaked a lot of people out over the years just by opening their eyes. Once they go down that path, there's no turning back and a lot of people can't handle waking up to the truth that's out there. It also helps that you have balls of steel!" Emma said with a giggle, breaking the intensity of the moment.

"Ha! Ha! Yes, balls of steel all right!"

"Woman, you got bigger balls than most men I know! Glad to have them stationed here!" Emma laughed.

"I'm thinking that Ms. Senator or whatever her name is needs to feel her balls squeezed for messing with my boss lady. What does Tomás think of all of this?"

"Oh, you know Tommy. Ego took a trip but he recovered nicely."

"That man loves you and only you, you know that, right?"

"Yes, I know."

"Good, 'cause I've never seen a man more smitten in my life. You should work that a bit more, get yourself some diamonds or something, girl!"

"That might work in your world," Emma replied, once again the laughter returning. "But I'm not sure how my chickens would react to such flash and glamor. It's time you lose all that big city attitude and come play in the poop for a while. It humbles a girl's soul...and from what I hear, it's good for your complexion!"

"You can try that shit with Tiffany; don't forget who you are talking to here," Jay said as she opened the barn door and gestured Emma inside.

124

Ridley finally sat down, her back and legs giving out beneath her. She was still surprised at how carrying such a small being inside of her could zap so much energy from her body. Bending slightly forward, she reached around and started to massage the tension from her back as she stretched upward. Finally feeling some release, she stood back up and went back to work.

The man who was brought in wasn't in as bad of shape as she had initially thought. Yes, he had some kind of element protruding from his back but other than that his vitals were strong. Looking more intently at the object, the look on her face spoke volumes.

"What do you think it is?" Ridley's mom asked her.

"If I didn't know better, I would think

that it's the handle of a toothbrush!"

"Really?"

"Problem is how much of it is in his body still. Obviously this is the handle, so is the head with the bristles inside?" Ridley asked more to herself than anyone.

"Man, I wish we had an X-ray machine here."

"Think we can stabilize him and take him to the clinic?"

"I doubt if anything is working down there. No sense moving him. Did you ever find out what was going on?" Ridley asked her mother.

"Sorta. Not entirely as pieces are coming in but it's not looking good." Her mother said. "Once we get communications back up at full tilt, we will know more."

"I love you, mom."

"Oh, I love you too baby. Things will be OK, you have to trust me. We have enough supplies to make it through any extended period of time."

"I know. Maybe it's with the baby coming but life has really changed, hasn't it?" Ridley asked her mother.

"Yes. Very much so. But we will get through whatever is thrown our way and it's our duty to help as many people as we can get through what's ahead as best we can."

"OK, back to work. We need to remove this object and get this guy back on his feet. I'm sure someone is missing him about right now," Ridley said as she lowered her head and started to re-examine his wound.

125

Angie dropped to her knees in the grass beside the tree where she had left Scott. "God, where did he go?" she muttered out to herself. He couldn't have made it far. Hell, she hadn't even been gone that long. Panic started to drift upwards through her body at the realization of how alone she was. All of her belongings were dumped all over the road a couple miles back. No one knew where she was and with no communications, she couldn't get in touch with anyone. "What the hell am I doing?" she blurted out. Scott was out there, hurt and needing help and all she could do was sit here and feel sorry for herself! Really? Was that all she was good for? Poor, poor Angie.

Standing up, she squared her shoulders. "Alright Chicky, time to get busy." Looking around at the area she left him she started looking for signs of which direction he may have taken. Slowly walking around the base of the tree, there were no signs other than heading out towards the road. Walking back in that direction, she knelt where he had been seated and slowly moved the grass aside and looked deeper for anything that could give her a clue. Ever so lightly pressed into the dirt was a set of footprints. Just the heel print of a boot. Following it, the imprint took her closer to the road in the direction that they had just driven past a day ago.

Looking in the direction the tracks went, she tried to remember what they had passed. A farm, there was a farm a few miles back. After that there was a rundown house that had a bunch of trash around it that had motorcycles parked outside. Nothing else much after that until they came into town but that was miles and miles away. Had he walked back to the farm? Had he hallucinated and taken off thinking he was going somewhere he recognized? Hell, were these even his tracks?

Walking along the edge of the road a dozen steps ahead, she kneeled down again. Running her hand over the tracks, her fingers identified the hoof print before her mind did. Horses.

126

He lifted his nose to the breeze and inhaled all the scents surrounding him. A hunter, his ability to separate the bouquets presented to him was like a magician shuffling cards until he magically found the one he needed.

He was used to the pack he lived with. Humans could learn from that. Many have it sunk deep into their skull that survival was about going it alone, not realizing that humans were just as much pack animals as the wolf. The sheep and the wolf mentality has overrun the preparedness population and people need to get past that, to learn from the wolf.

Emma journeyed down this path not long ago. She listened intently one day to the man on the radio when she still lived in the city. The full force of what he was saying sunk deep into her heart and made her weep. What can you do when your vote doesn't count, when your garden gets bulldozed, when you feel like your back is up against the wall? How do you fight back?

Is there a path to less intrusion, to less taxes, to more freedom? Where is the path? Who is going to go down the path first? Sadly, those people are ridiculed by the very hand trying to help them, those who want to take the very journey themselves but don't have the guts to take the first step.

Wrong is wrong. Wrong is out there and lives among us. When do you get tired of voting for the lesser of the two evils? Wrong cannot be fought unless you understand what you are fighting against. Wrong can be fought against by using its own energy against itself. Let the system destroy itself. Accelerate the process by backing your resources out of the system. The system may not collapse in your lifetime, but you have the ability to help set up future generations, your children's children, to have a better life even further away from the system.

Turn your back and distance yourself from the propaganda being spewed from the mouths of those creating the system. Turn your back and take a step. Now take another step. Stop enabling the enemy by being there and let nature take its course. Wars are won by using arms and information, with information being the more powerful of the two. How many ways are you supporting the system by everyday life? Is money as important as you think it is, as you are made to think it is? If they needed more money would they just not make more? So why do they need yours other than that they can use it to control you? Every generation that has collapsed has come out the other side with a new system. Stop holding on to the one we currently have.

Step back and evaluate your own alliances. You cannot find a solution to the problem from the very entity that created the problem in the first place. Step outside your thinking and build alliances of others to fight at your side.

Learn skills and develop the knowledge you need to enable yourself to live outside the trappings of society. Evaluate your needs from your wants. Be honest with yourself. Stack the deck in your favor and teach the knowledge and skills you have to those who come after you. To your children. To the children who will wish to run free in your pack.

Never call theft justice, never call captivity freedom and never equate safety with freedom. Never become an empathic sheep. Stop acting like you deserve the protection of the brave. For every one wolf, there are thousands of sheep. More people need to wake up to what is truly going on. Eyes need to be open. The issues that we are enduring right now are because we have earned it. Earned it by buying into the bullshit and compromising our principles. Accept that the deck is stacked against you; it's the first step in moving forward. It's time to take back the tool of your enemy, little by little, day by day. If you face a full frontal assault, you give support to the battle itself. Walk away. Withdraw and let nature take its course. Trust the human, that if you don't attack the being but plant a seed instead, their eyes will slowly open. Stop telling people what to do with the information that you give them, which you know to be true, and simply provide it to them. Let them chew it up and allow them the benefit of feeling the truth on their own tongue. And then, ask what they think you should do about the information. And when they ask you because they don't know, just know that it's time to keep talking to get more people to open up.

Take a step. Alone if you have to. Just take that step and show others that it can be done, that you can move towards the freedom that runs through the veins of the wolf. Others will notice. Keep moving. Keep talking. Before you know it, you will build a pack of like-minded people around you. Over time, your pack will grow and branch out to create other packs. Don't wait for those who don't want to step out. Let them be and move forward. You will be surprised by the wake you leave behind you when you start moving. Others will get caught up in it. Be a point of neutrality. A point of safety. A beacon of hope.

Her scent haunted him. Freedom haunted him. It bound him to this place as the overwhelming thirst to peregrinate the land dripped from his jowls into the hard ground below. His ground. Our ground. Lowering his head, he sniffed the dirt. It was getting harder to find her and little by little he moved closer. One day, with cunning patience, he would possess that which he desired most. One day, our children will be able to breathe free because of that which we help build now. If only we were brave enough to take the first steps. To release the bonds that bind us from the trappings of society that have been used against us to chain us down and use us as someone's slave. As sheep.

127

Chloe stared at the back of the man on the motorcycle. Strong, lean muscles extended out and gripped the handlebars. His hair curled over the collar of his jacket he sliced through the invisible forces and charged forth as a knight on his mighty steed.

Chloe quickly sat up and shook her head back and forth trying to remove the image. "What the hell is wrong with me?" she thought to no one but herself.

"You OK?" Megan asked from the driver's seat.

"Ya, must have drifted off a bit. Sorry," Chloe returned.

"Probably wouldn't hurt to take a nap. You've been driving nonstop and could use a break. Close your eyes and try and rest," Megan said, unknowingly putting a dose of motherly authority in her voice.

"You sure?"

"Yes. It's flat and reasonably straight across the top up here. Funny thing is I always thought you drove up one side of the mountain and down. I didn't realize there was like 300 miles between the up and down part. Seriously though, close your eyes and take a break. You're driving this thing down the other side and I need you to be wide awake and alert for that," Chloe added.

Chloe shot her a quick smile and settled back into the seat. Closing her eyes before she saw Michael again, she started counting sheep.

Up ahead, Michael steered the motorcycle with ease. The road was smooth and the scenery breathtaking as they headed up through the Sierra Nevada Mountains and into the Great Basin. One day he would come back here and take more time taking it all in. Right now, though, he needed to get these women to the farm. They would be safe and well taken care of there until the world sorted itself back out. Fucking idiots, he thought. Greed corrupted the best of men. Right now these men were quickly destroying everything he cared about. Based on his observations over San Diego earlier, he could guess that it had been pretty much completely destroyed. "What else was gone?" he wondered.

128

The group stopped for a quick break alongside the road they had been traveling on for miles. Not taking the chance of pulling over in a populated area, Michael felt more in control with vast openness around him. tomorrow they would drive down the Colorado Rockies and make their way east to Ohio. Right now, though, he was happy to be off the bike and getting some feeling back in his ass.

Setting his pack against the side of his bike, he pulled out a plastic bag full of papers and maps. Detailed instructions were written down. Looking at the distance across the top of the mountains, his best guess was that they should be to their first stop for breakfast and a refueling. Scanning for the corresponding notecard, he pulled out a small handheld radio and turned the dial to the on position. Dialing in the correct channel, he pressed the button on the side of the unit and spoke quietly.

"Adelina One Copy."

Releasing the button, static noise filled the air. Trying not to let the women in the RV hear, he put his back between the motor home and the radio and depressed the button again.

"Adelina One, Come In"

The static was quickly interrupted by a woman's voice. "Adelina One Copy."

Breathing out a sigh of relief, Mike quickly responded. "Bypass Adelina One. Resume at Zero Eight Hundred Shawna Two Over."

"Adelina One Out," came the female voice, followed by silence. Tucking the papers back into the plastic bag and securing the radio, Mike grabbed a quick drink of stale water from his canteen. Walking around the RV, he examined every inch of it for any kind of damage while the women were inside making dinner. He wasn't about to set foot inside the vast metal box with that much hormone imbalance going on. Kicking the tires, he was grasping at things now to make himself look busy.

A shadow crossed over his face as he looked up into the window to see Chloe walk towards the back of the camper. His eyes followed her form as she drifted into the shadows taking in all the less than subtle feminine aspects of her body. Kicking the tire again, he let out a yelp as he missed and his shin met the underside of the motor home. Oh boy, he needed to get his emotions under control. Limping back around to where his bike was, he pulled his pack off the back. Walking out from where the bus was, he found a spot to make camp that gave him a good vantage point just in case anyone came visiting.

He jerked his head up hearing the door open on the RV.

"Hey, you hungry?" he heard Chloe yell out to him.

Watching her bound down the step and walk towards him, he felt a tinge of excitement pulse in his crotch.

"Hey," her voice softened as she approached him. "You OK?"

"Yes, fine. Just tired. Everyone settled down inside?" he asked, motioning with his chin towards the motor home.

"Megan's mom is amazing! She is like super mom or something," she said with such a vibrant attitude that Mike had to wonder if he was talking to the same woman.

"Here," she added, handing him a plate of food. "Figured you might like to have this out here under the stars."

"Ya, thanks!" he said, taking the plate from her.

"So what's the plan, Michael? I know it isn't going to be all roses since we don't know what's going on down there," she said referring to their descent in the morning.

"We play it by ear. Our biggest issue is getting across the Mississippi. I figure if we head north through Nebraska we can skim along the bottom of the state into Iowa just north of the Missouri line. Let's just hope that the bridges are all intact. Gonna be a bitch swimming this time of year." Chloe didn't know whether to believe him or not. "You sure you know where we are going?" "Like the back of my hand," Michael answered.

129

Michael had grown up on a farm, and being the only male child, he bore the brunt of being the youngest also. He was essentially at the mercy of his sister. Twelve years spanned the difference in age between the two. When his sister was old enough to move out and get married, he was just learning how to hunt with their father. It was much like being an only child.

His father, their father was an avid outdoorsman. Michael remembered his sister showing him pictures of their father usually with some kind of wild game that had been killed. There were photos of the man as a child, always barefoot and with some kind of improvised weapon. Mike used to stare at the photos and envision what he was like as a young man.

When Mike turned 13, his father died from cancer. It was the hardest thing Michael had ever gone through in his young life, to see the man he idolized lose his battle against such a horrible, painful disease. Mike cried at the funeral in front of everyone and saw the people whisper. He was now the man of the family so how could he sit there crying? He needed to be tough, to be strong for his mom and his sister.

He spent way too many years after his father's death pissed off at the world. Feeling like there was no way out of his life in a small town, he joined the Army against his mother's wishes. Bottom line was that he was running away and he never wanted to look back.

A country boy out to seek his way in the world, once his superiors learned how good he was at tracking, they recruited him into Pathfinder's School. There he learned how to set up and operate drop zones, pickup zones, and helicopter landing sites for airborne operations, air resupply operations, and other air operations in support of the ground unit commander. He was the first line of defense and it was his duty to make sure the men who followed in behind him once he made the area secure and gave the word would be safe from enemy fire.

He learned a lot from the military, including how to be a brother. He had a sister he had barely seen since he was little and his mother was still alive but that was about it. It took a while but he realized he needed someone to watch his back like he did for others, and before long he had made long-lasting friendships with his peers. He would have given his life for any one of them, and that was hard for Mike to admit. Tough exterior at all times, no tears, he never wanted to be seen as a pansy again.

Now he was being questioned by this small imp of a woman standing before him. He felt the old feelings of anger brewing beneath the surface diminish as he saw the fear in her eyes. Those eyes locked onto his, losing him in the glossy moss-colored pools of glass and bore down into his soul looking for places to repair, to heal. She intrigued him. Watching the emotions dance across her face somehow reminded him of home, of wanting to grab onto her and protect her from all the cruelness of the world.

"Hey, stop looking so depressing. Where did all the spunk go from the bar?" he finally asked.

"Spunk. Interesting way to describe me. It's one thing to be a bit spunky when you are responsible for no one but yourself," she said, drifting off and looking at the motor home.

"But you feel responsible for these people you just met?" he asked.

"I guess I do," she replied, realizing for the first time it was the closest she had come to having a sister. "I like Megan and her family, a lot. We need to make sure nothing happens to them until you get us to my contact."

"Yes ma'am," Mike said smiling at her. Her contact. Hmpf! This should be interesting, Michael thought.

130

The sun streaked its way through the cracks in the boards and played with her eyelashes. Wanting nothing more than to roll back over and duck under the covers in protest, she tried to open her eyes. Mornings were always her favorite time of the day and today she wanted to just stay where she was and snuggle up against her husband. Raising her arm up and over, she began to turn when the searing pain reminded her she was only dreaming.

Her eyes flew open as the nausea caught up to her. Turning as best she could without jarring her leg, she relieved the stress in her stomach on the dirt floor. Tears streamed down her face as the acids in her stomach ate at the lining of her throat. The wrenching subsiding, Shelby reached into her apron and found the handkerchief she always kept there. Wiping her mouth, the memories of what happened the day before started flooding her mind.

The kids! Sitting up, she tried to turn her leg and was met with a blinding pain. Yelling for help would set the animals off in a scurry and she would likely be trampled. Frantically looking around, there was nothing at all she could use to get up. The walls of the barn were smooth and offered no opportunity for grasping. Shelby sank back in despair. She had to get up!

"OH Bella, how could you do this to me?" Shelby whispered out. The horse heard her name leave Shelby's lips and turned her head towards the woman. There, dangling from Bella's halter was one of the rein straps.

It was her only hope! Making kissing noises, Shelby gently tried to coax the pony over to where Shelby was sitting. "Gentle girl. That's it. Come on over here to mama," Shelby cooed. Bella clumsily meandered towards Shelby, making the woman nervous. "Please don't step on me again," Shelby breathed through her mouth. Shelby stuck her hands into her apron pocket like she was looking for a treat for the horse and it was enough to bring Bella closer. "That a girl. Easy. Easy. Almost," Shelby prayed.

The strap swung in front of Shelby as Bella brought her head down to investigate what Shelby had hiding in her hand. It was enough to allow Shelby to grab the rein. "Oh God this is going to hurt," Shelby muttered. Quickly taking her apron off, she tried to secure her swollen leg as best as she could. She then stuck the handkerchief in her mouth. Shelby was going to use it to keep from screaming out and scaring the rest of the animals. The last thing she needed was Bella bolting from fright. Pulling Bella's head down with the rein, Shelby was able to grab hold of the halter around Bella's face. Misty tugged on the halter as hard as she could as the horse tried to raise her head. Misty, holding on for dear life, cried out in agony as it was enough to bring Shelby up off of the floor. Sweat started to bead across Shelby's forehead as she became vertical. Grabbing a handful of Bella's mane, Shelby rested against the horse until the dizziness subsided.

Shelby opened her mouth and let the handkerchief fall onto the ground. Tears began to fall as the determination within the woman raged on. She was up, that was all she needed. Walking Bella over to the door, Shelby hopped with one leg trying to not use the damaged one. Opening the door, Shelby yelled out for her oldest child. "It's going to be OK," she said to herself. "It's going to be OK."

131

Megan snapped the binder closed and rested her head on top. It was one thing to be prepared. It was entirely different to be prepared with a special needs child. Being Robbie's mother had stretched her mind past the point of exhaustion trying to cover all the bases for his survival. And he would survive, Megan had promised herself. Even if it was the last thing she did.

Before they left home, Megan had attached homemade signs on each of the windows on the motor home. Heaven forbid if anything had happened to her, but if someone found them, they would need to know how to interact with her son.

The decal itself instructed the First Responders to check in the glove box for more information about her family, specifically about her youngest son. Robbie would not show pain if he happened to be in any so the medical team would need to take extra precautions with him.

"Oh Robbie," Megan sighed.

Months earlier the doctor had tried to convince her to give him a chip under his skin so they could track him if he attempted to run away as he got older. A child with Robbie's issue was known to run away before they would let anyone know there was a problem. The chip itself would not be noticeable and the earlier in his little life the doctors administered it, the easier it would be on his little body. He would adjust easier than if he was older and fought against the intrusion as kids with his diagnosis often did. It was a simple procedure. A simple prick of a needle would slip the device under his skin. They would monitor it for a while just in case an infection would set in, but it was a 30/70 chance for that.

Megan remembered sitting in the doctor's office just staring at the attending physician as they described the procedure. Lifesaving, they had called it. Hell! It was all the rage with the dementia patients, from the way they talked about its benefits. You would almost have to be insane not to take it!

She had gone home to think about it. Trusting her gut for a change, Megan realized that any time she was feeling overwhelmed was the wrong time to make a decision. And this was a huge one. While she understood the benefits of being able to not only track Robbie if he did run away in the future but also have his entire medical history implanted on his body so any medical facility could access it, something in her gut told her no. Something in her gut just didn't feel right.

After she had tucked the kids in bed later that night, Megan made herself a cup of tea and sat down at her computer. Article after article described the invasion that Robbie would endure. While the articles essentially described the same process to insert the chip itself, each one had a different spin on it. It was like the creators couldn't decide what came first, the chicken or the egg, and so spun a web to ensnare anyone who walked by.

The nagging feeling was getting worse the deeper that Megan dug into information about the implant.
Shutting the top of her computer, Megan backed away from the table. Not again. It was bad enough that she had caused Robbie's autism by not educating herself, but she wasn't about to make the same mistake twice.

Walking down the hallway, she stopped at his doorway. Nestled without a care in the world with his favorite stuffed toy, Robbie was at peace when he was asleep. With what little sleep he got anymore. He had been known to stay awake for over 20 hours at a time, which caused him to become quite agitated to the point he would just cry. Too young to communicate, Megan was learning to pick up on the little signals he would put out and she would try to give him as much comfort as possible without causing him more distress. It was a balancing act not for the faint of heart.

Silently approaching his crib, she gently laid his blanket over his bare legs. It was an action she performed multiple times each night as he was constantly moving, even in his sleep. Saying a prayer over him, she turned to leave when she noticed the baby monitor was turned off. Walking over, she turned the dial when the image flashed through her mind. While the chip was an internal GPS device, there had to be an external GPS device.

Walking back into the kitchen, she opened her computer back up and started looking. There had to be some kind of device that she could get that could help her keep track of her child.

"BINGO!" she said louder than she had intended. Reading further she discovered a wristwatch-type device that could also be attached to an ankle. A little over a hundred dollars later, and she had what she needed. Not only a GPS device for each child, but emergency alert bracelets and forms that she could fill out that that detailed each child's personal and medical information. Not only would this information be able to be printed but it also could be stored on a thumb-drive and worn by each child as a bracelet.

Megan read through more information including the six actions to prepare for an emergency situation

The first action was to assess the risks to your child. Was flooding or extreme weather a threat? Water was an attraction to anyone with autism, which made drowning the number one cause of death for people with ASD. Did she live near water, train tracks, other potentially dangerous conditions? Were house or wild fires a risk? Or were there escalating or other dangerous behaviors that might lead to an encounter with professional responders? What medications put your child at risk? What are the nonverbal, mobility challenges that you had to adjust to? Does your child have a service dog that you would also need to have preparations for?

The second action was to identify yourself. This included not only registering with her local 911 but carrying a card about ASD in her pocket, wallet, or pouch along with getting Robbie an ID bracelet or some other ready to wear identifiers. There were also phone apps with "in case of emergency" information. Megan took the opportunity while she was sitting there to use the ICE logo on her phone and ordered a kitchen magnet. She also ordered stickers and a magnet for the house and car window. She also decided to order a couple stickers at the last minute for the motor home window. It was a real balance concerning her need for privacy, labeling, predatory practices against a responder's need to know.

The third action she learned was to introduce herself to neighbors and coworkers. She needed to explain her situation and concerns about Robbie to family, friends, neighbors and coworkers. She would need to ask others to check on her and her family in the event of an emergency and be able to help as needed. She would need to include all the contact information in her plan.

The fourth action was to consult resources about emergency preparedness. Easy enough, as she could do this from her computer. She would need to prepare a checklist and keep ICE information with her and the kids at all times. She also needed to create a ready kit and Go Bag for each family member that would include tools to improve communications with responders: *a* 911 registry, communication board, device or phone apps and ID information. The most important thing was to practice. She would have to test her plan with emergency drills. She could use social stories, role play and video modeling. She could also plan a visit with police, fire and EMS before any emergency occurred.

The fifth action was to prepare for wandering, and this one truly scared Megan. She didn't know what she would do if Robbie ever wandered off and she couldn't find him. This is what had brought her here now on her research journey. She needed to utilize a tracking device and protocol already supported by her community, such as Project Lifesaver. If there was no locally supported protocol she could consult with local law enforcement for potential solutions.

The last action was to be an advocate for those who couldn't stick up for themselves. She needed to meet with local emergency responders BEFORE an emergency situation happened, which included the local law enforcement, Fire, EMS and Emergency Management personnel, 911 dispatchers and school officials. She needed to get comfortable talking about autism. Whatever she learned could help someone else someday.

How far she had come, she thought as she looked at Robbie sleeping tonight on the makeshift bed. High up in the Rocky Mountains with people she barely knew, she was trusting his life to them. She needed to talk with Chloe tomorrow about Robbie, just in case. While she didn't think about it, she also knew the possibility that she might not make it to Ohio and the more people who could take care of her children, the better.

Flipping the binder back open, she flipped through the pages. This was Robbie's binder and she had made it specifically for him. In it, several laminated pages were in the very front with his medical information but also an Emergency 4 All communication card.

To find out more about Preparedness with Special Needs, please visit our website at www.PrepperChicks.org

The communication card had small pictures that Robbie could easily point to that would help him be able to convey his needs without speaking. The right side of the card had a picture of a human body, both front and back, that he could point to and get across that he had pain. The left side had small pictures that he could also use to signify cold, hungry, bathroom or a plethora of other needs. Chloe needed to learn how to use this with Robbie.

Flipping to the second page, Megan would add Chloe as a point of contact under Robbie's personal information if Chloe would let her. She had to get Robbie used to other people other than just herself. Heaven forbid if something would happen to her, Robbie would freak out and in the circumstances they currently were in, who truly knew what the future held. They were family now, Megan thought, whether Chloe knew it yet or not.

132

The plan was in motion. Each guest was seated at the table exactly where Emma had requested. It was nice to have Jay and Tiffany there to help, Emma thought, as most of the work had previously been on her shoulders. It didn't help that Jay and Tiff were getting a kick out of all the sarcasm they were shooting towards Nina.

Ben arrived to the party all dapper and smelling like a French whore on a Friday night. He quickly attached himself to Nina's elbow and was obviously miffed when he realized his setting at the table was not near her. "Ben, play nice. It's my party and I want Nina to spend some time getting to know my guests. There will be time afterwards to mingle," Emma quietly whispered in his ear. Ben quickly shot her a look of disapproval but knew better than to make a scene.

"Everyone, let's mosey into the dining room and be seated. The food is getting cold!" Tom announced. "Mosey?" Jay asked. "You've been out here a long time, haven't you?" she said with a bit of laughter in her voice.

"And loving every minute of it!" Tom replied, smiling at his wife.

133

"Give me that tote over there," Shelby said as she pointed towards the outer wall. "There should be some medicinal herbs in there. Look for the jar that's labeled Comfrey." Shelby instructed. "Now, grab the chia bran and psyllium husk. A little bit of water too. We are going to need a bowl, too, and something to mix this all with."

The kids all set out collecting everything that Shelby was asking for. Like precision clockwork, each child brought the items to Shelby and waited for more instructions. Shelby added the dried comfrey leaves and started to chop them up. Adding drops of water at a time, she next added the chia bran and psyllium husk until she got a gooey paste. "Can someone grab me some tea towels and some plastic wrap please. Thank you so much, you are all such great children. Best helpers there are."

Taking the mixture, Shelby spread it on the towel and gently laid the towel on her leg. Two more applications and her leg was covered from the knee down in the towels and comfrey poultice. "Now, help me out here a bit," she said to her oldest, Missy. Handing the plastic wrap to the child, Shelby instructed her to wrap it snugly around her leg, covering the concoction she had already applied. "There. That should keep it in place and dry. Grab the tape and we can seal off the edges until I can get the doc out here," Shelby instructed.

"Now, grab me that metal box over there," Shelby pointed. "It's time to see how your father is doing."

134

"Miss Emma, I have so missed your cooking. What's for dessert?" Tiffany asked Emma as dinner came to a close.

"You actually have room for more food?" Jay asked in astonishment.

Laughing, Emma replied, "Only our favorite, Tiff. Coconut cream pie!"

"You better watch it." Tiff said jokingly to Jay, "Or I will replace your ass with someone who can make me a mean coconut cream pie!"

Emma walked around the table to where Tommy was sitting and slid her arms down his chest. "Sorry, luv, I'm taken," Emma said with a wink towards Tiffany.

Tom reached up and laid his hand on Emma's arms. "And don't forget it," he said across the table for all to hear.

Jay turned and looked straight at Nina and got the answer that she wanted. Based on the expression on her face, the woman was up to no good. Jay prided herself on her instincts and didn't care for the woman the first time they met. After what Emma had told her about Nina, even more so. This sealed the deal.

"How about a game of Conflicted?" Tom asked. "It's become a habit in our family to play a few rounds after dinner. With the kids not being here as often, it would be nice for you folks to sit in."

"Um, sure," Jay asked. "Walk us through the rules."

"How long will it take? I don't want to be rude but I do have some reports to go over before I retire," Nina said.

"We can just probably get through a couple cards pretty fast. We can play it by ear from there."

Nina stood and started to clear the table. The last thing she wanted was to sit here and watch Emma with her hands all over Tom.

"Well, let's get a move on then!" Nina said.

Emma walked back into the room with a tray of cups and a large pot of coffee. Walking back out, she could feel Nina's eyes dig into her as they passed in the kitchen. "Nina, could you grab both of those pies on your way back into the dining room?" And without waiting, Emma left to return to her guests.

Nina walked over to the kitchen sink and looked out the window. Her reflection caught her attention in the glass. Tilting her chin up in an act of defiance, she closed her eyes against the harsh reality staring back at her. What was once a young woman; the reflection could not lie and hide the details etched in her face. The last few years had taken their toll. Taking a deep breath, she turned and walked back into the dining room.

"Pie?" Tiffany asked staring right at Nina when she entered the room.

A bit startled, Nina walked around the table and sat in the open seat beside Tom before anyone else could snatch it up. Pie or Tom, there really was no choice.

Ben could feel the veins in his neck tighten and the warmth creep up into his face. "I'll get the pie," he spat out and stood to leave. He needed a quick escape and took any opportunity that presented itself, even to carry a pie or two.

Walking through the kitchen, he was a bit irritated when his head hit the wrought iron pan holder hanging from the ceiling. "Fricken spics," he snarled as he realized he was taller than anyone in the house. It would give him an excuse though as to why his face was so red so it wasn't all bad, he thought. Touching the area that hurt, he brought his hand down and noticed the red hue. "What's a little blood, aye?" he said as he turned to walk back into the dining room.

Ben walked back into the dining room and straight over to where Nina and Tom were sitting. "Excuse me, don't you have some medical training?" he asked Nina.

"Oh Ben! What happened?" Nina exclaimed.

"Damn pot holder jumped down and bit me. Can't tell what's going on up there. Can you take a look?" Ben asked Nina.

"Here! Sit here," Tom said as he quickly got up and moved.

"Uh!" Nina started to say, but caught herself. Last thing she needed was to show her hand, but it was quite obvious she was a little irritated.

Ben sat down where Tom had been, fully expecting Nina to look at the damage he had done to his head.

Instead, she rang the medic who had traveled with her group to come to the house and look at the gash. Moving out of the way, Nina's only option was to sit beside Emma. Damn it! She had the perfect opportunity to stick it to Emma and Ben had to come in and ruin things for her! Now she had to endure the rest of the evening sitting beside the woman she would like to throttle with her bare hands.

"Well isn't this cozy," Jay chuckled. "I

think I'll pour myself a cup of coffee!"

"And where's the damn pie?!" Tiffany

blurted out.

135

Chloe got behind the steering wheel as the rest of the crew took their seats and buckled in. If the descent out of the mountains into Denver was anything like the climb up the elevation, they were in for a ride. Taking a deep breath, she turned the ignition allowing the beast to roar to life.

Looking into the side mirrors, Chloe let out a deep breath. "Here we go, kiddos!"

Exclamations of joy could be heard from behind her. Small voices that Chloe was unaccustomed to but was gaining a deep appreciation of. For just an instant, Chloe thought about what it must be like to be someone's mom. To feel the unconditional love that she saw Megan soak up throughout the day. One day. One day she would have her own family, but right now this family was relying on her to get them safely to Emma's farm where they actually might stand a chance of growing up. A feeling of dread overwhelmed her for a minute as the reality of what the future held washed over her. Life would never be the same for any of them, let alone the children sitting behind her. They still needed a chance to grow into adulthood, a chance to be happy and laugh and not worry about where their next meal would come from. Looking into the rear-view mirror, Chloe looked at the kids getting buckled into their seats. This was their future, not hers anymore.

Chloe tilted her head slightly back, the determination on her face set her chin square. She had this.
She had to have this. Whatever it took, she promised herself as she pulled out onto the road.

136

Mountain Man scrambled to reach the small handheld radio when he heard Shelby's voice cut through the static. "Shelby! Come in!" he said as he depressed the button on the side.

"Joshua, is that really you? Are you OK?" Shelby replied with obvious desperation in her voice "Yes, yes. How are you and the kids?"

"Oh, we are fine," she said looking at the children to hush and keep their secret. "Are you in the house?"

"Not really, but she took the blast just fine. I'm in the back room and I haven't gone into the rest of the house yet. Shelby, I was out when the cloud appeared. I tried to get home as soon as I could but I'm just not sure. I tried to reach you all last night but I guess you couldn't find the radios."

Shelby closed her eyes against the tears and bowed her head. She had let her Mountain Man down. She had shut him out when he needed her most and now he may die from radiation poisoning. Her heart broke as the tears fought behind her lashes to escape.

Picking up the radio and bringing it to her lips, she pressed the button to talk but nothing came out.
Her hand collapsed into her lap. Damn it! She muttered to herself. She had to pull herself together. Taking a deep breath, she tilted her face to the heavens and waited for the strength she knew could only come from God.

Picking back up the radio, she pressed the button and said, "Mountain Man, I love you. Now here is what I need you to do."

137

Michael wasn't kidding about how beautiful the mountains were descending into Denver. Turn after turn, Chloe handled the motor home like a pro. She did have to remind herself to breathe after each descent, thinking that the one she had just conquered was the final one. The mountains had a way of teasing her, though, and Chloe was getting annoyed with their self-gratifying game. But they were stunning, Chloe had to admit.

As the road leveled out, Chloe noticed a few cars abandoned along the road. The farther they traveled into the city, the more apparent it was that there were more issues that they would face on this side of the mountains. Taking a deep breath, Chloe had to even wonder if they would make it to Emma's farm. Her spirit of adventure kicked in and she had to admit, what lay ahead will probably make for a good book!

Chloe's eyes caught Michael signaling to pull off the main road and follow him. Perplexed, Chloe had an odd feeling in the pit of her stomach. It wasn't fear. It wasn't distrust. She couldn't quite put her finger on it. Blowing out a deep breath from between her lips, she turned the big motor home and followed Michael.

Further back away from the main part of the city of Colorado Springs, nestled back along the mountains, was a small ordinary-looking farm. Following Michael into the driveway to the house, she was surprised that they weren't met by anyone. As they got closer to the house, a woman appeared on the porch and walked over to where Michael was parking the RV. Words were exchanged and the woman raised her arm and waved at Chloe. Instantly, Chloe felt at ease. Catching herself letting down her guard, she instantly scolded herself. She didn't know these people, hell, truth be told, she barely knew Michael. All in all, the only thing she could hold onto was that the person in Ohio she trusted with her life sent him to get her.

Chloe parked the RV and stepped out into the sunshine. Walking to where the woman and Michael were talking, she was surprised to hear them laughing.

"Chloe, come meet Shawna. Shawna, this is Chloe. The rest of the party will get off the bus soon enough, I'm sure," Michael said.

Chloe reached her hand out towards Shawna but the woman walked past it and gave Chloe a quick squeeze. "Any friend of Michael's is a friend of mine! No handshakes here, just hugs!" the woman said.

Taken aback, Chloe didn't know quite what to say so just hugged the woman back.

"We are going to refuel here and have some breakfast before we head out," Michael said.

"Here?" Chloe said looking around. "But, this isn't a gas station."

"Oh hun, you won't get within three miles of a gas station without being robbed or shot dead with what's going on out there," Shawna said. "Come inside and get some hot food in you, get a shower and we can go from there."

"Go on in with Shawna and I will get the rest of the crew," Michael said to Chloe.

Shawna hooked her arm within Chloe's and pulled her gently in the direction of the front door of the house. "Come, meet my family."

Chloe briefly looked back and saw Michael climb the stairs into the RV while Shawna escorted her into the house. Immediately inside the front door and Chloe was overwhelmed with the delicious smell of food. Real food. Not the packed stuff they had been eating in the motor home but real, cooked food. Obviously so did her stomach, as it made a loud, demanding grumble to feed it!

"I'm so sorry!" Chloe muttered, a bit embarrassed.

Laughing, Shawna motioned Chloe into the bathroom. "Wash up quick and let's eat. Showers after while we refuel," she said as the rest of the entourage entered the house. Chloe used the commotion as an excuse to disappear into the bathroom as the rest of the introductions were made. Walking over to the sink, she ran some hot water and splashed it on her face. Looking up at herself in the mirror, she was struck by the horror before her. "Oh girlie, you are one hot mess!" Her stomach growled from the lack of attention it was receiving and Chloe picked up the hint. Giving it a quick pat, she quickly dried her face and walked back out to meet everyone. Now was not the time to let vanity rule her senses.

138

Sitting around the table, Shawna introduced her family to her guests. I wish my husband could be here to join us, but he will be in as soon as the RV is filled."

"How in the world are you going to fuel the RV? Is there a station around here that isn't on the map?" Megan asked.

"Oh goodness no. We actually have a storage tank here on the farm. He is using that to refuel," Shawna responded.

"That's a lot of fuel, I'm not sure we all have enough money to repay you," Megan said.

"Don't worry about it. It's what we are here for. One day we will need something and someone will lend us a hand. It's how we work things out," Shawna explained. "This farm was created for this very issue. People coming down off of the mountains or going up the mountains. Either way, we are a stopping point."

"Stopping point? I don't understand," Chloe said, confusion written all over her face.

"To move people back and forth in case something happens and all normal activity ceases. We are what is called an Alpha Farm. We are part of a network across the country that was created for this very purpose."

"Oh," Chloe muttered, clearly still perplexed.

"Don't worry your pretty little head," Michael interjected. "Just know we will get you where you need to be."

Clearly miffed at the comment made by Mike, Chloe raised an eyebrow. "I think I will get that shower now," she said as she scooted her chair back.

"Oh! Certainly!" Shawna exclaimed. "Towels are in the hall closet. Everything else you may need is under the counter. Please, help yourself. If you need anything, just give me a yell."

Chloe stood under the hot water, letting it cascade down the length of her body. Closing her eyes, she replayed the last few days through her head. Little by little the tension released itself from her tired muscles. Raising her hands above her head and resting them on the side of the shower, she stretched her back. "Ugh," the sound escaped from between her lips. What had she gotten herself into? Wiping the water from her eyes, she lathered her hair with lavender-scented shampoo. It didn't really matter what she had gotten herself into, she had nowhere to turn back to so she was in for the ride, whether she liked it or not.

139

Angie kept off the main rode as best she could, Emma's voice echoing in her head. "Don't make yourself an easy target. Follow the road but keep yourself hidden as best you can in the trees or brush. If you have to cross a field, consider crawling down in the ditch until you can take cover again. If it really warrants it, detour around the area. Better to take the extra time than end up in deeper trouble"

Looking ahead, Angie saw where the trees abruptly ended along the edge of a field. Across the field was a small homestead. Scanning across the road, Angie's heart sank as she saw nothing but open field also. Damn it! There was no way to get up close to the home without the chance of someone seeing her. Checking the depth of the ditch that ran along both sides of the road, she would be an easy target if she tried to crawl along the ditch.

"Hell!" she muttered out loud. "I don't even know if Scott's here."

Trying to peer down the road, she saw no travelers in either direction. Taking a step out onto the road, she tried to see as far as she could past the farm to the only other house she remembered seeing. Nothing. Exasperated, she melted back into the woods for cover. She would have to wait for nightfall. Finding a spot that gave her concealment among some berry shrubs, she waited and watched for any sign of movement on the farm. Damn it! He had to be here. God, if whoever took him any further they could kill him. Sinking her face into the crook of her arms, Angie released all the horror of the last few days. Her body shook from the sobs raking through every muscle. "Lady, you OK?"

Angie stopped crying and laid as still as she could, not even taking the chance of breathing.

"Hey, lady. Are you OK? Get yourself out of those bushes before the snakes get you," came the voice again.

Snakes? Angie jumped up in sheer fright. If there was one thing that scared her to death it was snakes.
She had seen them occasionally at Emma's farm around the barn and she steered clear of them even though Emma said they were beneficial and would not harm her. Of course, those were black snakes that kept the mice population down in and around the outbuildings, but Angie sure as hell did not need one crawling up on her as she was laying out here.

Looking around frantically on the ground, it dawned on Angie that she had just been tricked. Slowly raising her hands, she turned and looked in the direction of where the voice had come from.

There, sitting on a horse, was a man who looked just like all the cowboys Angie had ever seen. Rugged face with hair peppered with grey streaks peeking out from beneath his Stetson, he wore jeans and a flannel shirt. The toes of his boots peeked out from the tip of stirrup.

Angie felt oddly at ease.

"Ma'am, please put your arms down. You're not being arrested. Just was wondering what you were doing out here bawling your eyes out?" he asked.

Angie slowly dropped her arms, looking into the man's bright blue eyes. "I.....I" she stammered.

"Here, you look like you could use this," he said as he tossed her a handkerchief.

Embarrassed, Angie picked it up off her shoulder where it landed. "Oh, I must look a fright," she murmured as she wiped her face.

"I've seen worse," the cowboy said. "Want to tell me what you're doing out here now?"

Not wanting to give out too much information, Angie finally said, "My car stopped running. I'm not sure what happened."

"Ya, lots of that going on" he said.

"Do you know what's going on?" she asked him.

"A little. Not sure if you really want to know though. Where are you headed?"

"Ohio," she let slip out without thinking.

"That's going to be a very long walk. Any other plans?" he asked.

"There is someone here in Tennessee that I can go to, I just need to figure out how to get there. Her name is Shelby," Angie said.

"Shelby, aye? Well then, we need to get you up to the house," the man said.

"Oh no, it's OK. I can figure it out."

"You don't seem to understand. You need to go to the house with me," he added with such sternness that Angie's body quivered.

"Um, OK," Angie finally said, clearly shaken.

Angie walked beside the man riding the horse until they reached the barn, her mind reeling from all the scenarios that were playing out. The man looked so kind but as soon as she mentioned Shelby he instantly tightened up. His manner abruptly changed and tenseness hung in the air.

Once at the barn, the man dismounted and tied the reins around a post. "This way," he said as he pointed to a rear door into the house.

Angie walked ahead of him, her heart pulsating beneath her shirt. What had she done? She had no way of finding Scott if she had gotten herself detained. And how long would they keep her?

The man turned the doorknob and motioned for her to go inside.

The familiar smell hit her nostrils and made her cringe. Why did the inside of his house smell like a hospital? The aroma of antiseptic was so strong it was making her eyes water. The pungent yellow, sickly smell of the air filled her lungs and made her want to turn and run back outside.

"Third door on your right," came the man's booming voice from behind her. Her muscles tightened as she listened to the tympanic rhythm of her captor's boots as they followed her.

Stopping before the door, she reached down and grabbed the knob, stopping for a brief moment before she twisted it and opened the door. "This is it, girly," she thought. Raising her chin, she would meet whatever was behind the door head on.

Taking a deep breath, she took the cold orb in her hand and turned, pushing gingerly at the rough wooden door.

140

Shawna hugged everyone as they loaded themselves back onto the motor home. "Be careful out there. Next stop is Betsy Four. You should be OK through Oksana Three," she said.

Chloe turned around and just stared at her "Oksana Three?" she asked.

"Have Michael explain, but you will be in good hands," Shawna said.

Chloe looked up as Michael was already pulling out of the driveway on the motorcycle. "I guess that will have to wait," she murmured.

Chloe waited while everyone buckled themselves into their seats, the motor starting to purr as it was warming up. Taking a deep breath, she put the gearshift into drive and moved the beast forward. First stop they made, she needed to have a conversation with the man in front of her. She had a lot of questions that need answered. First things first, if something happened to him, how the hell would she even find her way? He seemed to have all the knowledge about the actual trip itself and that bothered her. And what were these Alpha Farms? And who exactly was this man she was trusting with her life....

141

Betsy heard the faint crackle of a voice and turned the dial up.

"Betsy Four Copy"

Picking up the radio, she tried to get the button to depress but couldn't get it to go down.

"Betsy Four Copy"

Trying again, she finally got the mic to key. "Betsy Four, Over"

"Oksana Three Confirm two dash seven twenty four. Over"

"Betsy Four Confirm two dash seven twenty four. Over"

"Oksana Three Out"

"Betsy Four Out" Betsy said into the mic. "Please stay safe' my friend," she whispered.

OK. Seven guests are in route in two vehicles and should be arriving within twenty-four hours if all goes well. She felt her pulse increase at the prospect of her new arrivals. While it was dangerous to take strangers in, this was different. These people were somehow connected to people Betsy trusted. With word from Oksana, Betsy would need to keep her radio powered up as her next contact would be from the travelers themselves. In the meantime, she needed to make preparations. For her guests. This was why she was here. She was an Alpha Farm. It was the commitment she and her family had made to help others in case of a down grid situation. It wasn't a decision she had taken lightly as it did pose some danger first to take and strangers and second to break the rules of OPSEC, or operational security. Weighing it all out, she knew it needed to be done and she wanted to play an important part in the rebuilding of the country if something ever happened. People had to be moved, shuffled around if something happened. She had spent many an hour with the girls of the Alpha Farms, making sure they were all synced. After the Alphas were on the same page, Betsy oversaw a group of sister chicks in her area who helped on a more localized bases. A second tier of defenses.

Scenario after scenario was played out on paper along with every conceivable outcome. Was there room for error? Of course. They had to learn to improvise, to adapt to the situations, but the ultimate goal was always to overcome. This was not a game for losers as lives could be lost. It was all in or nothing.

Betsy set about tidying up the extra bedrooms that she had. She had some citrus cleaner she had made from orange peels and vinegar that would leave the rooms smelling fresh. Looking at the bottle, she would need to make more after this visit. Perfect plan she thought. She can make some lemonade for her guests and make some lemon cleaner instead of the orange this time.

Walking out to her greenhouse, she pulled a couple lemons from her small trees and took them back to the kitchen. Back in the kitchen, she sliced the lemons and used the juice for the beverage. Taking the peel, she put it all in a jar and filled the jar with white vinegar. Putting the lid on the jar, she sat it in the back of her cleaning supplies to marinate for at least ten days. That would give the oils in the lemon peels enough time to make the cleaner smell good while making it potent.

Picking up the seeds, she held them in the palm of her hand surveying their fleshing appearance. Popping them into her mouth, she sucked all the pulp from them. Keeping them in her mouth to stay moist, Betsy walked back out to her greenhouse. Finding an empty pot was not easy, as growing food was of utmost importance. Moving two plants together, Betsy freed up a pot for her newest prized possession. Three to six years from now, these tiny seeds would be producing their own fruit. They were more valuable than gold.

Betsy stuck her finger into the moist dirt and dropped the seeds into the hole formed. About a half an inch deep, she tenderly covered the seeds with dirt and sprayed the dirt until damp. Taking a clear piece of leftover plastic, she covered the top of the pot and wrapped a rubber band around it to keep the plastic in place. Taking a deep breath, she exhaled, "Please grow."

The country she lived in was spotted with pockets of power. Big cities in the east to Midwest were hit the hardest from whatever caused this catastrophe. Reports were coming in that an earthquake had cause the destruction, one that had hit the New Madrid area. Seemed unlikely considering the extent of the damage, but that was what it seemed was being echoed across the airwaves. Luckily for Betsy, her Sister Chicks had prepared ahead of time. While none of the city services were currently functioning, Betsy had backups to her backups. Water from her well, solar power with a couple small wind turbines with plenty of battery storage had Betsy not missing a step. The only thing she truly missed was the internet. She loved research and keeping in touch with people, especially her girlies, and this unusual silence was unnerving.

Next, she pulled some canned chicken from the cellar with some rice from the pantry. Her food storage was staged around the house for a reason. If someone stopped by purposefully to remove what food she had, she could show how little she had in her pantry without compromising her entire stockpile.

Adding the rice, chicken and enough water to cover into a ceramic pot, she took it outside and put it into her sun oven. It would take a couple hours to cook, but that was one thing she had now, time. She had to stay ahead of the meals and plan out hours or even days in advance what to cook as popping things in the microwave and expecting it to be ready in minutes, heck, those days were long gone. Mixing up a garden salad with fresh tomatoes and cucumbers, she set it into her small refrigerator that she bought in an RV shop. While it was the perfect size for a motor home, it looked extremely out of place in her kitchen. It was about half the size of her regular refrigerator. What made it priceless, though, was it ran off of her solar batteries and not regular electrical current. Mixing up her lemonade, she set it also in her small fridge to chill down before her guests arrived. All she had left to do was make a quick dessert and track down her husband who was in the barn tending to their animals. He would need to get the refueling station ready.

Walking back into the kitchen from the barn, she heard the crackle from her ham radio.

"Betsy Four Over," came the man's voice over the radio.

Betsy dropped her dish towel and headed into the living room where she kept the radio.

"Betsy Four Over," came the man's voice again.

"Betsy Four Over!" she shouted into the handset.

"Betsy Four Thirty Out"

"Betsy Four Thirty Confirmed Out," Betsy yelled back. Her guests would be there in thirty minutes Not a lot of time left!

True to his word, half an hour later a motorcycle came barreling up the driveway with a motor home not far behind. It had been a while since Betsy had seen an actual working vehicle as most of the newer ones were impacted by the supposed earthquake that the media kept dumping onto the emergency radio waves. Betsy went out to meet her guests from the porch, her pistol tucked ladylike under her apron… you know… just in case things didn't pan out the way intended.

"Michael!" Betsy exclaimed.

"Hey, Little Momma!" Michael cooed back.

Chloe was just stepping off the steps of the motor home as she witnessed the exchange of welcomes between what were obviously old friends.

"So you're Betsy Four?" Chloe asked, now even more intrigued. Here was this woman standing before her who Chloe would never in a million years was part of this...this... country wide spy ring of mothers going on. "Someone needs to explain to me what the hell is going on around here."

Over dinner, Betsy and Michael explained the network of women around the country that could be used to get people and supplies where they needed to go. They also explained the complex set of commands spoken on the radio along with the changes in frequencies. Chloe would need to learn them over time, but for now her mind was on overload.

"Next stop should be Dawna in Indiana for a quick refuel and then Ohio," Betsy said.

"Wow, that's going to go faster than I thought," Chloe chimed.

"Don't be so quick. Sounds like you have had a reasonably smooth drive here but that's about to change. You have a pretty significant river to cross and that's not going to be easy considering," Betsy said.

"Considering what?" Michael asked.

"They are all blocked. We've been out to look for ourselves. Part of the redistribution of wealth going on. Pay the price to cross safely on one end. Pay to get off the other end. By the time you are done, you won't have anything left... not even your life sometimes. It got pretty stupid around here pretty fast." Betsy added.

"What are we going to do now? Megan asked. "We've come this far to not make it?"

Michael was being unusually quiet. Chloe looked over at him deep in thought. "I think we need to stay for a couple days if that's OK Betsy... I want to check out these bridges," he finally said.

"Of course." Betsy said, knowing all the options going through his head. Hell, she had probably thought of some of them herself!

142

"I'm going, too, " Chloe said.

"Really? You think?" Michael said.

"Yes," She responded.

"Well, I think not. I work alone. Less mistakes that way."

"Tough titty," she quipped.

"What?" he half-laughed.

"I'm going. Get over it. If anything, use it to teach me some stuff I don't know."

She had him there. She was tough, he gave her that. Maybe he should teach her a thing or two.

"OK, fine. Be ready to go at 2300…" he said and walked away.

"But wait," she yelled after him with a wicked grin on her face. "What do I wear?"

143

Betsy and Chloe both walked into the room together dressed in Army fatigues, their faces painted in camouflage paint.

"What the hell?" Michael said laughing.

"WE are both going with you," Betsy said.

"Are you both out of your fucking minds?" he asked.

Exchanging glances and a hint of a smile, both women responded at the same exact time, "Yes."

"Ah come on Mike, let them live a little," Betsy's husband said.

"Oh! I love a man with your kind of thinking…" Betsy said as she winked at her husband.

"Ya well, don't get to excited. You get hurt and I'm kicking your ass," he said as he took his wife in his arms and kissed her forehead.

"Yes dear," she responded, squeezing him tight.

Releasing his breath from between his lips in a highly agitated manner, Mike finally walked to the kitchen table and laid out some topographical maps.

"OK, ladies. Here's the plan."

They spend the next thirty minutes reviewing their travel route and course of action. "If all goes well, we should be back before the break of dawn," Michael said to everyone. "Let's load up and head out."

"Wait, I have to pee," Chloe said as the room broke into laughter.

"Of course you do," Michael, said shaking his head. "Of course."

144

It became quite clear after a small amount of time that crossing any bridge within a day's travel was going to require a rather large distraction of some kind to get the motor home across. The motorcycle would be easy enough but a big lumbering RV full of passengers was going to need a pretty intensive amount of planning.

Two things came to mind for Michael: Compromise or deceit. Beg, borrow or steal your way across or create a distraction big enough that it takes out all operatives. Looking around at the two women with him, it could come down to both compromise and deceit.

"Alright ladies, I've seen enough. Let's head home," Michael said breaking the silence.

Gathering the supplies that they had unpacked, the trio headed quietly back out of their hiding spot the way they had come in. "Who does the boat service belong to that we passed on the way?"

"That's River Rat...or Jack but most people around here call him River Rat as he knows this river like the back of his hand. Why?" Betsy asked.

"How well do you know him?" Mike asked Betsy.

"Well enough but I really don't think he has the capability to get a big ass motor home across this river. I don't like the feel of this at all," Betsy said. "No one there is a local... why wouldn't any of our guys be over there? That would make it a hell of a lot easier!"

"No idea," Michael said quietly, obviously distracted by the question.

"OK, what gives Mikey? What's ticking away in that hard head of yours?" Chloe asked.

"I don't think we can do this," he finally said.

"Wait! What?! Can't do what? Get across that bridge?" Chloe asked.

"I don't know who 'we' is but us chickies can do whatever we need to do to get the job done and no pile of camo-dressed men guarding a bridge are going to stop us!" Betsy chimed in.

Michael smiled to himself in the dark. Just the response he was looking for. Any hesitation on their part could get some of them, if not all of them, killed. It was going to be all or nothing and he preferred they had total buy in of the plan. He just now needed to convince them that it was their plan they were creating.

The walk back to Betsy's house was quiet and uneventful. It gave Michael enough time to think about their mission ahead and pull together any possible variable that could deter it from success. His biggest worry was the two women walking beside him. It was one thing to trust your six to a trained soldier. Another to some housewives he hardly knew. Not much of a choice, though, he had to work with what he had and he was quickly running out of time.

Once back at the house, Chloe and Betsy made a bite to eat for them all and they gathered around the table to discuss what each of them witnessed at the bridge. Mike was impressed by the amount of detail they had gathered that slipped his notice. Piling all the info together gave them a clear cut idea of what they needed to do, and it was going to take all of them to get the job done. They finally broke for the night as the sun was starting to rise. They needed to get some sleep, and then get Megan and Betsy's husband involved in the plan and then put it all into motion before dusk.

Betsy climbed into bed beside her husband after making a final check on their security, four German shepherds that roamed the property at night. Betsy got them as pups and spent many rigorous hours with them training them for security. Each Alpha Farm in the network had some kind of canine security whether it was German shepherds or Great Pyrenees.

"You OK with all of this?" Betsy asked him.

"Do I have a choice? It should be me going through," he said.

"Just don't."

Betsy's husband had been injured in a car accident many years before. Wheelchair bound, he still managed to help around the farm with various chores but it still wasn't enough. The doctors had given him a bit of hope right before the grid went down with a new experimental surgery that may have given him partial mobility back in his legs but all hope of that was lost when the power went out. It was bad enough to have to deal with his restrictions but to have a rambunctious wife who took on most of the responsibilities around the farm left him fighting some days to keep a smile on his face. At first, he thought it was a great idea for Betsy to get involved with being an Alpha Farm, tonight though it really hit home how much danger it brought to his family and he honestly wasn't OK with that.

They both lay quietly wrapped in each other's arms, each contemplating what the next day would bring. Good or bad.

145

Nap time ended all too soon for the group about to set out. Showering after a quick bite of food, the group began to systematically repack only the necessary supplies they would need on the next phase of their journey. This left Betsy and her family with quite a stash of freeze-dried foods for her pantry. Michael kept all the medical supplies but wanted the RV as light as possible going over the small wooden bridge. The amount of firepower and manpower on the big concrete bridge made the smaller bridge the way to go.

If all worked out, Mike would take the motorbike and create a diversion. Chloe would follow in the motorhome while Betsy took Megan and the kids across the river via River Rat and his boat. They would meet up in a designated location further down the road away from all the commotion. If it all went according to plan.

The trio each bumped fists as a final goodbye, no words spoken, each knowing full well the others depended on them to get the job done.

Betsy set off with Megan and Megan's family to River Rat's boat dock.

Chloe climbed into the RV and buckled herself in. Her firearms were within reach and ready to go.

Michael mounted the motorcycle and turned the key. Driving off, he didn't look back. He was the point, the man out front to try and defuse the situation as much as possible before the rest came through. From the scouting expedition it looked like six guys were guarding the bridge at any given time. Three on each side. He needed to snipe off as many as he could before Chloe got there with the motor home.

Chloe then needed to get across the bridge as fast as she could before reinforcements arrived and sure enough as soon as the shooting started, they would be coming.

Michael got as close as he felt comfortable and turned off the motorcycle. Pushing it forward with his legs, he got it as close as he could and then parked it and walked the rest of the way to his vantage point. Laying on the ground, he pulled his night vision goggles out of his pack and laid them beside him. Next, he pulled his rifle out of the sling across his back. It was a Browning Short Trac .308win with an ATN X-Sight night vision scope. He bought it to go boar hunting but it would work just as well for what he was about to do.

Sighting in, he followed several of the guys around for a few minutes. Which to shoot first now becomes the question. Who's biggest? Ugliest? Location was what Michael was looking at. Who was in the way of Chloe getting the damn house on wheels across the bridge? Watching intently, he tried to calm his nerves as best he could. Listening, he waited until he heard the motor home behind him coming down the road. It was his cue. Squeezing his finger back, the first man fell with no issues. The second man right behind him. Repositioning his rifle to the other side of the bridge he sighted in and squeezed but did not meet his target. By now all the men were scrambling around, shouting orders. "Dammit" Michael muttered under his breath. He was hoping to get at least two on each side. Now all he had was two on one side. Chloe would have to do the rest.

Chloe rolled her window up. She had heard all she needed to. Michael was right on time. Pushing her foot down on the accelerator, she increased her speed to meet the barricade ahead. As the front of the bridge came into view, she saw the makeshift wooden barriers across the front. Her eyes drifted down to the body lying across the road under the barrier. "Oh God!" she screamed out to no one, her foot still increasing the speed of the RV.

The front of the RV crashed through the barrier, splintering it like small wooden toothpicks. It wasn't much time later that Chloe felt the wheel hit the body lying in the way. Fighting back the urge to vomit, Chloe increased her speed as she saw the other end of the bridge was blocked with cars instead. Shots rang out with a bullet crashing through the front windshield. Chloe ducked in her seat trying to make herself as small a target as possible. Ahead in the headlights she saw the men standing across the bridge, their rifles aimed at her. Pushing the lever of her seat into a lying back position, Chloe floored the gas. Holding onto the steering wheel as best she could, she tried to keep the RV straight without being able to see. Within seconds she felt the impact. The jolt had her sitting upwards again with her chest across the steering wheel. One man's eyes locked onto hers through the window and then they were gone along with the cars blocking the way. Chloe would never forget the look of pure terror on the man's face as the RV slammed into his body, melding it into one fused being with the metal of the vehicles around him. She kept driving as fast as she could, her body overtaken with extreme amounts of adrenaline. It wasn't until she almost tipped the RV over trying to navigate a curve that she realized she needed to slow down and continue to the meet up location. Little did she realize that Michael was right behind her coming across the bridge, eating the debris that she was spitting out from under the motor home. He didn't see the body and ended up flipping over end over end as what was left of a man's torso hit the front wheel of his bike.

Chloe drove to the designated pull off and waiting for the rest of her party. Betsy should be arriving soon with Megan and her family. Michael shouldn't be far behind. Actually he should have been there already, she thought.

A beating on the door had her jolting and reaching for her gun. "Chloe?" she heard Megan call out.

"Oh geez," Chloe responded.

"You OK?" Megan asked as she ushered the kids onto the RV quickly.

"Ya. Ya. You see Michael out there anywhere?"

"No. He's not here yet?" Betsy asked.

"I haven't seen him," Chloe said.

None of the women spoke, each looking from one to the other.

Betsy turned and walked over to where River Rat was. "We'll be right back," she said to Megan and
Chloe. "Don't do anything until we get back."

Chloe and Megan exchanged looks as Betsy got back into the boat with River Rat. Turning the boat, the duo headed upstream.

146

"Don't you dare tell my husband what we are doing," Betsy threatened the man steering the boat. Grinning a toothless grin, the man cut the engines on the boat and edged it close to shore. Hand over hand, grabbing the brush alongside the bank, he maneuvered the boat as close to the bridge as he could.

Betsy could hear moaning coming from on top of the bridge. Was it Michael? Trying to hear as best as she could, she just couldn't make out any familiar sounds. Double checking her Sig Sauer P938 Betsy waited as patiently as she could for River Rat to secure the boat. Stepping out into the mud, Betsy grabbed onto the debris to pull herself up the bank as quietly as she could. The moaning was coming from the opposite side of the bridge. Scooting back down the bank, Betsy pointed for River Rat to get the boat to the other side. Pulling the boat further upstream, River Rat pushed it away from the bank and allowed the current to carry them back under the bridge to the other side. Using the oar as little as possible, he managed to dock the boat and pull it back along the bank to the bridge trestle.

Once again, Betsy made her way to the top of the embankment and listened. The groaning was coming from not far away. Debris littered the road like a tornado had come through. Listening, Betsy still couldn't tell if it was from Michael yet or not.

It was now or never, Betsy thought as she inhaled. Getting to a crouched position, she quickly scurried in the direction of the noise. A soft gooey substance kept sticking to the bottom of her feet, like walking over the kitchen floor after someone used too much cleaner in the water. Getting closer, Betsy saw that it was Michael lying on the ground clutching his head in pain. Quickly kneeling beside him, she laid her finger across her lips to try and quiet him.

"Betsy?" he whimpered.

"Can you move?" she quickly whispered.

"Ya. I think."

"Let's go then. Come on, suck it up buttercup," she said as she helped him to his knees.

The world was still spinning for Michael but he fought against it. In a crouched position, Betsy hurriedly moved him to the side of the road and slid him down the bank. In minutes they were making their way downstream and back to the RV.

The sound alerted the people in the RV that they were friends. Chloe still had her gun pointed at the door as it opened, though. In came Betsy with Michael right behind her and River Rat pushing the injured man from the backside. Getting Michael strapped into a seat, Betsy turned to Chloe and Megan.

"You girlies got this. You have the maps. There are no more reasons to stop until you get to Dawna Five. I will radio ahead so she will be on the lookout for you," Betsy said. "We all need to go quickly now."

All three women, with tears in their eyes, knew what needed to be done. With a quick hug, Betsy and
River Rat descended the steps of the RV and disappeared into the night. Megan taking shotgun in the front seat, Chloe started

the RV and headed off towards their next point of contact: Indiana and Dawna Five.

147

Michael pulled the RV up the gravel drive and straight to the house and was perplexed about the amount of military vehicles scattered around the property.

"What has she gotten herself into this time?" he wondered out loud.

"Who are you talking about?" Chloe asked.

Turning, Michael grinned at Chloe as he descended the stairs and got out of the motor home.

Looking out the window, Chloe was impressed by what she could take in. The house was well constructed and inviting but Chloe imagined how easily it could be fortified. Barn, chicken coop, solar panels, windmill, yep, completely what she would expect at Emma's farm.

Chloe steeped off of the landing of the motor home and looked around. WOW. This was going to be her home. It was already so much quieter than LA even with all the military generators. "Bet there's a story there," Chloe muttered to herself. "Only Emma," she thought, smiling to herself.

Michael was quite a few steps ahead of her and walking towards the back of the house when the woman walked out of the house. A tall woman, she had light brown hair that fell like a waterfall down her back, ending mid-thigh. Jeans and a flannel shirt, she had no shoes on and began to run across the hard ground like it was soft layers of sand.

"Michael!" she yelled as she quickly closed the distance between them.

Chloe stopped and watched, confused by the sight before her.

The man and woman met in the middle of the yard. Reaching up, the woman laid both of her hands on each side of the man's face and held it like a precious gem. "OH! I've missed you!" she giggled out in pure joy as her hands melted around the man's neck. Pulling her close, Michael picked her up off of the ground in a tremendous hug. From Chloe's vantage point, the two had an obvious fondness for each other.

Leaving the embrace of the man, the woman caught sight of Chloe standing there staring.

"Chloe?"

Startled by the woman knowing her name, the expression on her face grew more perplexed as the realization hit her square between the eyes.

"Emma?" she stammered out.

Running towards her, the woman grabbed her in a bear hug and squeezed the last drop of fear out of her.

"OH MY GOD! I can't believe it's you! I can't believe I'm here!" Chloe finally mumbled out.

"Yes, it's me... and yes, you are finally here! You have got to be exhausted!" Emma said.

"UGH! You can't imagine! The stories I have to tell you!!" Chloe sang out in excitement.

"Later, we can talk about it later. Right now let's get everyone inside and settled. I have lunch ready for everyone," Emma added.

Michael had walked back over to where the two women were still talking and coming around behind Emma, he laid his hands on her shoulders.

"How?" was all that could escape out of Chloe's mouth as she pointed first from Michael and then to Emma, her eyebrows burrowed in confusion.

"Chloe," Michael said, "I want you to meet my sister."

148

As the door slowly opened, the details of a hospital bed unfolded. More and more, Angie pushed at the door until she saw the full view of the room. What once was someone's office, with the desk now shoved against the far wall, and had been crudely turned into a makeshift infirmary. Silver poles danced above the bed holding bags of clear liquid. The silence was broken by the constant bleating of the machines.

Angie saw the man lying on the bed, her mind blending him in with the décor of the rest of the room.

"You know him?" the cowboy asked.

Stepping further into the room, Angie walked over to the side of the bed. The man lying on the bed had an oxygen tube running under his nose. His hair was disheveled and now fell forward over his forehead making him look like a young boy. His face lax from the deep sleep he was in, Angie felt her knees buckle as the room started to spin. Blackness enveloped her as her body slumped to the floor.

149

"You're the Queen Bee?" Chloe laughed "I should have known!"

"Yes. Well. Some of the coop girls thought it was cute, and of course it stuck. I owe some sweet young girl who lives in a bus for the nickname," Emma said getting caught up in the laughter. "Let's get you all inside and cleaned up and fed. You all need some serious down time. Unfortunately we have some.... guests that won't seem to leave," Emma said with a smile to her brother. "We may have to put you up in a couple of the cabins until we can get this all straightened out if you don't mind."

Just then Megan's kids started coming out of the motor home. One by one they came out and looked around. "Who do we have here?" Emma asked, a bit puzzled.

"I brought some guests!" Chloe added hurriedly. "I hope you don't mind?" she said with a bit of a question in her voice.

"Not at all. If you felt a need to bring them, that's good enough for me. But we really will need to get some cabins open!"

150

"You have quite a house full here," Nina whispered to Emma, catching her in the hallway.

"Yes," Emma smiled. "I do."

"Is that wise considering?" Nina asked.

"Considering what?" Emma inquired, meeting Nina square on.

"Well, that we are using your farm here as our base camp. Our country is depending on us getting up and functioning considering all that is happening. I wouldn't want anyone to hinder our efforts. There are only so many supplies here also." Nina's vile words insinuated that Emma's family and friends were not welcome here.

"Don't forget whose roof you are sleeping under. Whose food you are eating. You are here as a guest only and if it comes down to choosing between you and my family, my family always comes first," Emma shot back.

"Oh, not me. Don't forget we are trying to rebuild this government of ours. Not the words of a Patriot to threaten to kick us out," Nina said. "What's that saying, to benefit the many?"

"I'm not sure who you think you are but I assure you," Emma said positioning her body to back Nina against the wall, "My family comes before you or anyone you brought with you."

"Even Tommy?" Nina spat back "You seem to have forgotten that I did bring him here from Washington."

Hearing Nina use the term of endearment that Emma used for her husband made her blood boil. Emma's eyebrow rose in reply to Nina's words. "You might want to leave my family alone," she said, tilting her head. Without saying another word, Emma turned and walked away leaving Nina wondering what fire she had just lit.

151

The smell of ammonia filled Angie's nostrils like a knife, sharp and painful. Coughing, she opened her eyes to see the cowboy had been joined in the room by two women. "Take it easy," the cowboy drew out in a soft comforting voice.

Angie grabbed her head as the room started to spin again. Once more the ammonia capsule was shoved under her nose and bringing her back to reality. "OH god, stop that!" Angie cried out.

"Slow it down then before you pass out again," the woman said with annoyance.

Pulling a chair over to where Angie was lying on the floor, the cowboy took her under her arm. "Here, let's get you up here and sitting down," he said as he helped her into the chair.

Angie sat up and saw Scott lying on the bed. The day's previous events flooded back like a rollercoaster

"Ridley, get her some water. She's looking a little peaked again," the older woman said.

The younger woman left the room as the older woman laid a cold compress across Angie's forehead. Angie felt an immediate relief. The younger woman brought back a bottle of cold water, and Angie took a couple sips, the coolness running down her parched throat.

"I take it you know this man?" the cowboy quipped.

"Yes. Yes I do. His name is Scott" she said, "I'm Angie."

"I guess I owe you an apology, little lady. My name is Jack and this is my wife Dee," he said as he motioned towards the older woman. "That there is our daughter Ridley." "How.... How did he..." Angie began as she melted into tears.

"Take it easy. Things are going to be OK. You're safe here," Dee cooed.

Handing Angie a box of tissues, Dee continued, "My husband found him along the side of the road and brought him here. He was in pretty bad shape."

"I...I stabbed him" Angie choked out.

Jack, Dee and Ridley exchanged glances above the sobbing woman.

"He's going to be OK," Ridley finally said.

The trio sat in silence as the woman calmed herself and brought her emotions under control.

"I am so sorry, but thank you for helping him!" Angie finally said.

"You mind us asking what happened out there?"

"Well, that's a bit of a story" Angie said with an uneasy smile.

"No worries, we can take our time."

Angie started telling the family about their trip out of Memphis and the truck stopping when the road buckled. She told them about the stranger who visited and how she had tried to stab him but had hit Scott instead. She broke down in tears finally, unable to speak further. The older woman took Angie in her arms and allowed Angie to purge herself of all the terror of the last few months.

"Jack, why don't you put on a pot of coffee," Dee instructed.

The old cowboy took the opportunity to leave the room and allow the women all of their emotional stuff. He didn't know how to deal with it; this was his wife's territory.

The women, on the other hand, knew exactly what to do and began piling on loads of affection. Ridley explained how her father had brought Scott in and how she had removed the shank without too much damage. She also told Angie how he should be waking up soon but would have to take it easy for a while before they could travel back to Ohio.

"Ohio? Oh! We actually were trying to get to someone down here that's closer," Angie said.

"Really? That might make things a little easier then. Where were you headed?"

"I have a map that a friend of mine gave me in case we got into any kind of trouble and needed help. I guess this qualifies!" Angie said with a lopsided smile. Digging into a pocket of her pants, Angie brought out a map that was sealed inside a plastic zip lock baggie. "The woman's name is Shelby."

Dee and Ridley looked at each other in disbelief.

"This friend of yours in Ohio, her name wouldn't be Emma by chance?" Dee asked.

Her jaw dropping, Angie finally replied, "Why yes, yes it is!"

"Well, welcome to the Coop Chickie," Dee replied with a grin. "Let's go get us a cup of coffee and chat."

Over the next hour, Dee explained to Angie a bit more about the intricate workings of Emma's mind.
Angie was intrigued about how elaborate the underground system worked of moving people around the country if there was a down grid situation. Each Alpha Farm, as Emma called them was set up as a command center including a communication system that would enable them to skip a ham radio message across the country if they needed to. Supplies such as food and medicine for external visitors were also a prerequisite of being an Alpha Farm along with water catchment systems and purification systems. Each of the farms was accentually self-sufficient. This allowed people to not have to depend upon the government to survive and to avoid the government-run FEMA camps. Their only other obstacle was transportation and with the locations of each farm or Alpha Farm, they were sensitive to the workings of the areas around them, most having grown up in their respective areas. Maps were exchanged among the farms with detailed information not only on roadways but also tributaries, railways, hiking trails and even bike paths. Whatever it took, this group of elite preppers had made a commitment to make sure that they could help as many like-minded people as possible when the time came.

"And Shelby is one of our Alpha Farms. Emma probably would have sent you there because she is one of the closest to Memphis," Dee added.

"Angie, come quick!" Ridley yelled from Scott's room. Looking at Dee with panic on her face, Angie quickly made her way to Scott's makeshift hospital room.

"Hey baby," came the words from that all-too-familiar voice.

"Hey," she whispered back as she bent over Scott's bed and gave him a kiss on his head. "How are you doing?"

"Peachy. Just peachy. Never felt better," Scott said, his voice showing the wear on his body from the last few days. "What is that smell?" he asked.

Not one of them had noticed that Cowboy Jack had started dinner for his hungry guests. Pulling out some home-canned jars of beef stew from the cellar, he had the stew and cornbread in the fireplace baking along with some homemade rhubarb wine he had made the previous year. It was enough to envy the best chefs in Paris, Angie thought.

"Hold on there, big guy," Ridley said. "You aren't up for all of that yet, especially the wine. Angie yes, you no," she said, pointing a finger at his disappointed face. "I'll mash up some of the stew to make things easier, but slow and easy. OK?"

"Yes ma'am," Scott shot back.

"I like that!" Ridley exclaimed. "Especially since you are almost my parents' age," she added without thinking.

"Ouch," Scott said, dramatizing how she had hurt his feelings.

Laughter echoed throughout the rooms of the house, the first since the calamity had started. It was a good start for all of them considering the times ahead.

152

While Emma's family was busy getting settled and exchanging stories in front of the fire in the living room, Nina gathered her closest advisors for a meeting in one of the tents set up in the field below the barn.

"We seem to have too many mouths here lately. Mouths talk and can sink ships," she said. "We can't risk letting our whereabouts known right now. There's just too much at stake. Our whole country is counting on us to gather it back together and rebuild."

"Ma'am, What are you proposing?"

"A relocation." Nina snapped back

"You want us to move everything somewhere else?" he asked in disbelief. "Do you know how long that would take?"

"I do know, "Nina said, shaking her head in agreement. "That's why I think Emma and her family need to be the ones to vacate."

153

"What are you proposing?" Ben asked, flattered that Nina confided in him.

"Well, after thinking about it, the only way this is going to work is if she is out of the picture. She has too much power here with these people. She is taking that power away from you! You should really be in charge but it seems to me that everyone looks to Emma for answers. You are the law here, damn it, not her!" Nina dug the knife in deeper until she was certain Ben's small, Neanderthal brain was riveting with anger.

"Ya, I can see what you're saying," Ben replied deep in thought.

This was too easy, Nina thought to herself... and just a bit more to send him over the edge.

"Once Emma is gone, her husband will follow. Good thing, too, because his advances are getting a little old and I'm not sure how much longer I can hold him off. He obviously hasn't had sex in a long time."

Ben's face turned red with emotion as the corner of Nina's mouth turned up. "Bingo," she thought.

154

Shelby talked Mountain Man on the walkie talkies several more times before she lifted the 72-hour ban of separation. The one thing that she didn't want to happen was her children to be contaminated from the fallout of the explosion that they witnessed over Memphis. She had walked Mountain Man through getting as much of the dangerous toxins off himself as he could. Staying away from him was the hardest thing Shelby had ever had to do, especially not being able to contact him and knowing how he was doing.

By the time they were able to leave their underground bunker, Shelby's leg had swollen and turned all shades of blues, purples and yellows. It was obvious she was in a lot of pain when Mountain Man entered the room and picked her up to carry her to the house. He had sent one of the older kids to the local doctor's house on Bella with another horse in tow, hoping he would bring the doctor back as fast as possible.

Laying his hand on her forehead, Mountain Man knew she had a high fever. Taking some cloths, he soaked them in as cold of water as he could get from the spring and laid them across her head, and then he waited.

What seemed like hours later, his son finally returned with the doctor. Ushering the man hastily into their bedroom, Mountain Man stepped outside as he shut the door behind him. His girls would oversee the visit but if there was one thing he couldn't stomach it was his wife in so much pain. He needed to be strong for her, and as tough as he was, Shelby had the ability to bring him to his knees. Walking into the kitchen, he looked around at what little mess he had left to clean up. Glass from the windows had covered the inside of the room when the initial blast happened. Most of it had been dredged from its resting spots and safely discarded but he figured he would be finding shards for quite a while.

Knowing how Shelby loved her tea, he set her wood stove to heat a kettle of water and filled her tea strainer with dried chamomile leaves. Turning, he went to the cupboard to retrieve her favorite cup when he noticed it sitting on the far side table. She must have been sitting here before the blast went off, he thought. Walking across the room, his heart was relieved to find the cup still intact and not broken save for a small chip on the side. Picking up the cup, he ran his thumb over the nick. "Ouch," he mumbled out as blood ran down the side of the china.

"Mountain Man!" he heard the doc yell out. Finding himself still staring at the blood flowing from his thumb, he quickly grabbed a towel and wrapped it up and headed off towards Shelby and the doctor.

Once in the room, the doctor instructed the children to "Stop hovering and go get about dinner," as he needed to speak with their father alone. "Don't worry about Shelby," he said. "I gave her a sedative and she will be resting for a while until it wears off."

"How's her leg, doc?" Mountain Man asked once the children were out of the room.

"That's what we need to discuss. It's not good, Jeremiah," he said using Mountain Man's given name. Having known the man since birth, he saw past his tough exterior and knew what he had to tell him would hurt him as much as it would Shelby "Her leg is destroyed. She is risking blood clots and further infection if we don't remove it immediately."

"WHAT! You mean amputate her leg?" Jeremiah wailed in disbelief.

"Yes. Right below the knee. I see no other choice," the doctor replied.

155

Nina set her plan in motion and was met with obstacle after obstacle. Ben was no help, as he was more concerned with getting into her pants than actually following her orders. Every time they were together, Nina spent more time shoving his hands off of her than working out the details to getting Emma off her farm. It was to the point that Nina was getting extremely agitated. This had to work and needed to be carried out with precision if she were to get what she wanted.

Ben was an expendable in her book, something she could afford to lose. A loose end that would have to eventually be disposed of. He had his purpose, but quite honestly, she could find any dimwit with an overactive libido to do what she needed.

Tom, on the other hand, was different. He was a challenge Nina couldn't just dismiss. She saw how he looked at his wife; the adoration was visibly written across his face. And who could very well blame him, Nina thought. Emma was every man's dream. She built Tom up on a pedestal and did whatever she needed to make sure he stayed there. A lady in public with the will power of a saint to control her tongue, Nina was positive she devoured her husband between her sheets whenever he needed it. Nina had tested both of her theories over the last couple weeks by not only pushing Emma past the point she had ever tested anyone, and still the bitch held her composure. And Tom, dear sweet Tom. Nina's advances had been dealt with by a cold wall that only a true gentleman possesses. If only she could make Tom love her the way he did Emma. She just needed to rework her plan some more. She would eventually figure it out, she always did, Nina thought with a frown. Damn it if this one was wasting too much of her time. She had a deadline to keep and the bitch was about to ruin it.

"A deadline," Nina thought.

"Dead…

Line…"

She let the words slowly roll over her tongue.

"Dead."

156

The doctor made arrangements with Jeremiah on when they would be removing Shelby's damaged leg. He would need to bring extra equipment in from his office and several of his staff to assist. The fact that they didn't have power was not helping the situation. The extraction of the damaged part of her leg would have to be done without any of the fancy equipment that present-day hospitals used.

Two days later, the doctor and two of his nurses arrived to begin the amputation. Shelby was given a sedative to hopefully help with the pain but without being able to use an anesthesiologist, they were hoping she would be strong enough to handle the pain if it wasn't enough.

"I want to explain this procedure to you, Jeremiah," the doctor said.

"I don't need to know. Just get it over with."

"Yes you do. And you need to know how to take care of her after this is over as you have no one here to help except you," the doctor returned, a bit irritated.

Jeremiah looked at the doctor with utter dislike on his face. He was a farmer and dealt with issues like this on occasion with his animals. Just never with someone he loved to the extent he loved his wife. Taking a deep breath and blowing out the air, Jeremiah looked at the doctor. "Alright."

"Have any coffee?" the doctor asked.

"Really! You want to take my wife's leg off but want me to fix you a cup of coffee first. Can't we just do this thing? If I hadn't have tried to find them, If I had been home, NONE of this would have happened in the first place!" Jeremiah screamed at the doctor, startling himself in the process.

"Do you need to talk about something?" the doctor asked Jeremiah.

Jeremiah fell back into the chair behind him and dropped his head into his hands, his elbows resting on his knees. His back started to heave up and down as the sobbing overtook his body.

The doctor motioned everyone out of the room. A man needed to cry and get it out of his system when he needed to, is what he always said. And this man had a lot of crying to do.

An hour later, Jeremiah walked outside to find the doctor sitting under a big tree in the yard. "Get it all out of your system?" the doctor asked.

"How did you know?" Jeremiah asked.

"Been in your shoes. I didn't get it out and ended up hurting the woman I love the most in the world even more by my actions afterwards. Listen, things happen that we have no control over. It's a part of life. But you can't get yourself all wrapped up in 'What Ifs' or it's going to eat away at your soul and turn you into a bitter old man. Deal with it and then walk away and get on with life. That family in there needs you right now. You, all of you," the doctor said pointing his finger in circles at Jeremiah.

"Not just parts of you."

"Yes sir," Jeremiah responded, "and thanks."

"My pleasure. Now, we have to get down to business. I would like to discuss putting the surgery off for a couple days, though, as Shelby's blood pressure is way too high right now," the doctor said.

"Won't that run the risk of the infection getting worse?"

"Well, I have her on some pretty strong antibiotics among other things. It's honestly me weighing the infection against a cardiac problem. I'm thinking right now let's give it a couple days, and no more than a couple to get her pressure down. She's been through a lot the last couple days. Hell, we all have," the doctor added.

157

"It's going to be about a full day's ride considering the shape you are in. I don't want to do anything to cause any setbacks," Ridley said to Scott.

"Stop babying me," Scott returned.

"Oh trust me. No petting pouters is my mom's philosophy in life and mine too. Suck it up, buttercup! So, that settled, we leave in the morning," Ridley said to the room.

"You're going with us?" Angie asked in astonishment.

"Sure! Why not? Besides, I have a mission that my mom is sending me on!"

"But you're pregnant!" Angie said.

"Yep! And not dying! So we leave in the morning. And I'm not going to wait for you so don't be late!" Ridley yelled over her shoulder as she walked out of the room.

"It will be nice to have a doctor along, even if she didn't finish college," Angie said to Scott.

"I'll be fine," Scott chirped back. "I wonder what this mission is she's on?"

"No idea. If she wanted us to know, don't you think she would tell us?"

"Excuse me, don't mean to interrupt but thought you folks would like something cold to drink besides water," Dee walked into the room with a pitcher of iced tea and sat it down on the side table.

"Ah, that's so sweet of you! How in the world did you get ice?" Angie asked astonished.

"I have one of those little table top ice machines. Hooked that bad boy up to one of our solar batteries and whammo! Ice. Consider it a delicacy going forward, so enjoy it!"

"What's the secret mission you are sending Ridley on with us?" Scott blatantly asked Dee.

"Scott!" Angie squealed.

"What? You want to know too, you just don't have the balls to ask!"

"Secret mission?" Dee repeated, thinking. "Oh! You must mean the quilt?"

"No idea. Ridley just said she is going with us on a secret mission you are sending her on."

Dee laughed. "Well, yes. I could see why she would say that!"

"Well? The suspense is making my wound hurt," Scott added, acting hurt and weak.

"Funny boy! No, actually, it was rumored that during the time of the actual Underground Railroad movement that quilts were used to convey messages to passerby's or visitors."

"Quilts? Really?" Angie asked.

"Yes. And don't forget, this was just rumored as I do not believe there was any evidence provided to back it up. Emma and the coop girls just thought it was a good idea and adapted it into our group. Anyhow. Supposedly, quilts were used to communicate information about how to escape to freedom. They say quilts were hung on the clotheslines to signal a house was safe for runaways, the colors and shapes of the blocks were then used to convey the message if you knew what you were looking for. I finished another quilt to give to a new coop girl who Shelby knows and needed to get it to her. We are going to use these to identify each other in case of an issue. I'll be right back."

"Wow, that's pretty interesting. Think there's any basis behind the story she just told?" Angie asked Scott.

"Possibly. Don't forget, history books are always written by the ones who won the battle. There's always two sides. Take the cowboys and the Indians. Cowboys win and it's was an epic battle. Indians win and it was a massacre. It all depends on which side of the fence you are sitting on."

"I get your point," she said, smiling at Scott.

Dee walked back into the room holding a beautiful handmade quilt. Trimmed in black with a solid black backing, the facing was of blocks of solid green with blocks of daisies in between. Directly in the center was a block with the silhouette of a woman holding a rifle with a feather in her hair.

Angie started laughing, "Emma has this same woman on the mantle above her fireplace. A friend of hers made it out of copper."

"Well Lonnet, one of the Sister Chicks in Kentucky made these specifically for all of us girlies. Aren't they beautiful? Now you know what to look for!" Dee said to Angie smiling.

"Does this mean I'm a coop girl now?" Angie laughed.

"I think you were all along, you just didn't realize it yet," Dee said, giving Angie a hug.

158

Scott, Angie, Ridley and Cowboy Jack were all saddled and ready to ride as soon as the sun came up the next morning. Dee had packed enough food and supplies for a week's worth of travel, which they packed on a fifth horse.

Sticking mainly to using a topographical map along with tributaries, the group arrived at Shelby's farm ahead of schedule. Word passed to Mountain Man that the group was approaching and he went out to meet them.

"Jack old friend! Ridley!" Mountain Man sang out as he approached their horses and reached up to give their hands a shake.

"Mountain Man, I have some guests I would like you to meet" Jack began. "This is Angie and Scott I'm thinking Shelby might already know of them."

"I've heard her talk, yes. Welcome, but I'm afraid Shelby is a bit under the weather. Bella trampled her leg and Doc is looking at removing it."

"What?" Ridley exclaimed, not waiting for an explanation as she took off towards the house on her horse.

"Come on to the house and let's get you all settled. How long can you stay, Jack?" Mountain Man asked.

"For a few days, anyways. Let's see how we can pitch in and help," Jack said more to Scott than Mountain Man.

The three men and Angie rode the dirt road back through the trees until they came to a clearing with a log home. Several outbuildings were scattered around the property. Angie loved what she saw before her. A self-sufficient homestead. Emma had taught her over the months how important permaculture was to the design of your land. It was one thing to plant your garden in neat little rows in raised beds. The concern was that anyone walking by could see it and instantly know you have food of some type.
In a down grid situation, Angie could appreciate that sentiment even more now. Riding back into Mountain Man's property, it would be easy for anyone who didn't know what they were looking for to just see a nice cabin.

Scott looked over and saw Angie sitting straight in her saddle with a big smile across her face taking it all in as they rode along the path. "You seem to be enjoying yourself," he said.

"Oh Scott, it's beautiful! The nut trees, the orchard. All the perennial herbs and plants. It's like uncovering layer after layer of paradise! And it comes back year after year! I guess that's why it's called permanent culture. And to think I spent years just growing tomatoes in a pot on my porch because the HOA wouldn't allow a garden. I could have planted all of this right under their noses and they would never have even known!" Angie rattled off.

"Beat them at their own game is what I always say," Jack added.

"Oh, If I could just go back and fix my life knowing what I know now!" Angie sighed.

"Move forward, young lady. Help those who don't get it and stop dwelling on the past. We have a lot of work to be done. This war isn't over until the last battle is won." Jack said seriously.

"War?" Angie asked.

"To live free like our ancestors fought for. To stop having Big Brother sticking his nose in where it doesn't belong. To stop paying for $1600 toilet seats while people in this country are starving. To stop the entitlement mentality that is so prevalent in this society. To stop wars because we can make a buck off of them. To let people breathe without fear, to create without condemnation, to start loving each other without rejection," Jack said.

"Wow, talk about a speech!" Angie laughed out. "But you're right Jack. If it's not us, then who?"

"It has to be us, it's all the world has left," Jack added.

They had reached the house and dismounted from the horses. Jack helped Scott down off his horse and checked his bandages. "All's good!" he said, giving Scott the thumbs up.

"I'm going to go check on my wife. Make yourselves at home. Jack, you know where everything is at," Mountain Man said. "You two can use the bedroom off the hallway with the blue walls. Jack knows where it is. Scott, you might want to go down lie down for a bit and rest." "Thanks for the hospitality," Scott said as Mountain Man disappeared inside.

159

"Oh Shelby! What happened?" Ridley said as she sat on the edge of the bed.

"Just got in the way of Bella's hoof. She meant no harm. It's not her fault. Doc says I need to have it taken off as the damage is too extensive. So the plan is to take the blasted thing off tomorrow. You going to stick around for the show?" Shelby asked through tears.

Ridley reached over and gave Shelby a hug. Sticking her face in Shelby's she started talking in a low voice. "I know I haven't finished school yet and don't have a fancy piece of paper, but could I look at it?"

"Well...I don't ..."

"Listen, a lot is going on in the medical world that your doctor here might not know anything about. When was the last time he learned anything new? When was the last time he was out of his four walls and saw the world and all the things that people are working on? Shelby, I mean no respect but he's old school. Let me at least try. Please!" Ridley begged.

"Let her try, Mama," Mountain Man said as he walked into the room and kissed Ridley on the top of the head. She was young enough to be his daughter but he had a fondness for her and her spunky spirit. Ridley reminded him a lot of his wife when she was younger.

Taking a deep breath, Shelby looked from Ridley to Mountain Man and then back again.

"Well, what do I have to lose? Oh! Just a foot!" she said trying to break the tension. "OK. Let's do this thing!"

Ridley jumped up excitedly hugged Mountain Man and then they both leaned over and hugged Shelby.
Ridley could do this. She had to do this. If there was anything she learned about in school it was repairing tissue. She seemed to have a knack for it, so she had gravitated to reconstructive surgery.

"I'm going to go scrub up and will be back. Where's your medical supplies?" Ridley asked.

"What medical supplies?" Shelby asked.

"Oh come now. I know all about the little project you and my mama have been keeping to yourselves. Where's the stash?" Ridley asked with her hands on her hips. She looked like she was twelve again, Shelby thought. All spice, attitude and mouth.

"Mountain Man, you want to show Lil Miss Know It All where the stash is?" Shelby said with the raise of an eyebrow.

"Sure thing, Mama," he said as he motioned the way.

Shelby laid her head back against the pillow and closed her eyes. It was the first time in days that she had seen the glimmer of hope. Not necessarily about her leg, but the attitude and hope in the spirit of the young folks. "We just might be able to save this country," she whispered to no one.

160

Nina stalked her in total silence, the wind masking any hint of her predatory existence. What the woman had would soon belong to Nina. Nina had dreamed of having the life this bitch had and now it was time to claim it for herself. After all, Nina was entitled to it since she was soon going to be reclaiming this fine cold, hard country underneath her belly right now. Might as well claim hold of this woman's husband and everything else she loved. Served the bitch right for not showing Nina more respect.

Nina had worked hard for where she was in her life, well except for her ex. He just wouldn't conform to her life anymore. Nina thought about Tomás. He was the kind of man who made women weep at night in bed, and Nina was tired of trying to scratch her own itch. She wanted to sink her teeth into him and devour his Latino blood. Fucking bitch was in the way though. Best she had gotten from him was politeness, and damnit, she wanted more. She knew he had it in him. She saw the way he looked at Emma. So the simple solution was little Miss Perfect needed removed from the scene so Tomás could weep in Nina's bed.

Nina blinked the mist from her eyes. It was a good night for death. It was the same kind of night when her husband had died. He should have known. He should have read the signs. It's not like Nina didn't throw them in his face. How comfortable people get when they think the person they love most has their best interest at heart. It was a game now for Nina and she enjoyed the sport of it. Her training in the military had taught her well. He had succumbed to her advances; given her everything she had set out to get from him, especially monetary security. The kids were an added benefit and sealed the deal. Cute kids and all, she thought, but would be considered collateral damage if need be.

Emma's blood running through Nina's fingers would put the finishing touches on Nina's dodecahedron of annihilation. This would be her last and final dispatching of life and Nina was planning on enjoying every last breath leaving Emma's body.

She demanded respect wherever she went and this woman had the balls to buck that? Who the hell did that? Who did she think she was? Nina had men groveling at her feet like she was the last bit of chocolate placed before a hormonal female, so why not this sorry excuse for a woman? Agitated, Nina rolled slightly to her left and heard a branch break beneath her. Damn! She was better than that but this woman just pissed her off. She needed to be more careful or her plan could get messy. Narrowing her eyes to a blur of lashes, Nina watched as the woman stopped dead in her tracks.

Emma could feel the wind taunting her. Something was wrong.

Emma knew that feeling well living in an old house with stories to tell. She had felt the souls of those lost convulse between the jongleur walls of the homestead. She felt a presence here with her tonight, an existence that Emma sensed coveted evilness.

Pausing, Emma sent up a prayer of protection. Lifting her chin, she felt the surge of strength enter her body. She was a warrior. It was time for this battle to begin.

Slowing opening her eyes, she slowly turned back toward where she knew her adversary was waiting. Taunting him, she waited.

The nemesis took the bait and stepped forward. It was too much of a fascination, this woman standing here so boldly.

Emma gasped in disbelief. "Nina?" she questioned.

"I love an element of surprise," Nina gloated. "I bet it won't surprise you though when I say I want your life. I want your husband in my bed, making love to me as your memory fades from his little brain."

Emma stood still, knowing the wrong move would be fatal. Let the woman talk, she said to herself.
Instead, Emma concentrated on the woman's taunting movements. She needed to figure out her weakness and allow Nina to play out her hand. She still had the element of shocked disbelief on her side and as long as the woman thought she was driving a wedge into her heart, it bought Emma time.

The woman kept talking, words rolling off of her tongue at an astonishing rate. She was cleansing herself, justifying the actions she was about to take. Her lust for blood was severely overriding all rational thought in her head. Emotions had a grip on her sanity and the high from the purge she was experiencing was a valorous kismet.

Emma waited. Silence wrapped itself around her like her grandmother's quilt.

The moon exposed Nina's secret first, glimmering off the blade of the knife she had hidden in her hand. Emma caught the reflection out of the corner of her eye. The fury brewing in her gut. Emma needed to control this anger or it would damage her soul. It would cause her to make a mistake that could cost her life. She was not misjudging the scene before her; this would end with blood spilt. Emma was determined that it would not be hers. The woman before her was a mess, divulging long kept secrets that should have been buried in her abysmal heart.

Nina brought the hilt down hard towards Emma, only to be caught off balance as Emma sidestepped. Nina tumbled forward but was able to recoup quickly, coming back around with another strike. This time finding flesh as Emma stuck her arm up to protect herself, the knife cut through her sleeve and opened a small gash.

Dixon came out of nowhere, putting himself between Emma and Nina. Her white knight. Her protector was here to fight to the death. His bark alerting everyone within earshot.

Nina calculated her move and drove the knife into his side, crimson staining his glorious white fur. He refused to give up the fight and grabbed her arm between his jaws.

Gasping in horror, Emma lunged towards Nina, only to be thrust backwards, hitting her head against a tree. Shaking her head, she couldn't pass out now. She had to stay in this battle!

Grabbing another blade from her leg sheath, Nina dug in again, this time finding Dixon's lung. Dixon let out a whimper and crumbled into the blood-soaked dirt, dragging Nina down with him. Nina digging the blade in deeper.

OH GOD! Emma's mind was whirling as she saw Dixon laying on the ground motionless, Nina still on him. Emma grabbed the back of her hair and yanked Nina off of the dog, stepping around her to get to Dixon.

Nina just sat there and watched the woman in her wretchedness, trying to stop the blood draining the life from the mutt. A smile curved her lips as she saw her opportunity. Standing up, Nina raised the knife and visually acquired her target.

Just as the metal on the blade caught the moonlight, Nina heard the impassioned snarl from behind her. Turning slowly, Nina looked into the eyes of the captor of her mortality. With the lunge of a locomotive, the wolf leapt onto Nina, knocking her flat on her stomach, knocking the air from her lungs. The wolf found her vulnerability and sunk his teeth into her neck, ripping flesh and bone as it raised its head towards the moon. Emma's tear-stained eyes looked at the beast, his lip snarling just before his howl wept into the night.

Silence crept in again as the wolf walked over to Dixon and began to lick his face, a quiet whimper escaping her throat. Emma stared on in silence. Was this where Dixon was spending his time, with this female? Were the puppies she had seen his? Lifting her head, her eyes locking with Emma's as if she was reading her mind, the wolf turned her muzzle towards Emma's house and let out a howl before she turned and melted into the night.

Emma quickly gathered her thoughts and knew she had to get Dixon help, the woman on the ground beside him was already dead and part of her neck ripped out from the tremendous strength the jaws of the wolf. She needed to get Dixon to Doc Scott's without Nina's henchmen seeing her. They shouldn't be concerned about Nina until at least morning, thinking she was in bed asleep. She had one chance, the tunnels.

161

Emma grabbed the wheelbarrow from behind the barn and got Dixon loaded as gently as she could. Setting off, she made it into the woods that she knew and loved so well. The going was rough pushing a 150 lb. dog, but she made it to the entrance of the cave.

Not many people knew what existed below the ground under Emma's property. Connecting her to each of her children's homes, along with several neighbor's homes, was a series of tunnels used by people who lived here in the 1800s. While the tunnels, or escape routes, were not literally underground, there were access levels to safe dwellings along multiple routes between homes. The tunnels themselves were usually not very long, but when Emma moved here, she opened them up, fortifying them, knowing that one day they would be put to good use. She knew that once the nation's historians died off, America would once again repeat its mistakes, as few had learned from the errors of the past.

She hadn't been down here in a very long time so it was slow moving. Glad she had a flashlight with her, she had several miles of darkness ahead of her to get to Scott's house. From there, she needed to get his assistant somehow, hoping that she was staying at the house while Scott was with Angie in Tennessee.

Hours later, Emma emerged from the cave at the back of Scott's property. One day she would have to tell him about this. Being as nosey as he was, she was surprised he hadn't discovered it yet.

Downhill from there, Emma got Dixon to the house. He was still breathing but was obviously in tremendous pain as each breath was quiet and labored. "Please, please answer," Emma whispered....

Emma was contemplating breaking into the house when Jane answered the door. "Yes!" Emma thought. "Jane, it's Emma, I need your help!" she almost cried out.

"Well of course, dear, what in the world is going on?" she asked looking down at the white fluff in the wheelbarrow. "Is that Dixon?"

"Yes, he's been hurt badly," Emma replied.

"Hurry. Wheel him to the garage and we can get him in through there without too much trouble," Jane said.

Emma pushed him towards the garage and Jane hurried ahead and pushed up the garage door. Wheeling him down a hall in the back of the garage, Emma pushed him into a dark room. Taking down some oil lamps on the shelf, Jane quickly got some light going in the room and set about getting the examination table ready for Dixon. Cranking the table as low as she could get it, she motioned for Emma to help her get Dixon lifted to the table.

Emma slid her hands under Dixon's hips while Jane took his front shoulder and head. Ever so gently they tried, but neither could get him up there without causing him more pain. Jane ran from the room and came back in a few moments with her soporific husband rubbing his eyes. With all three of them in sync, they managed to get the dog up on the table. Jane's husband went about making the dog comfortable while Jane quickly got to work getting her medical instruments. Listening to every inch of him, she informed the duo that she needed to get Dixon into X-ray as soon as possible and they couldn't be in the room. Reluctantly, they both left. Jane's husband put on a pot of coffee and both of them paced back and forth until Jane appeared.

Almost an hour had passed when she finally came out of the room.

"I think he's going to be OK," she said.

Emma melted into a puddle on the floor, tears finally busting through the tough composure that she had been grasping for all night. Jane knelt beside Emma and wrapped her arms around her, feeling Emma's body unleash the fear that had manifested itself there. Motioning for her husband to grab a towel, Jane brushed the hair back from Emma's face and handed her the soft cotton to weep into.

"Honey, what happened?" Jane asked.

Emma took a deep breath and looked up finally. For the next hour they talked about the events beforehand as they all watched over Dixon.

Content that she knew Dixon was in good hands, Emma knew she needed to get home before anyone noticed she was missing and before the sun came up to welcome the day. This was one day that Emma was not looking forward to.

Giving Dixon kisses all over his sweet face, and hugging deeply the loving people who would be watching over him, Emma made her way back to the cave. The trip home was much faster without having a dog to push. Feeling her way along the walls, Emma emerged from the exit with just the light from the moon. Knowing these woods was a sense of relief as she made her way back to where Nina's body was lying.

As she exited the woods, she saw the faint glow of multiple lights in the area where Nina should still be. Quickly back tracking, Emma made her way back into the tunnel. "Shit," she said. She needed to get to the house before anyone found her. Feeling her way back along the wall, she finally found the indentation to the false door. Prying her fingers into the cracks, she pulled with all the strength she had left. This off shoot led to her basement and under the bench she used to store her root crops all winter. Piled with potatoes, squash and onions, she was wondering how hard it was going to be to get the trap door to open and how quietly she could get it open. "Shit," was all she could think as she made it to the end of the tunnel. There were voices coming from the room and she couldn't quite make out what they were saying.

162

"Tell us what you know!" They were screaming at Tommy, blood dripping from his ear. Tying him to a chair, his arms pulled behind him and secured with handcuffs, the men in uniform were no longer friendly to their host.

Trying to focus, Tom looked around the room for something, anything that could help him. Racks of canning jars that Emma had filled over the summer from their garden covered several walls. Wooden crates of potatoes and squash lined another. Baskets of apples sat around the room from the fall harvest of their orchard. He was glad Emma talked him into putting in the orchard. The grandkids loved the applesauce she made every year for them, he thought. He was concerned about the location since there weren't a lot of ways to water the trees there but once Emma showed him the benefits of adding swales, the trees were able to flourish in an area of the farm that once was impossible to grow anything.

His jaw moved awkwardly as the soldier hit him once again. "Where is she at?" Tom heard him say as blood began to stream from the cut on his lip. Once again Tom's face absorbed the blow from the soldier's powerful arm. Again and again the bones in his face were rearranged like a jigsaw puzzle. Blood sprayed across the room as teeth were dislodged from their socket.

"Let's take a break for a bit," Tom barely heard above the ringing in his ears. Not being able to see from the swelling setting in, Tom tried to keep from passing out by concentrating on the voices yelling at him.

A man shuffled down the steps into the root cellar and was taken aback by the scene he was witnessing. Walking across the room, he whispered in the ear of the soldier in charge. Looking behind him, the soldier addressed the man casually leaning back against the wall.

"Sheriff, we think we found her," the soldier said.

163

Emma tried to hear what the voices were saying but she couldn't make out the words through the door. "Damn it! Who the hell would be in the cellar this late at night? Just a few more minutes and she would have been inside the house and no one would have known she had left! Back tracking, she would have to use the exit through the spring house. The only problem was she would have to sneak across a section of the backyard and onto the porch before she could get into the house through the kitchen door. "Deep breath, girlie" she said to herself, trying to calm her nerves.

The spring house was set back in the bank behind the house and always stayed cool. It was a good thing for the water pool to keep it chilled, yet another for the amount of spiders that lived there enjoying the dark mustiness of the small room. Peering out the door, Emma could only see part of the yard and house. There just was no way to see behind the building and up the bank to where Nina lay in the dirt.

Edging herself out the door, she kept her back tight up against the building and in the shadows. Easing herself to the corner, she peered around the side as best as she could. The light was glowing from the back porch. "Shit," she mouthed not allowing sound to exit her lips. Looking around, there was no way she could get through the porch and into the kitchen without being seen.

Frustrated she leaned her head back against the spring house and closed her eyes. A silent breeze blew across her lashes. Opening her eyes, Emma saw the moon glistening off the metal of the TV tower that ran up the side of the house. "Oh ya!" Emma said louder than she should have. Waiting, she listened for anyone approaching. With enough time passing, Emma scurried uphill across the yard towards the shadows beneath the tower. Just as she almost reached the sidewalk going alongside the house, her foot slipped and she landed face down in the dew-covered grass. She lay as still as she could.

164

The two men picked Emma up by her upper arms and damn near ripped them from their sockets as they escorted her into the house. Sitting her down at the kitchen table, one man stayed with her as the other walked down the steps to the root cellar. Emma swallowed as she had a feeling this wasn't going to end well.

Hearing the approaching footsteps of several people coming up the stairs, Emma was surprised to see Sheriff Olan coming through the door.

"Ben! There must be some kind of misunderstanding here!" Emma said directly at him.

"I doubt it," he replied. "Where the hell have you been?"

Emma looked at the man standing before her. She had never seen him filled with so much anger.

"Fucking answer me!" he screamed at her, making her jump in her chair.

"I...I" she stammered.

"We found Nina's body," he hissed at her.

Not being able to talk, she just stared into his dark eyes.

Walking over to the door that led down into the basement and root cellar, Ben yelled "Bring him up." Emma's could feel the contents of her stomach rise up to her throat.

Staring at the entrance into the basement, several soldiers emerged dragging a limp body. Emma gasped in horror as she recognized the tattoo on the victim's shoulder. Tommy's griffin that he had gotten in Germany when he served in the Army was partially hidden by the blood that was smeared on his arm, but Emma recognized it immediately. She had spent countless hours tracing the outline with her fingers late at night while they lay in their bed together. She loved to watch him sleep, listening to him snore, trying to memorize every detail of the man she adored.

The soldiers dragged Tommy's lifeless body over and dumped it in the middle of the floor.

"Now, what were you saying?" Ben said as he turned to look at Emma.

165

The two men flanking her would not allow her to leave the chair she was sitting on. Pushing her down as hard as they could, they underestimated the strength she possessed.

"Nooooooooo!" she screamed out when she saw Tommy's body lying on the floor. Struggling against the men, Emma didn't hear what Ben was saying to her as the men picked Tommy back up and took him out the door.

"Stop!" she screamed "What are you doing? Where are you taking him?" she was screaming through her tears.

"You fucked up big time and now it's time you learned a lesson," Ben spat back at her. "Keep the rest of the people in this house locked in their rooms and don't let them out," he instructed his men.

"Leave him the fuck alone you fucking asshat," she snarled back as she frantically tried to free herself. Just one hand was all she needed.

"You want me, you fucking come here and get me. Be a fucking man for a change. Leave my husband out of this!" she screamed at Ben.

"You've fucked up my plans for the very last time. Hell, I didn't even get me a little bit of the Latino bitch before you had to off her. That pains me, Emma. That truly pains me. I was planning on ruling these here United States with her as she rebuilt them, but no, you had to go put your meddling ass nose into things and destroy the chance I had. Do you know how long I've waited for this? How long I've waited to rip that fucking smile off of your face? Since the day I met you and your pansy-ass husband. Fucking spic lover is all you are. You have no business being called a white woman with a dick like his being shoved in you. Fun and games are all over now though, aren't they, little Miss High and Mighty."

Emma stared at Ben. "It was you," she said under her breath.

"Me what?" Ben replied.

"The little girl over in the next county. The one that lost her baby after she was brutally raped. She kept telling me the man her kept thrusting his little penis into her kept calling her a Latino bitch, just like you just referred to Nina as. It all makes sense now," Emma said in disbelief.

"You're sorry ass can't prove a fucking thing. Little penis, whatever," he said as his face turned a more intense red than before.

Grinding her teeth, Emma looked at the sorry excuse of a man standing before her. The anger was coursing through his veins. If she stood any chance of saving Tommy, God, if he even was still alive, she had to get this prick out of her face.

Sheriff Olan turned to walk out the door. Looking back at the pile of distraught woman lying on the floor, he walked over and grabbed a handful of her hair. "Don't leave this house," he whispered in her ear.

"Fuck you," she screamed as she lunged for his throat.

Backing up, Ben smiled when she missed him. To save face before his men, he released her hair and pummeled the side of her head with his boot, sending her back down onto the floor. Pointing down at her with his finger, the smile left his face. "Don't leave," he said.

Emma lay on the floor sobbing, several men guarded her from leaving, even if she wanted to. Was he alive? Was he one of the voices she heard when she was outside the cellar door? God, if she had only walked through that door it might have saved him. What had she done? These thoughts all screamed within her head.

Picking her up by both arms, two men heaved her up the stairs into her own bedroom. The room she had shared with her husband. Barely being able to walk into the room, she collapsed along his side of the bed, her mind reeling from the all the events that had just unfolded. What if he was gone? What if she never saw him again? She frantically tried to recall the last moment they had together, the arch of his nose, the smell of him. Her body shook from the gasps of breath that she struggled to take. The pain was just too much as she couldn't catch her breath. Frantically grasping at the bed, trying to grab onto something to stand, she ended up pulling the bedspread down as she fell backwards, hitting her head and knocking herself unconscious.

166

As the moon started to part way for the morning light, the alarm on the nightstand started to play the last song that Tom had programmed to awaken them to begin the day.

Emma could barely hear the words as the song played against the silence. They tried to push their way past the fogginess in her head, past the pain…

….a story to tell….wounds to be healed… Is there… beauty in this mess…from the ashes… Where? ~ so tired of holding on ~ let go, move on ~ Meaning here? In this mess?

The tears fell silently over her lashes and down her face. Damn it! She never asked for this…. Why! There has to be a reason! Her faith wrestled frantically within her spirit, screaming out for answers.

Cry out….. She was crying damnit… God, why won't you hear me….
Take this…take the pain….The words were coming faster…embedding themselves into her soul….strength… she had to find the strength

Just keep breathing?

Keep breathing…. Keep breathing she chanted to herself over and over as the sobs raked her soul.

Her shoulders shook with such fury as the pain engulfed her, bringing her straight to her knees… "God please!" Her soul screamed out. "I can't do this… I don't want to do this…Take this from me… make the pain stop!"

….a road I didn't plan….how did I get here… I'm trying…. to hear…. that still small voice ~

That still small voice.... Be still.....still...and know....

I'm trying to hear above the noise... The noise was getting louder....so loud... It screamed in her head and ripped her heart from beneath her chest....tightly squeezing all the life from her innermost being...The pain was enormous....The pain.... hurt.

Her fists pounded the floor with intense fury as her voice screamed, "Take this! Take it all! I don't want it! I never did and you just gave it to me anyway..... How could you do this? This isn't fair! I can't do this!" Her voice turned to a whimper as her feelings betrayed her. "Please," she begged as she lowered her head into her hands as the torrent of tears broke through. "God please," barely escaped her lips as her body shook with torment.

Though I walk.....

Though I Walk through the shadows
I am so afraid... so very afraid...God I am so fucking afraid... Please don't leave me....

Emma curled up on the floor beside her bed, her body exhausted. The stains on her face had almost dried. Her breathing came in deeper gasps and finally evened out, her muscles started to relax. "Listen ..." she heard cutting through the noise... "Listen to me..."

I need you now.... Now more than ever...

Her eyes closed, she let her soul escape from the emotional prison she had been holding it in. She finally felt peace... His peace.

Dragging her weary body to the window, she looked out across her land, a land that would one day gather her dust back to itself and allow her to rest. Raising her chin in defiance, her warrior spirit returned. She knew what she had to do.

She blew out the candle and watched as the smoke drifted toward the stars. What a beautiful night it was, soon to be lost to the morning. The clouds danced playfully in front of the moon causing shadows across the open field.

If she stared hard enough, she could just barely make out his figure coming out of the tree line. Tears ran down her cheeks as she tried so hard not to blink, for she knew if she drew her lashes even slightly together, he would be gone. She turned away quickly…one day soon they would be together again. Until then, she had work to do.

Taking a deep breath and straightening her back, Emma turned and ran downstairs and back into the kitchen just in time to witness the unspeakable. A beast of a dog was hanging from her wrought iron pot rack in the middle of the room, his beautiful white fur had been slit and his hair stripped from his neck down and now hung from his feet in a pool on the floor beneath him.

A knife had been thrust into his body with a piece of bloody white paper. On the note, written in a color of lipstick that Emma could not ignore, were the words…… "One by one, all you love will die the exact same way."

Thank you and please consider leaving a review for

Alpha Farm, The Beginning at Amazon.

Please visit Annie's website, www. AnnnieBerdel.com

The author welcomes any comments, feedback or questions at
AnnieBerdel@yahoo.com

ABOUT THE AUTHOR

Based in Indianapolis, Annie Berdel is a self-proclaimed advocate
of educating women in the art of personal protection and self-
reliance.

As an aspiring writer, Annie took her advocacy and dove into the
dystopia genre with strong female lead characters.

A passion for firearms, herbal medicine, knives, slingshots, home
canning, Kali street fighting, Kempo karate and furry animals fuels
the fire and adds countless stories to be told beginning with her
inaugural book "Alpha Farm, The Beginning".

Wife, mother, business professional and bibliophile, in her spare
time, Annie likes to stretch the boundaries of survival in a Post-
Apocalyptic scenario.

Wanting to leave The Big Blue Marble better than she found it for
her children and grandchildren, Annie is always learning, always
loving and always looking for ways to help people become self-
reliant and better prepared for whatever may come.

Made in the USA
San Bernardino, CA
29 August 2014